AUTHOR NOTE

Thank you for buying my book!

Crossing Lines is the follow-on to the Amazon #1 Best Selling thriller **Killing Hope** and prequel to **Taking Liberty**.

The events in this novel are a continuation of those featured in the first Gabe Quinn Thriller – therefore, it is recommended to read all three in the correct sequence to ensure the best reading experience, as some key aspects of **Crossing Lines** are a carryover of situations introduced in **Killing Hope** and extended into **Taking Liberty**.

Crossing Lines
(Gabe Quinn Thriller #2)

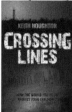 

Also available in eBook and Audiobook formats

Killing Hope
(Gabe Quinn Thriller #1)

Taking Liberty
(Gabe Quinn Thriller #3)

 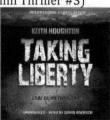

CROSSING LINES

GABE QUINN THRILLER #2

KEITH HOUGHTON

ISBN: 1490423397

Keith Houghton

~ For My Children ~

Jason, Gemma and Rebecca
*Who outshine the sun with their
brilliance and warmth*

Keith Houghton

CROSSING LINES

"How far would you go to protect your children?"

Keith Houghton

PROLOGUE

The corrugated metal deck inside the van was a cold gauntlet repeatedly knuckling her in the face. She could feel the soft flesh around her eye beginning to buckle where her abductor had struck her, once from nowhere and again as she'd crumpled to her knees under the force of the first blow. It smarted, throbbed like a bad toothache. There was blood on her cheek and forming a gooey patch on the metal flooring. Probably, the socket itself was fractured. Definitely blackened. He'd hit her with a sledgehammer – a big fist with thick fingers curled tight – one hand clutching her shoulder while the other one inflicted the sucker punch. Her knees had buckled. Fireflies flew. Then he'd knocked out the lights with the second strike.

She'd come to in the back of the van. In the dark and feeling woozy. Flat on her stomach and being banged around as the driver cornered too fast. Her wrists were bound behind the small of her back, so tight that the bindings bit into the skin. Same with her ankles. A gag of sticky duct tape covered her mouth. There was no sense of time, of orientation, of the identity of her attacker. Just the hard rumble of the road jarring against her cheekbone and the distant whimper of a small, frightened child coming from deep within.

Not for the first time she clenched fizzing teeth and strained against her restraints. But the plastic ties were unyielding and happy to chafe her skin all day long.

There was no escape.

No way of knowing where he was taking her or what would happen once they got there.

Fear and pain she could live with.

It was the uncertainty that was killing her.

1

Running five miles before breakfast had got me back in some kind of a shape. Maybe not the sculpted shape ripped from hours of chipping away at it in the gym – the infomercial kind of shape – but enough to keep me off the mortician's slab.

I guess you could say, from the top down, things were looking up.

The subtropical sun was a hot shrug on my shoulders as I left the main drag and hit the home straight running. My father used to say that legs ran in the Quinn family, and I guess he was right. Running had always come easy to me. As a stringy teenager I'd run the banks of the Mississippi River, through the parks in Memphis, every morning before loping off to school. *'Keep going like that and someday you'll run for your country'* my father had said on more than one occasion. *'You got stamina, kiddo, just like your Pop – of the bull-headed variety that takes you places'*.

I'd never made it to the Olympics, but I had inherited several traits from my father – the running gene being the only one to ever get me out of trouble.

I snatched a swig from a glucose drink and checked the time. I was ahead of my standing best by over thirty seconds. An improvement, five days running. Not bad for a guy in his fifties.

As usual, my dawn outing had taken me through the island's wildlife refuge: a four-mile loop cutting across a picturesque bayou. Lazy waters and flying fish. Miles of untamed swamps and overgrown mangroves. It was a great place to focus on absolutely nothing and to pretend that the falling of feet was all that existed. Essentially, escape. Better still, I was enjoying a newfound health. I was trimmer and leaner than ever. Even my old knees were less shaky – but maybe through other reasons, I guess. Quitting the badge and coming to Florida had done me a world of good. It had given me a whole new lease on an old property. Picking up the pieces again. But looks can be deceptive. On the outside I was a summer retreat with wildflowers blooming in the window boxes. On the inside I was a winter hideaway with ghostly sheets draped over the furniture.

Can't win them all.

Up ahead, I could see the gray metal rooftop of Jack's place glimmering above the palms lining the roadway. A quarter mile distant. A sliver of insipid yellow walls through breezeless trees.

I increased my gait.

Jack Heckscher and I had met for the first time one steamy afternoon at the tail end of May. We'd clicked like two halves of a bad penny. Some things are like that. Several mornings each week, I'd been hanging out at the Sanibel fishing pier – not because I had any keen interest in fishing, but rather to absorb the chummy atmosphere of men sharing in one of mankind's oldest pastimes. There was something fundamental about what went on there, on that wet wooden jetty, with the tang of salt and the reek of bait. Something that nudged at the hindbrain, said: *this is what it's all about*. I'd noticed Jack there most days; cussing out catches onto the weathered timbers. That particular morning he'd been doing his best to land a speckled sea trout that was giving him the slip. In my curiosity I'd ventured a little too close and Jack had thrust a net in my hands. "Don't just gawp," he'd hollered, "Give me a damn hand!" And together we'd landed the biggest catch of the day.

We'd been just about inseparable since.

I drained the last of the energy drink as a lone heron sliced silently across the sky.

Keith Houghton

Jack was my generation. An old-school cop retired from the Houston Police Department. He was opinionated and pessimistic, much like me. He'd lost his wife and seen enough of life to realize he'd missed living it and wanted to go out with a bang. We understood one another, Jack and me. You could say, we related. Emotionally, we'd been dealt a bad hand and lost heavily. Where we differed was that Jack had won a sizeable sum on the Texas Lottery and come here to live the dream. Me, I'd come to Sanibel to escape a nightmare.

I dropped into a final short sprint, forced tired legs to fire like pistons one last time. I reached Jack's place at full speed, turned sharply onto the property and almost ran smack-bang into the tailgate of a Lee County Sheriff cruiser parked on the sandy run-up.

I came to a juddering stop with my palms flat against the trunk.

Jack's citric green Range Rover was hunkered in the open-plan garage beneath the raised house. The deputy's white cruiser was blocking it. The latter hadn't been here when I'd left on my run.

I am many things – incurious not being one of them.

I circled the green-striped cruiser and peered through its tinted windows.

As far as I knew, Jack didn't have any contacts in the local law enforcement. Like me, he'd left all that behind. Unclaimed baggage. My own dealings with the City of Sanibel Police had been sparse – more out of courtesy than anything else, and the fact my old Captain had asked them to 'keep an eye' on me. Like I needed it. Like *they* needed it.

Through the driver's window I could see a darkened computer screen jutting out of the dash. A bunch of papers fanned across the passenger seat. A foam *Island Java Cafe* cup in a holder on the armrest. The keys were still jammed in the ignition. Our visitor hadn't been here long; I could hear the engine tinkling as the heat tried to dissipate, not fast enough.

One more thing caught my eye: a dog-eared photo taped to the dash. I cupped a hand against the glass to get a better look. It depicted a red-haired girl of about nine or maybe ten, with pale arms wrapped adoringly around a black Labrador dog.

For a moment my heart burned. I backed away, instinctively, as bile surged in my throat. But this wasn't the 7th Street Bridge. And that wasn't Jennifer McNamara, slain at the hands of *The Undertaker* seven months ago.

"Detective Quinn."

I turned sharply toward the house, eyes narrowing against the morning sun.

A thin-faced deputy from the Sheriff's Office was pushing open the bug screen door and coming out onto the raised wooden porch. A disheveled-looking guy in cargo shorts and a baggy Hank Williams tee followed him. With his shaggy gray hair and knotty eyes, my landlord and friend, Jack Heckscher, looked about as gnarly as a chunk of dried-out driftwood.

"There's been an incident," the Sheriff's deputy said without preamble as he started down the wooden steps. "Detective, you need to come with me."

I went to say something, saw Jack shake his head, and thought better of it.

The deputy opened the passenger door and I climbed inside.

2

Ordinarily, I would have insisted on showering first. Maybe grab a cup of hot black for the road. But the urgency in the deputy's voice and the grimness fixing his expression was enough to trigger obedience.

Impolite as it was, I'd just have to smell.

I had a sudden pang that perhaps my daughter, Grace, had been involved in an accident. She lived nearby, on the mainland, in a cramped apartment in Fort Myers – one of the reasons I was down here in the first place. Only one of the reasons. No one had called. Fingers crossed.

"What kind of an incident?" I ventured as the deputy backed the patrol car briskly out onto the street and headed north, returning the way I'd come. I was on the backseat, slithering around in nylon running shorts, looking at the back of his head through a wire grille.

"Not my place to say," he answered.

I saw his pale blue eyes find me in the rearview mirror; saw that look of recognition when the penny drops. Somebody had told him to keep his mouth shut. Somebody that knew I'd start asking all kinds of awkward and unanswerable questions, and didn't want to cause a fuss out in the open.

"Just sit tight, detective. The Sheriff will fill you in."

It was in my nature to press further, but I had the good sense to know it wouldn't do my blood pressure or me any good. Sometimes sitting tight is all that stops us from running.

We came to a stop sign. The tight-lipped deputy made a right onto the lengthy Sanibel-Captiva Road and we accelerated east at a steady rate. We slipped out and around a slower-moving delivery truck, drove in silence for about a mile along the tree-lined route. The air-conditioning was on; I could feel sweat patches cooling against my skin. The deputy kept it tight to the speed limit, kept his eyes away from the mirror, effectively avoiding any chance I had of using Jedi mind tricks.

Something big.

That was my first thought.

Maybe nothing personal. But big all the same.

Large enough to warp space and suck me in.

Let's get something out in the open: Sanibel isn't exactly a hotbed of crime. Not many tourist spots are. Not these days. The island seemed safer than most. Stuck in a bygone era where doors could be left unlocked at night and neighbors borrowed sugar without asking. Just about the only offense I'd seen committed on a regular basis involved unleashed dogs spooking birds on the public beach.

I leaned back and stewed in my own drying sweat.

There were another two Lee County Sheriff's cruisers and a pair of Sanibel Police patrol vehicles parked helter-skelter outside an unassuming medical center on Palm Ridge Road. A newish Ford Explorer, white-with-a-green-stripe and sporting the Sheriff's decals, was parked in the shade of a fishtail palm.

"Inside," the deputy said without going into detail.

I cracked the door, got out, felt the heat rush in, and then hopped up the sandy steps.

I knew it existed, but I hadn't had reason to visit the medical center before today. Meds make me run a mile. It didn't look anything special: just one unassuming unit in a long row of unassuming businesses – flamingo-pink stucco walls and olive-green metal roofs. Sanibel's equivalent of a strip mall.

I pulled open the door and entered an air-conditioned holding area.

The insides of the medical center on Palm Ridge Road were as unexceptional as the outsides. A pine receptionist's desk occupying one side, but no receptionist. A pair of matching couches in a palm leaf fabric, facing one another across a pine coffee table. Outdated copies of *Men's Health* and *Florida Realtor* magazines stacked on the wicker surface. The prerequisite potted plants in need of dusting. One or two thrift store prints. And finally a waft of colliding colognes coming from a group of sour-faced law enforcement personnel gathered around a water dispenser at the head of the room.

"Good morning, folks," I announced in a cheery voice.

All I got in return were sourpuss looks.

A middle-aged Hispanic woman, with short mahogany hair and wearing the dark green uniform of the Sheriff's Office, separated herself from the team huddle and reached out a hand. No wedding band, I noticed. A dime store watch. Basic makeup. She introduced herself as Lee County Sheriff Torres.

We shook hands, brisk and business-like. No smiles. No first names. Fine with me.

"Sheriff," I acknowledged with a respectful nod. "Mind if I ask what this is all about?"

"I was hoping you could tell me."

No giveaway in those jet-black eyes. But something important enough to roll the big cheese herself all the way from her cozy mainland office this early on an otherwise humdrum Tuesday morning.

Behind her, the other uniforms were watching in tense silence.

I shrugged. "Sorry to disappoint you, Sheriff, but whatever it is, I'm retired; I don't do this kind of thing anymore. My professional opinion no longer holds water."

She indicated a dimly-lit hallway leading away from the reception area. "It's through here."

"What is?"

"Something you really need to see."

I glanced at the boys huddled around the water dispenser: still deathly quiet, still pensive, complexions pallid, all eyes on me.

"It's not a request," she added.

"Seems like I don't have much choice, do I?"

I tailed the Lee County Sheriff along the narrow corridor to the back of the building. We passed well-equipped examination rooms with their blinds drawn against the rising sun. No patients. No disinterested doctors *umming* and *ahhing*. On a workday, and at this time in the morning, the medical center should have been opening up shop: at least one doctor on duty, a nurse or two, reception staff – all gearing-up for the day's cavalcade of shell-lacerated feet and bug-bitten legs. But the place felt as cool and as friendly as a morgue.

"You okay with bad smells?" Torres asked as we approached a brightly-lit doorway at the far end.

"Are you kidding?" I snickered. "This running gear hasn't seen detergent since June. It'd have to be really bad to beat me right now."

But there was no contest. The stench escaping from the room at the back of the medical center threw me on the mat and beat me into submission, hands-down.

3

I tell myself I don't get fazed easily. It's a lie.

Never used to be this way.

When I'd first started wearing the badge, back in Memphis as a snot-nosed rookie, I'd had a cast-iron constitution. One of those kids who could stuff his face with hot chilies while watching a horror movie and not blink. The streets had hardened me. Even the worst homicides hadn't dented my armor. Then I'd met Hope, started a family, become less detached. Raising kids had reduced my reserve. Then middle age and becoming a grandpa had softened me up. These days, I wept like a baby, even over commercials.

The stink in the back room of the medical center on Palm Ridge was thick. An invisible fog of putrid particles. Palpable. Heavy molecules snagging on nasal hairs. It came from a *thing* lying on an examination table. Only way to describe it: a *thing*. Not every day you get to see one, in the flesh – or without. It was a monstrosity so ugly and so vile that it didn't belong anywhere on this charming snip of land. Anyplace at all, for that matter, outside of a deranged imagination.

Torres offered me a scoop of tiger balm to go under my nose. I shook my head; the stench was keeping me focused.

There were two men standing near the *thing*, either side of the examination table: a short, sandy-haired knucklehead wearing a tight black police uniform with golden regalia; and the other a thin red-head sporting a blue plaid shirt over creased chinos. The Sheriff introduced them as Police Chief Cooper and Doctor Osman, respectively.

I could see their noses were trying to crawl up inside their faces. I wondered if mine looked the same.

"Gentlemen," I acknowledged with a stiff nod.

I'd already met Chief Cooper, in passing, shortly after taking up residence on the island. We'd hit it off like a cat and dog in a hen loft. What Cooper lacked in height he made up for it in girth. Cooper was a burly gorilla with a lipless mouth and a Neanderthal brow. One of those countenances whose outlook is dark cloud turning thundery later. He'd made it clear from the get-go he thought I was trouble.

I hadn't argued; my reputation preceded me everywhere I went.

"Good God, Quinn," Cooper breathed as he weighed me up and down. "What abomination this side of weird are you supposed to be?"

"A healthy one?" I answered.

In my shabby running shoes, sleeveless royal blue *Memphis Tigers* jersey and skimpy Nike running shorts, I must have looked like a reject from an early '80s pop video. The sweatbands were an afterthought and clearly a mistake.

I thumbed a thumb at the *thing* on the examination table. "Unlike that. You thinking of opening up a Ripley's Believe It Or Not on the island, Cooper?"

He made a snorting sound. "If I do, you can rest-assured that the Celebrity Cop exhibit will be center stage."

Sheriff Torres sighed loudly, "Boys, will you please save the ego bashing until you're outside in the parking lot, or preferably out of my county altogether." She nodded toward the *thing*. "They found it on an exposed sandbar north of Bowman's Beach. About three hundred yards out in the direction of Blind Pass. So far as we know it was washed up after dark."

Bowman's was a nice stretch of public beach clinging to the northwest side of the island, facing the Gulf. Roomy. Spectacular sunsets. Popular with sun-seekers and shell hunters alike. I'd been there a few times, seen beached whale tourists barbequing themselves to a crisp, but I hadn't seen anything quite like this.

"At first they thought it was a loggerhead," Torres continued. "There was no moon out last night, which made it hard to tell for sure in the dark."

"A sea turtle?"

"You find them nesting up and down the beaches this time of year."

I stared at the *thing* on the table.

This was no sea turtle. In fact, it was the worst case of mistaken identity I'd seen since I'd been framed for murder in Vegas at the start of the year.

It looked like a prop from a horror movie. No two ways about it. Painted latex and dyed gelatin. Approximately the same size and shape as a loggerhead, but that was as far as the similarity went. I could see how the mistake might have been made in the dark and from a distance. It reminded me of black-and-white images I'd seen on one of those paper-thin TV shows, those that try to explain the unexplainable, but leave the viewer more undecided than they were before they started. Those same TV shows described such things as dead flotsam, thrown up on stony beaches across Maine and into Nova Scotia, Ostensibly they proclaimed them as the remains of beached sea monsters, exhumed from deep ocean graves, when in actual fact they were the boneless bodies of rotting whales.

But this was no carcass of an orca.

This was something much worse.

I curled a lip. "They?"

"Kids," Chief Cooper grunted in a tone that showed his disapproval. "A bunch of twelfth graders. They called it in around four o'clock this morning."

"What were they doing on the beach in the dead of night?"

"Breaking any number of city ordinances. What do you think?"

I stuck out the lip. "Unlike you, Cooper, I'm not paid to think; that's why I'm asking you." I glanced at the Sheriff for back up

"Most likely they were prospecting for shells," she said with a tight shrug. "We get our fair share of treasure seekers this time of the year. They come from all over. Some are kids, but mainly they're serious collectors. They know the beaches are patrolled throughout the day, so they hit them after dark, especially at low tide."

I nodded. I'd been here long enough to notice the endless processions of visitors doing the daily *Sanibel Stoop* as they shuffled zombie-like back and forth along the unswept beaches, searching for that one rare find to justify all the neck ache and the doctor's bill.

"Did they touch anything, these kids?"

Cooper made another snorting sound – must be his signature tune. "You kidding? They high-tailed it out of there like the devil himself was on their heels. Called nine-one-one as soon as they were safely on the Causeway."

I shook my head. "City kids. You got to love them. Still, I guess I would have run a mile too, coming across this thing in the dark. Mind if I take a closer look?"

"Be our guest."

The *thing* was sitting in a sticky pool of stinking fluid, on a clear plastic sheet that had been thrown over the examination table to protect the vinyl. It was a gray-white lump of fish-nibbled blubber, asymmetrical, its humped and lumpy surface shot through with purple lacerations. The bottom half was dusted with sand and broken bits of shell. Something like a bloated tentacle hung loosely on one side. Something like a stump sticking out of the opposite end. I could see semicircular bite marks from a big fish, probably a shark. Rents revealing a bluish interior and spongy yellow fat. Brown streaks that looked like mud. Splinters of white that might be broken bone. The impression of a shattered rib cage, maybe.

At first glance, you could be mistaken for thinking it was part of a dead seal. A bulbous chunk of waterlogged muscle, pecked at by predators.

But I'd seen this sight before.

And it didn't belong in any ocean.

I glanced at Osman. So far, the doc hadn't spoken a single word. Wasn't sure if he were exactly breathing. Looked like if he opened his mouth any longer than a few seconds he'd barf. Rimless eyeglasses protected his soft brown eyes. But I could see the thick lenses weren't enough to shield him from the grotesque *thing* stinking up his surgery. Osman was the kind of underwhelmed country doctor who was happy to bandage up the needy and hand out candy to well-behaved patients. Not cut out for regurgitations from hell. But who was? Just about the grossest thing to ever come into his surgery prior to this morning was a bad dose of acne.

"Any idea how long it's been in the water?" I asked.

He swallowed down something icky. "Best guestimate between three and four weeks." His answer was quick, terse, practiced. A longer sentence would have meant projectile puke, for sure.

"As long as a month?" I blew out a silent whistle. "In this heat and in the middle of summer, that has to be some kind of a record. I mean, doc, I'm no marine biologist, but I've been up and down these islands and witnessed firsthand the nature of the wildlife you have here. Sure, it's pretty cute from a distance, but up close it's pretty dangerous. I've even seen that big black saltwater croc you keep hidden away for special occasions. There's no way this much would be left after a month in the open water."

"You're right," Sheriff Torres interceded. "We think it spent most of that time in a saline swamp,'

"The mangroves?" The northeast side of the island was overrun with them. I'd explored a fair portion by kayak, and even rubbed shoulders with the occasional manatee. But I'd never seen anything like this. "Explains why it smells so bad, I guess."

Not just extensive decomposition, then: brackish water. The stagnant green goo in the bottom of a flower vase. The *thing's* insides must have been sodden with it.

Doctor Osman lifted a metal bowl from a trolley. "I removed these from the flesh." He showed me the contents.

Several long green pods that looked like out-of-shape runner beans. They were mangrove seeds; I'd seen the swamps carpeted with them.

"We think the last high tide pulled it out," Torres said.

"Okay," I began with a nod, "I can see where this is heading. You've got something pretty nasty here and no one wants to make a decision. It's one of those days. So level with me, Sheriff. What's really going on? Why isn't this body in the city morgue and why isn't your Major Crimes Unit on the scene?"

4

Thinking back, I should have called it a day then and there. I should have thanked the Sheriff for including me in her little shindig, hit the road and ran back to Jack's place nonstop. But I was hooked. Being reeled in. Not by the fact there was a mashed-up human torso on the examination table in Doctor Osman's surgery, but because my instincts were screaming blue murder.

"Ultimately, keeping it here it was my call," Sheriff Torres admitted. "The Chief was all set to ship it out to the mainland. He didn't want you involved at all."

"None of your business," Cooper agreed, gruffly.

"So exactly why am I here?"

Torres' dark eyes stayed on mine. "Simply put, I want your professional opinion."

She'd said it without having to think twice. Another rehearsed statement and enough to arouse my suspicion.

"You mean you want to pick my brains?"

"I like to use everything at my disposal," she answered. "Just so happens you're the best police detective currently on the island."

"Probably the only one," I corrected. "And as I've said but no one seemed to notice, I'm retired."

"My point exactly. " Cooper folded his arms across his chest and gave me the full force of his thundery countenance.

I deliberately loosened up my shoulders. It was too early in the day for confrontations. "Looks like you have this all figured out, Cooper. So before you hear mine, what's your professional verdict on this – what do you think happened here?"

A gloat hooked up the corner of his lipless mouth. "Easy. Some unlucky tourist wandered a little too far off the beaten track and ended up gator bait. Case closed."

"How about you, doc? You concur with the Chief?"

All at once, Osman looked like he wanted to flee the scene. He didn't like being caught in the middle of a muscle spat, or outmanned on his own turf. I couldn't blame him.

"There is evidence of rotational shearing," he began edgily. "It's exactly what you see in alligator attacks."

I nodded. "Sure, that's right. I've watched National Geographic just like you. Those big jaws clamp down. Teeth sink in. The gator goes into a spin. Limbs are ripped clean off. Makes a real mess, don't it? Cooper, you had any reports of missing tourists?"

I saw his arms tighten across his chest, pushing his pectorals into perfect peaks. He was sweating despite the frigid atmosphere. I was being a pain in his ass and it showed.

"There's no big mystery here, Quinn. Some visitors come by themselves. It's not unreasonable to presume weeks could pass before they're missed back home."

"But you think this is a homicide, don't you, Sheriff?"

"I sure do."

"Why is that?"

"Call it a hunch."

I nodded. Hunches are as good as a third eye in police work.

Cooper grunted: "What about you, Quinn? You think you're so smart. Let's hear what the world famous Celebrity Cop has to say."

"Well, that's easy. I agree with the Sheriff. This is definitely a homicide. And I think you're being overly defensive."

Cooper glowered. Cooper had it down to a tee.

"Truth is, I've seen enough murdered bodies in my time to recognize one when I see it. Plus, there are ligature marks on the body."

Deathly silence. I love surprises – especially by my own doing. Cooper shot a querulous glare at Osman – who was wearing the face of someone just caught with his pants down. He'd missed the linear bruising I'd noticed the moment I'd examined the body and now he was racking his brain for a believable excuse to appease the chief.

Torres stepped into the uneasy silence: "Show me."

"Sure. You got a magnifying glass handy, doc?"

With a nervy hand, Osman pulled open a drawer, fished out one of those handheld illuminated magnifiers they sell in Staples. I ignited the lamp and held it over the base of the stump. Torres leaned in for a closer look. I pointed out the faint purplish rash forming a two-inch-wide stripe.

"Resembles the Milky Way on a clear night," I said.

She nodded, "So I see. What are we thinking – heavy duty rope maybe?"

"More like cable ties. Remember, this flesh is bloated, which means the bruises are too."

Skin is porous. Immersed in liquid for days on end, dead fat and muscle act like sponges. Given time even bone swells up. This body had ballooned to double its size – imagine half the *Michelin Man* after a road traffic accident – but not before being ravaged by an untold number of fish, reptiles and insects.

Cooper jumped in on the act. "Let me see that."

Torres stepped aside. I held the magnifier steady. Cooper made a disgruntled noise. Flicked the light on and off a few times. Made the same piggish noise again.

"Could be anything," he said dismissively. "Damage from tree roots. Anything. Doesn't prove foul play one bit."

"It does when you couple it with the next piece of evidence," I said. "Doc, you got a pair of tweezers around here?"

Osman obliged; he was getting into the swing of things now. I stepped around Cooper, leaned in with the magnifiers and tweezed a small sliver of dark polyethylene from a crevice in the flesh. I held it up to the light, squinted.

Torres was hanging on my shoulder, "Looks like a shred from a garbage bag. They sell the exact same kind down the road at Bailey's General Store. Green with yellow ties."

"But it still doesn't prove murder," Cooper argued through clenched teeth.

I turned. "What is it with you, Cooper? Isn't a dead body with evidence of garbage bags and cable ties good enough for you? I just handed you a smoking gun here. You should be on your phone and dispatching men to scour the mangroves."

Cooper's lipless mouth folded over itself to form a sour-pop-sucking expression.

All at once I could see why the Lee County Sheriff and the Sanibel Police Chief were at loggerheads: news of a murder on the island would be bad for business. Damage the vacation industry – at least in the short term. Neither wanted it. Cooper was happy to sweep it under the carpet. Ship it back to the mainland as quickly and as quietly as possible. Pretend the gruesome carcass had never been found. The Sheriff couldn't. Duty forbade it. She suspected foul play and was obliged to investigate. Both were acutely aware that an island crawling with boys and girls from the CSU would spell temporary death to the island economy.

In other words, an island murderer would kill tourism.

"Quinn's right," Torres said to Cooper. "We need to search the swamps, and preferably before the next high tide."

Cooper started to object. Another thing he had down pat.

I cut him off at the pass: "Cooper, whether you like it or not, you have yourselves a homicide. And where there's a homicide there's a murderer. He bagged this body and secured it with cable ties, then dumped it in the bayou, where it remained, casseroling for a few weeks in its own juices before the gators and the crabs got wind of it. Then they tore it up. Chewed off limbs. Made a real mess. Then the last high tide caught it up and swept it out to sea, where it got nibbled at some more before washing up for those kids to find. Like it or not, this is definitely a homicide."

Cooper looked like he had a bad taste in his mouth.

I turned to the Sheriff. "But what I don't understand is why I'm here. Let's be honest, you didn't need my opinion, second or third. Your mind was already made up before I got here. You knew this was a homicide. I just plugged the gaps. Helped you make your case for the defense. But there's more to it than that, isn't there? You admitted you broke procedure by bringing the body down here instead of shipping it straight out to the Coroner's facility. I'm guessing that's not something you do every day. So what's the real reason you wanted me to see it, Sheriff? Why'd you really want me to see it?"

I saw Sheriff Torres fill her lungs, then give the doctor the official nod.

The green-faced Osman lifted another metal bowl from the trolley. He handed it to me with cupped hands, as though it contained an unexploded bomb and I was expected to defuse it.

There was a length of yellow rubber in the bottom of the bowl. Curled like a slice of thick lemon peel.

I made a frown. "What is this?"

"You tell us, Quinn," Cooper said with a smug hiss. "It has your name all over it."

5

A wheel clipped a pothole, smashing her bruised face against the cool metal flooring. She struggled to roll onto her side, to alleviate the constant pummeling sending flashes of pain through her skull, but the van's sinuous course made it an impossibility.

Vaguely, she had a sensation of street lighting sweeping through the vehicle, at regular intervals. City streets – which meant their destination wasn't remote. No secluded cabin in the woods. A house or an apartment, with neighbors and maybe a nosy curtain-twitcher to notice her abductor carrying her inside.

Through blurred vision she'd tried examining the insides of the van, vantage point permitting, to remember details, as best she could. But there were no identifying features, at least none that she could make out in the semi-darkness. No crates bearing company logos. No old delivery notes screwed up on the floor. Just a nondescript work van, newish and plain white. A blend-in.

But there was a smell. Something that clawed at her nostrils. Something that had been transported at an earlier time and left a bad residue. Something she was yet to place.

The van bounced through an intersection and she winced as pain sprang through her broken eye socket.

Bile gushed into her mouth.

She felt panic rush to the surface as the puke pressed against the duct tape, going nowhere. All at once she couldn't breathe. She struggled to draw air through her nose, to swallow down the sour acid.

Her lungs were on fire.

The panic continued to plume. For a moment she thought she was going to asphyxiate on her own vomit. Then the van rolled around a corner and the bile exploded through her nostrils.

6

There was a note pinned to the bug screen door when I got back to Jack's place:

Gone fishing. Back later. Pancakes the way you like.

Jack's lime-green SUV was still shading itself under the awning – which meant one of his fishing buddies had picked him up. It also meant he wouldn't be home until gone dark. Probably exhausted. Definitely smashed. Same old same old.

I pulled open the screen door and pushed my way inside. It was cooler indoors, but not by much. Overhead fans struggling against the rising summer heat. I moved between rattan furniture. Soft furnishings in tropical designs. Faded prints listing on whitewashed wooden walls: scenes of anemic herons standing solemnly against washed-out seashores. Very Floridian. I liked it.

In the open-plan kitchen area I found a plate of pancakes on the granite counter, and a brief smile passed over my lips.

At first I'd been reticent about moving in with Jack. Not because I was worried people might get the wrong idea. I'm a modern guy; I'm comfortable with my heterosexuality. And besides, I was through worrying what people thought of me anyway. Hateful headlines had hardboiled my head. I had long since accepted that people gossiped no matter how much I beat myself up. Truth was, I'd been more concerned that my lodging at Jack's place would be an imposition on a burgeoning friendship. And impositions quickly become burdens.

I hadn't given in to his suggestion of moving in together. Not right away. I was happy with the arrangements I'd made since coming to Florida, which basically involved spending precious time with my daughter, Grace, in and around her busy work schedule. Plus, crashing on the sofa in her cramped Fort Myers apartment and eating everything in her fridge. I hadn't wanted commitment in any shape or form. Sometimes the ties that bind are better left cut. In fact, and in spite of more heartache than any heart should bear in one lifetime, I'd begun to embrace life again. I don't know, maybe it was deliberate. Self-preservation. God knows, I needed a break – not just from my old life, but from me, too, I figured. The old me. The me who harbored fugitives and lacked the guts to be open about it. And so I'd shut it all out. I'd spent long lazy days roaming the barrier islands protecting the Gulf Coast. Exploring the sweeping shorelines of Lee County, from Boca Grande in the north to Lover's Key in the south. Kayaking the shallow bays and mangrove swamps. Essentially, doing everything I could to keep from under Grace's feet, and to stay one step ahead of my demons. So far, the storm-proofing had worked. I'd shuttered up tight and buried the past, with no intention of exhuming it.

But sooner or later everyone's debts are called in.

And Jack hadn't taken no for an answer.

"Damn it, big guy. Consider it doing me a favor," he'd argued over beer on the evening he'd raised the subject of co-habitation for the third or fourth time. "Most days, we're hanging out together as it is. You practically live here. I've been rattling round this island for six months now. I need the company. Sure, I'd prefer something a little more blonde and maybe longer-legged, but when you reach my age you take whatever scraps are left on the plate."

The idea of two grumpy old men shacking up together had sounded like a bad sitcom. And probably it was. Time would tell. For now, it helped facilitate my escapism. And, shameful as it was, I was okay with that.

I poured a cup of strong black from the coffee pot to go with the pancakes, slid onto a stool at the breakfast nook and shook out the morning paper.

The headline warned of a bad hurricane brewing out in the Caribbean. Heading this way. It told of Jamaica deluged by rains, of shanty dwellings wrecked, and of lives lost.

Locally, no mention of any murders.

I wolfed down the cold pancakes, threw the coffee down my neck, then shrugged out of my running clothes and showered off dried sweat. I dressed in a white cheesecloth shirt and tan summer slacks, stepped into deck shoes, and sprayed deodorant until I coughed up a lung. Good as new – or as good as it got.

The inside of Jack's swanky Range Rover was cocoon warm. It smelled of hot leather and Californian cherry. I started it up and cranked the air-conditioning to max. I backed it out of the shaded garage and turned it around on the sandy run-up. Then I headed south to West Gulf Drive, made the left and drove east, smoothly along the island's evacuation route.

We all have secrets.

Obsessions.

We think we control them.

We don't.

7

The van had come to a stop a while ago, after what had seemed like an eternity of corners and intersections. For now, she had no way of knowing if this was their final destination or a temporary stopover. No overhead lighting to speak of, or the sounds of other vehicles coming and going, so it was unlikely they were parked in a gas station. The driver – her attacker, her abductor – had snuffed the headlights and killed the engine. He'd climbed out and locked the door behind him. He'd left her facedown in the dark and the silence, with just the thudding of her heart and the specters of her imagination to keep her company.

She ran through a mental checklist, assessing her physical state. No need to worry about her psychological state. Not yet. Her hands were tacky with blood. Wrists red-raw and greasy, lacerated where she'd fought in vain to snap her shackles. Face swollen and sore. Right eye completely closed. Cheek scuffed and bloody. In fact, her whole skeleton ached from the bumpy ride, especially her left hip. It pulsed with pain. Something was digging into it, something other than the metal flooring. She realized with a start that her assailant had neglected to frisk her either before or after punching her to the ground.

For a moment she experienced a rush of adrenaline-fed hope.

8

The morning was heating up, fast.

I had a meeting, arranged in advance to take place in a coffee shop situated in one of the island's boardwalk-covered shopping centers. Big glass windows overlooking a fountain. It was a nice location, filled with wooden-fronted boutiques selling expensive bric-a-brac to dollar-heavy tourists. Jimmy Buffett searching for his flip flop from speakers disguised as rocks. The usual prehistoric foliage and morning scavengers.

I was early. So, too, was the other party.

I studied the man facing me across the marble-topped table. There was a steaming cup of Peruvian black between us. It wasn't his.

He went by the name of Hives – like the rash. I didn't know if it was his first name or his last, or just something he'd picked up along the way. Truth was, I didn't care much either way. Hives had come highly recommended. Reportedly, better than good at his job. That was all I needed to know. He was a three hundred pound African American with a French bulldog face: roundish and flat, with bulging eyes that seemed too close to his ears to provide proper stereoscopic vision. His shaven head sported sickle scar over one ear. Not much of a jaw line hiding beneath folds of fat. The protruding eyes were a product of proptosis, I suspected, rather than surprise at the confidential information I'd just revealed to him.

"Sure I can't get you a drink?" I said. "Coffee? Hot chocolate? Rumor has it they make a to-die-for iced tea here."

"I'm good, Mr. Quinn. Thank you all the same, but no; I have bladder issues, you see. Medication does its part, but this heat makes it difficult."

My cell phone rang. Indifferently, I glanced at the caller ID.

Eleanor Zimmerman – my old psychiatrist friend from Internal Affairs back in LA – had called just about every day since I'd landed in the Sunshine State. Normally, I'd ignore her calls. Today would be no exception.

"Lady trouble?"

I glanced up at Hives.

"The expression's a dead giveaway," he smiled. "The widening of the pupils and the slight flushing of the cheeks.'

"Maybe I need to work on my poker face."

"Or maybe you should tell her what's really on your mind. Not that it's any of my business, Mr. Quinn. Just saying it like it is."

I let the phone ring until it went dead.

Don't get me wrong; Eleanor and I are friends – more than friends if she had her way. Eighteen months ago, Eleanor was assigned to debug my brain following the murder of my wife. I'd disgracefully objected, threw tantrums like a spoiled brat and did everything I could to avoid the subject. Following my failure to apprehend the serial killer known as *The Undertaker*, the promise of another psychological inquisition had spurred me to abandon California altogether. It wasn't her fault. But right now I could live without the psychoanalyzing or, for that matter, Eleanor's attempts at wooing.

I stuffed the phone in a pocket. "Do you have everything you need?"

"I do."

"Any questions?"

A wry smile plumped his thick lips. "Plenty. But I suspect you'd rather I didn't ask them."

I'd only been in his company ten minutes and already he had me figured.

"You understand I want absolute discretion?"

He nodded, "Diplomacy is my middle name. Consider this doctor-patient privilege. Like lawyer confidentiality. What you've just shared with me will go with me to the grave."

It was my turn to nod. Although Hives had me mostly worked out, I was still trying to weigh him up. Under different circumstances, I would have checked deeper into his background, studied his handiwork for myself, that kind of thing. But with retirement came limitations, even with my contacts.

"You do know who I am?"

He gave me another wry smile. "Sure I do. It would be remiss of me if I didn't make a point of researching my clients prior to accepting their business. I know who you are, Mr. Quinn. You're former LAPD senior homicide detective, with a closure rate hovering in the upper eighty percentile. If memory serves me correctly, they also made a movie out of one of your more colorful cases."

I couldn't hold back my snicker. "Trust me, they took creative license on that one."

Hives showed his big ivory teeth. "No worries. I'm more of a documentaries kind of guy. Animal Planet. Anything without humans getting in the way."

"You understand I need to keep this quiet?"

"My lips are sealed."

"No paper or electronic records whatsoever."

"Absolutely." He tapped at his temple. "Got me a computer right up here. Secure and more reliable than any super-cooled mainframe. Better yet, only me with the password."

"And if anyone asks, this meeting never happened."

More flashing teeth: "What meeting?"

"You don't even know me."

"We never met, Mr. Quinn."

I made sure no one was looking our way before sliding an envelope across the tabletop. It was a plain white self-seal, as thick as my hand.

"First installment. You can check it. All used bills. Enough to cover your travel costs, hotel expenses, that kind of thing, plus a little extra to treat you to that habit I know you have."

He smiled broadly. "What can I say? The ladies have a thing for me."

"I'll wire more when it's needed."

Hives kept his protuberant eyes on mine as he fingered the envelope.

"It's all there," I said. "Go ahead: count it if you like."

"No need, Mr. Quinn. In my game, trust is everything."

Someone rapped knuckles on the windowpane next to my face. I turned to see Chief Cooper leering through the glass. He looked like a thundercloud on a sunny day. He made one of those *I'm watching you* gestures with two fingers, then continued to the coffee shop entrance.

I gestured to the envelope lurking under Hives' hand. "You might want to put that away; we're about to have company."

Hives shifted it under the table – just as Cooper came directly over.

I straightened in the bench seat. "You following me, Cooper?"

He ignored the question, went straight for the slap down. "You girls seem to be having a whole lot of fun. What's going on here?"

I sighed loudly. "Aside from the police harassment?"

"Who's your guest?"

"No one you need to be acquainted with."

Cooper focused his glower on Hives. "What's your name, boy?"

Hives kept his bulging eyes on me.

I sighed again, loud enough to draw the attention of the other patrons scattered throughout the coffee shop. "Really, Cooper, shouldn't you be out writing parking tickets instead of pestering the people who pay your wages?"

Cooper's stormy countenance swung back in my direction. He dropped his knuckles on the tabletop like a gorilla posturing for a scrap. "You think you're smart, don't you, Quinn? You breeze in here, set up camp on my turf and then sweet-talk the Sheriff against me with your fancy words and your hotshot holier-than-thou attitude. Are you deliberately trying to make me look like an idiot?"

I got to my feet. "Not deliberately. You make it easy. Now won't you excuse us; we were just about leaving."

Hives got to his feet: a three-hundred-pound unmovable mass.

Cooper backed away a little. Cooper isn't the tallest tree on the island.

"This isn't over, Quinn," he warned as we walked away. "I'm watching you. I have you in my sights. You hear me? Don't give me any reason to arrest your sorry ass and throw away the key."

9

The single-floor office block was located a half mile behind the Edison Mall in downtown Fort Myers, or thereabouts, on a backstreet plot bordered by a dilapidated chain-link fence and three other equally rundown parcels of land. The fence sagged in places, with entire sections overgrown by thick glossy shrubbery. The building had been built around thirty years ago, back in the boom. From up in the air it was a swastika-shaped low-key affair, split into eight rentable units, set back from the street within a wraparound parking lot of undulating asphalt. On the ground, it wasn't dissimilar from the rest of the aging buildings hereabouts.

I parked the Range Rover round back and climbed out into baking heat.

I'd been in Florida for months now and I still hadn't fully acclimatized to the tropical weather. Sunscreen and antihistamines helped, but they didn't do a damn thing to alleviate the unrelenting temperature.

I remembered a lyric from an old song: '*most killing is committed at 90 degrees; when it's too hot to breathe; and it's too hot to think*'.

The office block looked like a flaky tombstone jutting out of the broken blacktop. Six of the units were unoccupied. Realtors had propped *Space for Lease* boards in the smoked-glass windows. Looking like they hadn't moved in years. A shifty-looking guy driving a black pickup was using the office farthest from the street for storage. There was a red Jeep Wrangler parked near the back of the property. Here all week. Not sure if it belonged to the shifty-looking guy or if it was abandoned. Tennessee plates and a dream catcher dangling from the rearview mirror. Otherwise, the lot was empty.

I stared at the plain blue door set into the side of the building as I walked toward it. The doorway to a humdrum office, innocuous in every aspect. Looks can be deceptive.

I slipped a key from a pocket and slid it into the lock, opened the door and sealed myself inside.

Ask any woman and they will concur that men possess the unenviable ability to conveniently snub emotional issues. Blame genetics and social imprinting. I know I do. From an early age, men are taught to be strong, to keep a stiff upper lip in the face of adversity, to believe that tears are a sign of weakness. In other words, we are conditioned to be assholes.

I loitered in the darkness, shoulders pressed against the hard wood of the door for long quiet moments.

I am not the fastest croupier in the casino. Fate had dealt me a crap hand and I was dealing with it the only way I knew how: badly – the asshole way.

It was refreshingly icy in here; a result of keeping the blinds drawn and the air-conditioning chugging away at full blast, twenty-four-seven. The premium wasn't an issue; things can spoil in too much heat. And there were things in here I wanted to keep fresh. Vivid. Partly out of habit, but mostly out of a bizarre sense of masochism.

No one knew about this place. Not even Jack.

I'd rented the small office a week after moving in with Grace. Paid a year's rent in advance. Cash. No plastic ties. I hadn't intended to rent it, at first. I had intended to leave all my baggage behind in California. Not just my meteoric career, but also my demonic history. No such luck. You know what they say about best-laid plans. Florida had offered the promise of a new start. I'd bought into it like one of those naive tourists happily handing over their life savings for a smidgeon of a timeshare. Coming to the Sunshine State and shucking off the yolk of my past had been a way out. An escape. A chance to put everything behind me once and for all, rightly or wrongly. I'd believed it. Embraced it. Convinced myself that I needed the break to get my house in order. Who was I kidding?

I flicked on lights. Fluorescent tubes flickered and fired up.

I'd kept things simple in here: a tidy desk in the middle of the room, a plastic swivel chair, a battered laptop hooked up to the internet, a phone, notepads, sharpened pencils, a coffee pot with carcinogenic sludge evolving in the bottom.

Just the bare essentials for hunting killers.

Beyond the desk, the wall was a mosaic of photos and newspaper clippings, cut down the middle with a three-inch gap. It was a reflection of my cluttered brain: a multicolored maelstrom of photo evidence and paper trails connected by color-coded strings. Every shred of evidence collected from the last two major cases I'd worked before handing in my badge was here, at a glance.

In reality, a nightmare that would be any psychologist's dream.

The wall catalogued two serial killers and their work, both still at large and on the run. Both keeping a wary distance from me. Both connected through me.

The Undertaker and *The Maestro*.

One had killed my faith.

The other had killed my hope.

These were my obsessions.

My purpose.

My reason for getting up in the morning and putting one foot after the other.

I checked my watch: I had the rest of the afternoon free to chase specters.

10

Stress had pulled her into a dreamless sleep. She had no idea how long she'd been unconscious, floating around in her sea of pain. She came to as the van's rear doors swung open, silently on well-greased hinges. She tilted her face to get a better look at her abductor, but all she saw was a big bear clambering into the van. A bear that stank of human sweat and traces of cheeseburger. Suddenly any hopeful thought she'd had of raising help was gone, replaced with a renewed dread that burned in her belly.

The bulky bear filled the doorway, silhouetted against the growing dawn light. Behind him she could see the shadowy wall of a building and a slight angle of roof. It looked like a suburban dwelling. Could be anywhere.

She tried to squirm from his grasp as he reached in and grabbed a handful of her hair. Then he was hauling her out, dragging her facedown along the van's metal floor. No consideration to her discomfort. No thought for her dignity. She thrashed and she screamed. But her bonds limited her movements, and the duct tape muffled her voice. He hauled her free of the metal flooring, so swiftly that her legs fell from under her and slammed into hard concrete. Her knees flared with pain. Ankles cracked. Joints jarred. Her whole body convulsed with agony.

Still gripping her by the hair, he proceeded to drag her across the rough cement. Skin scuffing from her kneecaps. Feet scraping. Scalp screaming.

One of her shoes came loose and dropped behind. Her unprotected toenails scraped along the unforgiving ground. It was the most she could do to remain conscious.

No prince was coming to find the owner of the missing shoe.

11

The dimly-lit sports bar and grill located near the center of the island is one of those old-worldly establishments that harks back to a kinder era of bubblegum and hula-hoops. It stands on sturdy stilts above an open-sided parking garage, with shiny aluminum steps ascending to a short wooden promenade. I'd heard it had been re-roofed and virtually rebuilt after Hurricane Charley had stormed the island back in 2004, but you couldn't tell; they'd done a good job.

There were two glass tankards on the lacquered tabletop. Frothy amber beer on square paper napkins.

I toyed with the idea of making a start. Then decided it would be bad manners.

I'd spent most of the day exploring dead ends in my private city office, checking emails and reading homicide headlines – anything to banish an image burning in my mind's eye. It was one of those nagging memories that kept resurfacing in spite of its weight, like a drowned body. Not the macabre memory of the mutilated monster lying on the examination table in the Palm Ridge medical center. This was something else. While undoubtedly unpleasant, I could live with the gruesome image of the limbless and headless corpse in Dr. Osman's surgery. Over the years, I'd worked enough homicides to desensitize and dissociate. Irrationally, it was the picture of the little girl taped to the deputy's dash that was haunting me. I knew it was crazy. Knew that the photo of the deputy's daughter was far removed from the nightmare I'd witnessed seven months ago beneath the 7th Street Bridge in Los Angeles. But my mind had a mind of its own. And I wasn't in complete control of it.

Guilt tattoos itself into memory with indelible ink.

I forced my spine against the wood-paneled back of the booth, and let my gaze rove across the craze of framed photographs covering virtually every square inch of wall space. In every one of them, the restaurant owner was posing with famous sports stars, politicians and Hollywood celebrities. Cheshire Cat grins and forced handshakes. Autographs that would make a killing on eBay.

I checked my watch: 7:15 p.m., on a humid Tuesday in early August.

The place was busy and filling up fast; plenty of evening fixtures to watch and cheer at on the flat screens arrayed around the U-shaped bar. Various sports, some reruns and some piped in from overseas. Happy patrons stacking up drinks and making private wagers. Slapping backs and laughing. Everything warm and friendly.

A million miles away from evil.

Wasn't that the reason I was here?

I saw my friend Jack enter the bar and drift my way, sharing pleasantries with barroom buddies as he came. He had on a jazzy Hawaiian shirt over loose green linens. Leather bracelets and beads. Camouflage Crocs. Unruly gray hair finger-combed back from a craggy jaw coated in gray stubble. Every bit the sixty-year-old hippie.

I hadn't seen my friend since the deputy had whisked me away to the Palm Ridge medical center earlier in the day, and I could tell from his face that he wanted answers.

He slid into the facing bench seat and scooped up the beer. "Cheers, big guy. You have no idea how much I need this." He put it to his lips. "You really shouldn't have."

"I didn't."

He paused with froth in his stubble. "You didn't?"

"No, I really didn't."

He lowered the tankard and repositioned it on the napkin. "Okay. I get it. You got a date. You lucky SOB. So

I guess we better make this quick, then. I'm dying to know: how'd it go this morning, with the Sheriff?"

I leaned across the table and kept my voice low; there were ears everywhere – one or two who I knew wrote features for the local rag. "Jack, this is just between you and me, right? So make sure you keep it that way."

Jack leaned in, "Hey, see this face? It's the definition of discretion."

"I mean it."

"My lips are zipped. Now stop yanking my chain and spit it out."

"All right." I glanced around, suspiciously. No one was paying attention. "They found a body. Some kids. Late last night. Out on the beach past Bowman's. At first they thought it was a boating accident or maybe an alligator attack."

"But it wasn't."

"The Sheriff suspected foul play and I confirmed it."

"That why they hauled you in?"

"Partly." Another visual sweep of our noisy surroundings. "There were ligature marks and signs that the corpse had been wrapped in garbage bags."

Jack smiled. "Jesus, Mary and Joseph. So they got themselves a homicide. I'll be damned."

I leaned back and ran a finger over the condensation frosting my beer glass. "Want to hear the best part? At first I thought they wanted my professional opinion. You know me: I don't mind giving it, even when no one's asking. But the Sheriff had already made up her mind it was a homicide even before I got there."

"I hear the Sheriff's a smart gal. Single, too. So why'd she need you on her side?"

"Because neither Chief Cooper nor Doc Osman was of the same opinion as her. It was two on one. Cooper and Osman were as good as playing tag partners. Come to think of it, the doc looked nervy as hell the whole time."

"Like he didn't know what he was doing?"

"For sure, he didn't. His whole medical career up until this morning consisted of prescribing antihistamines and handing out hydrocortisone to itching vacationers. But it was more than your regular nervousness, Jack. Like he'd worked out his responses beforehand and didn't want them to sound, I don't know, stiff."

"Maybe he set the whole thing up."

I smiled at the thought. "Jack, seriously, Osman couldn't pull off his own sweater, never mind a murder. Besides, why would he do such a thing?"

"To make a good impression on the Sheriff. I read someplace the Lee County ME is retiring shortly. No better time to put in his tender. No better way than to diagnose murder."

I didn't think about it too long; it didn't feel right.

"Of course he'd need help," Jack continued without waiting for me to poke holes in his theory. "Someone with authority. Someone who could help him realize his bid."

"You mean someone like Cooper?"

"Damned right I do. Cooper's a prick. You said it yourself they were as thick as thieves."

"And you're right; I don't like Cooper either. He's a snake in the grass. More bad blood than a day-old corpse. But I can't imagine him killing somebody just to give Osman a leg up."

"Unless Osman has something on Cooper."

Now I laughed. "Jack, you have a vivid imagination. Osman would need balls of steel to go up against the chief. Sure, Cooper's a wolf in sheep's clothing, but he doesn't strike me as the kind to roll over that easily. Want to know the real reason they hauled me over there?"

"Sure, why not? You have my interest piqued."

I dug out my phone and brought up a photograph I'd taken in the examination room, right before being asked to leave and to delete it.

Jack squinted at the picture, frowned. "Am I supposed to know what this is?"

I stroked the screen. The image expanded. Against a background of silvery metal, a strip of curved yellow rubber – about three inches in length and a half-inch wide – was curled up like a wounded grub. Both ends of it were ragged, as though wrenched apart by force.

Jack was shaking his head. "Still not seeing it, big guy."

I sighed. "It's a piece of one of those promotional wristbands. Like the kind they sell to fundraise or promote public awareness."

"Like this?" He held up his wrist. Amid the leather-and-bead bangles I could see a sliver of red silicone.

"Exactly. What's that one say?"

"I'd kill for a Bud."

I shook my head and tapped the screen again until the slice of yellow filled it completely. Then I pointed a finger. "See the words engraved in the silicone?"

Jack's eyes narrowed. We are both of that age where reading glasses are an annoying necessity, acknowledged but rarely accepted.

There were two words impressed into the broken wristband, same color as the background. Hard to make out unless magnified. The first one was badly scuffed, with the forward half of it missing. The second word was clearly visible.

"Something Cop," Jack read out loud. "Is this the best photo you could take?"

"Jack, it's the *only* photo they'd let me take."

"So what's the word before Cop? Looks like it ends in *rity.*"

"That's because it does. They think the *Celeb* got eaten by a shark."

I saw realization chase away his frown.

Hardly anyone had referred to me as *Celebrity Cop* since I'd packed my bags, got on a plane and escaped to

Keith Houghton

Florida. Everyone with the exception of Cooper, that is. I'd been landed with the ball-and-chain moniker a few years back, during a cinematic homicide case involving the brightest Hollywood stars. Chasing down a deranged killer fixated on strangling media personalities with the nation's flag had catapulted me into the public eye. In and around the hectic investigation, I'd endured forced talk shows and stressful news channel appearances. All high profile nonsense that had achieved absolutely nothing except making me a household name. I've said it before and I'll say it again: limelight only makes me look green. The Star Strangled Banner Case had been brought to a successful conclusion and subsequently closed. But the nickname had stuck, in my back, like a dagger ever since. I had thought I'd left the handle far behind in LA. I was wrong.

"The dude must have been in your fan club," Jack said with a wink.

I shuddered at the thought. I knew there were fan sites on the Internet – another result of my brush with stardom – dedicated to following my cases and broadcasting my life worldwide, warts and all. But this was something new. I hadn't seen one of these wristbands before, with my nick on it. And I was uncomfortable with the thought that any misguided 'fan' of mine should meet with such a grisly demise.

"They know who the unlucky bastard is?"

I put my phone away. "Not yet. The body was badly mutilated. Missing its head and limbs. It was bloated beyond recognition. Jack, you should have seen that thing. It had been in the water for weeks. You could hardly recognize it as being human, let alone make a positive ID. They're submitting DNA to the FBI database. Hoping for a hit in CODIS. But it could be a while before the results come back."

Jack was looking at me from beneath a frown. "Are you even interested when they do?"

I shrugged.

48

"Jesus, Mary and Joseph. You're thinking about going out there, aren't you?"

"Out where?"

"Bowman's Beach, for chrissakes."

"I very much doubt it. The Sheriff said Forensics didn't find a thing."

"Never stopped you before."

"What's that supposed to mean?"

"You know exactly what it means, big guy. The whole world knows what you're like.'

"They do?"

"Sure, they do. You're obsessive. You like to hang out at crime scenes and soak up the ambience." He leaned closer, voice low: "Especially homicides."

"Sounds like somebody's a tad jealous."

Jack pushed himself back and let out a long breath. "Well, you got me there. Sure, I miss my old life sometimes. The thrill of the chase. The excitement that comes from the crime. All those killings. But taunting you, big guy, more than makes up for it."

I straightened my spine as I saw a blonde-haired woman enter the sports bar. I puffed out my chest a little and put on my best face.

Jack saw my feathers unfurl and turned to see who had brightened up my mope. Then he scuttled out of the booth and smoothed down his hair.

"Hi, y'all!" the blonde smiled as she floated over. One of those ruthless smiles that pulls out your own teeth.

"Hi yourself," Jack whooped. He threw big arms around her and gave her a friendly hug. Lifted her onto tiptoes. She hugged him back.

"Okay, break it up you two." I got to my feet. Opened my arms.

She slipped out of Jack's embrace and swooned into mine. We hugged each other. Longer. Harder. It felt good – as it should.

"Hi, Daddy," she whispered in my ear.

"Hi, Gracie."

The crowd at the bar cheered as the designated hitter struck a home run.

I let the hug linger, and Gracie let it too.

12

This time in the morning, the sandy parking lot near the picturesque lighthouse was overrun with those holidaymakers crazy enough to vacation during the hottest month of the year, but smart enough to take advantage of the low season rates. An army of sun-seekers heading for the glistening beaches, armed with coolers, beach towels and e-readers. The happy clapping of flip-flopped feet against the gentle splash of waves.

Paradise, for the living.

It was barely mid-morning, Wednesday, and the sky sizzled. The island was basking in the sixth day running of uninterrupted sunshine. Several degrees above the seasonal average. No sign of the regular and predictable afternoon showers or T-storms in almost a week. I had a feeling it was thanks to the embryonic hurricane sucking up moisture down near the neck of the Gulf. But I'm no meteorologist. There was a cliff of white haze towering out at sea – storms brewing on the horizon. I had the Range Rover's climate control on max, but the invisible block of ice was beginning to melt through the open door as Jack unloaded his fishing gear from the backseat.

Beyond the gnarled sea grape trees rimming the sandy shoreline I could see pick-headed pelicans skimming turquoise water.

Like I say: paradise.

But even paradise had its pitfalls.

"Listen up, big guy, I'll hitch a ride back with one of the boys when I'm through. You go enjoy yourself or do whatever it is you do with your day when you'd rather not hang out with your best buddy. Don't worry about me. I'm a survivor."

"Sure you don't want me to come pick you up maybe later? I don't have any plans that are set in stone."

Jack popped a straw Stetson onto his head. "Positive. I know you're itching for it. You go get Bowman's Beach out of your system. Don't worry about me. The weather's fine and the fish are flying. I'll be home for dinner – maybe even with dinner. Take it easy, big guy. And don't do anything I wouldn't do."

He slammed the car door, hefted his fishing gear over his shoulder and marched off in the direction of the fishing pier.

I heard the air-conditioning relax a little.

Jack knew me better than I knew me.

I rolled the Range Rover toward the beach park exit and then drove it northwest across the island, slowing at the *first come, first served* intersections. Stopping for lines of smiling cyclists crossing the highway at the yield points. I'd soon learned that patience was a requirement for island living. This time of year, the long spit of land teemed with tourists. Thousands of sandal-wearing sun-lovers riding up and down the bikeways. Many more swarming around the little knots of specialty stores like wasps on dollops of honey. All of them making the most of the fine Florida weather before the rains returned in earnest.

I was halfway to my destination when I spotted a black sedan pop up in the rearview mirror. It was a nondescript generic with Orange County plates. Orlando, or thereabouts. Newish. Probably a rental. A male driver wearing a hat. I'd noticed it a few times over recent days. Each time following at a discreet distance. Not every single journey. But enough to rouse suspicion. I hadn't mentioned it to Jack. Jack would have challenged the driver, warned him to steer clear the old-fashioned way – with a promise of violence and no coming back. Jack was much more hands-on than me. Old school policing has little time for subtlety, I guess.

I pulled into the gas station on the corner of Periwinkle and Tarpon Bay and climbed out into scorching sunshine. I gave the old timer sitting on a stool forty bucks for thirty dollars' worth of gas, and made polite chitchat while he filled her up.

The driver of the black sedan was watching from the sidewalk. He'd parked the rental out front of a store adjacent to the gas station and was doing his best to look nonchalant. Hands stuffed in pockets. Working so hard at pretending to be doing absolutely nothing that he stood out like a clown at a funeral. That kind of forced *I'm just standing here watching the world go by* attitude is a magnet to a police officer, even a retired one. The guy might as well have had a neon sign on his head saying *Crack for Sale*.

I studied him out of the corner of one eye. He was an ordinary-looking guy in a short-sleeved board shirt, blue jeans and snakeskin boots. Late twenties to early thirties. Olive-skinned and long-faced. Maybe more Native American than south of the border. He was a sturdy-looking guy nonetheless – toned without being overly muscled – with the inklings of a closely-shaven head hiding under a trendy fedora. Too far away to make out his features in any real detail.

I was wondering why he was following me, or who'd paid him in the first place.

The old timer shook off droplets from the nozzle and clanged it against the metalwork. I got back inside the Range Rover and backed it into a vacant parking bay five spaces down from the black sedan. Then I entered the general store, keeping an eye out for the guy in the snakeskin boots. It was cool inside. The smells of fresh bread and coffee, fruit and breakfast. I took my time moving through the grocery section. I was curious to see if my tail would follow. Thirty seconds later, he did. Side-on, I watched him feign interest in a chilled glass cabinet filled with homemade fudges.

But his attention was aimed my way. Not openly, but I could *sense* it.

Lately, I'd adopted a more passive disposition. Partly because I was getting too old for all the anxiety, but mostly because Sanibel had a soporific effect. I'd told myself that coming to the island called for a different approach. No more gung-ho, door-kicking-in, bullets-flying mentality. I was retired now. A regular member of the public. Chilling out would help keep the Band-Aid stuck down on old wounds.

But not today.

Today didn't apply.

The guy with the snakeskin boots had been following me all week and I wanted to know why.

I started walking toward him.

He didn't budge. Not one inch. He kept his hands jammed in his pockets while he gawped at the rainbow-colored candies.

I stopped a foot short and peered into the chiller cabinet. We were in each other's personal space. I could smell his cologne: something woody. I could feel the heat coming off his body. From this angle, I couldn't see all of his face, but what I could see seemed like it had come out in sympathy with his snakeskin boots. Just about the worst case of acne scarring I'd ever seen in my life.

"The rocky road's a good choice," I began conversationally.

He didn't flinch. Didn't react. Inside, this boy was as cold as an ice statue.

But I could feel the tension. See it in his jaw as his facial muscles tensed over clenched teeth.

I wondered what his problem was.

This guy was in good shape. No doubt about that. Plenty of gym time – probably at the expense of a daytime job and a serious relationship. There was a tattoo on his forearm: a stylized phoenix with jagged flame wings. I'd seen similar tats on military personnel and federal agents.

He had that air about him: institutionalized. Maybe even an ex-con.

"You from round here?" I asked.

The guy in the fedora turned and strolled away. Wordlessly. Like I wasn't there. He didn't even acknowledge my question with so much as a glance. He just upped sticks and left the store.

I lingered, mulling it over.

By the time I got outside, the black sedan was gone.

I started up the Range Rover and headed out.

13

Bowman's Beach is one of the island's best-kept secrets. It is located far enough from the umbilical roadway connecting Sanibel to the mainland to prevent all but the serious shell hunters from making the long trek. That said, the sandy parking lot was full to overcapacity by the time I got there, and a handwritten sign confirmed it. I left the Range Rover tucked on the roadside. Jack wouldn't be happy; he was slightly precious about his brand new ride. I cut through the parked cars and crossed the bridged freshwater bayou to the beach. Beneath the blazing sun, the luminous sand was blinding: a broad stretch of brilliant white, sloping toward calm azure waters. Filled with sunbathers and multicolored parasols. Kids with inflatables. Teens playing volleyball. Parents frying to a crisp. I pushed sunglasses to the bridge of my nose and turned immediately right as I hit the grassy backwash.

According to the Sheriff, the mangled corpse had been found on a sandbar on the way out to Blind Pass, but closer to Bowman's.

I headed north through razor-sharp dune grasses, skirted humps of sea oats, crossed lines of flowering railroad vines. My board shoes crunched shells as I went. It was hot, sticky work. I opened my shirt and let the warm sea breeze ventilate.

A half mile later, I changed tack. I cut down to the water's edge. There was a long section of beach where the tide had gouged out a yard-deep drop onto harder, wetter sand below. I stopped at the lip and shielded my eyes against the pearlescent water.

There were hardly any zombies doing the Sanibel Stoop this far out from the public access, just one or two star-crossed lovers, hand-in-hand, sifting shells and kicking through the warm shallows. Not a care in the world. The occasional prehistoric pelican dozing on a lazy swell. And something that shouldn't have been here on such a pleasant day at the beginning of August.

I flattened a patch of broken shells with my foot and seated myself on the edge of the drop-away.

I'd spent the last six months running away from it. Storm-proofing. Kidding myself that these kinds of horrors were either in another time and another place or safely stowed behind steel shutters.

"Death has a way of following you around, Quinn." Chief Cooper had told me in no uncertain terms the first time we'd met. And, damn him, he was right.

About twenty yards out, the top few inches of four bamboo canes were sticking out of the clear green swell. Gaudy black-and-yellow police tape connected them together to form a square about four yards along each edge. A snowy egret was staring at me from its perch atop one of the canes.

This was the spot where the kids had stumbled across the washed-up carcass.

Yesterday, it had been laid bare beneath a moonless sky.

Today, the crime scene was three feet underwater.

I scooped up a hot handful of crushed shells and let them sift through my fingers. I gazed out across the silky water and thought about the bad people I'd put behind bars. Thought about the ones who had evaded capture and still posed a real danger to the general public, including me. With the memories came faces, names. Not only killers, crazies and monsters, but also friends, colleagues and family who had paid the ultimate price for my obsessions. I thought about my last two partners, Harry Kelso and Jamie Garcia – both of whom had been slain because of me. I was under no illusions. Cooper was right:

people died around me. I'd lived it. Seen it. Survived to tell the grim tale. No such thing as coincidence, remember?

I tasted something unholy in the back of my mouth, and swallowed it down with a shudder.

They'd found a bracelet with my moniker on it. Stuck in the bloated flesh of a mutilated corpse. Here, on this beautiful secluded beach. No matter which way I cut it, the wristband linked the grisly homicide to me.

It wasn't my problem. Not my case. So why couldn't I let it go?

14

She had no concept of time, which meant she had no idea how long she'd been unconscious. Minutes, hours, days. It was impossible to determine. She'd woken with a hangover head and a dull ache in the whole of one side of her face. Sharp pain in her hands and feet. Wherever she was, it was dark. Not pitch black, but dark enough to make it almost impossible to define proper shape in the space around her. Just indistinct impressions of formless things. Wherever she was, she was flat on her back, naked and spread-eagled, so that she formed a letter X on what was a soft surface. A folded blanket or even a comforter. Her wrists and ankles were still tied. But the position had changed: they were no longer bound together with plastic ties behind her back. Her new restraints felt razor-sharp, already biting into her chaffed skin. Experimentally, she tried to draw in her arms and legs, but winced as stinging pain lanced through her limbs. She tried lifting her head, but experienced yet more excruciating pain sear across her face. There was something crisscrossing the bridge of her nose, she realized. Something hair-thin and knife-like. She tried twisting her head to the side and fresh pain bit into her skin. Instinctively, she shied from it. Blinking away tears. Wires. That's what pinned her down like a butterfly to a board. Her captor had looped wires around her wrists and ankles, and strung them across her face and torso, so that she couldn't move without inflicting severe self-torture. Suddenly, fear welled within her. Frantically, she probed the claustrophobic duct tape with her tongue, trying to loosen it up, to work it aside, to breathe through her mouth. But there was no give. Her scream came out a terrified whimper.

15

I'd barely driven a mile from Bowman's Beach when I spotted the black sedan again in the rearview mirror. Fifty yards behind. Staying put. Same driver wearing a fedora.

Snakeskin.

Curious, I let him follow as I drove eastward across the island, taking the long sweeping curves of the evacuation route at a steady pace. For now, I was happy to play his game; free time was something I had in abundance.

Sooner or later he'd show his hand.

I'd be ready.

There are several ways to tell if someone is shadowing you. One of them is to break routine. Do something unexpected. See how they react.

As the road straightened out, I swung the Range Rover sharply into the driveway of a big house hidden behind the trees, and stamped on the brake.

The black sedan slowed, hesitantly – as if Snakeskin were thinking what to do next – then the vehicle sped up and shot past with a growl of tires.

I let it go out of sight around the next curve before backing out and giving chase.

Over the years, my rollercoaster career has attracted an endless procession of followers, bunny boilers, groupies, fame-hunters. Most of them fall away once they learn how humdrum my real life actually is. Those that stay the course are either full-blown stalkers or unshakable crazies looking for their own fifteen minutes.

I wasn't sure yet which category my stalker fit into.

There was a chance he was a hard-nosed reporter sniffing out a scoop. Six months ago, when I'd disappeared from public life, one or two newshounds had come sniffing after me for interviews, for exclusives, for weeks. I hadn't given them the satisfaction, and hadn't been hounded since. But things change. Murders happen.

I arrived at the busy intersection where the causeway joined the island to the mainland and looked left and right for the black sedan. I spotted it directly ahead, across the intersection, on the pavement leading onto the road bridges. Four cars ahead.

I waited my turn, impatiently watching my stalker get farther and farther away, then crossed the intersection with a squeal of tires. Accelerated onto the first of the three long bridged roadways reaching out to the mainland.

The black sedan was about a half mile ahead. A dozen vehicles in between us. I kept my distance as we crossed the long straight roadway stretching on stilts over San Carlos Bay.

Dovetailed bridge sections slapped rhythmically against the tires.

Up above, lines of dispersing vapor trails crossed the blue sky. Down below, motorboats plied the cerulean waters of the intracoastal waterway. To the side, pelicans kept pace without batting either an eyelid or a wing. You might say, one of those brightly-colored Disney days where evil is a figment of somebody else's animation studio.

My cell phone rang and skipped around on the dash. I picked it up and squinted at the name on the screen. Then I put it back, unanswered.

I followed Snakeskin across the island cays linking the bridges, wondering what his game was. Believe me, I have just about seen everything there is to see. No great surprises left anymore. Only one kind of people interested in making my professional acquaintance these days: vultures.

I passed through the open toll station at the end of Sanibel Causeway and accelerated onto the wide pavement running northeast. The black sedan was doing the same. Fifteen cars ahead now and overtaking slower-moving vehicles. The speed limit didn't hold me back. I leaned on the gas until there were three cars between us. Kept it there. Traffic was light. Mostly heading the opposite way, back in the direction of the beaches. Sunlight glinted off windshields. The rumble of the road and the whirr of the air-conditioning. Regular folks going about their regular business. Not me.

I had no idea where the chase would lead. But it was the most fun I'd had in ages.

Leafy suburbs of gated communities with terracotta roofs passed by. Small, cream-colored strip malls set back from the roadside. I saw signs for US-41. Saw the black sedan signal and take the right-hand offshoot toward Fort Myers. Traffic started thickening. More black sedans joining the chase. I kept a sharp eye on my target. Not quite like shadowing a specific yellow taxi in New York City, but not a million miles away either. He turned left onto US-41, heading northbound on the sunbaked Tamiami Trail.

Again, the phone vibrated on the dash. Again, I ignored it.

It's easier pigeonholing the past when the sun shines.

After a half mile I noticed his left blinker light up, saw him move into the left-turn lane at the upcoming intersection. There weren't any other vehicles between us now. The signals were on green. The black sedan made the left down the side of a gas station. So did I, about thirty yards behind. I thought he was going to turn into the station, but he continued down the quieter side road and made a right into the parking lot of a small hotel.

I slowed the Range Rover to a crawl. Nothing behind. Nothing up ahead. The hotel parking lot was mostly empty: a handful of cars scattered around the blacktop. The black sedan rolled into a parking bay near the main entrance. I pulled over on the street, mostly obscured by a palm tree sprouting out of the sidewalk. Saw the driver's door open and Snakeskin climb out. Boot heels hammering. Didn't look like he'd noticed me. I waited until he'd disappeared inside the canopied main entrance before pulling into the property. I didn't know if Snakeskin was holed up here or if he was making a social call. Either way, it gave me the opportunity to investigate closer. I left the Range Rover down the side of the hotel and walked back through the heat to the entrance. Shielded my eyes against the noonday glare as I peered inside the black sedan.

Okay, I'm nosy by default. I also have an aversion to stalkers.

There was an opened bag of potato chips on the passenger seat. Cajun herb and spice flavor. Crumbs on the velour. An opened bottle of spring water in a cup holder: one of those pull-up drinkers. A casual shirt thrown on the backseat: white with a black panel. A bunch of folded papers that looked like car rental contracts and a driver's map of Florida. I could just make out computer print on one of the sheets, maybe the first few letters of the word *Dollar*, but no driver details visible.

I checked the doors: locked.

I went round the front and peered through the fly-spattered windshield.

There was a paper parking permit hanging from the interior mirror. One of those hangers advertising local attractions. A room number, handwritten in thick black marker pen.

I returned to the Range Rover and repositioned it so that I could monitor the black sedan from a safe distance. I was in no hurry. No pressing engagements. No one to rush home to. I tuned the in-car stereo to a local rock station and sang tunelessly to a *Journey* hit – something that had been covered a few years back and gleefully throttled by a popular TV show. I drummed palms against the steering wheel. Thought about the last ludicrous stakeout I'd been involved in and how it had ended with an innocent kid being shot and the Department being sued.

In some ways my life read like a Scorsese movie script.

Less than ten minutes later, Snakeskin reappeared, wheeling out two carry-on suitcases: those hard-shelled indestructible kinds they sell at the airport, with the slogan that even if you don't survive the plane crash, your baggage will.

I watched him heave the cases into the trunk, then get in the rental and pull out of the lot. I didn't give chase. I waited until he was out of sight before going into the hotel.

A brown-haired, beige-suited girl with too much makeup was manning the front desk. She was by herself in the pleasant reception area. I could smell coffee and hear elevator music playing somewhere not distant enough.

She smiled through glossy lips as I approached. "Good afternoon, sir. How may I help? Do you have a reservation?"

"Actually," I began with an affable smile, "I need the name of one of your guests. The guy wearing the fedora. The one who just left?"

I saw her smile wane.

Invariably, waning smiles signify an imminent withdrawal of cooperation. Normally, they are quickly followed with evasion and obfuscation. Sometimes, foot chases.

"I'm sorry, sir, but I'm unable to disclose that kind of information." She batted her eyelashes, as if to reinforce her stance, as if I'd buy it.

"I'm with the police."

It was worth a try.

It was like throwing up a blind and letting the summer sunshine in. Her smile returned anew. "Okay. Great. In that case, I'll be happy to help. Can I see your identification?"

I made an awkward face. "Now that's just the thing, you see. I don't seem to have it with me right now."

I patted out pockets. Saw her smile begin to falter. "The thing is, and I know you'll understand, I'm here on vacation. You know how it is. You leave your stuff in the room safe, for safe keeping, and then you forget to get it back out again."

The blinds dropped and the smile vanished. In and out like the sun on cloudy day. I could see she didn't believe a word I was saying. Neither did I.

I produced my driver's license and tapped a finger against the photograph. "See. That's me. You may recognize my face. Some folks know me as the Celebrity Cop, from LA."

She peered at the picture, twisted a ruby lip, and then shook her head. "I'm sorry, sir. It's hotel policy. You'll have to come back with proper authority."

"Even if it's my suspicion the guy in the fedora is a felon?"

"I'm sorry, sir."

The telephone gurgled at the end of the counter. The receptionist excused herself and answered the call. I pulled back, pretending to be admiring the lobby. She accessed a booking on a computer screen. I waited until she was preoccupied, then slipped into the elevator area. I could hear the receptionist still talking into the receiver; she hadn't noticed my skullduggery. I gave the elevators a pass and went straight to the stairwell. Made my way to the second floor without looking back.

I didn't know what I was hoping to achieve. Nothing good ever comes of sneaking around. I'd learned that lesson several times.

Luckily, the hotel was quiet. Everyone out in the sunshine. No sign of any guests. Just a housekeeping cart parked outside one of the rooms. The sounds of a vacuum cleaner coming from inside.

I made my way along the green-carpeted hallway until I came to the room with the same number as the one I'd seen on the parking permit. I put my ear against the wood and listened. It didn't sound like anyone was home. There was a *Do Not Disturb* swingy on the handle. Electronically locked.

I shucked off my shirt, rolled it into a tube and tucked it in my waistband at the small of my back. Then I returned to the room where the maid was busy cleaning. I picked up a clean towel from the cart and poked my head into the doorway.

"Hello," I hollered above the noise of the vacuum cleaner. I repeated it twice, louder each time, before the din died.

A maid wandered out of the bedroom area, eyeing me curiously.

I held up the towel. "I needed a fresh towel and grabbed one from your cart. I hope you don't mind?"

A nervy smile broke out across her round face, "No, no. Not at all. Take as many as you need. What room are you?"

"Right at the end of the hallway." I confirmed it with a gesture. "But the thing is, and this is embarrassing, I locked myself out when I came for the towel. And I'm not really dressed for going downstairs. Could you let me back in? I'm sorry to trouble you and all."

"Of course. It's no problem." She rummaged a master key card from a chain attached to her belt. Then I followed her to Snakeskin's room. She dipped the card in and out of the slot and opened the door.

"Thank you. Much obliged."

"You're welcome. Have a good day."

I waited until she'd gone back to her cleaning before going inside.

Snooping always gives me the jitters.

I shouldn't have been doing it.

Never stopped me before.

It was dark in the second floor guest room of the hotel in Fort Myers. The heavy drapes were drawn, leaving a crack of brilliance down the middle. I could smell toiletries and something sickly. I unrolled my shirt and put it back on. There was a bathroom to my immediate right. I caught the reflection of a fifty-something guy with a Mallen streak moving across a darkened mirror. Me. I ventured deeper, in and out of a shaft of dust motes. There were clothes on the carpeting. Randomly dropped. Two beds. One made. One not. Brown blankets and white sheets tangled and humped in the middle. A set of drawers with a TV on top. Nothing on the nightstand. Just a regular hotel room in a regular part of town.

I walked over to the window and flung back the drapes.

White-hot midday sunshine flooded the room.

I turned to look for a suitcase or something to identify my tail.

And that's when I realized I wasn't alone.

16

"I thought dispatch was joking." The Lee County Sheriff was shaking her head as she came down the hallway toward me. "But here you are. We meet again."

I was doing my best to look like an innocent bystander. Casually leaning against the wall outside the second floor room of the hotel in Fort Myers. Maybe overdoing it. I even had a plaintive look on my stupid face. Definitely looking guilty.

Behind Torres, farther down the hall, two deputies were on turn-away duty. Another guarding the guest room door. The maid and her cart had been cleared out, together with any guests found lounging in their rooms. Boys from the Major Crimes Unit were on their way.

"I thought you said you no longer did this kind of stuff?"

"It's a long story, Sheriff."

"They always are. Especially where you're involved, I hear. Care to give me the synopsis?"

I didn't hold back much. I told Torres about my tail and how, out of sheer curiosity and having nothing better to do, I'd followed him to the hotel. Playing it back out loud sounded juvenile. Lame. I saw her sigh once or twice and knew she was thinking the same.

"You do understand you're confessing to breaking and entering?"

"Just the entering part," I corrected through a stiff smile. "The maid let me in."

"Under false pretenses. The girl on reception said you impersonated a police officer."

My plaintive face was back. "Extenuating circumstances." I'd been doing it for years.

I could see Torres run through the implications of my trespassing. I'd gained access to a private guest room, illegally. Masqueraded as a cop and got myself in a knot of trouble. She ought to be arresting me and filling out awkward paperwork. I'd made things difficult and we both knew it. But I had discovered a dead body.

Torres sighed. "You know, if you didn't come with cast iron credentials, I'd take you in. It's only because I trust your judgment that I'm overlooking this. Please don't give me any more reasons to side with Chief Cooper."

"Can I politely state for the record that Cooper is an ass?"

She tittered. "You may. And you won't be the first, or the last. He does have a habit of getting under the skin."

"Incidentally, he paid me a visit."

"I take it not out of courtesy."

"Does he even know the word exists?"

"Possibly not. What did he want?"

"A shot across the bows."

"Ignore him."

"I did."

The deputy drew aside as we entered the room.

We stepped around clothes scattered on the green carpeting. Came to a stop next to the unmade bed – where the naked body of a woman was tangled up in the bed linens.

In the harsh light coming through the window, the quiet hotel room had become a brightly-lit crime scene.

"Did you touch anything?" Torres asked.

"I checked her vital signs. Two fingers, like this. Hovered my cheek over her mouth to feel for breath. There wasn't any."

"Did you attempt CPR?"

"No point. She's been dead a while."

Torres didn't ask how I knew; she, too, had seen dead bodies before. After the first handful you get to recognize the telltale signs.

"Everything was exactly the way you see it now. Only the drapes were closed."

Torres moved down the side of the bed to get a better angle.

The dead woman was in her thirties. Thicker in the midriff and classically pear-shaped. Long blonde hair with three inches of darker roots. Skin paled by death. She had red bracelet marks on both wrists. The same red necklace bruising on her throat. A dribble of crusted vomit over cold blue lips.

Three lengths of thin black tubing, each about a yard long, were on the white bed sheet near the top of the mattress. They looked like dead vipers. Coiled and twisted.

Sheriff Torres nodded, "She was strangled."

"Or a sex game gone wrong."

She glanced my way. "Explain?"

"See those ligature marks on her wrists? She was tied to the bedposts with two of those restraints. That's classic dominance. The other was used for another reason: to simulate asphyxiation during orgasm."

Torres made a '*I don't need to know how you know how*' face.

"There's also an empty condom wrapper on the bathroom counter," I added, "but no signs of a condom – used or otherwise."

"You love this, don't you?"

"Unfortunately, I have a knack for it."

"Okay. So let me get a handle on this: you're saying he tied her up first, raped her, and then strangled her."

"No," I countered again. "I'm saying, aside from the outcome, all this was consensual. As far as I can see, there are no signs of a struggle. Look at her clothes and shoes. They're discarded in a trail leading to the bed. That implies they were peeled off along the way. Usually by people in a hurry to get things underway."

"You're saying this was mutual?"

"The sex part definitely. I'm not so sure about the end result. Notice the vomit on her cheek and in her mouth? It means she was alive after the tourniquet was removed."

"So how'd he kill her?"

I shrugged. "I'm not sure he did. I've seen these kinds of things turn bad in the past. Innocent sex games ending in tragedy. I'll lay odds there are drugs involved. It's something for your ME to rule in or out."

Torres gave me a long, lidded look. "Why do I have the feeling there's more to this than meets the eye?"

A deputy stuck his head into the room: "Sheriff, Forensics downstairs."

We rode the elevator to the ground floor. There were more deputies in the lobby, plus several black-uniformed officers from the Fort Myers PD. Sheriff Torres gave the official nod to the techies from the Crime Scene Unit and they crowded into the elevator carriage, armed with kit bags and resolute expressions. Through the main entranceway, I could see various patrol cars and an assistant from the Coroner's Office wheeling a gurney toward the doors.

"I need to see your bookings," Torres instructed the dumbstruck girl behind the counter.

The receptionist looked a little less bright than she had done thirty minutes earlier. A little more green. I wondered if I looked the same. Discovering a dead body on your watch can do that kind of thing.

Wordlessly, she spun a computer monitor round to face us. She tapped a nervous red nail against an entry on the screen.

"The room's registered to a Carole Quayle," Torres read out loud. "Checked in last Friday for a one week stay. Is there another name on the booking?"

"No. Just the one."

"But there have been two guests staying in that room."

The girl looked puzzled.

"A man," I said before Torres could say it. "About six foot, medium build, bad skin, wears a fedora. The one I asked you about earlier."

"Yes, I did see him passing through. But I didn't know which room he was in. I'm sorry."

"Were you on the desk, Friday, when Ms. Quayle checked in?"

"Yes. But as far as I can remember, she was alone."

Torres pointed to the screen. "I'm going to need a printout of her booking. Together with a list of all your guests during the last week."

"No problem." The girl set about spooling up the printer.

Torres turned to me. "And I need you to give a description of this man to my detectives when they get here. Then go through the motions with a sketch artist. If he did kill her, we'll need to get eyes out for him as soon as we can."

"What about the rental car? They have tracking devices."

Torres got on her radio to dispatch and issued an All Points Bulletin.

"We'll bring him in and see what his story is. Then see how it matches up with the ME's findings. In the meantime, have you any idea who he might be and why he's following you?"

"Aside from a stalker, I don't, on either count. Like I say, I saw him first a couple of days ago."

I didn't mention the ex-military tattoos. Or the fact his body language had been wound up tight like a jack-in-the-box.

"How about before that? Maybe back in LA?"

I shrugged. Hard to say for sure. Los Angeles was a big place. And I'd come into contact with a lot of strange strangers over the years.

"Someone you might have upset, for instance?"

I'd upset a lot of people. Get to the back of the line.

"An ex-con?"

I made a face.

Torres saw she was wasting her time. "Either way, until we know otherwise, we have to treat him as our number one suspect in a potential homicide."

The receptionist placed a printout on the counter. "There's an outstanding balance," she said. "Items from the mini bar."

I glanced at the sheet. "Any phone calls?"

"Yes."

I went to pick it up. Torres beat me to it.

"Look, Quinn, I appreciate the cooperation. I really do, but this isn't your investigation. If my detectives come across anything pertinent to you, I'll have them get in touch. In the meantime, please try and stay out of trouble."

I hung around the lobby until the detectives showed. A man and a woman. Efficient and friendly – not their names. I gave them Snakeskin's description. They told me to stay put; a sketch artist was on her way. They made note of both my cell and Jack's home phone numbers and told me to be available for further questioning. Then they interrogated the receptionist before heading upstairs to the crime scene.

A TV news van entered the hotel parking lot. Sheriff Torres went outside and spoke with an NBC reporter. They shot some footage before making camp out on the roadside.

I hung around some more. Helped myself to the complementary coffee. Watched the police procedures as officers came and went. Information passed to and from. The sketch artist arrived. I spent thirty minutes guiding her pencil. She was good enough to mold my fudgy descriptions into an exact likeness of the guy in the fedora – or as close as my aging eyesight could give. She thanked me and left with the Sheriff.

Finally, the CSU cleared out, making way for the ME's assistants to take the elevator to the second floor and bag the body. They were wheeling it out on the collapsible gurney when everyone in uniform started running toward the main doors.

I collared a flush-faced deputy as he tried to rush by. "What's with all the excitement?"

"The perpetrator's vehicle has been found."

I put down my coffee, almost spilling it, and joined the scramble.

17

The most excitement Fort Myers had seen in months – me, too, for that matter – at least that was the impression I had as I kept pace with the cruisers converging on the location of the sighted vehicle. A minimum of a dozen PD and Sheriff's units already ahead of me, with more joining the stampede as we charged northbound on US-41. I could even hear the *thump-thump* of a helicopter as it chopped above rooftops, obscured by the brilliant sunshine. A few of the squad cars leading the race had their red-and-blues flashing in unison with their screaming sirens. Adrenaline pumping at full throttle. I was exceeding the speed limit by a reprehensible amount, but no one noticed.

As we passed Page Field, the high-speed convoy made the next right onto Fowler, stemming the flow of traffic at the intersection. I kept my foot on the gas. Determined to keep up with the race leaders. We came to the busy intersection with Colonial Boulevard and sped through it, loosing sparks.

Up ahead I could see the stream of police vehicles turning right, cutting through a plaza of automotive repair shops. Mystified mechanics and puzzled customers watched as the convoy bounced along the side road. One flashy cruiser after another. The wail of sirens blasting off the walls. I brought up the rear. Weaving around parked cars and pedestrians. The procession caught the next left and started to slow.

I made the turn with my foot off the gas. Brake lights lit in front. The convoy slowed to a crawl. I eased off some more. The sirens stopped. The lead cars had arrived at their destination and were taking up positions around a single-story building set back from the roadside. One by one they rolled onto the wraparound parking lot, until they had the place surrounded. Two-dozen or more police cars and Sheriff's Office cruisers, all facing the plain white building. Roof lights crackling.

I left the Range Rover butted up against the curb and leapt out. Cops and deputies were leaping out of their own vehicles, drawing weapons and using car doors as shields.

There was a black sedan parked round back. Nose-in to the building. Straddling two parking bays, on an angle.

It was the same black sedan that had been following me the last few days.

"That's as far as you go!" an officer yelled in my ear. He grabbed me by the arm and brought me to a halt. He was big enough to absorb my momentum. He pushed me to the rear of his cruiser, hand raised in my face. "Please, sir, for your own safety, stay back!"

I gaped at him with big fearful eyes.

I had a flame of adrenaline burning in my chest. But not for the same reason as the armed officers training their guns on the culprit's car.

The black sedan was parked outside a rundown office block.

The same office block with a space rented out in my name.

18

Someone bellowed: "Car looks clear! The suspect must be inside!"

Inside.

My chest was on fire. Rack of ribs, flame-grilled.

Inside meant inside the office block.

Inside my office.

The black sedan was pointing accusingly at the blue door.

A blue door whose key was in my pocket, burning a hole.

A barrel-chested police officer with sergeant stripes snapped out orders. Four uniforms sprinted to the black sedan, their weapons trained on it like eagle eyes. Two covered their colleagues as they flung open doors and declared it empty.

A siren gave a short blast. The Sheriff's white Explorer bumped up onto the parking lot and rocked to a stop. Torres tumbled out and ducked into her Stetson. She saw me but went straight over to the sergeant in charge. They conferred. Gestures that pointed to the office block and its surroundings. The sergeant nodded. Torres wasn't his boss, but she held the highest rank of anyone here. He waved at his men to secure the area. Uniforms scurried around, stooping behind parked cruisers as they went. Endless hours of police training coming into practice. If Snakeskin was in there, he wasn't coming out, except in cuffs or a body bag.

A helicopter roared overhead, obscured by the afternoon sun. I couldn't tell if it belonged to the police or a TV news station.

Torres retrieved something from the trunk of one of the police units and came over.

"Here," she said, "put this on. Don't argue now; I don't need any civilians getting caught in any crossfire."

I looked at the Kevlar vest in her outstretched hand, made a face. "Sheriff, there's no saying he's inside. Or that he's armed and dangerous." My voice had a desperate quiver to it.

Torres noticed, made note, but didn't comment.

"The car looks like he dumped it," I offered feebly. "He's gone."

"Quinn, I don't know how you do things in LA, and frankly it's none of my business, but here we follow procedure. Now wear this and stay put, or return to your vehicle immediately."

Her dark eyes meant business. I accepted the vest and sealed myself inside.

Maybe it was the heat, but I could feel my blood pulsing through my body.

Several uniforms hunched their way to the other office units. Tried the doors. I saw them peer through windows, then look around the *Space for Lease* boards. Formalities and a risk of liability meant they had to make sure the area was secure before proceeding.

There was no sign of the shifty-looking guy with the black pickup. And even the red Jeep Wrangler that had been here all week had disappeared.

"The car's a Dollar rental," Torres told me as I did my best to hide my unease. "Rented out in Ms. Quayle's name."

I had one eye on the blue door. "Explains the room number on the permit."

"She picked it up from McCarran Airport, Friday."

"She drove here from Orlando?"

"Probably a tourist. It's what they do. They spend a few days doing the theme parks, then come down here to find the real Florida."

I was willing the guy in the fedora to come strolling out. Save me from a dozen nosy cops poring all over my private stuff.

The pulsing blood in my veins had begun to thud.

"We're running checks on her right now. Her driver's license is registered in California. You ever run into her?"

I let out a nervy laugh. It sounded misplaced and inappropriate. Guilty. Sheriff Torres was running through a checklist and crossing out dead ends. Doing it by the book. My reaction wasn't just thought-provoking, it was unprofessional.

Snakeskin had followed me to the office.

And I'd missed it.

A dark-colored SWAT van came hurtling down the street and mounted the curb, came to a stop behind Jack's Range Rover. A no-nonsense, green-suited SWAT team bailed out and started kitting up. Sheriff Torres excused herself and went over to strategize with the stern-faced Watch Commander.

I realized I was on my toes and forced my legs to relax. One or two cops were staring. Probably wondering who the hell I was and why I looked like a flummoxed teenager whose parents were about to find a stash of porn magazines under his bed.

I should have run to the Range Rover and hightailed it back to Sanibel, never looking over my shoulder. Pack my bags and catch the next plane to anywhere that wasn't here. But I didn't. My legs were rooted to the hot blacktop. I couldn't flee even if I wanted to. And, believe me, I wanted to.

Things were about to get real icky, real quick.

And I was in the middle.

The practiced SWAT team strutted their stuff flawlessly. Heavily-armed and flak-jacketed, they spread out in pairs and ran over to the office building. Started inching their way along the flaking walls toward the plain blue door. Taut silence descended as every uniform braced for possible confrontation.

"This is the Police Department." The police sergeant was using a bullhorn. His amplified voice boomed across the parking lot. There was a whine, then a crackle. "We have the place surrounded. Come out with your hands in the open."

No one came out.

The blue door remained defiantly closed.

The sergeant repeated his request.

Same result.

By now there were two SWAT members on either side of the blue door. Two crouching and two leaning over their comrades, covering with their submachine guns. Four highly-trained professionals with rifles butted against shoulders and intentions steely. A fifth appeared with a handheld battering ram. His partner was spooning him from behind, aiming his MP5 over his colleague's shoulder. Everything tight and well-practiced. At any other time it would have been good to watch. Not this time.

The only sounds were the distant whirring of rotor blades and the bass drum pounding behind my ribs.

I glanced at Sheriff Torres. She was standing with the stern-faced Watch Commander and the police sergeant, back by the SWAT van – coordinating from the sidelines like coaches at a football game.

Torres had her cell phone to her ear.

She should have been watching her deputies. She should have been monitoring the situation as the assault played out. But she was staring straight at me.

I realized with a start that maybe she was speaking with the realty company responsible for leasing out the office space, and that right now she was discovering exactly whose name the unit was rented out to.

The bass drum quickened its beat.

All that was missing was the marching band.

But they would come.

I saw the SWAT guy with the battering ram adopt an attack position.

They were about to break into my private lair. Expose my obsessions. Make me look foolish, probably live on TV. Not the first time.

I had to stop them. Somehow.

I drew a fiery breath and stepped forward, automatically. Started to raise my hand in objection.

"Wait!"

I froze.

The command had come from Sheriff Torres. It echoed across the parking lot, drawing everyone's eyes. I turned to see her marching toward me. I had a sudden sickly, gut-kicking feeling that she'd uncovered my dark secret and it was about to be laid bare for all to see. Innards picked at by the vultures. But she wasn't looking at me anymore, I realized. She was looking through me. Past me. She marched right by, as if I didn't exist, right into the middle of the assault arena.

"Listen up!" she shouted to the men and women in uniform. "The suspect has been sighted in the vicinity of Edison Mall. We need to move out, now. Let's go, people!"

19

I exhaled dragon breath.

My secret was safe. For now. But the relief was short-lived. I watched, numbly, as Torres instructed a pair of deputies to stay with the victim's rental while everyone else jumped back in their cruisers and headed out. Finished at the hotel, detectives and techies from the Crime Scene Unit were on their way to investigate.

And I was knee-deep in dung.

Forensics would have a field day in that office. They'd find my prints all over the place. On every scrap of information pinned to the walls. Fall over their own feet with excitement when they found the laptop containing traces of every Internet search I'd made in the last six months, and then some. Everything I'd amassed on two serial killers. Everything I knew about *The Maestro* and *The Undertaker*. A lot of stuff not even in the case files. Not to mention emails, records, personal data and just about every bit of incriminating evidence they needed to make me look like a complete and utter nut job.

I caught Torres' attention as she was about to get back in her vehicle. "Sheriff, the mall's a big place; you'll need every available man. I've got this. Let me hold the fort here until Forensics arrives. It's just an abandoned car. No big deal." It sounded desperate, pleading. I hoped she hadn't noticed.

But Torres was no fool. She confirmed it with a suspicious frown.

"I'm serious," I continued before she could protest. "The fun's over here. Take your men. I have this covered. I know the drill. I won't let anyone within fifty yards of this vehicle until your detectives show up."

I saw her think it through. We both knew I was right. The mall contained dozens of shops to process. Four big department stores. Hundreds if not thousands of shoppers. Plenty of places to hide and avoid capture. Limited police personnel. She'd need all the muscle she could muster just to cover the exits alone.

She chewed it over as the SWAT van made a U-turn in the street and sped away.

I kept the desperate pleading from screwing up my face any more than it already was. Hoped my shaky voice hadn't given the game away. Six months of sitting in a rocking chair, pretending bad things happened to other people, had softened my normally masterful poker face. Ask Hives.

"What's in it for you?" she asked, throwing me off balance.

"Let's just say it'll make me feel better and go a ways to make amends for my little fiasco at the hotel." It didn't sound sincere. I wouldn't have believed me; I couldn't expect Torres to be any less forgiving.

But Torres desperately wanted to trust me. I could see it. I wondered why.

"Okay," she nodded at last. "But, please, do not touch anything. I mean it, Quinn. I've had enough surprises for one week. Leaving you here goes against everything I believe in. But I trust you – so don't mess up."

She made a sharp gesture to the remaining deputies, who promptly got in their cruiser and joined the police posse racing west in the direction of the mall, sirens screaming.

Torres got in her Explorer, her eyes never moving off me all the time she was backing out onto the street.

I waited until she was out of sight before slipping the key from my pocket. Made sure I was alone. No deaf deputies skulking around back. No nosy helicopter hovering overhead. I reckoned I'd have a couple of minutes at best to clean out my stuff before the cavalry arrived. Less than two hundred seconds to tear down six months of work and hide it away in the trunk of Jack's Range Rover. No sweat. I was pumped.

I ran on wobbly legs to the plain blue door, twisted the key into the lock, and then paused again to make sure I wasn't being watched.

The bass drum banging away behind my ribs had slowed its beat, but not by much.

I went inside and reached for the lights. Strip bulbs sputtered into life.

My jaw sagged.

Snakeskin wasn't here. But he'd been in here.

The guy in the fedora had ransacked the office. My office.

"Damn you, Snakeskin."

Every single photograph, newspaper clipping and handwritten post-it relating to The Undertaker Case was gone from the wall. All that remained was a big empty space, with a random scattering of poster putty and general blankness.

Even worse, there was a gap on the desk where my laptop used to be.

Strangely, all of *The Maestro* material remained untouched.

Heart burning, I retreated back outside, where I scooted straight to the abandoned black sedan and tore open the passenger door. Quickly, I checked the glove box: nothing. Checked the foot spaces: nothing. But my stuff could still be here. I scanned the insides, frantically, even peeped under the foot mats. The rental documents were still scattered across the backseat. No signs of the bag of potato chips or the water bottle. Looked like he'd wiped everything down. Not the actions of the innocent. I leaned over and popped the trunk, closed the passenger door and went round back.

I'd seen Snakeskin put two carry-ons in the trunk. I lifted the lid and looked inside. There was just a single shiny suitcase in the roomy space. Nothing else.

It looked like a James Bond jetpack.

It had two shiny steel clasps; inviting access.

Without thinking, I reached down and released the locks.

The clasps snapped apart on highly-sprung springs.

I cracked the lid.

But something prevented me from lifting it more than an inch. Not an obstruction. A hunch. I'd glimpsed something inside. Something that made my belly burn with abrupt adrenaline.

A wire.

Instinctively, I closed the case, stepped back and slammed the trunk lid.

I didn't have any time to do anything else. Not even to contemplate turning around and running for my life.

An invisible fist punched me in the gut and sent me flying across the parking lot.

In the same instant, the black sedan lifted a few feet off the cracked asphalt and, with a deafening roar, burst into angry orange flame.

I hit the deck hard, seemingly head first, followed by the rest of my ragdoll body.

I thought I wasn't going to black out. I was wrong.

20

Punch drunk. That's the best way to describe it. Like I'd been slugged in a heavyweight title bout and hit the canvas hard enough to loosen teeth. The world was spinning, blurrily, on a right angle. I tried to shake my head, but only succeeded in making everything spin even faster. I coughed up something foul tasting and spat it out. Whatever it was it didn't get far; it clung to my lips and tried to crawl back inside.

Tremendous heat against my skin and a high-pitched ringing in my ears.

I was on my side, I realized. Flat against hot asphalt. Eyes stinging, watering. Bubbling noises coming from my throat. Reality coalescing from someplace high up.

I knew what had happened, but my brain was still playing catch-up.

Most of my blurry vision was filled with the burning wreck of the sedan. Searing red flames and acrid smoke gushing from its smashed windows. A writhing black column billowing upward into the clear blue sky, alive with sparks and blistering paint particles. The sharp sounds of creaking metal and popping plastic. The smarting smell of burning rubber and the chemical taste of ignited gasoline.

No idea how long I'd been out of it.

I coughed up mucus. The world spun.

Several vehicles were screeching to a halt along the curbside: police units, an EMS van and two gleaming fire trucks. Cops and paramedics running toward me at an odd angle, avoiding bits of fiery wreckage. Firefighters rolling out hoses. Someone bellowing orders and gesticulating. Organizing mayhem.

I rolled onto my back, crunching crumbled glass fragments under my shoulders. Somehow I managed to lift my trembling hands and count my silhouetted fingers.

All present and accounted for.

But I didn't breathe a sigh of relief.

Snakeskin had planted a bomb in the suitcase. Triggered it to explode the moment the lid was opened.

By a miracle I'd escaped certain death by the skin of my teeth.

I coughed, eyes streaming, bones aching.

It started snowing paint flakes.

21

"The bomb was in the trunk." I shouted above the lion roaring in my ears. My voice sounded far away, like a faint radio station drowned out by static. I raised its volume, but it made no difference. "In a piece of carry-on luggage."

I was propped up in the back of an EMS unit, on a collapsed gurney, trying to hear Sheriff Torres' voice above the unrelenting screaming in my head. I told her to speak up, but she responded with a weary frown.

"Maybe I should try the bullhorn," she shouted. "It's a miracle you're alive and in one piece, Quinn. If it hadn't been for the body armor . . ."

She didn't need to complete the sentence; we both knew that the Kevlar vest had probably saved my internal organs from being brutally compressed in what would otherwise have been a fatal blast.

I caught sight of my warped reflection in a shiny aluminum side panel. A mad professor in the rubble aftermath of blowing up his science lab: ashy wild hair blown back from a sooty face.

A paramedic finished checking my vitals and gave a thumbs-up. Just a few scrapes and bruises. Rattled bones. A concussion for a few days, with instructions to take it easy and lay off any alcohol. Two blood-shot eyes and a heavy metal band thumping out a rock version of *The Devil Went Down To Georgia'* in my head. Pills to go.

Not bad for the survivor of a car bomb.

I thanked the paramedic and climbed out of the ambulance. "I guess I owe you one, Sheriff."

"I don't do IOU's," she protested. "It's entirely my fault. I should never have put you in the line of fire. It was reckless and irresponsible."

"I'm fine," I coughed.

In truth, my ears were ringing, blood fizzing in the back of my head. Nostrils and throat tarry. I stuck out my chest and erupted in a fit of coughing. When I looked up through tears, Torres was shaking her head, matronly. I could see my superman antics didn't impress her. I'd been a whisker away from death, on her watch, and the thought was weighing heavily on her sense of responsibility.

"Ideally, you should take a ride to the hospital. Get yourself a thorough check-up. At least a CT scan. You took a nasty knock back there."

I brushed burnt paint particles from my ruined pants. "I'm fine. Honestly. I'll live. I'm told I'm thick-skulled."

"That's one way of saying it."

The cops had cordoned off the parking lot. Black-and-yellow tape running the entire length of the sidewalk adjacent to the property. Beyond the assembly of police cruisers and fire engines, curious onlookers had started to gather, some of them holding cell phones aloft and snapping pictures. Uploading live video to YouTube. Behind them, there was a white news van with a cameraman standing on the hood, and a reporter speaking into a microphone.

The Fort Myers Fire Department had doused the inferno and was rolling up hoses. The billowing black beanstalk had disappeared, but the air still stank of wet rubber burn. As for the black sedan, it was unrecognizable: a twisted, blackened metal skeleton sitting in a lake of frothy foam. Dripping and steaming.

Even with all their high-tech magic, the Crime Lab would have a hard time pulling a white rabbit from that mess.

A somber-looking FMFD captain waded over. It was over ninety degrees in the shade, but he wore his flame retardant gear and red helmet without breaking a sweat.

"What's the verdict, Jim?" Torres asked.

"Too soon to say for sure, Sheriff. Hazmat and the Bomb Squad are on their way to evaluate. First impression points to some kind of a chemical bomb. We'll know more once they run the tests." His eyes turned on me. "You're a lucky guy. You closed the trunk?"

"Yes. And the suitcase."

He nodded, "Containing the blast was a smart move. Saved your life. Some of those high-end polycarbonate cases are almost indestructible. It could have been much worse. How you feeling?"

"Like a punch bag."

He continued nodding. "You sure had an angel on your shoulder today." He reached out and shook my hand. "No doubt about that." His eyes moved back to Torres. "Lifting gear's on its way. Once Special Services are through, we'll have this out of here by nightfall."

"Thanks, Jim. Keep me posted."

"Will do."

The captain nodded and returned to coordinating the cleanup.

A helicopter buzzed by overhead. Cameras flashed.

Torres reached over and tugged a shard of plastic from my hair. "I'm compelled to ask it, Quinn: do you think this is all a coincidence, this guy following you and the body washed-up on Bowman's Beach?"

Truthfully, I hadn't connected the two. Wouldn't know where to begin. My gut told me the mangled corpse had nothing to do with me. I didn't feel the same about Snakeskin. Snakeskin had invaded my personal space. He was here for a reason, and not one I'd like.

"Sheriff, if you know anything about me you'll know I don't believe in coincidences. But I don't think the two are connected." I glanced at the office building – *my office* – as Crime Lab techies came in and out. "Do we know what he was doing here, the guy in the fedora?"

Torres blew out an uneasy breath. "It looks like he was using the office to run a private investigation of some kind."

"He's a PI?"

"I wouldn't go as far as to make that claim just yet. Not until we get a positive ID. But he was definitely snooping into something."

I nodded, playing along. "Any idea what?"

"One of your old cases, as a matter of fact. Probably the reason why he had you in his crosshairs."

I feigned surprise.

She smiled. "That's the same face I made when I found out."

She indicated I should follow her. I did.

"Since you're now involved," she said, "I guess it'll do no harm if you take a look while you're here. See if anything rings a bell."

I was under no illusions. Torres wanted to gauge my reaction on seeing the setup. I'd do the same. Two dead bodies, a shrine dedicated to a serial killer, and me in the middle were more than enough to wag tongues. Once she discovered I'd rented the unit and it was my stuff lining the walls, it would be game over.

I had to stay on my toes. Think my way out of this mess.

Damn Snakeskin.

I kept the stupid look on my sooty face as we circumvented frothy foam.

The explosion had painted zebra stripes all over the flaky white walls. Intense heat had blistered the blue door paint. In fact, the door was completely off its hinges, and on the floor in the blackened doorway. The smoked glass in the window frame was gone, blown inwards. Several roof tiles ripped loose and missing. We stepped over the door. Windshield crumbs crunched underfoot. Inside, the desk and chair had been flipped over by the force of the blast and smashed into the far wall. Pencils and papers all over the place. The office looked like it had been hit by a tornado.

But most of the Piano Wire Murders stuff was still intact, plastered to the far wall.

The two detectives I'd met earlier were here, together with a pair of Crime Lab boys taking photos and assessing the place for prints and identifying evidence. They acknowledged our presence before resuming their business.

I have learned never to underestimate friend or foe.

Like I say, Torres is smart. You don't get to be Sheriff of anywhere without being at the top of your game. I had a feeling the only time wool was pulled over her eyes was when she wore a sweater – which wasn't very often in this climate. It would be difficult explaining away my prints all over the evidence, and her buying it.

All the same, I maintained a mystified expression, while my thoughts raced furiously.

I stepped around debris. Then I deliberately placed hands on the upturned table and chair, pulled them out of the way. I sensed Torres was about to say something, then decide against it. We both knew the CSU would automatically rule out any prints that belonged to me, now that I'd touched the office furniture.

Strike one to me.

"Any idea why he'd be interested in the Piano Wire Murders?" Torres asked, hands on hips, poised to study my reaction.

I responded with a stupefied shrug. I'm good at it. The guy in the fedora had just escalated his status from stalker to bomber in the space of a heartbeat. I was still computing, by abacus. I needed a breather to think, time to assess. My brain had gone soft since coming to Sanibel and now turned to mush with the impact of the bomb.

But I did know one thing: I knew without any doubt that Snakeskin wasn't interested in the Piano Wire Murders. Not one bit. He'd left all that in place. He wasn't the least bit interested in *The Maestro*. But I wasn't about to share it with Torres. His interest was in The Undertaker Case. With *The Undertaker*. That's why he'd taken all of those case notes with him and left these behind. I didn't know why he was interested. But I was already speculating.

I scanned the mosaic of Technicolor photos and monochrome newspaper clippings, as if for the first time – in fact, I made a point of making it look like the first time. Pictures of *The Maestro's* victims. Razor-sharp wires cutting through flesh. Bloodstained clothes. Letter X incisions where two wires crossed their faces at the bridge of the nose. So much blood. So much death. So much inhumanity.

I spotted a headline cut from a national paper: '*Maestro Writes Celebrity Cop Dirge*', and kept my expression stoic.

Torres looked on. I didn't know what she was thinking – probably about coincidences despite my reassurance to the contrary, definitely about two homicides in as many days, a bomb, and me in the thick of it – but she was definitely thinking something.

Under pressure from the blast wave, one or two of the yellow post-its had come unstuck and had fluttered to the floor. Showing interest, I plucked several from the carpet tiles.

I could sense Torres tense as I corrupted yet more evidence.

"Sheriff, take a look at this. We have a serious problem."

Torres came a curious step closer. "What is it?"

"See these notes?" I waggled one in front of her face. "This is my handwriting."

Her brow crinkled. "You're sure?"

"Positive."

"How does that one work out?"

"Because they're mine. That's how. I wrote these notes."

I saw Torres' eyebrows dip in the middle and meet. I'd just presented her with a puzzle that tied me directly into the office and a bomber, but would hopefully get me out of the corner I'd painted myself into.

Disclose a minor indiscretion to hide a larger one.

I showed her a post-it. Kept the stoicism fixing my face.

Her frown lingered. "Yours?"

It was a single-word question demanding anything but a single-word answer.

I knew I had to construct my response carefully. Convince Torres to accept my off the cuff explanation, without making it sound spurious and ad-lib. But her probing eyes were drilling through my defenses, trying to strike a vein of truth.

I scanned the colorful collage, "In fact, now that I look at it, this is probably all my stuff." I tapped a finger against a Polaroid snapshot. "See these. I recognize these pictures. They're copies of our originals, taken by the LA Crime Lab the year before last. These printouts, too: copies of our case notes. It's all mine, Sheriff. The guy in the fedora is using my stuff." I looked back at her, letting some of my genuine fear show through.

I could see she was struggling to believe me. Fair's fair, right?

She drew a big breath. "Okay, let's backtrack. Make some sense out of this. If these are yours, as you claim they are, how'd he come by them?"

Part of being a good detective is being a great salesman. I have found that the best lies are those that contain a thread of irrefutable truth.

I looked her in the eyes and spun my web: "There's only one explanation, Sheriff. He stole them from my home in California."

"Your home?"

"Sure. Don't tell me you've never taken casework home with you. It might be against the rules, but we all do it." I jabbed a finger at the wall. "These were in my house. All of this stuff. In my basement. Back in Alhambra."

Not a lie – just a tall order to buy.

But I was willing to sacrifice a knight in order to save a queen.

The kink in Sheriff Torres' forehead twisted. "You're saying he burglarized your house?"

"I'm saying it certainly seems that way. All I know is that the last time I was home, which was back in January, these were there, in my basement." Another truth. Torres was starting to buy into it.

She reached for her radio. "I'll have the Alhambra PD make a house call."

"No," I said, maybe a little too forcibly.

I noticed a spark of suspicion ignite in her eyes.

"Sheriff, please, it's a sensitive point. The house is full of my wife's personal things. Stuff I want to keep private. Things that have remained undisturbed since her murder. The last thing I want is some nosy beat cop poking around."

Her hand moved away from her radio.

I breathed with relief. "Trust me, Sheriff, I'll handle this. I have friends in the police department. I'll give them a call. Right away, as soon as we're done here. Make sure the place is secure."

"There's a chance he left forensic evidence there."

"And I'll get my colleagues to check it out. Go over the place with a fine-toothed comb if need be. But I doubt he left anything behind. It looked like he wiped the rental down. It wouldn't surprise me one bit if the only prints they find in here are all mine."

22

Shakily, I drove back to Sanibel, following signs pointing to the beaches.

My head was splitting, woozy. Back aching. Shoulders sore. It felt like I'd just survived a car bomb. I gobbled down two of the paramedic's pills. Coughed one up and swallowed it again.

I felt bad about lying to Sheriff Torres.

She seemed like a good cop.

But darkness leaves little room for light.

The hotel homicide was her domain. No disputing that. She could keep it. I had no beef there. But the guy in the fedora was my business. Mine. He'd made it that way the moment he'd started following me. Reinforced it by stealing my stuff. Then cemented our relationship by trying to blow me up. Snakeskin belonged to me. I wanted to know why he was obsessed with my obsession, and why he'd rigged a booby-trap bomb in the rental of a dead woman. I needed to find out who he was, and fast.

As a matter of courtesy, Torres promised to keep me in the loop. She didn't have to; guilt can bend rules. "I'll have Chief Cooper keep a man on you," she'd said as I'd climbed back in the Range Rover, a little stiffly.

"That won't be necessary, Sheriff. But thanks all the same. I'm an ex-cop, remember? Plus, I live with another ex-cop. I think between us I'll be okay."

She hadn't looked happy about it, but she knew better than to duke it out with an old stubborn mule like me. "All right. But don't say I didn't offer. Now go home and get some rest; you look like shit. And please stay out of trouble, at least for the next few days."

A smirk crept across my face at the strangeness of it all.

Three days ago, I was a nobody. And happy to be – if happy were the right word – as happy as a man on the run could be. Just another faceless retiree, stooping for shells on a paradise beach. It had taken several long months to drag myself out of the quagmire of my old life and two days to get sucked right back in.

Some people are born for the job.

And some people die for it.

Without slowing, I drove through the SunPass lane at the Summerlin Road toll station and accelerated onto the three-mile-long series of road bridges piggybacking the sandy cays to Sanibel.

I had to remind myself that there was no way Snakeskin could have anticipated my opening the carry-on. Any number of passersby could have come across the abandoned car and pried into the carry-on's contents, and especially the cops. If he'd wanted me dead, there were far easier ways to go about it. Plus, he'd had ample opportunity over the last couple of days to gun me down or even run me over. Planting a bomb just to take me out – on the slim chance I'd find it ahead of a snoopy police officer – sounded far too elaborate. Out of the ballpark and into the rough.

I ran through the facts I knew as the concrete balusters flickered by. Snippets of aquamarine water, like pictures in a zoetrope.

Snakeskin had first appeared a couple of days ago, driving a black sedan rented out by a woman called Carole Quayle from CA, now deceased. He'd tailed me around the island, on and off to the mainland. At some point, he'd seen me use the office. Maybe he'd jimmied the lock, snuck in, and seen what was going on in there. I'd followed him to the hotel just off the Tamiami Trail. He'd disappeared inside – no longer than ten minutes – before driving to the office and abandoning the rental. While I had been preoccupied at the hotel, Snakeskin had removed all trace of The Undertaker Case from the office, left an activated bomb in the car, and then . . . what? Where'd he go?

He'd left in the Jeep.

The realization slapped me on the jowls.

It was obvious, now that I thought about it. The red Jeep Wrangler had been there all week, minding its own business at the back of the lot. It hadn't been there when the cops had stormed the place today.

Unless Snakeskin had caught the last bus to Nutsville or thumbed a ride, there was only one conclusion: the red Jeep Wrangler belonged to Snakeskin.

Find that and I'd find him.

23

Spread yourself too thinly and you risk becoming transparent.

Jack wasn't home when I arrived back at his place. Maybe for the better. Knowing him, he was probably still out fishing or being mischievous somewhere. Maybe both.

I booted up his home computer, used it to access all my sensitive log-ins and promptly changed all the passwords. Snakeskin had my laptop; I didn't want him stealing my identity or trashing my virtual life. Luckily, I kept most of my personal files in cloud storage. I checked and they were still there.

I went to my room, threw ruined clothes in the trash and showered paint particles from my ashy hair. I scrubbed soot and vaporized gasoline from bruised skin. Winced when the water hit the soft spot on the back of my head where the blacktop had clipped me hard. Blood clouded the water at my feet. I thought about the last bomb blast I'd survived back in Vegas, and then chastised myself for not keeping in touch with Sonny Maxwell more than I had.

Senior Inspector Sonny Maxwell and I shared a secret.

Not so much a *'til death do we die* secret – more a private confidence.

Seven months ago, a psychic serial killer had stalked the streets of Los Angeles, before causing more murderous mayhem in the glittery Las Vegas hotels. *The Undertaker* had believed in a prophesy of doom, and this had led him to kill in a bid to prevent infanticide. We hadn't bought into his misguided insights. But our dismissal of his claims hadn't stopped the killings. Working with the FBI, the Vegas Metropolitan Police had launched the biggest manhunt in Nevada history. Even the National Guard had come out to play. But only a final face-off at the top of the Stratosphere Tower in downtown Vegas had quenched the killer's thirst for blood and brought an end to the killings.

There had been a suitcase then, too. Much like the unassuming carry-on today. Maybe even the same make and design. Seemingly innocuous and small enough to fit inside overhead compartments. It had been left in a hotel suite in Caesar's Palace. The room had belonged to a man called Candlewood. The suitcase hadn't. Our team of cops and Feds had swept the suite for traces of *The Undertaker*. On my instruction, the Special Agent in Charge, Marty Gunner, had opened the carry-on. It was a mistake. The resulting explosion had blasted a gaping hole in the flank of the hotel, wrecked the suite and caused major damage to the rooms directly above and below.

Sonny and I had survived the blast out of sheer luck.

Marty hadn't.

I thought about *The Undertaker* while I dried off and got dressed.

Some demons are here for the long-term.

Since faking his own demise in spectacular fashion, the psychic killer had gone to ground. As far as the Feds were concerned, they had their man: Harland Candlewood, a scapegoat framed by *The Undertaker*. Candlewood had been the head of a biotech outfit in Boston called Harland Labs. The killer had believed one of their future vaccines would kill instead of protect. Wipe out millions of baby lives. He'd taken it on himself to dispose of everyone involved in the program, embarking on a killing spree that had culminated in Candlewood's death. But *The Undertaker* hadn't killed Candlewood. The Feds had. A posse of FBI thugs, to be exact, metering out vengeance in the wake of Marty Gunner's murder. Under instruction from Norman

Fuller, the Director of the FBI, the Los Angeles Police Department had closed the case on *The Undertaker.* I hadn't.

And neither had Sonny Maxwell.

What unnerved me this time round were the similarities: a rigged suitcase containing liquid explosive. And me.

But Snakeskin wasn't *The Undertaker.* No way in hell.

I poured a lemonade from the fridge, suckled a long pull, swallowed down two more analgesics, and then went out onto Jack's sunny, bug-screened lanai. It was still hot. Late afternoon in early August hot. White egrets standing stock still on the edges of the algae-covered backwater like plastic ornaments. Cicadas swinging chainsaws. Bugs skittering on the water. My concussion made everything look hazy, as though I was viewing the world through greasy eyeglasses.

I eased down the sunshade a little and fell into a padded lawn chair.

Motives are the currency of crime. All of us have them, not just the felons. Motives control our actions and can lead investigators straight to the source. Money, greed, revenge, passion, hate – you name it, these things motivate criminals. Most of the time their motives are excuses: the guy who holds up a convenience store because he's spent the rent money on a flash plasma TV; the jilted lover who is unable to accept the fact his halitosis is a mountain no woman can climb; the son who exacts revenge on his father for failing to save his mother from the hands of a killer.

Identifying motives can help an investigator understand a criminal's reasoning. Understand a criminal's reasoning and you're halfway to anticipating their next move.

Or so the story goes.

Right now I had no idea why Snakeskin had been following me. Or if he still was.

Without a motive, I couldn't predict what he might do next.

But I knew where to start.

I scrolled through the contacts on my cell phone, looking for a number I rarely dialed these days. I should have called Sonny. I should have caught up on her life in Vegas, asked how her three kids were doing, apologized for staying out of touch and being an asshole. I didn't.

"It's me," I said when the call was answered by a soft male voice.

"No kidding, man."

"Is this a good time?"

"For what, the end of days? You got your foil hat there? I know I have mine."

"To speak."

"I guess. But you better make it quick; Winston's about to wipe over my table. I had a spillage, man. I'm dealing with damage limitation here."

"I need a favor."

"And it's the only time you call."

"Dreads, I'm sorry; it's been a long time. I know you're busy doing your exposés. I promise I'll keep it quick."

"Hey, it's your life, man. Don't matter to me what you do with it. I don't exactly worry about you and keep a candle lit."

"Aren't you the least bit curious where I've been all this time?"

"I know where you are."

I knew that he did. "That's right. I forgot. We're interfaced."

"Remotely networked," he corrected with a sigh.

Dreads is an epithet for a freelance writer, working on conspiracy theories from a bar near my Californian home in Alhambra. I didn't know his real name. Never had reason to ask. I knew which mud flats I wanted to poke a stick into and his wasn't one of them. Dreads and I weren't friends. We were acquaintances. He was paranoid and I was a cop. He was also a computer genius. I'd employed his skills several times in the past to unearth sensitive information. Illegally obtained, I know, but about a week faster than conventional methods and usually more accurate.

Investigators will use whatever methods are at their disposal. Ask Torres.

"I've been meaning to ask: how's the current exposé shaping up?"

I heard him pause, then: "Why are you asking?"

"Consider it showing a friendly interest."

"I thought you needed a favor?"

"I do. But that doesn't stop me from showing willing."

I heard him sigh again. "It's going slow, man. Real sluggishly slow. Some minor setbacks here and there. Mostly technical BS. I'm working on it."

"Has anyone been asking after me?"

"Like who?"

"Like the police, or anyone."

"Like your pheremonal girlfriend?"

I smiled at his concocted expression. "Has Eleanor been troubling you, Dreads?"

"Man, since you left, she's been like the cat that lost the cream. She comes in here with her chin scraping the floor. She drinks herself to sleep most nights. Man, will you do me a favor? Don't invite me to the wedding."

A nervous chuckle escaped before I could catch it, "Listen, about this favor. I need you to run a plate. Get me everything you can on the owner. Not just a name and an address. I want employment details, plus police records if there are any. Consider it a matter of urgency."

"No problem. But just to let you know, it could some time; they've installed new firewalls on the DMV system."

"Dreads, I have every confidence in you. I know you love a challenge. You got a pen?"

24

Night or day, she had no idea which. It was like being blindfolded and manacled in the solitary confinement of a padded cell.

She'd tried to maintain some degree of mental time, but had given up after slipping in and out of a tortured sleep filled with shadowy nightmares. With no change in her surroundings or her state, it was impossible to keep track of the minutes and the hours. Her body clock had tried its best to readjust, to keep step, but with no external references with which to align, it had settled into an almost catatonic state.

She wondered if this is what it felt like to be buried alive.

She'd tried listening for recognizable sounds, anything to shed some light on her whereabouts. Distantly, she'd heard the intermittent rumble of traffic on a street. The occasional faraway voice, the bark of dog, a distant police siren. Closer to home, she'd picked out the creak of timbers and the cracking of plaster as her prison breathed in the summer heat, and also the growling of her own belly as it demanded to be sated.

The world around her was static, but her internal processes weren't. It had been hours, maybe days since she'd last eaten anything, and her digestive system was letting her know about it. Sensations to defecate and urinate had come and gone. She'd determined herself to maintain her dignity as long as physically possible. But she knew, if her situation remained unchanged, it was only a matter of time before her body expelled its waste products with or without her consent.

One thing she was clear about was that lack of food and water had made her weak. Dizzy and disoriented. Probably, she slept more than she realized. She knew a human body could only function so long without nourishment before it started eating itself from the inside out. She knew that vital organs would begin to shut down as her dehydration increased. Three or four days without water would finish her off.

She did not know how close to that deadline she was.

The thought made her tense. And tensing caused the steely wires to slice deeper into her flesh. She willed away the pain. But there was only so much compartmentalizing a mind could do under such duress. Ironically, pain meant hope. Once she became numb to the pain it was a slippery slope to oblivion. She wanted to cry, but she refused to. Shedding tears meant losing valuable water. Her papery skin had already started to itch all over, and her cracked lips had long since shriveled from the duct tape. A tongue as dry and ridged as corrugated cardboard. Saliva turned into hardening glue.

There was a fine line between survival in the short term and staying alive for the longer duration.

The way she saw it, she had two choices: either stay as still as she could and hope that rescue came soon, or fight against the restraints and hope to escape. Both had merit. Both had penalties. She had no way of knowing if rescue was coming, or if she could even escape should she throw off her razor-sharp bonds. She did know that staying absolutely still helped stem the bleeding from the lacerations already crisscrossing her body, and that breaking free came with an undeniable risk of fatal blood loss and reducing herself to so much chopped liver.

So far, she'd survived by refusing to panic.

But the longer she remained captive, the weaker she got. And the weaker she got, the more she felt panicked.

At this rate she'd die of thirst before she bled out.

25

Lately, my philosophy had become: *let somebody else carry the can.*

Selfish as it was, it had kept me from going insane since fleeing California. In fact, I'd gone out of my way to dodge death of any description. No scary movies. No late night chillers. No impromptu visits to the local morgue. If I so much as caught a whiff of something hinky I'd run a mile in the opposite direction.

So far the avoidance tactics had served me well – up until this week, that is.

Life doesn't always pander to our wishes.

I received a call from Sheriff Torres the following afternoon, Thursday.

She sounded tired and a bit irritable. Keeping a lid on the island's first murder in half a century was taking its toll. Not surprisingly, I hadn't seen any mention of the murder in any of the Fort Myers papers, and the local *Islander* rag sheet seemed more worried about the fate of the native raccoon population should the hurricane presently revving up in the Caribbean decide to pay a visit.

The Fort Myers News-Press had run a small column on a dead woman found in a hotel just off the Tamiami Trail, but no information whether it was a homicide or an accidental death. The car bomb had found its way into the public arena disguised as a wiring-loom fire. No questions asked. And no word about Snakeskin or the location of his Jeep Wrangler.

"Thought you'd like to know we found the dump site for the washed-up body," Torres told me down the line, before I could ask the nature of her call. "Can you meet me at Ding Darling?"

Not a request.

I contemplated stating a case for her case not being my case, and then thought better of it. Try as I might, I hadn't been able to completely brush aside the images of the mutilated corpse. Maybe visiting the dumpsite wasn't such a bad idea. It wasn't like I had to squeeze it into a busy itinerary or anything.

"Sure, Sheriff. Give me twenty minutes."

Jack had taken the Range Rover out for the day. I donned a straw sun hat I'd picked up on sale in a local souvenir store, then walked the mile to the National Wildlife Refuge otherwise known as *Ding Darling*.

It was another glowing pearl of an afternoon in a long necklace of sizzling summer days. But gray-bottomed clouds were invading from the south, out in the direction of the hurricane whirling round in the neck of the Gulf. I didn't mind the walk one bit. It gave me time to think — pretty much all I'd done since the bomb blast.

I'd racked my pulverized brains, trying to figure out Snakeskin's game plan. Turned out I knew squat. I wasn't happy about nearly being blown up, or about sitting around while Snakeskin roamed free. That was the trouble of living on a paradise island — paradoxically, as a human being I was in my comfort zone, but as a lawman I was stuck up a prickly tree. I'd gone online several times, searching high and low for anything I could find to identify my stalker-bomber, but came up blank. I hadn't heard a peep from Dreads and I was beginning to think I'd been left high and dry. Illegally accessing federal computer systems takes time and patience, I know. Time, I had earned aplenty. Patience had to be learned. I had discovered a tattoo similar to the one imprinted on Snakeskin's arm — the stylized phoenix with jagged flame wings — but it was available through countless parlors. No hope there.

I found Sheriff Torres outside the Visitor Center, posing for vacation snaps with sun-kissed kids in bright summer colors. She politely disengaged herself and waved me aside as I approached.

"Looks like you're the celebrity cop in this neck of the woods," I said with a smile.

She smiled back. "One of the perks of the job."

"They like you. The kids. You have any of your own, Sheriff?"

She shook her head and chuckled. "Heck, I missed that boat a long time ago. Think it sank without a trace."

"What about Mr. Torres?"

"Which one – my brother or my father?"

"You've never married?"

"Why, are you proposing?" She saw me flap and added: "Relax, Quinn. Right now I'm married to the job. And I'm happy with that. Say, how'd it turn out for you, back at your house in Alhambra?"

I performed a deceitful shrug. "Exactly as I thought: no fingerprints. They think the lock on the backdoor was probably picked. Aside from the case documents in the basement, nothing missing."

The lie hung heavy in my stomach. I'd anticipated her question. Practiced my fake response until it sounded real. Torres seemed to accept it without suspicion. I hated myself for it. No choice.

That was it: my *Get Out of Jail Free* card was now used.

My cell phone rang. I glanced at the caller ID, then denied the call.

We climbed into the Sheriff's gleaming Explorer and passed through the gateway onto Wildlife Drive. The five-mile-long roadway was built atop a stout dike, snaking through the scenic Sanibel Bayou. We were waved past the payment booth without incurring a charge. We kept it to a crawl, respecting the low speed limit as we moved around parked vehicles and jaywalking sightseers. This time in the afternoon, the habitat crawled with visitors: snapping photographs of their loved ones against the lush greenery or tentatively trying to spot alligators lurking in the exposed creeks and muddy inlets. It was an altogether different place than in dawn's early light when I ran the same route. Then I was pretty much alone.

"Any news on our mysterious bomber?" I asked conversationally.

Over the last twenty-four hours I'd made a few forays away from Jack's place. Kept to my routine. Kept an eye out for Snakeskin and his red Jeep Wrangler, or any other vehicle following more than once. But I hadn't glimpsed a thing.

"Forensics failed to lift any useable prints from the hotel or the office other than yours. We've circulated his description. But we don't have a great deal to go on."

Truth was, half of me hoped she'd come up with something to point me in the right direction, while the other half hoped she wouldn't. Like I say, Snakeskin was mine.

"What about the type of bomb he used?"

"Our analysts are still working on it. So far, it looks like a chemical make-up of gasoline and thermite."

"Napalm."

"Or at least a rudimentary homemade version of it. I see you know your stuff."

"Comes from coming into contact with it once or twice."

I didn't mention it was a similar concoction used in Vegas by *The Undertaker*.

For a moment I wondered again if the two were indeed connected, then discarded the bizarre notion. I'd seen the guy in the fedora – the bomber. I knew what *The Undertaker* looked like. It wasn't him. Sometimes our brains see convenient connections where only our demons exist.

We came to a raised section of road where the dike bridged a narrow inlet. It was a popular fishing spot, crowded with tourists going starry-eyed as local fisherman landed snook and redfish. We waited for the way to clear before proceeding.

"Have you given any thought about why he's interested in The Maestro?"

I hadn't – simply because he wasn't. But Torres didn't know that.

"That office was like a shrine," I said as I looked out the window. "Maybe he's a fan."

"Or he's out for revenge."

I let her see my impassive expression.

"Either way, he's dangerous. Had that bomb gone off in a crowded area it would have been a whole different story. Incidentally, how's the head?"

I touched the lump on the back of my scalp. The concussion had kept me waking throughout the night and feeling nauseous. I'd been popping pills all morning – no martyr here, not these days – but the meds hadn't completely removed either the pain or the dizziness. Only time would do that.

"You should keep out of the sun for a few days. Drink plenty of water."

The road curved westward. I dropped the visor against the sudden overwhelming sunshine. The Sheriff did the same.

"What about Carole Quayle?" I asked. "Any more news on her?"

Torres gave me a sideways glance. "Your hunch was right. She wasn't strangled. It was a drug overdose. The Coroner's verdict was returned: death by misadventure. She had toxic levels of MDMA and cocaine in her system."

"Killed by an adverse reaction to ecstasy. What a waste."

But no proof that Snakeskin had force-fed her the drugs. The evidence in the hotel room had pointed to a mutual sex and drugs party gone bad. The ME had confirmed a lack of foul play – or at least none provable.

My view of Snakeskin wasn't cleansed by his lesser wrongdoings.

"Do we know what she was doing here?"

"We contacted her next of kin. Apparently, Quayle was a fiction writer. Her family said she was in Florida doing research for her new book. According to her mother, her itinerary included Orlando, Naples and Miami."

"Plus, a fatal stopover in Fort Myers. What kind of fiction did she write?"

"Crime."

I smiled at the irony.

We passed a family on bicycles. Smiling faces puffed with heat.

"We also have a dilemma," Torres said. "There are people who think it strange we have our first island murder in fifty years, same time you're here. Then another dead body the very next day, and you're the common denominator."

"Law of averages," I answered, maybe a little too quickly.

Torres glanced my way again. "I'd like to think so. But you don't believe in coincidences, do you?"

I said nothing. Another nail in the coffin.

The roadway straightened out. Tangled trees thinned enough to open up expansive views of the glimmering estuary on either side. The Sheriff leaned on the gas a little. We passed a group of birdwatchers with big zoom lenses mounted on tripods.

"The other day," she said, "after we met at Doc Osman's, I read your jacket properly for the first time. Of course, I knew a bit about you beforehand. Who doesn't? I read the papers. Watch CNN. I also make a point of knowing which celebrities take up residence in my county."

"Must keep you busy. I hear Captiva's a regular east coast Beverly Hills. Did it make for an interesting read, my jacket?"

She chuckled. "I wouldn't recommend it as bedtime material, if that's what you mean. I don't believe I've ever seen quite so many dead bodies outside of a Rambo movie."

Now it was my turn to titter. "Well, I guess some people attract trouble and some trouble attracts people."

"Ask me and that sounds like an excuse."

"You're right. It is."

We shared a laugh. It was natural, unforced. It was a side of Torres I liked.

The tangled greenery closed in again. We passed the entrance to the cross-dike, connecting the Drive to a sandy foot-trail running back to the Visitor Center – my jogging route.

"Truth is, Quinn, I'm undecided exactly how to classify you. More often than not you get your man. Occasionally he gets you. I might be the unglamorous sheriff of an unglamorous county – compared with what you're used to – but that doesn't make me naive. I've been in this game long enough to know how pressure systems work. None of us are made from steel."

"So what's your dilemma, Sheriff?"

"Oh, it isn't mine. It's more the mayor's grievance. Your being here doesn't bother me in the slightest. If anything, I'm rising to the challenge. But he wants you off the island and out of the County altogether."

I let out a grunt; I'd seen it coming since Tuesday.

The island murder was a problem. A huge problem. A tourism killer. Like it or lump it, I was part of it. Right now they couldn't fix the murder. But they could fix me. They could remove the troublesome Celebrity Cop from the game before the media got a handle on the story. Avoid potential bad publicity. It was all BS. Politics. But that's the way of the world these days.

"In other words," I said, "he wants you to run me out of town. Is that the real reason you invited me out here, Sheriff, to do the mayor's bidding – break the bad news gently?"

Torres laughed. "No need to go getting all bristly on me, Quinn. This isn't the Old West and that sure ain't my style. You've seen it with your own eyes: I'm a people person. I like doing business face to face. The very last thing I do is run errands for the mayor. I'm just giving you a friendly heads-up. Like I say, I have no problem with your being here at all."

"Unlike Cooper."

We passed a tall wooden observation tower crawling with sightseers. It was a double-tiered structure of planked platforms, wheelchair-access gradients and zigzagging steps. A prime location overlooking a vast expanse of the Refuge, dotted with sediment bars and surrounded by a thick, impenetrable green wall of mangroves.

"Cooper's bark is worse than his bite," Torres said. "He's just pissed about this murder, that's all. It's on his patch, and so he's taking it personally. Not because he's an asshole – which, I admit, sometimes he is – but because he's territorial."

I nodded. "Always a killer. I had a cat like that once. Back in Tennessee. It took exception to a Rottweiler muscling in down the street. It spent the whole of one summer taunting it. Up on the fence. Driving the poor mutt mad. Then it got a little too cocky, a little too close for comfort. The only part of the cat the Rottweiler didn't rip to pieces was its damn tail."

Torres chuckled. "Give Cooper a chance. Despite his prickly exterior, he's a good, God-fearing family man. He's not all bad. He went up against the mayor on your behalf. Put in a decent bid for your defense."

"He petitioned to keep me here?" The surprise came out in my tone.

"Oh dear. I think that came out wrong."

"No, Sheriff, you hit the nail on the head. I get it. Cooper thinks I'm a suspect." I didn't hide the undercurrent of annoyance keeping the statement afloat. "That's why he doesn't want me to leave. He thinks I'm involved. And that's the real dilemma. The mayor fears bad press and wants me gone, while Cooper thinks I'm implicated in the murder and wants to pin it on me."

"Which is made all the more complicated by the fact Cooper and the mayor are cousins. And I don't mean of the kissing kind. They might be blood, but they rarely see eye to eye on anything."

"Small man syndrome," I said with a smirk.

"Make that small men syndrome."

Now I knew her struggle: Sheriff Torres was caught in the middle. She was attempting to mollify both showmen trying to outmaneuver one another in a political wrestling ring, with Torres refereeing from afar. Only a matter of time before the one with the biggest hat won the match.

As for me, I was a cranky gator in the middle of the road, and no one could decide what to do about it.

"So what finally brought Cooper round to your murder theory?"

"The Coroner confirmed it. He's in agreement with you about those purple bruises being ligature marks. He also found evidence of serrations on the bones of the proximal phalanxes."

I straightened my spine. "You mean that thing had fingers? I didn't even see the hand."

"It took the best part of Tuesday and overnight just to dehydrate the body. I hear once that swelling went down the hand popped right out, together the stumps of four fingers and a thumb."

Take a rubber glove, turn it inside out, pour in some water and squeeze the wrist.

"The ME thinks the digits were manually severed just below the middle knuckle, probably by a sharp cutting blade with a serrated edge."

"Like a Bowie knife?"

"Or a power tool."

"Sheriff, it sounds like somebody didn't want you identifying that body."

Torres didn't respond. I knew what she was thinking. No spur-of-the-moment murder, this. No jilted lover exacting revenge with a carving knife. No proprietor mercilessly gunned down in a dime store hold-up. This was something much darker and much more evil. This killing had been planned and executed with meticulous precision. It took balls to chop another human being up like that. Brains to cover it up so carefully. And insanity to believe they'd get away with it.

We arrived at a slightly wider area of the Drive. The Sheriff slowed the Explorer and pulled it to a stop on the right, behind a solitary Sanibel Police unit.

This was the start of the Wulfert Keys Trail.

I'd walked it, once. Nothing to write home about. The trail was a power company service road that ran at a right angle from the Drive for about a quarter mile before dead-ending in the choppy waters of the Pine Island Sound. Not much to see other than the big concrete pylons towering out of the water, with their heavy power line loads. Maybe a wild rabbit or two if you were lucky.

A bored-looking police officer was perched on the hood of his car, arms folded, a ball of hardening gum keeping his tongue busy. He spat it into his hand and stuck it to the face of his wristwatch as Torres and I climbed out into air as hot as a steam room.

I ducked into the straw hat. The Sheriff put on her Stetson.

We exchanged pleasantries with the cop before crossing a wooden bridge spanning a rusty canal. The shallow orange water smelled bad. Like the back room of

Doctor Osman's medical center, bad. I could see tree crabs scuttling along exposed mangrove roots. Slender seedpods sprouting out of stinking sludge.

"We think the killer dumped the body at the top of the trail," Torres told me as we headed out. "Before it was swept up and dropped on Bowman's Beach."

"I'm surprised the tide took it that route." We were on the other side of the island. A lot of water and bits of land to get in the way.

"The currents can be unpredictable this time of year. It looks like the intracoastal waters carried it northward around Captiva before the loop current brought it back south. Otherwise, we'd be none the wiser."

"The perfect crime. Any news on an ID yet?"

She shook her head. "Even post-marked urgent, the DNA results won't be back for some time. There's no saying we'll even get a hit in CODIS."

We marched along compacted gravel to the incessant whine of insects. Not saying much, and not having to. What waited at our destination was enough to bite tongues. On either side, the dense red mangrove swamps sweated under the unforgiving sun. It was like being the main course at a BBQ.

Torres saw me flapping a hand over my superheated face. "Make the most of it. This is just about the last of the sun we'll see in a while. Haven't you heard? There's a hurricane on its way. Maybe as soon as Monday."

"Should be interesting; I've never seen one up close and personal before."

"Trust me, you don't want to. I was here when Charley hit. It's scary."

"Then I'll try my best to stay out of its way."

The service road terminated in a lollipop of land edged by craggy boulders. At about ten yards back, someone had planted a bamboo cane in the edge of the path. A ribbon of yellow-and-black police tape hung limply from the top of it. The Sheriff stepped down onto a narrow beach of firm, coffee dregs sediment. I did the same. Our shoes squelched sludge. I could see tracks from innumerable overlapping boot impressions. Crushed seedpods. Thumbnail crabs scurrying sideways out of our way.

"That's the spot, right there," she said.

A yard or so in front of us, the mangroves loomed up out of tannic water to form an impenetrable wall of labyrinthine limbs and snarled vines. It looked like the rest of the swamp. Completely ordinary. I didn't know what I'd expected. Maybe shreds of garbage bags still snagged on prop roots. Broken tie wraps. Human bones. But there was nothing out of the ordinary here. No signs other than the police tape and the footprints to show that something bad had happened.

The wildlife and the Crime Lab crew had cleaned up.

But I could feel it. Sense the evil residue. Even in the dazzling sunshine it was as tangible as it had been beneath the 7th Street Bridge seven months ago. Real enough to give me a chill on one of the hottest days of the year so far.

Torres' coal-black eyes were on me.

All at once I knew the real reason for her inviting me out here on such a punishingly-hot afternoon. And I couldn't escape it.

"You know," she said as she tipped her Stetson against the searing sun, "it's always interesting to see a suspect's first reaction to a crime scene. Good thing Cooper isn't here; that look you just made had guilt running right the way through it."

26

No matter which way you dice it self-preservation is selfish.

Coming to Florida had been the complete and undeniable act of a desperate man trying to escape his conscience. On reflection, not my proudest moment. But sometimes our protection instincts outweigh obligation. I empathized with the Sheriff's predicament, but I was determined to keep the island murder from taking up any more space in my brain than it deserved. I had more important fish to fry. The island murder would take care of itself. I was more concerned with finding the identity of my stalker-bomber before he struck again.

I was almost at Jack's place, working up a sweat, when my cell phone vibrated.

"Dreads, you got that information for me?"

"All in due course, man." I heard him say. "First things first: I got a ping from your laptop, about an hour ago."

"A ping?"

"Think of it as kind of a confirmation signal, when it connects online."

"Okay. So Snakeskin's accessing the Internet with my laptop."

"Was. He disconnected five minutes later."

"Did it give you enough time to delete my stuff?"

"Plenty."

"You should have called me."

"I did, man. But you didn't pick up."

True. I'd been with the Sheriff and in a position where talking with Dreads would have opened up an awkward line of enquiry. "So where's he at?"

"As the crow flies, less than a mile from your location."

I hastened my pace. "A coffee shop or something?"

"The IP resolved to a public Wi-Fi hotspot on Periwinkle Way. So, yeah, possibly. Look, man, do you want me to permanently disable the rig next time it pops up?"

"No." I fell into a jog. "Let's track him. I want to know where he goes and what he's up to. Can you remotely monitor and record his online activity?"

"Was Oswald a fall guy?"

By now I was sprinting the last hundred yards, holding down the straw hat from blowing off my head. Deck shoes slapping pavement.

Another thought occurred: "Dreads, what about the webcam? Can you enable it without him knowing?"

"Better than that, man, I can stream the video to a server, record everything. You can watch it back at your leisure."

"What about that license plate?"

"Don't push me, man. I'm almost there. I'm working through a dozen proxies. Hopefully, within the next hour."

I thanked Dreads and disconnected the call.

Snakeskin was here. On the island. Within reach, within minutes. Maybe still enjoying a cappuccino in a coffee shop on Periwinkle. It was too good an opportunity to miss. I could grab him and question him, and all before the cops did.

At speed, I made the sharp turn into the sandy run-up outside Jack's yellow-painted house and skidded to a stop like a hitter reaching second base.

There was a red Jeep Wrangler with Tennessee plates parked in the shade underneath the house.

Snakeskin was here.

27

Years of conditioning made me reach for my sidearm – before I remembered with a blow that I hadn't carried the Glock in half a year.

Damn!

Adrenaline blossomed through my chest.

Then instinct kicked me up the rump.

I ran, stooping to the windowless fascia next to the wooden steps and planted my back against the painted boards. I wasn't sure if I'd been seen. Wasn't sure if Snakeskin was up there inside the house, right now, watching me. Wasn't sure of anything other than he was here, somewhere. I snatched a glance at the Jeep parked in the shade. I had no idea how long it had been there.

What was Snakeskin doing here?

He'd already invaded my personal space back at the office. Now he was inside Jack's place. What was he looking for?

I listened for sounds of activity coming from within the house. But the racket of crickets in the undergrowth was all-prevailing.

For a fleeting moment, I contemplated calling the cops. Then decided against it. I wanted to interrogate my stalker-bomber on my own terms, and in private. Involving anyone else would just make things a whole lot more complicated. I wanted to know why he'd taken my case notes, where they were and how I could get them back. Most of all, I wanted to know why he wanted them.

I hooked my hat on a nail sticking out of the fascia and ran hands through damp hair.

One thing was clear: I was defenseless in the thin summer shirt. Deck shoes were no match for pointy snakeskin boots. I had no way of knowing how armed my foe was. I needed a weapon. Something better than fists. A baseball bat or a tire iron would do. I sucked a deep breath and worked my way along the side of the house toward the carport. Taking it slow. Listening. Watching for movement anywhere on the property. The back end of the Jeep was jutting out a little from under the house. Maybe I could pop the hatch, grab a tire iron, feel a whole lot safer.

I inched my way closer. Peeked into the garage.

Everything looked in its place: a workbench over in the far back with an array of old tools pegged to a board, a battered chest freezer to one side with various paint cans stacked on the top, storage bins lined up, a plastic hopper containing gardening stuff, a hose reel, some work boots, the usual suspects.

No sign of Snakeskin.

I moved behind the Wrangler. Waited, listened, scanned full circle, then listened some more. Then I reached around the spare wheel for the tailgate handle. I waited again. Heart racing. Listened. Then I curled fingers under the metal latch, kept my eyes on the dark recesses underneath the elevated house, and popped the catch.

Silently, the tailgate swung aside, and then fresh adrenaline bloomed in my chest.

Snakeskin was lying on his back in the small cargo space.

He was facing the hatch, knees up, his legs angled apart, shoehorned in.

At first I thought he was dead.

But then I saw the bulky gun in his outstretched hands a fraction of a second before I heard him say the word *'Gotcha'*, followed a fraction later by intense pain as the twin barbs from the Taser buried themselves into my sternum and discharged their fifty thousand volts without prejudice.

28

I must have blacked out. I seemed to have gotten it down pat lately. No dreams. Nothing. I rejoined reality with a thud. As if my unconscious soul had been dropped back into my body from a great height. Skeletal muscles fizzed. Aching in the back of my head. Something that tasted like bile and blood in my mouth. I tried to spit it out. Failed.

I blinked against harsh light. My vision shimmied, and then stabilized. I blinked some more, and the focus hardened.

I was in the house. Inside Jack's place. In the living room, to be exact. In a chair. One of the heavy, straight-backed carvers from Jack's carved dining set. I was sitting perfectly upright in the way that finishing school kids sit with books stacked on the crowns of their heads until either they learn good posture or that those with flatter skulls have an unfair advantage. I was facing the tiled entrance area of the house, with the glass-paneled front door in the center. Unable to move. I tried. But it was no good. My legs were bound to the chair's legs with translucent white tie wraps, pulled tight, two around the ankles and one behind the knees. One of my deck shoes was missing. My arms were fixed in a similar fashion to the chair's arms, two wraps around each wrist and one in the crease of the elbows. Again, pulled tight enough to dig into the skin and hinder circulation. Ballooned veins and chili pepper fingers. Something that looked like a nylon cord – a washing line, maybe – was looped several times around my upper waist and the chair's sturdy wooden back, just below the ribs. Restrictive. It was interfering with my diaphragm. Try as I might, I couldn't move, could hardly breathe.

No doubt, I was in a fix.

I tried spitting out the foul-tasting mucus again, then realized there was a three-inch-wide band of duct tape sealing my mouth. I pressed my tongue against it. It was tacky, with no give.

I swallowed the icky mucus and gagged.

A bubble of blood emerged from a nostril and inflated to the size of a grape before popping.

Snakeskin wasn't taking any chances.

I couldn't move. Couldn't speak.

But I was alive.

There was a sensitive bulge on the side of my tongue where teeth had clamped involuntarily under fierce electrocution.

The son of a bitch had hit me with a Taser. The memory came back with a jolt.

He'd lain in wait. Snakeskin. Placed the bet I'd inspect the Jeep. Then gathered up his winnings as he'd hit me with enough volts to make my eyes light up and my fillings spark.

But I was alive.

And that was the important bit. Crucial. Two possibilities sprang to mind: either he didn't intend on killing me, or he did but wanted to torture me first.

Either way, it didn't look promising.

But I wasn't dead yet.

There was something strapped to my lap. It looked like a portable DVD player, screen tilted up and open. Underneath my right palm was a small remote control, taped to the chair arm. A yellow post-it on the DVD player that read:

Play Me.

I didn't, not straight away; I was noticing other stuff.

Snakeskin had been busy during my blackout.

A web of steely filaments crisscrossed the room in various directions, heights and angles of inclination, to form an intricate network of hair-thin wires attached to windows and doors. It was like one of those scenes from a spy movie, where a dozen laser beams promise death at the slightest touch.

To complete the analogy, there was a bomb at the center of the array.

No mistaking it.

I didn't know what was more apt: to laugh or to cry.

It looked like everything I imagined a homemade bomb to be. Straight out of a Hollywood thriller. I didn't know if Snakeskin had purposely designed it this way – for effect – or if he'd been brainwashed by B-movie reruns and he didn't know any better. All that was missing was an ignited fuse and a signpost with the word *BOMB* on it.

I twisted my head for a better look.

The bomb was on the dining table, about five feet away, level with my face. Snakeskin had dragged the robust table into the living space. He'd left the three remaining chairs standing on the red Persian rug that covered the floorboards in the dining area.

Vertebrae clacked as I twisted some more.

The contraption consisted of three plastic bottles and an oversized digital clock, bound together with silver duct tape. No finesse. Nothing fancy. The readout looked like it had once been part of a radio alarm clock; it was still attached to a sliver of green circuit board. The bottles looked like regular soda bottles with their labels removed. Each contained liquid of varying yellowness. Thin colored cables connected the clock to a small gray box that I guessed was the battery, probably from a cell phone or camcorder. More curly cables ran through holes pierced into two of the bottles, then back to form a circuit. Every taut cable crossing the room converged on a series of micro switches soldered to the circuit board. Trip any wire and the whole thing was rigged to explode.

If there were a chemical bomb stereotype, this was it.

Six blood-red numerals blazed away on the readout, denoting hours, minutes and seconds:

00:05:00 and unmoving.

Snakeskin had neglected to set the timer.

I tried mouthing the words *'stupid sucker'* but only succeeded in blowing out more blood bubbles.

There was no sign of Snakeskin anyplace close. It was deathly quiet. Even the overhead fans were still. Looked like he'd left me here to die.

I refocused on the DVD player.

Play Me.

I curled fingers to expose the remote control, stabbed at a green triangle-shaped stud. Immediately, the contraption on my lap stirred out of standby. LED lights glowed. I heard the disk start to spin. A second later, the screen brightened, but not by much.

It was the recording of a man.

Snakeskin.

He was in a darkened room. Looked like a hotel room with the drapes drawn. He was sitting on the edge of a bed. Looked like an unmade bed. There was a picture on the wall behind him – maybe a sunset on crashing waves – but the lighting was too dim to pick out any proper details. In the camera angle, I could see his lower torso, illuminated in the insipid glow coming from the camcorder's uncomplimentary bulb. An open shirt hung loosely at his sides. An exposed stomach with distinct abdominal muscles under tight skin. A black tattoo surrounding his navel: concentric circles, crossed lines, a tiny stick man near the top. My stalker's upper torso and head were out of shot, lost in the shadows.

He spoke in a gruff voice – like that of a heavy smoker – cut through with a Southern twang. It was surprisingly resonant considering the tiny speakers.

"The Good Book teaches us to take an eye for an eye. It urges us to fight fire with fire. That those who live by the sword shall die by the sword. Are you a God-fearing man, Detective?"

I peered at the dark image, trying to make out clues.

"If you are, then I suggest you start praying. You see, you don't have long left on this earth. You've outstayed your welcome. In fact, mine will be the last face you see before oblivion sweeps you up and casts you into the fire where you belong."

I was beginning to get a bad feeling.

It was like watching a horror movie, where the lead man was about to get axed.

Then it got worse: Snakeskin leaned forward, into the cold bluish glow coming from the camcorder, so that his head came into shot and his face emerged from out of the darkness. It lit up in an intricate mosaic of blue-white light and sharp shadows, six inches from the lens.

All at once I was face to face with my stalker-bomber.

The little boy inside of me pulled the bed sheets over his head.

Something terrible had happened to Snakeskin.

He looked like Freddy Krueger, but without the striped shirt, the razorblade fingernails, and the movie franchise. Now that I could see the whole of his face front-on, I realized that what I had thought to be a bad dose of acne scarring was something else entirely. Poor eyesight and distance had blurred it. Smoothed it over. Now I could see clearly in the sterile light. Perhaps too clearly. The whole of the skin on one side of his face, head and neck looked like plastic that had been molten and bubbling before solidifying hard. Craters peppered his face like the surface of the Moon. No right eyebrow. A shriveled ear. An eye that was a murky white orb, sightless, as unblinking as a ball of ice.

The home movie had just got R-rated.

"That's right, Detective. Take a long, hard look. I used to be somebody. Not bad-looking. Pick of the gals. Things going my way. I had a career, a life, dreams and hopes like the next man. That was until our lines crossed. Now look at me: I'm a ghost. A nobody. A freak. Some might say, a humiliation. And guess what? You did this to me. That's right, Detective. You killed me. And now it's your turn to experience the living hell I've endured these last seven months."

A crooked smile rippled in his slash of a mouth. A torn gasket under pressure. He brought his disfigured face right up to the lens, so that his bird egg eye filled it.

"It's time to reap what you sowed, Detective. An eye for an eye, remember?"

I glanced at the bomb.

The digital timer was in the process of counting down:

00:03:46 and falling.

Unwittingly, by using the remote control, I had activated the bomb.

When I looked back at the screen, Snakeskin had pulled back and was *beaming*.

I expected to feel panicky. I didn't. I was about to be blown up. Plastered across Jack's living room walls. Brighten the place up. And yet I felt no real sense of urgency. Was it normal to feel so damn calm about dying?

Snakeskin wanted payback. I wasn't sure exactly how I figured into his disfigurement, but it was as clear as the melted nose on his face that he believed I was in some way responsible. And the price for my crime was cremation.

Thinking about it, maybe I wasn't panicked because, deep down, something inside of me knew I didn't deserve to remain living. Let's face it, I'd let serial killers go free. Time and again I'd failed to protect those close to me. Failed as a father, a husband, a cop, and as a protector of the people I served. Maybe this was a good thing, a long time coming. Maybe this was karma, redressing the balance of my sins. Maybe the world would be a quieter place without me. Maybe.

I looked at the readout and deliberated on my own fate.

Had it come to this: my choosing whether to live or to die? There were abundant reasons why I shouldn't go on living. So what did I have to live for other than a slow decline into permanent retirement, while the killers I'd failed to catch or kill kept on killing? Is that what I wanted? Is that the way I wanted to go out, dribbling into my breakfast cereal, catheterized and unable to remember my own name? Who did I have to live for? Certainly, not for me. Not for any of the families of the victims whose killers still roamed free because of my bloodied hands. Who, then? My kids, definitely. Grace and George. I needed to stay alive for them, for different reasons. My grandson being raised by his mom in New York. Now there was the definition of hope, wasn't it? Didn't I have a duty to protect him from the evil stalking this world, from the demons lurking in the shadows, from the monsters under his bed? Then there was a vow I'd made on my wife's deathbed to avenge her murder by hunting down *The Maestro* and rubbing him out of existence. The real question was: did my life have more meaning alive or dead?

I looked away from the readout and made a life-changing decision.

I had three minutes to break free. I could do it. It's surprising how much you can fit into three minutes. The record books are full of such death-defying feats. Panicking just clouds judgment and forces mistakes.

I reexamined my predicament.

At a push, I could tilt forwards onto my toes. Slam the rear chair legs into the wall. Smash the chair up, rip off the cable ties and get the hell out of Jack's place before everything went toast. Less than one minute, easy.

But there was one big flaw in that plan: Snakeskin had fixed wires from the bomb to each of the chair's legs. Moving so much as an inch would trip the switches.

Maybe it didn't matter that I'd chosen to live.

Snakeskin had fixed it for me to die.

A clenched fist uncurled a *'you're screwed'* finger in my belly.

I fought back a sudden rush of fear. Forced myself to breathe through snot and blood.

Now that I'd decided to live, I really wanted to.

I wanted to avenge my wife's murder. I wanted to bring justice to those I'd failed to apprehend. Most of all, I wanted to see my grandson grow up and think of me as his hero rather than the old fool who could have but never did.

I'd been in worse scrapes. I was sure I had. Somewhere. Sometime. I'd come through every one of them. Worse for wear, maybe. Beaten, battered, broken, bruised. But alive. I wondered how many times I could cheat death before it caught me out. Would this be the one? Was Jack's place about to become my funeral pyre?

I emitted a muffled growl of defiance at Snakeskin's grinning image.

The second thing to do in any potentially fatal situation is to reassess. The first is to cuss out loud. Preferably, very loud. Since I couldn't even murmur – thanks to the duct tape – I skipped the first and went straight to the reevaluation.

Under pressure of time and excitement killers make mistakes.

In their haste to flee a crime scene they often leave doors open.

Maybe Snakeskin had made an oversight.

I strained my wrists against the plastic shackles. Twisted my forearms as far as the binds holding my elbows would allow. Pulled. Pushed. Saw my hands go purple. Skin chafe. The flesh would give before the cable ties did. A slim chance I could get them through the ties, but I'd lose a good deal of flesh and muscle in the process. End up with skeletal hands. No chance of getting my feet through those around my ankles, not at that angle, not without breaking bone and triggering the bomb.

I was stuck.

A human fly in Snakeskin's spider web.

Stay calm.

Not easy, not when the clock read:

00:02:49 and falling.

I studied the crossing lines, working out what went where.

Wires from windows to bomb. From doors to bomb. From chair to bomb. Tripwires, stretching six inches above the floor, across the archways leading to the various rooms surrounding the living area. Military style. Every base covered. If anyone so much as tried to enter the arena it would blow them and me to smithereens.

The cables running from the chair legs were as stiff as guitar strings.

I couldn't risk moving the chair away from the bomb. That was a no-brainer. Or was it? Moving *toward* the bomb would slacken the tension.

Snakeskin had made an error.

A sudden crazy thought washed over me: maybe I could disarm it, if I got close enough. I'd seen movies. I knew it could be done. All I needed to do was break the circuit and disable the timer.

How hard could it be?

But real life doesn't emulate art. This wasn't a Hollywood film set.

The likelihood was I'd trigger an explosion and never know anything about it.

But I had to try. Only my miserable life to lose.

I held my breath and shifted my weight. The chair squeaked an inch across the varnished floorboards in the direction of the bomb. Four lines sagged simultaneously. I breathed a bubble of red snot with relief. That gave me five feet of loose wire to play with. If I was careful, I could roll onto my tiptoes and get face to face with the bomb.

After that, it was pure guesswork.

Inch by inch, I pushed the chair closer to the dining table. It scraped wood, leaving gouges. Jack would be mad. The lines drooped. I pushed some more, until the wires started coiling on the floor, then I tipped forward onto my toes. The chair lifted with me. Now I was stooped, legs and back forming a right angle. I shuffled the last few inches to the edge of the table, wary of snagging the wires near my feet, and looked more closely at Snakeskin's bomb.

Three soda bottles taped together. Two larger than the one in the middle. The two outer ones were filled with a translucent, slightly yellowish liquid of different tones. The smaller bottle contained a darker, amber-colored fluid. Wires, ending in metallic electrodes, floated within the substance.

The amber fluid was the catalyst. The detonator. The two outer bottles probably contained an accelerant and something highly flammable. It wasn't a bomb in the explosively destructive sense of the word – more an incendiary device. A firebomb. Probably identical to the one Snakeskin had hidden away in the carry-on, filled with homemade napalm. It was designed to spread explosive fire in close quarters and fry everything it came into contact with.

Snakeskin didn't just want me dead; he wanted to burn me first, while I was still alive.

He wanted me to melt, like him.

An eye for an eye.

I dragged a deep breath through my snotty nose and leaned even closer.

I knew the basics of how electrical circuits worked. Break the circuit and you break the signal. Simple, right? It was the rule of thumb for all bomb disposal experts faced with defusing a booby-rigged explosive device up-close: stop the electrical impulse from reaching the detonator – in this case a chemical catalyst – and the bomb would be disarmed.

Simple.

Yeah.

But not if the circuit had a feedback that triggered the bomb if any of the wires were cut.

What choice did I have?

Visually, I followed the paths of the colored wires as they looped to and from the circuit board. The setup looked straightforward enough. 7th Grade Science Fair simple. In fact, the longer I looked, the more I was convinced that simply detaching one of the wires from the battery would be enough to disable it.

Snakeskin had messed up big time.

He hadn't anticipated I might actually attempt to disarm the bomb, and so hadn't factored in a tamperproof system.

All I needed to do was unhook the red wire from the battery terminal.

But how?

My hands were tied.

The chair impeded my reaching any higher than the tabletop.

And teeth were out of the question.

Then the situation worsened. I heard Death approaching on his pale horse in the form of Jack's Range Rover rolling across the sandy run-up outside. I heard the echo of the engine as the vehicle slid into the garage under the house. Heard the sound die, a door open and close.

Time to panic.

Jack was about to enter the house. Trip the wires. Flamethrower us both in fiery death.

In my belly, the clenched fist punched me in the ribs.

A droplet of sweat dripped into my eye. It stung. I blinked and shook my head.

One of Snakeskin's wires ran straight from the bomb to a little looped pulley system rigged between the front door and the jamb. It meant that as soon as the door opened inward even a fraction, the wire would pull tight and flip a micro switch on the circuit board, a few inches from my face.

Instant incineration.

I heard heavy footfalls on wooden steps.

I twisted my head, glaring at the front door. I saw Jack's shaggy silhouette appear in the glass panel.

I might have screamed a warning – maybe I did – but the uncompromising duct tape prevented anything but a whimpering mumble from leaking out.

Jack was about to come breezing in and blow us both to fiery hell, and there wasn't a damn thing I could do about it.

29

People say that in the last few seconds before death they see the whole of their life flash before them.

Mine didn't.

The only thing I could see flashing in my vision was the decrementing timer.

I gaped at Jack's silhouette as it reached for the door handle. The fist behind my ribs punched me in the heart. Hot lava flooded my lungs. My eyes found a previously unseen telephoto setting and zoomed in on the doorknob, until it became the center of my universe. A big, nickel-colored hub with the rest of reality revolving lazily around it.

I would have puked, but the duct tape promised a drowning if I did.

Suddenly every nerve in my body was as taut as Snakeskin's web.

Highly-strung and screaming out blue murder.

Cold sweat erupted from every pore.

I heard the bug screen door screak on its flimsy hinges.

I saw the knob begin to turn.

And still I didn't experience any flashbacks.

Something made Jack hesitate. I didn't know what. Maybe divine intervention. Sometimes instinct nudges the subconscious. All I saw was the doorknob rotate backwards, followed by a screak as the bug screen snapped shut. Then Jack's silhouette appeared in the window next to the door. I saw his hands move to his face as he cupped his eyes against the glass.

"You in there, big guy?"

Nothing but a soggy murmur in reply.

He peered through the bug screen covering the pane. I wasn't sure how much he could see. Compared to outside, it was dark in here. It would take a few moments for his sun-hardened pupils to soften up. Time was critical.

I heard him call: "Now I see you. Oh my. Looks like you got yourself in a scrape there, big guy. Is that what I think it is?"

I nodded, vigorously. It was the most I could do.

He scanned the scene: wires crisscrossing the room in every conceivable direction, with me, doing the Sanibel Stoop, standing next to an unexploded bomb, looking like I'd soiled my pants.

"Give me two minutes," he called and disappeared from view.

I heard him clatter down the wooden decking, back the way he'd come.

I glanced at the clock. Sweat was running into my eyes.

The readout read:

00:01:22 and falling.

Two minutes was a luxury I couldn't afford.

30

Distantly, I could hear movement under the house. In the garage. Things being thrown around, willy-nilly. Stuff falling. Clanging. The rattle of metal against metal.

There was a loud bang.

I jumped, then cursed against the duct tape.

I peered beyond the table toward the dining area. A hump appeared in the middle of the Persian rug. There was another bang. The hump grew. A bubble of carpet expanding upward. There was movement beneath the hump – like the moment before the alien baby bursts through John Hurt's belly in the movie – then half the rug flapped aside to reveal a raised section of floorboards. It was a hatch. Cut into the floor and leading straight down into the shadowy parking garage. I watched the lid flip back fully on its hinges, and Jack's tousled head appear in the gap.

"Don't look at me like that," he said as he hauled himself into the house. "You never know when you might need a priest hole."

The timer read:

00:00:38 and falling.

Nimbly, Jack stepped over the wire spanning the invisible divider between the living room and the dining area. He ducked under another. Scissor-jumped the next. He was barefooted. Moving like a Ninja. My heart was thrumming. Sweat smarting eyes. There was a pair of wire cutters in his hand. And a cold resolve fixing his gaze.

Without stopping to assess the situation, he snipped every wire connected to the trip switches. One by one, in quick succession, as if he'd done it a thousand times. I flinched as the cutters made the first contact, then

137

the second, and then the next. Jack didn't. Jack was cooler than an Eskimo naturist. As the metal web fell apart around us, Jack dropped the cutters on the table and grabbed the bomb in both hands.

"Be right back, big guy."

I watched, unmoving, as he scuttled to the hatchway and dropped feet-first though the hole in the floor like a Navy Seal hitting the water.

I caught a flash of the timer just before it vanished from view:

00:0:17 and falling.

Five seconds later, I heard a thud. Five seconds after that, Jack reappeared in the hatchway. He pulled himself through the floor as if it was something he did every day, like Grisly Adams climbing into a tree house. Then he dropped the lid, unfolded the Persian rug across the boards, quickly kicked out a kink and smoothed it flat.

There couldn't have been more than two seconds left.

Distantly, I heard a muffled *thwump*, followed by a muffled *thrud*.

The boards under my feet wobbled.

"Houston, we have liftoff," Jack said as his steely eyes found mine.

It all seemed a little surreal. Like a scene from a bad sitcom, but without the canned laughter or the fakery. I should have been deliriously happy. I wasn't.

Jack tore the tape from my mouth.

I spat out mucus, coughed up blood. "What did you do with it?"

"I put it on ice, in the freezer. Some of those old chests are built like tanks. Now keep still, big guy. Let me get you out of this."

Jack used the wire cutters to snip my ties. The chair crashed to the floor. I caught the DVD player as it fell free.

I thrust out a hand at Jack. "Give me your car keys."

"Why?"

"Because this guy's a showman. He'll want to see the pyrotechnics up close."

Jack handed them over. "Just what the hell is going on here?"

"I'll explain on the way. Come on."

We stepped through the slackened web and hurried outside. The Range Rover was parked in the place where I'd last seen Snakeskin's Wrangler. We jumped inside. I threw the rotary gearshift in reverse and heard tires spew out grit and shells as the vehicle tore backwards out of the sandy run-up. It bumped straight out onto the street, still facing Jack's place. I hit the brakes and snatched a quick look left and right.

About a quarter mile down the roadway, a red Jeep was parked up against the verge. Snakeskin. I threw the shift into Drive, just as the Jeep slewed fully onto the road surface and kicked up tire smoke as it sped away in the opposite direction.

He'd made us.

I yanked the steering wheel fully to the right and stamped on the gas. The Range Rover fishtailed as it straightened out, screeched, and then we were accelerating after the fleeing felon. Racing down Rabbit Road on a hop.

Snakeskin had been watching from a safe distance, waiting to see Jack's place go up in a ball of flame. Waiting to see me get incinerated, and possibly Jack too. He must have been so disappointed to see us giving chase.

"Who'd you upset this time?" Jack asked as we charged down the road at an increasing rate.

"Trust me, Jack, you don't want to know."

The Jeep reached the intersection and made a right onto Sanibel-Captiva without signaling. Seemingly, without slowing. We reached the intersection seconds later. There was a steady stream of vehicles heading to the right, headed off island, all equally spaced. Rush hour. I braked at the last second and slotted the Range Rover into one of the small gaps, accelerated with inches to spare. The driver immediately behind us honked his horn.

"Those liquid explosives aren't nearly as easy to mix as you might think," Jack said. "You know I'll keep jabbing away until I take you down."

I did. Like me, Jack was nosy by nature. Once he had his teeth in something, he wouldn't let go until he'd shaken out every last detail.

I swallowed blood. "Who he is, I don't know exactly – other than he blames me for his life being a crock. I'm guessing he's a professional. You saw that setup back there. It's likely he's either government or military trained."

"Yeah, and with a sick sense of humor."

I told Jack everything I knew about my stalker-bomber as we followed the flow of traffic going east. I told him how Snakeskin had tailed me for days; the encounter in the general store; the hotel; the dead woman; the car bomb; the office robbery; Snakeskin accessing my laptop; the Taser; the recording on the portable DVD. I could tell by Jack's silence that he didn't like the fact I'd kept him in the dark, especially the fact I'd almost been killed the other day, or that his lovely island home had very nearly been razed to the ground.

"So this guy with the pizza face –"

"Snakeskin."

"– you're absolutely sure the both of you haven't crossed paths before now?"

"I think I'd remember."

I'd thought about it long and hard, more so since seeing his liquefied face on the DVD. I'd tried visualizing him prior to his meltdown, but I couldn't get beyond the horrific disfigurement.

"All I know is he blames me for turning him into Freddy Krueger. That's it."

The line of traffic crossed the intersection with Tarpon Bay Road and curved round onto Palm Ridge. Late afternoon sunlight was throwing shadows across the gray asphalt. The island roads were narrow and winding, leaving little leeway to pass any of the vehicles ahead in safety, and especially not in the rush hour. I could see brake lights coming on as vehicles began to back up at the intersection with Periwinkle.

"Take the next left," Jack said. "Short cut."

Not much traffic coming the other way. I jumped the Range Rover across the oncoming lane and gunned it down the side road. Hardly any traffic on here at all. I'd been this way before. The road curled round in a crescent and rejoined Periwinkle, cutting out the bottleneck. I held it tight around the first chicane and then floored it. The engine growled with unleashed pleasure. The speedometer hit forty and kept going. We flew by the City Hall and the Sanibel Police Department. Then I hit the brakes just before the tight right turn. Swung the vehicle into the bend. Tires squealed with delight as they clung to the road surface. We leaned with the suspension. Then I gunned it again, down the home straight. I could see a steady stream of traffic moving leftward across the end of the road. I stamped on the brakes again and left parallel lines of smoking rubber on the pavement.

I glanced to our right, searching for the red Jeep, hoping our racy detour had propelled us ahead. But there was no sign of it.

Jack pointed left. "There, dammit. He beat us."

I nudged the Range Rover into a gap. More honked horns, from both directions. Now we were part of a long procession of vehicles heading down Periwinkle in the direction of the bridges leading to the mainland. Five cars between Snakeskin's Wrangler and us. Better. But no chance of getting any nearer until we left the island, providing that's where Snakeskin was headed.

My cell phone rang. I rummaged it out.

"Dreads?"

"Hey, man. I ran that plate. The vehicle's registered to a dude called Gary Cornsilk. He's from Jackson, Tennessee. I ran a basic background check like you asked."

"And?"

"There was nothing on the system."

"What does that mean?"

A weary sigh: "It means his personal information is protected."

"Military?"

"Not quite. I dug deeper and found his discharge papers. Up until January this year, Cornsilk was a government suit." I heard him whisper: "He worked for the Bureau."

"He's ex-FBI?"

Jack glanced in my direction. My mind shifted up a gear.

"What's he been doing since January?"

"Unknown, man. It looks like he dropped off the radar. I'll need to do some more digging. In the meantime I'll text you his home address and contact numbers."

"Thanks, Dreads. I owe you one." I swapped ears on the phone and hands on the wheel. "Did you find out how he came to leave the Bureau?"

"He failed his mental health reviews following a debilitating injury."

It sounded like Snakeskin all right.

"Do we know how he got damaged?"

I imagined Dreads shaking his dreads. "Give me a chance, man. I'll need to do some more digging. I'll be in touch."

The line went dead.

"So, this pizza face, he's an ex-Fed?"

I nodded at Jack. "Explains the elaborate setup, I guess."

"No, craziness explains the elaborate setup. This guy's a serious nut job. And a dangerous one at that. A bad combo in anyone's meal deal. What did you do to piss this guy off?"

"I have no idea."

I looked at the red roof a few cars ahead, at the Jeep being driven by Gary Cornsilk, my stalker-bomber. I didn't recognize the name. I couldn't recall knowing any Cornsilks back in Tennessee. Why was an ex-Fed with a melted face trying to cremate me alive?

We arrived at the intersection where the causeway connected Sanibel to the mainland. Most of the vehicles were taking the bridge, being waved through by a traffic cop. Snakeskin made the left. We waited our turn, and then did the same.

The road inclined onto the first of the long bridges.

"This is it, big guy. Now's our chance to get closer."

No sign of any immediate traffic coming the opposite way; just one or two vehicles in the far distance, on the sandy cay between this bridge and the next. Plenty of time to get right behind Snakeskin. Maybe even nudge his tailgate. Force him to pull over on one of the causeway islands. Find out why he wanted me dead.

I stamped on the gas. The Range Rover dropped down a gear, then underwent a burst of fierce acceleration. The vehicle crossed the double-yellow line in the center of the pavement, moved into the oncoming lane: forty, forty-five, fifty. We passed two vehicles, three. Then Snakeskin noticed our sneaky move and took evasive action. Jack's lime-green Range Rover isn't exactly a blend-in. The red Jeep sprang out in front of us and began to hightail it.

"Don't let him get away," Jack urged. "Give this baby some throttle."

I had no intention of letting my stalker-bomber escape.

Tires clapped frantically as we sped along, wrong side of the roadway. Balusters blurred.

But the red Jeep was keeping its distance. The needle on the speedometer swept up to sixty, sixty-five, seventy. There was traffic coming straight at us, head on. I braked and pulled back into the right-hand lane. No choice. Snakeskin did the same. Horns sounded.

We hit the first island cay still doing fifty. Weaving in and out of slower-moving traffic.

Then I heard it: the long, shrill wail of a police siren.

In the rearview mirror I caught sight of a City of Sanibel Police pickup racing down the middle of the road behind us. Red-and-blue turret lights crackling. Must have been sitting on the shoulder, behind a palm.

"Damn it," I breathed.

Jack twisted round and made a face. "Aw, to hell with them. We'll stand the speeding ticket. Just don't let pizza face give us the slip."

We raced onto the second road bridge. There was a gap in the oncoming traffic. The red Jeep sprang out again, into the oncoming lane, and accelerated. I did the same. Behind us, the police pickup copied the maneuver.

Despite the air-conditioning, sweat was pooling under my arms.

"Keep pressing, big guy. Force the mistake."

"You're enjoying this, aren't you?"

"Damn right I am. Best bit of fun I've had all day."

I floored it. The Range Rover rocketed across the pavement and came within a foot of the Jeep's tailgate. A second later, the police truck was right up our own tail pipe.

"This is the Sanibel Police! Pull over! Now!"

The amplified command came in and around the swirling sirens.

But it was wishful thinking; there was nowhere to pull over, just a death-drop into the crystal-clear waters below.

More onrushing traffic. I saw the red Jeep cross the median lines and slip back into the right lane. More horns blared. I waited until the very last moment, then leaned on the brake and dipped back in line. Through the mirror I saw the hood of the pickup dip sharply as the cop hit his own brakes. The vehicle pitched and lost momentum. It swerved into the lane behind us, missing a collision with the oncoming traffic by a whisker.

Jack was chuckling. "You know, he's going to nail your ass to the wall for that maneuver."

We hit the second and last island cay. We were doing seventy, easy. White concrete giving way to black asphalt. Strips of beach and palm tree-shaded picnic areas. The roadway split into two – the inside lane becoming a parallel run-off that looped back beneath the final bridge for traffic returning to Sanibel. It was bumper-to-bumper with stopped vehicles. Everyone had gotten wind of the chase and had moved aside, allowing us a straight run across the cay. One or two drivers with their smart phones poking through windows, videoing our mad dash.

Up ahead, tearing toward us down the last hump-backed bridge, I could see a white Sheriff's cruiser, its red-and-blues popping like firecrackers. No other oncoming traffic.

The police pickup nudged us from behind. The Range Rover bucked and skewed. I had to ease off the gas to compensate, brake. The gap between Snakeskin and us immediately widened.

Jack glared. "He's getting away, dammit!"

"We won't make it," I countered. "They're going for a pincer movement. Force us off the road."

"So let them try. Floor it, big guy!"

I hesitated. It was too close to call. Snakeskin's Jeep reached the bridge a split second before the approaching cruiser performed a textbook maneuver. It turned side-on across both lanes and screeched to a smoking stop as the red Wrangler sped up the incline beyond it.

Roadblock.

Nowhere to go.

And we were doing fifty.

I slammed the brake to the floor and threw the steering wheel hard to the left. In the exact same instant, the police pickup shot through a gap in the parked traffic to our right and careened down the run-off lane. The deputy in the parked cruiser went wide-eyed as the Range Rover screeched toward him on an angle across the asphalt, burning rubber as it went. I yanked on the handbrake and we slid sideways across the oncoming lane, still doing about forty, then spun through a half circle, going backward, missing the retaining barrier by inches. The SUV bucked like a bad-tempered mule as it hit the uneven off-road surface, going the wrong way. The steering wheel tried to wrest itself out of my grasp as we were thrown about in our seats. Teeth chattered. Bones rattled. Shells and pebbles clattered around the fenders. The rear tires hit softer sand and our speed was sucked out from under us. We came to a juddering stop, snapping our heads against the headrests.

We were about a yard from the lapping waters of San Carlos Bay. Rear wheels buried a foot deep in broken shells.

Through a cloud of settling dust, the blood-red Wrangler was just visible as it sped out of sight over the curve of the bridge. The final bridge leading to the mainland, and escape.

Snakeskin was gone.

And Jack was cussing like he'd wacked a thumb with a hammer.

When I looked back through the windshield, I could see two Sanibel cops and a Sheriff's deputy approaching us with their weapons drawn.

31

The Sanibel Police Department is located on the second floor, west wing of the wooden Sanibel City Hall. Its pristine holding area consists of an alcove at the back of the main office space, behind a grille of hard wire mesh. Basically, it is a small rectangular room with two short metal benches fixed to opposite walls. No window. No frills. No cable TV.

It didn't look like it had seen too much activity either. No names of detainees scrawled on the walls. No Roman numerals counting days held in captivity. In any other workspace it would have passed as a secure area for storing sensitive documentation. Here, it was a gray-painted pigpen.

I had my shoulders wedged against plain plaster, watching Jack on the facing bench as he strummed out a silent tune against his thighs with his thick fingers.

We hadn't been arrested exactly. But we hadn't been cautioned and released either. Causing chaos on the otherwise orderly Sanibel Causeway hadn't gone down well with our uniformed pursuers. After a rough frisking for concealed weapons or illegal substances, I'd passed the field breathalyzer and politely refused the sobriety test. Jack had offered to do it in my stead, taking immense satisfaction from standing on one foot and touching his nose, even when it hadn't been requested of him.

Overhead fans circulated cool air.

Not counting the both of us, there were seven people in the tidy office space. They were mainly civilian administrators – clerks filing paperwork or updating computer data – with two uniformed officers typing up reports at their stations. Every now and then, a female

147

dispatcher would issue updates into a desk microphone. Every now and then, she would receive echoed responses separated by long periods of noise squelch.

It was all efficiently laidback, like everything else about the island.

Jack's eyes were closed. Not quite dozing. His lips quivered as he murmured along to whatever melody was buzzing round in his head. Before surrendering to his meditative state, Jack had told everyone within earshot that his rights had been violated and that justice would prevail. It hadn't expedited our release.

We'd been here over an hour, watered, but as yet no offer of a restroom break.

I'd spent the time thinking about Snakeskin and his homemade incendiary devices, trying to fathom out why he blamed me for his disfigurement. Okay, so I'd upset a lot of people over the years. Couldn't argue my way out of that fact. It was impossible to keep track and tabs. Some people I'd upset indirectly – such as family members of those criminals I'd put behind bars. Some were connected more tenuously – such as misguided groupies and reporters I'd shunned. But not all of them wanted to avenge my actions. Or maybe they did, but only a few had the guts or the mental incapacity to see it through.

Gary Cornsilk.

That was my stalker-bomber's name. He was an ex-Fed from my home State. He'd been forced into early retirement on the grounds of mental health, following his debilitating injury. I'd seen his physical disability firsthand – his liquefied face – and knew that his psychological problem was no less hidden. Additionally, I knew he was interested in The Undertaker Case. Why else would he have taken all the case notes from the Fort Myers office? The more I thought about it, the more I was convinced it was this that connected us together. What I couldn't figure out was how exactly.

I looked at my cell phone in a tray on a nearby desk, together with the rest of our personal effects. I wondered if Dreads had unearthed more information and left a voicemail.

"Jack, I've been meaning to ask, what made you think twice about entering the house, before, when I was all hooked up to that bomb?"

"Instinct," Jack answered without opening his eyes. "And maybe your shoe on the steps."

I laughed. "Saved by a size nine. Thanks, Jack."

"For what?"

"For saving my life."

"Don't mention it, big guy. I know you'd do the same for me."

"I mean it."

He cracked open an eye. "So do I. Want a hug?"

My smile lingered, "No."

"Definitely not going to get all mushy and sentimental on me are you?"

"Do I look the type?"

I heard the main doors suck inwards. Chief Cooper entered the station. There was a glower on his Neanderthal brow – the kind that announced he'd just stepped in something undesirable on his way in. He brushed off the attempts of one of the clerks to part with his signature as he came storming toward us. I could see a hint of mild amusement behind his thunderous glower. Cooper didn't like the thought of my being here, on his turf, but he couldn't help but be secretly gratified by it either.

He came right up to the grille and sneered through it.

There was a book in his hand. It didn't look like the Holy one. I wondered if he was about to throw it at us. I could see he wanted to.

"This here's the riot act," he said, "and I'll be damned if the two of you don't pay attention and listen to every last word of it."

32

By the time we arrived back at Jack's place the sun had set and a warm blanket of darkness had draped itself over the island.

I rolled the Range Rover underneath the house and killed the engine.

A City of Sanibel vehicle recovery unit had winched the SUV out of its sandy resting place and towed it to the police station. Aside from a few pebble scuffs, the paintwork had escaped relatively unscathed. Not like me. I'd come away from the chase with three things: a speeding violation against my license, a ridiculously hefty fine for reckless driving, and the knowledge that Snakeskin was out to get me.

I left the headlights on as we climbed out and crossed the shadowy garage to the old chest freezer.

After placing the bomb inside, Jack had padlocked the lid. Despite the ferocity of the incendiary blast, the lock had held.

"You were right when you said they built these things like tanks."

Jack jangled a key into the padlock. "Best damned way to keep the coons out of your perishables. Besides, combustible bombs are all talk. They're mostly superheated gas and flame. What they lack in explosive energy they make up for it in pretty pyrotechnics. Now try not to breathe any of these fumes, big guy. They're most likely lethal."

He rattled the padlock out of the latch and flung back the lid.

A wave of noxious gas and black smoke rolled over us. I spluttered and flapped hands at the caustic odor. It was like breathing pure sulfur. The stench was indescribable. Hellish. Something that sucked all the oxygen out of the air and clawed alveoli from the lungs.

We peered inside.

It was like looking into the mouth of hell. Everything was scorched black, including the lid. The exothermic reaction had melted the thick insulation and caused it to exude and bubble, creating tentacle-like stalagmites that reached out in every direction. Deep-sea smokers formed from solidified magma. The entire cabinet was crisscrossed with black skeletal fingers, turning the chest into a webbed chasm that seemed to descend through the bottom of the freezer, all the way to the center of the Earth where Satan sat grinning.

"That could have been me," I realized.

Jack dropped the lid with a thud. "And when we find Cornsilk, it'll be him."

Against the buzz of katydids we retreated to the house, put on lights and cracked open a couple of beers. We moved the furniture back to where it should be, and then tidied away Snakeskin's mess. We coiled up all the snipped wires and dumped them in the trash.

I ejected Snakeskin's DVD from the portable player and put it in Jack's machine. Then we watched a rerun of Snakeskin's little demonic speech, over beers.

The homemade movie didn't look any less creepy the second time around. Stress hadn't caused me to miss anything. Visually, Snakeskin was just as scary. Just as stomach-turning. He was sitting in his darkened hotel room with his toned skin glowing ghostly in the camera. Up close and in real life, he looked nothing like the sketch artist's drawing I'd given back at the hotel. Every cop in Lee County was searching for a normal-looking guy with acne, in a fedora. Not someone who'd stand out like a grapefruit in a coconut shy. Maybe for the better.

"He's one ugly as sin bastard," Jack breathed when the show was over. "Play it again. Only this time freeze it on that belly tattoo of his."

I replayed the video from the beginning – hairs still doing handstands on my neck – then paused it on a clear shot of Snakeskin's primitive cave painting.

"That's the Maze of Life," Jack said. "A Navajo design. It's supposed to symbolize a person's journey through life, with those twists and turns representing the choices we make."

I raised my beer in salutation. "Jack, I am hereby impressed."

"Don't be; I used to date a Shawnee girl who made Hopi jewelry." He guzzled beer. "So what do you intend to do about him, this pizza face?"

I stared at the frozen image. Rubbed the rim of the bottle over my grizzly chin. What was I going to do when I caught up with Snakeskin? I had a growing list of bad people I was chasing after. Did I have room for another?

"See who can strike the biggest match, I guess."

"What about that lady friend of yours – Sheriff Torres – you going to fill her in?"

I shook my head. "Jack, truth is, I don't like withholding information from Torres. She's good people. She doesn't deserve my deceit. But right now I guess I don't have much of a choice. Snakeskin is my problem. He's interested in one of my cases and he blames me for his Freddy Krueger makeover. Bringing in the big boys will just complicate matters."

My cell phone hummed on the coffee table. I picked up. It was a text message from Dreads.

"Cornsilk's address and cell number," I said. "Someplace outside of Jackson."

"Look familiar?"

"Nope. A few details from his FBI jacket, and . . ." I felt the blood drain from my face.

Jack leaned forward. "Okay. Who died?"

"Me, for a second. I just found out why he blames me for his disfigurement."

33

Time had no bearing out here on the edge of nothingness.

Life had no meaning in this dark limbo between heaven and hell.

Thought was something that came and went like a fair-weather friend.

She knew the end was approaching, swiftly with every slowing beat of her heart.

In some ways she welcomed it.

Her struggle to keep hold of this little spark of life was over. She'd tried her best to stay conscious, to resist, to live. But her energy was all but spent.

It was time to let it flutter away like a freed butterfly.

In her mind's eye, a rectangular aperture opened in the air near her feet, flooding her in brilliant light. She stirred, screwing her eyes against the blinding glare. She sensed something move through the radiance: a Being with shape and form, floating silently toward her across her purgatory prison cell.

She forced her drifting mind to stand still and hold on.

This was important.

Her time had come.

She felt something caress her arm, several times, in different places, and then the other. She tried to move, to respond to the touch, but her body was uncooperative. She sensed movement. She saw more light shine and glint through her wavering vision. Not sure if it was still in her mind's eye or for real. Something stung her arm. A minor scratch compared with the pain she'd experienced. Pain now numbed by a nervous system sending scrambled messages. She felt something cold nip under her hot skin, on the inside of her elbow, followed by a cooling sensation travelling into her shoulder.

Take me with you, she thought. I'm ready.

She tried to make out the face of her angel. She strained to see the face of the supernatural Being plucking her from her grave. But before she could bring her crusty eyes into focus, the heavenly doorway slammed shut, plunging her into an interminable blackness that rushed in from every point and beat her frail mind into submission.

And so she fell from the brink of heaven, tumbling head over heels, through an infinite abyss of warming emptiness, all the way back to her personal hell.

She landed with a bang.

And renewed pain exploded through her like fire sweeping through a cornfield.

34

Fridays, the wildlife refuge is closed to the general public. It means I have to run the long beach with the rest of the island's fitness addicts. The only difference is, I do it early, usually before the sun and the zombies come out to play.

This particular Friday it was less of an inconvenience.

Being seconds from a fiery death had left me itching to burn things off.

I'd started running again for two reasons: to promote physical health and for the sake of my sanity. We all need time out. Okay, so I'd had more than my fair share since coming to the island, but adaptation doesn't always harden. Running gave me time to think. Working out helped me work things out. I liked to think of it as a twofer.

Besides, there was no better way to loosen up all those tight and sore muscles.

At this hour, the beach was all but deserted; just one or two crazy people pounding the sand through the murky dawn light, far ahead, not coming my way. Flamingo-pink cloud feathering the east. One or two bright stars still twinkling in the west. Silky water that seemed to stretch up and forever into an indigo sky thickening with cloud.

It was still warm, but I could feel a coolness in the air that hadn't been here yesterday. A change in the weather was imminent, thanks to the hurricane choking up the mouth of the Gulf. There was a big thunderstorm on the horizon. The occasional violet flash of violent lightning illuminating the seascape.

I concentrated on thinking things through, planting one foot after the other onto the hard sand left by the retreating tide.

Running is easy. Exorcising ghosts is a whole other marathon.

A lot had happened this week. More than it had in six months.

There was murder on my mind.

Something about Tuesday's grisly discovery didn't feel right.

I couldn't shake the image of the Sheriff's face as she'd caught me reminiscing over a past I'd tried and failed to put to rest. I was undecided if her reason for showing me the dump site on the Wulfert Keys Trail was purely to gauge my reaction on Cooper's behalf or something more calculated. Torres had read my jacket. She'd have known I couldn't let sleeping dogs lie. I wondered what other skeletons she'd seen in my closet.

The island killer was either physically fit or well-prepared. Maybe both. I'd walked the trail. The dumpsite was located four hundred yards from the parking area on Wildlife Drive. Either the killer had carried the body firefighter-style all that way in unrelenting heat or he'd used something to cart it the quarter mile to its watery grave. The latter pointed to a perpetrator with roots in the community: someone with access to a hand truck or a wheelbarrow. The former indicated a killer fitter than most Olympians.

Occam's razor. I have learned the hard way that the simplest explanation is often the right one – however unbelievable it may turn out to be.

Madness cannot be quantified.

I reached the turnaround point of my run, slowed, and performed stretching exercises as I gazed out across the silvery water.

Muscles not as tight now.

A pair of early-morning pelicans skimmed the undulating surface. Silently. Keeping perfect formation before rearing up and diving into the smooth water.

They wolfed down their catch and flew on.

Cooper and his boys were in for a tough time. Without an identity to start off the investigation, things would be painfully slow.

You'd think finding a killer on an island would be plain sailing. After all, there are only so many residents to check out – just over six thousand locals at the last count. Everyone knowing everybody else. Lots of thumbs in lots of pies. A finite number of suspects. Twitchy drapes. Your business being my business. Difference was, Sanibel was a vacationer magnet. On any given day, several hundred sun-seekers crossed the three-mile causeway from the mainland and back again. Many thousands more lodging in the numerous hotels, cottages and condo rentals clinging to the sweeping shorelines, all coming and going on a weekly basis. Finding the island killer would take more than Cooper and his unfounded suspicions.

I quit stretching and started back the way I'd come.

My thoughts returned to my stalker-bomber.

I was in no doubt that Snakeskin wanted me dead. More than that, he was a sadist. He'd wanted me to know he wanted me dead and maybe to suffer a bit first.

And now I knew why.

On the sly, Dreads had gained access to Snakeskin's closed FBI file. Following his disfigurement, Snakeskin had undergone psychological evaluation. The Bureau called it counseling. But it was actually designed to sift out potential breakdowns of the kind that involved going into the workplace one morning, armed to the hilt, to put a bullet in anyone who had so much as smiled out of place.

Snakeskin had failed his tests.

Further reading revealed that Gary Cornsilk had been part of an FBI Special Weapons and Tactics unit based in Jackson, Tennessee. One freezing night back in January, they'd been scrambled on a reconnaissance mission to a small farmstead near the South Fork tributary of the Forked Deer River system. They'd gone in under the cover of darkness in a military-style Bell helicopter. Their mission: to gather information on a serial killer – at that point in time known to us as Ethan Davey Copes – then secure the premises and await backup. But it had transpired that the farmstead had been abandoned years before and showed no signs of recent activity. Even so, the SWAT team had carried out their orders and gone in. Gary Cornsilk and his Watch Commander had entered the main building through the front entrance. And that's when all hell had broken loose in Jackson.

I hadn't seen it coming. Neither had the FBI tactical unit.

The serial killer had anticipated our prying into his past and rigged a booby-trap bomb to blow up the moment anyone trespassed inside the farmstead. Some kind of hydrazine nitrate cocktail, if I recall rightly. In any case, a liquid explosive so destructive that it had turned the farmstead into a raging inferno, lighting up the dark winter sky like a huge bonfire.

Cornsilk had been badly burned in the explosion.

To some extent he'd been lucky; he'd lost an eye, his looks and his career. Two of his colleagues hadn't been so lucky; they'd lost their lives.

Cornsilk blamed me for ruining his life.

It was my investigation that had sent him to that fiery farmhouse on that cold winter's night. My serial killer that had planted the booby-trap bomb and caused Cornsilk's horrific injuries.

Snakeskin blamed me through my connection with the killer. Blamed *The Undertaker* and me equally. And that, in a nutshell, was his misguided reason for trying to incinerate me and for stealing all the case notes from the office in Fort Myers.

Cornsilk wanted to send us both to the same fiery hell he'd experienced for himself.

I glanced up from my pounding feet. There was a guy standing ankle-deep in the shallows, about fifty yards distant. He hadn't been there when I'd passed this way fifteen minutes earlier. As a precaution, I slowed. He looked taller than Snakeskin, but I didn't want to take any unnecessary risks.

The guy was gazing out to sea. Nothing unusual in that. People stand around in the Sanibel surf all day long, doing precisely the same thing. What struck me as odd was the time of day and the fact he was wearing a tailored black suit with his dress pants rolled up to the knees. There was a pair of leather shoes on the drier sand behind him. Socks stuffed in tight no doubt.

"This is bloody fantastic!" I heard him holler as I neared. "First time I've seen a dolphin in the wild."

I dropped into a stroll and came to a stop a few yards short.

"There," he insisted, backing it up with a gesture. "Tell me that isn't a dolphin."

He still hadn't so much as glanced in my direction.

In the early dawn light it was hard to define detail out on the water. Like trying to trace the profile of a raincloud against the night sky. I looked in the general direction, saw what could have been a shadow moving through a swell. A moment later, something that may have been a dorsal fin broke the surface, briefly, before sinking away.

"Shark," I concluded.

Now he glanced my way. "You are pulling my leg."

"I'm afraid not. No curved silhouette."

The guy backpedaled out of the shallows so fast he almost tripped up over his own feet.

"Easy," I warned.

"Never mind easy. I saw Jaws as a kid. The first time round. Never been swimming in the sea since. Bloody sharks. Hate the buggers."

"You're British."

He glanced at me for the second time, this time through a scowl.

"The clean accent," I said.

"Oh, yes, my giveaway British accent. What is it with you foreigners? Don't you know there's no such thing as a British accent?"

I spun out a mystified smile. "There isn't?"

He picked up his shoes and peered into them, as though expecting to find them filled with crabs. "No, not as far as I know. I am British, but my accent's English. Are you sure that was a shark?"

"No doubt."

"Bloody hell." The guy hopped into his socks and stepped into his shoes. Then he stuck out a rack-of-ribs hand. "The name's Stone. Mason Stone. Not to be mistaken for Sean Bean."

"Gabe Quinn." I accepted the handshake. It was strong, assertive. "Bean? Like the film actor?"

"Unfortunately, yes. Everywhere I go, people insist I'm his spitting image. Can't see it myself."

I could, now that he'd pointed it out. Even his deep tone sounded similar. Mason Stone was well-built. A couple of inches over six foot. Heavier than two hundred pounds. None of it fat. A sprinkle of salt-and-pepper hair shaven close to match the thick stubble coating his jaw line. Early fifties, at a guess. One of those dilapidated faces that looked like several hapless tenants had lived in it.

He smiled at me. "It's a pleasure to finally meet the illustrious Celebrity Cop."

Instinctively, I pulled away.

"No need to worry," he said quickly. "You and me, Quinn, we're on the same side. I'm here because of Sheryl Klaussner."

35

I hadn't heard that name spoken out loud in over a year. Maybe longer. But there wasn't a day that passed when I didn't think it.

"Why is the US government suddenly interested in Sheryl Klaussner?" I asked as I withdrew a little bit more.

Thick furrows formed on his brow. "Who said I work for the government?"

"The suit speaks for itself. Better than department store, but not quite designer. At a push, I'd say Saks Fifth. A conservative tie with a ten-dollar throwaway shirt. But the biggest giveaway is the standard-issue Glock clipped to your belt."

The furrows softened. The guy calling himself Mason Stone reached inside his jacket.

I tensed, automatically, even though there wasn't a whole lot I could do to protect myself against a bullet. Not in my fashionably reinvented running gear.

He saw my reaction and chuckled to himself as he produced a leather wallet and flipped it open.

"Relax, Quinn. I'm really not the enemy."

In the burgeoning dawn light I could see a shiny gold shield with an eagle perched on the bezel, the unmistakable blue bold typeface sitting alongside a passport-style photo of an unsmiling Mason Stone. It looked like the shot had been taken after a heavy night on the town; could have been done this morning by the looks of things.

"So how does a Brit get to be a special agent with the FBI?"

"I suppose dual nationality helps." Stone snapped the wallet shut and stuffed it away. "English mother,

American father. Plus about ten years former Chief Inspector with the London Metropolitan Police. Look, is there somewhere we can talk?"

"About?"

"Sheryl Klaussner, for starters."

"You have a car?"

He pointed to a nearby condominium complex. "Through there."

I wanted to know why the FBI had sent a special agent all the way from Pennsylvania Avenue to Sanibel Island. I didn't want to find out on a beach where the sand flies were about to rise for breakfast.

We crossed a raised boardwalk over dune grasses and cut through the manicured grounds of the condo resort. It was library quiet. Still early. Holidaymakers tucked up in their turned-downs. Dawn light stealing across steely water. We followed a cobbled pathway toward a white Dodge, parked nose-in against a fenced-off pool area. Stone popped the locks and we climbed inside. The vehicle smelled of citrus trying vainly to mask cigarette smoke. There was an opened packet of wintergreen gum in one of the cup holders and a handful of quarters in the other.

Stone shook out a cigarette from a crumpled pack. "Do you mind?"

I nodded to the *No Smoking / No Fumar* sticker stuck to the visor. "I don't if they don't."

"Trust me, they don't."

All the same, he slid down the driver's window before lighting the cigarette with a gold-colored Zippo. Then I watched him suck pleasurably before exhaling a lungful of smoke out into the air.

"It's nice here," he commented, "apart from the bloody sharks. I can see why you decided to make it your new home, Quinn. It's a long way from the LAPD. So what happened? They leave you with too few reasons to stay?"

"No, too many reasons to leave. Look, Stone, I don't mean to be rude, but what is this really all about?"

"Like I said: Sheryl Klaussner." He breathed smoke. "Any chance of you going back?"

I lowered the passenger window and let the gentle breeze blow through. "Thing is, I have a new life now. Far away from serial killers."

"But not bombers."

I shot him with a stare. Smoke trickled out the corner of his mouth like vapor from the muzzle of a gun. There was something in his gaze, like the dark glimmer of cold water in the bottom of a deep well.

"What do you know about that?"

"Enough." He leaned over, popped the glove box and brought out a manila folder. "The Lee County Sheriff flagged it up to us the other day. But, like I say, that's not why I'm here." He propped the folder against the steering wheel and opened it up. I could see a dozen sheets of paper, mostly full-color copies of crime scene photographs and one or two wordy documents.

He handed me a printout.

"What's this?"

"Consider it a personal invitation to a very special club."

I scanned it over. It was a document of big, legal-looking paragraphs in a small, inelegant font. There was an official Federal Bureau of Investigation letterhead at the top – including the blue-and-gold Department of Justice seal and Pennsylvania Avenue address. Space for two signatories at the bottom. Norman Fuller, Director of the FBI, had already signed one. The other was blank.

I felt my brow curl like drying paper. "You want me to join the Bureau?"

The notion seemed about as bizarre as believing there were no sharks in the Gulf of Mexico.

"Not me personally. If I had my way I'd be back in California, asleep. It's the bigwigs. But there really is no need to get all uppity, Quinn. Read the fine print; it's a temporary contract. One case only."

I smirked. "Is this somebody's idea of a joke? Who put you up to this, Stone? Bill? Was it him? It's the same kind of dumbass prank he likes to pull."

I discarded the paper on the dash. The breeze lifted it up and threw it back on my lap.

Stone blew twin spouts of smoke through his nostrils. "It's a good deal, Quinn. You should take it."

"I thought this was about Sheryl Klaussner."

"And so it is. And that's why you should sign your life away on the bottom line."

I let out a tired breath. "Look, Stone, there's no deal the Bureau can put together to get me back in the thick of things. I'm happy where I am. I don't need charity."

Stone studied me with suspicious and strangely saddened eyes. "So that's it. You're definitely never coming back, even temporarily? Even if I told you The Maestro is conducting his dirges again?"

Maybe it was the sweat cooling on my skin that caused the sudden shiver. Or maybe it was the ice pick thrust suddenly into my chest by Stone's revelation.

He slipped another sheet of paper onto my lap.

It was a standard school photograph of a sandy-haired teenager with freckles and a silver-and-blue retainer, shot from the chest up against a sky-blue background. He looked happy, round-faced, with the world at his feet.

"That's Zachary Innes," Stone said. "That's how he looked before he disappeared earlier this week. And this is what he looked like when a couple of hikers found him in Griffith Park, yesterday."

He slid another picture over the top. This one showed the same boy in a full-length view. Only this time he wasn't smiling. Far from it. He was gaunt, features pale and drawn, bound with loops of wire to a thick tree trunk. The wires were twisted so tight that they cut deep into the flesh and down to the bone, holding him in an upright position against the corrugated bark. Clothing torn and caked in dried blood. Exposed skin heavily lacerated with deep purple gouges, crisscrossing, as if an enraged lion had mauled him.

For the first time in a long time I had bile in my throat.

Stone slid another photo onto my lap before I could speak. It was a close-up of the boy's head and shoulders.

Two scalpel-neat lines crossed his lifeless face to form a letter X. They overlapped at the bridge of the nose, where a pair of wires forced his head back against the tree. Glazed, bluish eyeballs bulged from a bloodied mask.

Stone put a red-seal evidence bag on top of the picture. By now my pulse was racing. Through the clear plastic I could see a postcard-sized slip of white paper. On it, drawn with a red fiber-tipped pen, was a five-line music staff.

"It was pinned to his shirt."

Blood coagulated in my veins.

I had pictures just like this one. Images of tortured victims, malnourished and bled to death by a sadistic monster, with the same signature notes left with their drained bodies.

"Sheryl Klaussner," I began through gritted teeth, "how does she factor into this?"

"She's missing."

I looked up.

"A neighbor alerted the authorities after she noticed the lock on Sheryl's front door was busted in. When the police arrived they found evidence of a struggle. They flagged it up to the US Marshals. We have no idea when she went missing; the neighbor couldn't recall seeing her all week."

"She was abducted? By who?"

For long, aching seconds, Stone stared at me with his dark, baggy eyes. He tapped ash out the window. "I'm sure you've already figured it out."

The ice pick buried itself deeper into my chest.

Eighteen months ago, a West Coast serial killer had abducted, tortured and eventually killed several children, teenagers and young adults over a period of several terrifying weeks. As far as we knew, he'd imprisoned his victims in various locations – usually basements – for the best part of a week each time. Sometimes longer. Sometimes several at once. The killer had used piano wires as restraints – which meant that any attempt at escape had resulted in sliced flesh. In every case bar one, his victims had died from hypovolemia: a fatal amount of blood-loss due to exsanguination. The only abductee to survive, escape and live to tell the tale had been renamed and relocated by the US Department of Justice. I knew the survivor as Sheryl Klaussner: *the one that got away*. And I knew her abductor as *The Maestro*.

It was a nauseating thought, to think that *The Maestro* was back to his old tricks again. He and I had an old score to settle – a fight to the death, his or mine.

"But Sheryl's in the Witness Protection Program," I protested. "No one knows her new whereabouts or even her new name. Maybe she isn't even missing. Maybe she went away for a few days and burglars trashed the place in her absence." I sounded like a desperado. "How can you be sure it's him?"

Stone pulled a long, contemplative drag on his cigarette. I got the impression Stone never did anything in a hurry, or without thoroughly thinking it through first. He blew smoke through the window, as if he had all the time in the world, then handed me another eight-by-ten photograph.

"Recognize this?"

It was the picture of a living room. An ordinary-looking living room with white walls and green-upholstered furniture. Teak cabinets on brown carpeting. A few cheap prints in plastic frames on the periphery. It was a living room replicated in a million homes across the nation. The only difference here was that somebody had painted in blood on the wall behind the couch: a huge, hand-drawn pattern of five parallel lines crossed with musical notes.

I recognized it instantly.

I didn't want to believe it.

But here was the proof, in red and white.

I'd seen the same rendition in several Los Angeles homes eighteen months ago. And again, today, in the evidence bag from the Griffith Park crime scene. There was no mistaking what it was, what it represented and whose hand had drawn it.

It was the opening eight-note motif to Beethoven's Symphony #5 in C Minor – otherwise known as *The Maestro's* signature tune.

"The Bureau wants you on board, Quinn." Stone said. "Just for this one case. The Director feels your experience is invaluable. It would be negligent of us to ignore that. You know The Maestro better than anyone alive. This is your case and it can be again. Put it this way: it's the only way you'll ever get another bite at the cherry."

Temporarily joining the FBI: the only way to catch up with The Maestro once and for all . . .

Privately, I'd been chasing *The Maestro* since he'd gone to ground eighteen months ago. Longer, if I counted the weeks he'd terrorized the West Coast before disappearing. I'd compiled new notes on an increasingly scarcer scale. Once or twice the cold trail had warmed slightly. I'd even come face to face with my nemesis in Rochelle Lewis' backyard in Boulder City on a cold winter's night in Nevada – albeit masked by darkness and blood smarting my eyes. In some small, irrational way I had thought his killing days over. A mad spate and then nothing. He'd crawled back under his rock. Gone into retirement, like me, sipping tequilas on a porch in the sunshine. But now he'd killed again and abducted the one person who had escaped him the first time.

I stared at *The Maestro's* broad red brushstrokes as blood banged in my temples.

On coming to Sanibel I'd made a promise to remain retired, to chase two killers by my own means and at my own pace, to turn my back on all the pain and anguish associated with my life in California, to escape to the sunshine and the hope of absolution.

Now I realized it had all been folly.

The Maestro had struck a chord in me – one that resonated with one word: retribution.

There was a reckoning to be had.

I couldn't ignore it.

"There's a conflict of interest," I murmured over a drying tongue. "The Maestro murdered my wife."

Stone flicked the butt of his cigarette through the window. "We know. But the Bureau isn't interested in conflicts of interest. We're interested in catching this creep once and for all. By any means. The question is: are you?"

36

Her thoughts were less fluid now. No longer streaming over one another in a mad torrent of unfathomable information rushing her into oblivion. Structure had returned. Islands of coherency where she could take refuge from the incapacitating flow and mold thought without being swept away. Physically, she was still extremely weak. Unable to do little more than gently test her restraints before exhaustion pulled her back into feverish sleep. Mentally, her faculties were clambering ashore one by one, shaping self-awareness and the stark reality of her nightmarish predicament.

Experimentally, she curled tight fingers and toes. Felt hot electricity flash through the numbness.

She was still trapped beneath the wire mesh pressing her into the soft surface. Still cocooned in a warm, fudgy darkness. Still imprisoned. She had no idea how much blood she'd lost. No idea which of her organs was on the brink of self-destruction. The hardened saliva glue in her mouth had softened. Her tongue was more pliable. Skin still itching like the worst case of prickly heat ever.

But she was alive.

She didn't know for how much longer.

Her captor had brought her back from the brink for a reason.

Somewhere deep within her she had a disturbing feeling that something terrible was about to happen, and the thought of it terrified her beyond words.

37

Those close to me know two things about me for sure: I'm stubborn as a mule and I don't believe in coincidences.

I shielded my eyes from the bright overcast as Jack hauled my suitcase out of the trunk and extended the retractable pull handle with a snap.

"It's a crock of shit," he said, "that's what it is. I'm serious, big guy. This is one huge mistake. You're going to get yourself killed. And the best part about it is you don't owe them a damn thing."

I gathered up my suit jacket from the passenger seat and slung it on. "Jack, we've been over this a dozen times. Spent the whole ride out here arguing it over. I told you: the FBI can go screw itself. It's other people I owe."

"Yeah, well, dead people don't come looking for unpaid dues."

I made a face.

I couldn't blame my friend for being cross. Candidness can expose weaknesses. Over the last few months, Jack and I had shared histories. No holds barred. We were cast from the same mold. Old and wily ex-cops. But Jack could do something I couldn't. On some levels he'd mastered the ability to dissociate, to wholly separate his past from his present. I hadn't. Not completely. To some degree I envied him. I'd gotten adept at sidelining, but not at forgetting. Wasn't sure I wanted to go the whole nine yards.

"I also owe it to me," I said, as I looked him in the eyes. "Jack, I need this closure. For me."

"Sure, big guy. Like a bullet in the head."

Sometimes there was no winning with Jack.

We were at Southwest Florida International Airport, in an open-air parking area next to the private charter concourse. We were under an overcast sky, darker cloud thickening from the south. Looked like heavy rain on the way. Possibly the first of a band of thunderstorms clearing a path for the upcoming hurricane. I was leaving and so was the sunshine. But I wasn't taking it with me. Where I was going it was always cold and dark.

Before dropping me off at Jack's place, Stone had told me he was leaving for LA at 9 a.m. sharp, today, with or without me. It was five minutes until his deadline.

"It's still a crock of shit."

"That may be, Jack. But it's my crock of shit. The Maestro killed my wife. He's still out there because of me. I had two good chances to end it and blew both. I lost my Hope and very nearly my sanity in the process. Now he's killed again and kidnapped another. Their blood is on my hands, Jack. Try as I might, I can't paper over those cracks."

Again, I wasn't sure I wanted to even if I could.

"Damn it, big guy. It's not your fight. You did your bit. Don't forget why you came out here." It came from the heart, I knew, but through grinding teeth.

Jack dearly wanted me to stay. I'd carved out a life here on Sanibel. I was comfortable. We were set in our ways. But we both knew I couldn't let it drop. And I knew I didn't deserve anything like comfort.

My friend was looking at me with wounded eyes. In some ways I felt sorry for him. We were cut from the same cloth, but wore different clothes.

I thrust out a hand. "Take care of yourself, Jack. I can never repay you for your hospitality, and for saving my bacon."

Jack brushed my hand aside and slung his big arms around me, gave me one of those hugs normally reserved for bears. "Maybe someday we'll get even."

I reciprocated the hug. It felt good. Even at this hour of the day, I could smell beer on his breath. Feel sandpaper stubble prickle my cheek. I blew straggly gray hair out of my face.

"You do know Cooper will be pissed when he finds out you've left without asking his permission."

I smiled. "Screw Cooper."

With *The Maestro* back on the scene, I'd decided to put the island murder to the back of my mind, and not think about it again. Same applied to my stalker-bomber, Gary Cornsilk. If and when he made another explosive appearance, I'd worry about him then, but not a moment beforehand. I'd packed enough clothes for a week or so. I didn't want to think beyond that. I was focusing totally on *The Maestro* now. This was my time. My chance.

Jack squeezed some more. Vertebrae crunched.

"Give them hell, big guy," he said as he withdrew. "And don't forget there's a maniac out there trying to kill you."

I waited until he'd driven away before grabbing the carry-on by the retractable handle and clattering my way across the no-park zone.

Special Agent Mason Stone was standing just outside the shaded entrance of a small terminal building, smoking a cigarette. He wore a sagging face as craggy as a Cornish cliff. Shirtsleeves rolled up to the elbows. Loose body language that spoke of a guy comfortable in his own skin and indifferent to anyone who thought otherwise.

"You make a lovely couple," he grinned as I trudged over.

38

When it comes to domestic flights, top government agencies on a deadline rarely fly economy; they charter. The FBI is no exception. In this case, a twin-engine Gulfstream jet, hunkered down on the warm asphalt, with its turbines purring like electric whisks in melted chocolate.

I coughed against fuel fumes as we crossed cracked concrete.

A fresh-faced pilot in a crisp white shirt welcomed us onboard, then pulled up the steps and sealed the hatch behind us.

Unsurprisingly, we were the only passengers.

I dropped into one of the luxurious cream-colored leather armchairs and stowed the carry-on under a table. I'd flown in an identical FBI charter earlier this year, chaperoned by a pair of knucklehead G-Men from LA to Las Vegas. This one looked the same: cozy in a penthouse wardrobe kind of way. I could even hear a faint bubbling of music being piped from concealed speakers in back. It sounded more Stravinsky than Snoop Dogg.

Stone seated himself in the facing chair as the plane began taxiing toward the airstrip. I buckled up and double-checked the mechanism.

"You're a nervous flyer," Stone noted.

"I've been told it's a control issue. It's a statistical fact that most plane crashes occur during ascent or descent. I'm okay once I'm up there."

He gave me a sideways look of hesitant suspicion. It was an expression I was beginning to think of as his trademark stare.

"If it's any consolation, Quinn, I've survived a plane crash. You probably remember it: two-thousand-and-nine, the US Airways plane that went down in the Hudson River, where everyone survived?"

I nodded with gritted teeth. It was no consolation.

"Lightning rarely strikes the same place twice," he added as the plane accelerated sharply, pushing me deeper into the seat.

I clamped both hands over the ends of the armrests in anticipation of what was to come.

Stone was smiling toothily, deriving a little pleasure from my greening pallor.

The Gulfstream jet climbed steeply for what seemed an eternity before breaking through the thick cloud deck and leveling out into glorious sunshine. I unhooked talons from the chair.

Stone popped his safety belt. "There's a help-yourself bar service if you're thirsty. Some nibbles. Nothing fancy."

"I'm good, thanks."

"How about some breakfast then, my shout?"

I smiled thinly and shook my head. My belly was still playing catch-up somewhere down over the dwindling cityscape.

Stone got to his feet and went to the back of the plane. I heard him slide open a divider door and rummage around in a small galley. Through the window I could see an undulating layer of lumpy cloud, stretching out beneath us as far as the eye could see. Dazzling blue up above. In the far distance a towering grooved wall of gray cloud rose so high that it looked like it touched space itself. It was the outer edges of the hurricane, threatening landfall in the Gulf in a few days' time.

Maybe it wasn't such a bad idea to get out before it hit.

Stone returned a minute later with a cream-cheese bagel and two foam cups filled with black coffee. He put the coffees on the table between us.

"It'll help with your fear of flying – the pteromerhanophobia. Don't ask me to spell it."

"I'm impressed you can pronounce it. Thanks."

He gobbled a hearty bite out of the bagel and leveled his gaze on mine. "First things first. Did you sign the contract?"

I reached into my jacket pocket and handed over a folded sheet of paper.

It was like parting with a death warrant. A signed pact with the devil. My loyal and devoted services in return for a fat FBI paycheck and a stab at nailing *The Maestro*.

"You know, Stone, yesterday had somebody told me I'd be sitting here now, riding shotgun with a Fed on my way back to California, I wouldn't have believed them."

"Well, that's the nice thing about life. It's full of surprises." He scanned my signature at the bottom of the sheet. Then he folded it away and reached into his own jacket, which was hooked over the back of his chair. "You should be grinning from ear to ear. You made it the easy way, Quinn. It took me three applications and a marriage to get accepted." He handed me a black leather wallet. "Here, consider yourself temporarily deputized. Welcome onboard Special Agent Gabriel Quinn."

I looked at the gold shield and the big blue FBI letters, and let out an ironic snort. Some techie had transplanted my old photo ID straight from my LAPD badge. Not a bad touch-up job. "You boys sure know how to work fast when you want to. Shouldn't there be a swearing-in ceremony or something?"

"Would you want one?"

"Not particularly." I stuffed the wallet in a pocket.

"Our practices differ than the LAPD's in quite a few areas. You'll find that as we go along. Since your assignment is impermanent, you won't be expected to undergo the standard twenty weeks agent training at Quantico, but you will be expected to familiarize yourself with FBI procedures. Spend a couple of hours reading the technical blurb. Then Bob's your uncle."

I frowned at his British idiom.

"Is that what happened in your case?"

"More or less. I'd applied three times and got nowhere. Then I was leading an international team with the help of Interpol, hunting down a killer responsible for thirteen separate murders – homicides, as you call them here – spanning five separate nations. Over this side of the pond, I made the right impressions in the right places and subsequently got an invite when the case was wrapped up."

"I'm impressed."

"Don't be. The fact my uncle on my father's side is a US Senator weighed heavily. The truth is, you can have all the qualifications you need coming out of your ears, but at the end of the day it always boils down to who you know. Just like you."

"Me? How do you figure that one out?"

"Before, back in the car, you mentioned Bill. You meant William Teague, from the BAU, didn't you?"

"You know Bill?"

"Not as a friend, like you do. Our paths have crossed once or twice. You have to remember, Quinn, the Bureau's a big employer, spread thinly across a big country. I know of his work and I've even speed-read one of his books. I know the two of you have worked some pretty high profile cases over the years. I'm sure he'll be pleased to hear his recommendation paid off."

"Bill recommended me to Fuller?"

I thought about Bill Teague, my old friend from the Bureau, while I sipped coffee. I hadn't seen Bill since Jamie's funeral back in January. Hadn't spoken to him at length since saving his life at the hands of *The Undertaker* in the Stratosphere Tower in Las Vegas. In fact, I'd gone out of my way to avoid contacting him – just as I had with everyone else associated with my old life. Self-protection can have shameful side effects.

"I'll be perfectly honest with you, Quinn, even without your friend's recommendation, the Director speaks highly of you. Like I say, he considers your experience an asset. Don't underestimate his generosity. You caught the killer of his niece."

"Is that how history sees it?"

"What other way is there? Your investigation led to the identification and the direct capture of Harland Candlewood: The Undertaker. Didn't it? Or am I missing something? Perhaps the Director feels he owes you one and this is his way of expressing his gratitude."

I shuddered at the thought. When it came to *The Undertaker's* true identity, Stone was as clueless as the rest of the FBI, including its director.

"So how are we going to play this, Stone? This was my case. I know it intimately, but I have a feeling you like to run things your way."

Stone smiled toothily. "For now, we're working under the remit of a federal task force in conjunction with the LAPD. You and I will be looking after the Bureau's interests."

"But I'll be reporting directly to you, right?"

"Do you have a problem with the arrangement?"

"No. Just checking out the lay of the land."

For a second I wondered why he'd chosen that word: *interests.* I hadn't known Stone long, but I sensed he was anything but careless. Not necessarily persnickety, more like conscientious. He saw the thought cross my face, and mistook it for something else.

"Will that cause a problem: working with your old colleagues at the LAPD?" He leaned forward a little, put bare forearms on the table. "Because I know you didn't quit the force for the fun of it. I know what happened, seven months ago, with The Undertaker Case. So if you have a problem with anyone in Central Division, any issues personal or otherwise, I need to know about it now, before we get into this. Not when we're hot on the heels of a serial killer. Most of all, Quinn, I need to know I can trust you."

He studied me again with his deeply soulful eyes. There was contained hurt in that gaze. Something terrible had happened in his past, enough to alter forever the way he viewed the world, and its inhabitants.

"Can I trust you, Quinn?"

"You don't need to worry about me, Stone. I do enough worrying for the both of us."

There it was again: his signature look.

I wondered how much he knew about my past, and how much he believed. Certainly everything that was already on paper, in my LAPD jacket. The cases I'd worked; the killers I'd put away, killed or failed to catch; the innocent people in my life who had died along the way, mostly through association with me; every anesthetizing lie that had ever been told in the papers and on air, and the painful truths that never went away.

I could see he wanted to believe me, but my history made it difficult. Who could blame him for airing reservations? In his shoes I wouldn't be happy about working with me either. I was trouble. A maverick. I got people killed. I kept horrifying secrets. Truth was, my issues were stacked up like a game of Jenga. Pull out the wrong support and the whole wall of self-protection would come crashing down on everyone around me.

"If we are to be partners in this," Stone continued contemplatively, "I need to know you'll have my back when I need it. When the shit hits the fan, and it will, I need to know I can count on you to back me up one hundred per cent. We have to be straight with each other, from the start, or this won't work. No disrespect to you, Quinn, but you haven't exactly got a glowing record when it comes to keeping your partners alive. I need to know I can trust you to look after my interests and not just Gabe Quinn's."

I was holding my breath. Probably looking like I was sucking a lemon.

The Undertaker had murdered my last two partners within a week of each other. Both because of me. And Stone knew it. He wanted reassurance he wouldn't end up number three.

I offered a stiff nod. "Relax, Stone. I'm in this to the death."

"So long as it's not mine." He hefted a satchel onto the table and emptied out a pair of wafer-thin tablet PCs. "Here, take one. They contain everything we know about The Maestro and the Piano Wire Murders. Plus a whole load of FBI procedures you could do with memorizing." He glanced at his watch. A nice chunky Swiss number. "We have approximately four hours to our destination. That gives you plenty of time to shake off the cobwebs and find your legs. I have paperwork to do and some beauty sleep to catch up on." He picked up one of the PCs. "Do you mind?"

"Be my guest."

I powered up my own tablet and flicked through the collection of folders on the main screen. All but a few files belonged to the original LAPD investigation. *My case.* Grim reading in any light: coroner's reports; witness interviews, sworn testimonies; crime scene photos in all their gory detail, eye-popping images of lacerated flesh, blood-soaked clothes, drained corpses, crisscross cuts on pale faces. There was the new Griffith Park crime scene data of the murdered Zachary Innes, together with more snapshots taken in Sheryl Klaussner's home: a smashed table lamp, a chair on its side, signs of a scuffle. I took my time poring over them. I found only two things missing: the crime scene photos of my own home, with my wife wired to the master bed, and the sparse information I'd acquired over the last eighteen months during my personal mission, including my run-in with the killer in Rochelle's backyard.

I worked my way through the amassed data. I knew it all off by heart, but I pretended to peruse it all the same. As far as Stone and the authorities were concerned, I'd abandoned the investigation after the murder of my wife. As far as I was concerned, they were wrong.

I glanced at my new partner. He was prodding the screen of his tablet with thick, blunt fingers. Exuding an air of calm determination. Mason Stone was a man competent with his role and comfortable in himself. Someone just like me – before my world had imploded.

I turned my gaze to the window. There were long breaks in the cloud deck. Streaks of aquamarine water visible through deep rifts.

I hadn't bargained on being thrown in at the deep end with a new partner and new rules. Hadn't bargained on no longer being in control of my own case. It was too early to tell how I felt about either. The one thing I was absolutely sure about was that somehow, from out of the blue, I was back on the official hunt for Hope's murderer. And I wasn't sure if it should do, but it felt good.

39

I must have dozed off myself, because I jumped awake to the sound of a classical piano playing from Stone's cell phone. He nodded at my return to reality as he picked up.

I yawned, stretched and checked the time.

We were two thirds of the way through the flight, it seemed. Maybe more. Somewhere over southern Arizona or even New Mexico. Stone and I had shared few words over the last couple of hours, those that we had mostly being work-related. Our dialogue hadn't advanced to partner level just yet. No easy jokes or friendly strolls into personal spaces. No arrangements to go for buddy drinks and a ball game. I'd learned that Stone was something of an FBI case breaker, moving from field office to field office, around the country, wherever his expertise was best suited. He'd been in LA the last week, assigned directly from Pennsylvania Avenue to help break the reawakened Piano Wire Murders. In passing, I'd probed a little into his background with the Met and Scotland Yard. He'd thrown me a few vague scraps – nothing I couldn't have learned from a quick Google search – that had left me with the impression that Stone harbored secrets.

Then again who didn't?

Stretching, I worked my way to the back of the cabin while Stone listened to his call. Beyond the small, fully-equipped galley was another door. I snooped around the galley a little, inspecting drawers and their contents, before locking myself inside the lavender-smelling lavatory.

The guy staring back at me from the tinted washroom mirror looked older than I remembered. Gray highlights in the sterile lighting. A healthy Floridian tan on the curdle.

"What the hell are you doing, Gabriel?" I asked my gawping reflection. "Look at you: on your way back to California after all that has happened. Back to a life you left behind. On purpose, remember? Here you are: crossing every damn line you ever made. What are you thinking? You failed to catch The Maestro the first time round. What the hell makes you think you'll be any more successful this time?"

My reflection stared back, idiotically. We both knew the answer and were both too afraid to say it out loud.

I ran the sink and splashed tepid water over gritty eyes.

There was still time to back out, I knew. The FBI contract had a twelve-hour cooling-off period. Nice of them. I could rip it up, tell Stone to turn the plane around. Return to vegetating in Jack's lanai with a beer and full belly. Pretend that monsters under beds were merely the products of overactive imaginations. But all I could think about was Hope. My beautiful wife. My beautiful murdered wife. The mother of my children and the love of my life. Mercilessly slain by *The Maestro* as part of his evil game to have me dance along to his funereal dirge. My life was bigger than me. Hope owned my soul. Who was I to deny her mortal justice?

When I opened the concertina door, Stone was standing in the galley, filling two cups with steaming coffee from a metal flask.

"That was base camp on the phone. There's been a new development in the case. Your friends at the LAPD just found a woman's body bound with piano wire. Once we touch down we're going there right away."

"Sheryl?" I dared to ask.

Stone just shrugged. "That's all I know. Here, drink this. You look like you need it."

40

Sixty anxious minutes later, the Gulfstream jet squealed as it left hot rubber on the apron at LAX. An unmarked black Chevrolet Suburban picked us up and whisked us out of the airport at a lightning pace. The driver wore an earpiece and a granite façade. One of those faces that looked like it would split in half if he so much as tried cracking a smile.

"We're going straight to the crime scene," Stone told the driver as we jumped on the sun-bleached Century Freeway and headed east, faster than the speed limit.

I'd spent the remainder of the flight on the edge of my seat, dreading facing the fact that Sheryl Klaussner had already lost her life and part of our mission had ended even before it had begun.

Stone rolled the window down halfway, then tapped out a cigarette and lit it. "I've scheduled a case meeting for three this afternoon. The Federal building on Wilshire. The whole task force will be there. You and me, Quinn, too. Think you can handle a crowd?"

"Sure." I checked my wristwatch: a few minutes past one on a sunny day on the West Coast. I reset it back by three hours.

Wind tore smoke from Stone's lips. "Good. Because I'll need you to bring the team up to speed."

"Me?"

"Why not? You're the expert. No one knows The Maestro like you do."

Familiarity breeds contempt.

The cigarette glowed brightly as he sucked oxygen through it. "Look, Quinn, everyone understands your situation. Not exactly the new kid on the block. But not far from it. No one's expecting you to come in all guns blazing. It's going to take a couple of days for you to acclimatize. To get a good feel for this case again. All I'm asking is that you go through the motions and give it your spin. If it helps, Lieutenant Walters will be there, backing you up."

"Jan? She got that promotion at last?"

"My understanding is, they assigned her to Cold Case Homicide a few months back."

I nodded. "And now she's back working the Piano Wire Murders. Nothing like being thrown in the line of fire."

Detective Janine Walters had worked at Central Division longer than anyone I knew. She'd played a key part in every team I'd led. She was a conscientious detective throughout and also a loyal friend. Appointing Jan to oversee the CCH section of Robbery-Homicide was a smart choice in anyone's book.

Stone's cell played its piano concerto. He excused himself and answered.

I turned my gaze to the manmade Californian landscape as it slid by. Everything seemed just a little less lush than I'd become accustomed to of late. Fewer palm trees, more decay and absolutely no sign of any crossing gopher tortoises.

Four hours from Florida and already I was missing the Sunshine State.

Maintaining his speed, our driver chose the Los Angeles exit at the interchange and we raced north on Harbor Freeway, weaving in and out of slower traffic heading downtown.

I settled back and thought about Sheryl Klaussner, silently cursing *The Maestro* for finally finishing what he'd started.

Two Thanksgivings ago, *The Maestro* had abducted a twenty-three-year-old student nurse on her way home from a college study night. Six days later, that student nurse had escaped *The Maestro's* snare, through a combination of luck and sheer determination. Her name was Sheryl Klaussner. She'd lost a third of her blood supply and suffered terrible wounds during her six-day ordeal. But she'd managed to lead us right back to the rented house where he'd kept her locked in the basement for almost a week. Unsurprisingly, *The Maestro* had cleared out in the interim, taken all his belongings with him, and doused the entire place with spray bleach. He hadn't left us any DNA evidence to go on and the identity he'd used to rent the house had turned out bogus, but not before leading us on a wild goose chase for several frantic days. Having been kept in the dark the whole time, Sheryl had never seen the face of her abductor. But she had been able to describe some of his unseen characteristics, such as his speech and his sociopathic tendencies. After her recovery, the Department of Justice had offered her a new life far away from *The Maestro's* hunting grounds. The DoJ had given Sheryl a new identity and relocated her to an undisclosed location. No one outside of the DoJ and the US Marshal Service had been privy to the information. Not even me.

So how had he found her a second time?

We exited onto the busy Santa Monica Freeway and charged eastward, crossing in and out of slower traffic lines. Glassy downtown skyscrapers rose on our left, glinting in the sunlight.

Stone was off his phone and taking it all in. Having spent most of his life in England, I figured Los Angeles was still relatively new to him. I wondered how it stacked up to London or Leeds. Different accents. Same problems. Better weather.

I noticed we were heading east toward the LA River. Something stirred in my gut. Something that couldn't be attributed to travel sickness.

"Where's the dump site?"

"The Seventh Street Bridge." Stone saw my stricken expression, and pressed home his advantage: "I know its significance to you, Quinn. It's where The

186

Maestro orchestrated his final set piece, the last time round, before vanishing into thin air. I know what it means to you."

"You should have told me."

"Why, would it have made any difference?"

All at once, my mind was in a daze. Revisiting the scene of at least two terrible murders wasn't my idea of a fun day out. Over the last eighteen months or so, that part of the artificial river channel running beneath East 7th Street had become the gateway to Hell as far as I was concerned. A personal anathema that had me in its grip and refused to let go. The last thing I wanted was to go back there. Period.

Stone's eyes were studying my adverse reaction. If I hadn't known any better, I would have sworn he was enjoying seeing me squirm.

"Why do you suppose he's used it again?" he asked. "Picking up where he left off?"

"I doubt it. The Maestro never once struck me as the sentimental type. Far as I know, he never did anything without good reason. More likely it's a ruse to get me here. Back in the game. And I guess it's worked. Here I am. He'd know I'd take the bait."

"That's what happened with The Undertaker, isn't it? He knew the Seventh Street Bridge held bad memories for you and that's why he chose to dump the little girl's body there."

I shuddered. Couldn't stop it. Stone had hit an exposed nerve.

Things just kept getting worse.

January this year, *The Undertaker* had employed the same tactic with his second victim: a ten-year-old child from Seattle. He'd left the murdered body of Jennifer McNamara beneath the 7th Street Bridge, knowing my bloodied history with *The Maestro* twelve months earlier. Then he'd used both to lure me into his twisted mind games of cat and mouse that had culminated in my leaving the LAPD.

"The Maestro is a sick bastard," I breathed. "Don't underestimate him."

We crossed the LA River and passed under the sign for San Bernardino. The driver followed the long, curving off-ramp, then made two right turns until we were on East 7th Street.

I had a ball of acid rolling round in my belly.

I didn't want to be here on a sunny day in August. Didn't want to see Sheryl's lifeless body, starved and drained of blood. But neither was my call.

Once again I was a reluctant passenger being ferried toward his fate.

No one asked me to like it.

We cut through industrial buildings. Some abandoned. Some for lease. All white hulks crumbling beneath a glorious Californian sun. The road leading to the Union Pacific rail yard was badly cracked and pitted. Symbolic of the urban decay hereabouts. Up ahead, I could see several black-and-white patrol cars and a black mortuary van with dark windows. A couple of officers were leaning against hoods. Our driver hopped the Suburban over the rusty metal tracks set into the pavement. We crossed an open space of dust and windblown garbage. Then he brought our ride to a stop alongside the Coroner's vehicle, nose-in against a long, linked procession of unmoving freight cars.

We got out and put on shades.

There was a tremor in my gait.

The police officers straightened as we approached. Stone flashed his badge. Disinterested, they waved us through and went back to their lighthearted conversation.

"Bloody cops," Stone grumbled as we crossed oily shingle.

We moved in the direction of the manmade river channel. My pulse was thudding in my ears. Tall pillars and riveted stanchions rose to our left where the overpass bridged the LA River. I could hear the sounds of road traffic crossing the span, thundering in the cavities below. Diesel clawed at my throat. We stepped over crossing rail lines. Stone pointed to a gap in the chain-link fence. We ducked through the torn panel and eased our way down the steep concrete slope. Loose grit skittered ahead of us as we went. Beneath the bridge was a sight that had become painfully familiar to me: gaudy yellow-and-black police tape cordoning off an area deep in shadow. It was the same place I'd found another of *The Maestro's* victims, Leo Benjamin, and then another child, Jennifer McNamara, twelve months later. Same place, same damn cordon, same gutted feeling. Different serial killer.

The ball of acid bounced into my esophagus.

A plain-clothed Hollenbeck police detective and two more officers were manning the tape. Off to one side, a pair of label-and-bag gurney pushers from the Coroner's Office were waiting to cart the body off for processing.

Stone flashed his badge again. The lead detective detached himself from his conversation with the uniforms and came over.

He was a thickset guy with sandy hair and the kind of skin that reddens in daylight. He wore a thin sports jacket and a grouchy face.

"Fuck me. About time you boys showed. She's beginning to turn ripe in this heat."

We ducked under the tape.

"Has anyone touched anything?"

"What do you take us for, morons?"

Stone opened his mouth to agree, and I quickly interjected: "Forensics?"

"Been and gone. As requested, I made sure SID didn't interfere with the body. Everything's exactly the way it was when we got here. That good with you fellas?"

"Just show us the girl," Stone grumped.

We followed the detective into the shadow. I expected it to feel cooler. It didn't.

Above us, the thunder of traffic rolled around the vaulted carapace like ghosts bemoaning the dead.

I stripped off the sunglasses. "Who found her?"

"A guy walking his dog called it in just after eight. Looks like the killer dumped the body during the night. The first responders had to clear away rats when they got here."

There was a woman's body strapped to one of the concrete support pillars. The same support pillar where I'd found Leo Benjamin's dead body the year before last. As with then, she was held forcibly upright against the graffiti-covered cement, bound to the column with coils of silver wire. Her clothing – a black t-shirt and faded black jeans – were caked in layers of dried blood, ripped and chaffed to the threads. Gaping straight-line wounds showed on her exposed flesh where the thin metal restraints had sliced down to the bone. There was a pool of congealed blood and skin on the gritty concrete below her. Bloody, torn stumps where the rats had gnawed away toes, tendons and cartilage. As with all of *The Maestro's* victims, two wires crossed her face at the bridge of the nose to form the letter X.

Her straight, vinyl-black hair had blown across her face like a mourner's veil.

Days without food and water had turned her skeletal.

Acid seared the back of my mouth.

A foot or so above her head, *The Maestro's* musical motif calling card was painted on the face of the pillar in bright red blood. In a sick twist, he'd repainted over the original drawing left after his killing of Leo Benjamin.

"This isn't Sheryl Klaussner," Stone breathed as we looked on.

The wounded little boy inside of me curled into a fetal position. "No. But I know who she is."

41

Unsurprisingly, the old neighborhood had survived in my absence. Summer had greened up the trees and yellowed the lawns. One or two of the nearby houses had enjoyed new licks of paint. Summer flowers in window boxes. Everything looking smaller than I remembered. Drabber. Across the street, the Pearson's had a new Nissan utility vehicle, and farther along, the Kowalski's had a realtor's sale sign in the shade of an overgrown California lilac.

I hadn't come straight home. By request, the Feds had deposited me at the San Gabriel Cemetery a few blocks to the north. I'd hung around the graveyard for a while, picking out weeds from Hope's graveside, before walking along quiet roads to my house on Valencia Street.

And now I was here. Back where it all started.

I hesitated for a moment to survey the home I'd shared with my family for many happy years until evil had trashed it.

Fading paintwork, flaking where boards turned corners. Grubby windowpanes in need of a wet sponge. Sagging eaves. A balding lawn hedged in by three-foot-tall wildflowers. Weeds sprouting through fissures in the driveway. Altogether, it looked like nobody had lived here the last six months.

Heavy hearts make for heavy feet.

I lugged the carry-on up the front walk. It bounced over cracks.

The flap on the metal mailbox on the wall next to the front door was wedged open with mail. Before leaving for the East Coast, I'd arranged for all the important stuff to be forwarded to Grace's apartment in Fort Myers, and then on to my new home on Sanibel after the move. Most of this would be junk: fast food flyers and offers of home improvement loans – both of which I could do with right now.

I fumbled house keys into the lock, and then hesitated before opening the door.

No one had crossed this threshold since I'd run away to Florida. Despite my lies to Sheriff Torres, everything would be just as I'd left it: an empty fridge, used towels in the wash basket, devils chewing on nails in the corners. Same as it ever was.

I drew another deep breath and cracked open the door.

The air was dry, musty. Like an attic in summer. Undisturbed long enough for the everyday dust to settle in a fine coating across every horizontal surface. Silent and still. As if the house were in a coma.

I pressed the door shut behind me.

"Anyone home?"

The words were sucked instantly into the walls, deadening the sound. No one called back. No surprise.

I dropped keys on the hall table and automatically glanced at the answering machine. The little red light was blazing away like The Cyclops' angry eye. I'd forgotten to unplug the infernal thing before moving States and now the message memory was full. Priorities. It would have to wait.

I folded away the extendable handle on the suitcase and hefted it up the stairs.

My home in Alhambra has four bedrooms and two baths. In its heyday, when the happy sounds of teenagers had filled these spaces, two had belonged to my kids, with another for storing all the useless paraphernalia that families amass. These days, the storage room had a camping cot in it – a single mashed pillow and a jazzy sleeping bag – and the master bedroom hadn't been slept in for the last eighteen months.

I left the carry-on next to the cot and moved along the short landing to the master bedroom. Placed a hesitant hand on the brass doorknob. The metal was cold. Chill seeped into my skin. I pressed my other hand against the green-painted wood, then followed it with my brow. I let the door take my weight for a while. It didn't creak, but my neck did. I closed eyes, summoning – as I had done countless times before – the strength to turn the doorknob, to go inside the place where Hope had been brutally attacked by *The Maestro* and left to bleed out. But like every time before, fear and grief forced me back down the stairs.

I thought I heard her murmur my name – a distant, muffled cry for help – but knew it was just a demon playing tricks.

42

Fact: I didn't want my old job back. That was clear. But I did want to smooth down any bumps my resignation had raised with the LAPD, especially now that we were all going to be working the same case together again. Six months had passed. I wasn't the same person. I'd grown. Hardened a little. Relaxed a little. I liked John Ferguson, my former Police Captain. He'd been tolerant with my maverick ways when external pressures demanded otherwise. I'd done the dirty on John and the Department, after promising not to quit and then doing exactly that. Common courtesy dictated that I make the first move and apologize for wasting everybody's time. Essentially, grovel. A lifetime ago, I had been a man of my word. But then my belief system had been turned inside out. Nowadays, even I didn't believe me.

I plucked up the courage to call Ferguson as I drove my old car west into Los Angeles.

"Special Agent Stone's already filled me in," he told me over the phone, his voice still as whispery as wind through reed. "Gabe, it's a huge career change. Bigger expectations. In many ways bigger pressures. They tell me it's temporary – just until you break this case. But what happens if the hunt goes on for weeks or even months, or if it remains unsolved? Are you ready for that? Are you sure you want this?"

"John, the Feds have offered me another chance to nail the son of a bitch who killed Hope, and that's the only thing I'm sure of right now. If I turn it down I know I'd look back and hate myself for not trying. I'm just about as keen on the idea as you are. But teaming up with the Bureau is a necessary evil."

"The bastard has you over a barrel, He knows your weakness. Give me the nod and I'll speak with the Commissioner about getting you reinstated, in some capacity. I can't promise anything, but I'm happy to give it a shot. At least then you'd be your own boss on your own case."

"And I sincerely appreciate it, John, I really do. But we both know how things would turn out. I've always been an unsafe bet. We both know that. I wouldn't trust me to housesit your dog without encouraging a home invasion."

I heard Ferguson pull a smile: popping air bubbles in tightening cheeks. "It sounds like Florida's been kind to you, Gabe. You sound brighter. I'm happy for you."

"Trust me, John, it'll be short-lived."

I didn't say that sometimes blowing away dust can exhume the past.

"Still, if you change your mind, you know my number."

I did. And I wouldn't.

43

Los Angeles fried.

I left my car outside a sushi place on Santa Monica Boulevard and weaved my way along the busy sidewalk with the sun beating down on my neck. I didn't look like a newly-appointed federal agent. Not sure what one looked like anyway, aside from green and keen. I had on a loose, short-sleeved shirt open at the collar, with a pair of faded Levis and shabby sneakers. But I wasn't trying to fit the bill. The FBI badge in my jeans' back pocket was a means to an end. That's how I'd decided to think of it. A one-way ticket to a final destination.

Catch the killer. Avenge my murdered wife. Go back to Sanibel. Simple.

If only life was.

I waited for a gap in the lines of traffic before crossing the street.

The big smoked-glass building I was headed for looked like a bank. A cube with flattened corners. I went up to the entrance and tried the door. It was locked. I cupped a hand against the pane and peered inside. No signs of any activity. I could see a wide entranceway with black leatherette walls. Chrome rivets holding everything together. Concealed lighting. Framed posters of toned and tanned bodies scantily clad in leather and chains. Images that wouldn't have looked out of place in a subversive slasher movie. To the left, a barroom. Those tall, high-stem tables that patrons stand at rather than sit, sprouting from the floor like black dahlias. Cozy booths in back. To the right, a larger space, mostly shrouded in darkness. A tangle of lighting equipment barnacled to the ceiling.

I wrapped knuckles against the door, my wedding band rattling loudly against the reinforced glass. After a few seconds, a big guy in a black Dungeons & Dragons t-shirt, with a big gut, tattoos and facial piercings, wandered into view.

"Read the sign, buddy," he bellowed. "We're closed."

I showed him my shiny new FBI badge.

He came to the door and popped the locks.

I stepped back as the door sucked inwards. Caught a swirl of cooler air and the sound of distant drumbeats escaping onto the sidewalk.

"Yeah?"

"Tyler Cummings?"

"Yeah, so? And, what?"

"Can I come in?"

"You have a warrant that says you can come in?"

"Do I need one?"

He thought about it for a second, and then stepped aside reluctantly. I pushed through the doorway. It was cool inside the nightclub. The insipid scent of rainforest air freshener ineptly trying to mask the darker stench of musk and booze. I could hear dance music in the background. Turned low. Unmelodic modern. Not my scene – even though I'd spent a forgettable night here at a fancy dress policeman's ball, last January.

"So what is it, officer? You thinking of signing up for membership or something?"

"Official police business," I answered, then corrected myself: "FBI business, that is. You are Tyler Cummings, the proprietor of this place?"

"Yeah, and what of it?"

"I'm here about your girlfriend, Stephanie Hendricks."

I sensed his body language stiffen immediately.

"Stevie? What's she done now? Robbed a bank? I haven't seen that slut since she cleared out last month and took all of our savings with her. Frickin' bitch. You can tell her she's a dead woman when I see her."

"You can do that yourself," I said. "We found her body this morning, down by the LA River."

He gaped at me like he'd just pissed his pants. Maybe he had.

44

Confirming the identity of a decedent by way of viewing the deceased isn't like picking out finger food at a buffet.

I ferried my silent passenger, Tyler Cummings, to the Coroner's Office in Boyle Heights. I'd told him we'd already identified Stevie's body, and that a visual confirmation wasn't necessary, but he'd insisted. In his shoes, I'd have done the same. I have learned that denying or delaying such a request only leads to further heartache and can even give a person false hope that the authorities are somehow mistaken. There is no substitute for seeing a dead person in the flesh. No way to ignore those cold-light-of-day facts.

Besides, Tyler was feeling miserably guilty.

He didn't breathe a single word all the way there; he just stared through the open window while he wrung his hands repeatedly. I felt bad for him. His last exchange with Stevie had been bitter. A bust-up that had ended in her walking out. Now he knew that those were the final words she'd ever hear him speak. I could see he was beating himself up about it. I let him.

Through black-tinted sunglasses, I watched the LA streets slide by.

The Maestro had double-dipped his bait.

He'd known I'd be unable to resist revisiting the 7th Street Bridge once I'd heard he was taking bookings again on the killer scene. Absolutely knew I'd be suckered in if he killed someone I knew and left them there for the rats to enjoy.

I'd met Stephanie Hendricks a couple of times during *The Undertaker* investigation, earlier in the year. Even shared a dance and drinks with her in the nightclub that masqueraded as a bank – not that I remembered, given that she'd drugged me with Rohypnol at the time. A friend of hers, Tim Roxbury, who also happened to be an Alhambra PD motorbike cop, had insisted Stevie had had a thing for me. She'd even written her cell number on the back of my hand. I'd left it there for a couple of days before scrubbing it away. Unsure why. I'd never called her. Now, for some irrational reason, I wish I had.

Finding one to love is hard. Losing a loved one is harder.

I accompanied Tyler inside the Coroner's building on Mission Road, but didn't go all the way. I watched through a glass partition as the ME's assistant pulled back the white sheet to expose Stevie's head and shoulders. I saw Tyler's big gut tremble, felt my own do the same. Even in life, Stevie's complexion had been snow white. Long, raven-black hair. A Tim Burton face with silver piercings. Losing most of her blood and body fat hadn't paled her skin in the slightest. She looked asleep. The corpse bride, cut and bruised. Tyler rubbed the back of a big hand against his damp face. He sniffed. All at once his bravado and anger were gone. So, too, was his ex.

I offered him a ride home. He declined. Fine by me.

45

In the first few hours following her abduction she'd commanded herself to keep calm, to stay in control no matter what happened, that help would be on its way and that this state of duress was temporary. Then, as those first hours had slipped away and her situation had worsened, her thoughts had turned more to survival than rescue.

Forced to accept her incarceration, she'd spent a long time thinking about her life and those in it. People she interacted with. Some she even loved. All of whom would never see her alive again should things continue to go south.

She'd made mistakes. Times she should have dug in her heels instead of running. Times she should have bolted instead of standing her ground. People she should have spent less time with. People she should have invested more of herself in. Retrospectively, she could have made better decisions. Followed her heart instead of her head. Followed her head instead of her heart.

None of which mattered now.

For the millionth time since the start of her ordeal, she thought about the one she loved. The one she had always loved. Never to be.

She was dying.
She'd made her bed and now she was lying in it.
Her love would die with her and he would never know.

46

The FBI field office in Los Angeles is situated inside the federal building on Wilshire Boulevard, opposite the Veteran's Cemetery. I left my car in the tree-edged parking lot and passed through the security screening process without too many raised eyebrows. It helped I was in possession of a bona fide FBI badge. An illuminated building map revealed which floor to aim for, and I rode the mirrored elevator with another half dozen people wearing *Visitor* passes.

This was my first time here in my new official capacity and I felt like a fraud – kind of a new kid joining class halfway through the semester. One with good grades and a record of expulsion. All eyes on me.

An efficient coordinator holding a tablet PC greeted me. She checked my badge, tapped manicured nails against the glass screen, and then led me through a large open-plan work area to a glass-paneled office.

"I'll let SAC Stone know you're here," she said before leaving me to it.

I surveyed Stone's domain while I waited. It was nothing like I'd expected. In one corner, a glass-topped desk with a big brown leather chair tucked behind it. A computer screen sprouting out of the uncluttered surface. A flat keyboard and mouse. A phone. Empty in-and-out trays. The usual office necessities gathered in little groups. By the looks of it, everything new. There was a long, comfortable-looking brown sofa pushed against the opposite wall, with big green cushions to complement the potted plants either side. No personal items such as photos of Stone with his wife and his kids – presuming he had any. No framed memberships to scholarly clubs. No British paraphernalia or Union flags. Not even a photo of him with the Queen. But there was a large white panel on one of the walls, completely covered in photographic and written material pertaining to the Piano Wire Murders.

Someone had been busy.

I scanned the array of color images and monochrome printouts. The before-and-after portraits, from smiling, happy faces to bloodied death masks. It was all here: from *The Maestro's* very first Californian victim, then all the way though to Zachary Innes; the kid found in Griffith Park, Thursday. More than eighteen months of accumulated data. All very impressive, but none of it leading to a capture.

It was like having the world's most expensive Bugatti, without the wheels. Great to look at and to admire, but going nowhere fast.

I drifted over to the window. There were two homicides missing from the wall: my wife's and Stephanie Hendricks'. I thought about Stevie as my gaze roamed the stately green lawns of the Veteran's Cemetery far below. How had she ended up dead at the hands of *The Maestro*? Why had he chosen her out of everyone I knew? How had he even known about our connection? He'd left her beneath the 7th Street Bridge for me, on purpose, as a statement, to invite me back to the dance. Another delicate butterfly killed by my flame.

"The view's bloody amazing, isn't it?"

I turned to see Stone coming through the door.

"It's nice," I admitted.

"Get over yourself, Quinn. It's more than nice. It's yours."

"Mine?"

"For the duration of your tenure, it is. We had to put you somewhere." He joined me at the window. "What do you think? It's pretty bloody impressive if you ask me. Look: you can even see the Getty Center from here."

What did I think? I hadn't been with the Bureau two minutes and already owned prime real estate. But at whose expense?

Stone gave me a friendly pat on the back. "For God's sake, man. Don't look so put out. Rank hath its privileges. Come on, I'll introduce you to the ADIC and get you sworn in. We have a case meeting in less than an hour, and I need you on the ball."

47

At five minutes before three in the afternoon on a fairly pleasant August day in West Los Angeles, a handful of Feds gathered in my new office overlooking the crinkly green slopes of the Santa Monica Mountains. Two homicide detectives from the LAPD, Fred Phillips and his lieutenant Janine Walters, both old friends of mine, joined them. Everyone faced a large flat-panel monitor that had been wheeled in for the occasion and connected to a tablet PC. Their arms were folded and their expressions were firm. Everyone focused on the reason bringing us together. We breezed through introductions – warm hugs for old friends and spirited handshakes for new – and then got down to business.

If I was rusty, no one remarked on it.

If anyone thought I wasn't up to the task, they didn't mention it.

I knew every scene of the Piano Wire Murders like one of those black-and-white afternoon matinees they play over and over on cable. I knew it so well it felt like I'd written it myself.

I ran through a recap, explaining how *The Maestro* had first appeared on our radar the year before last. Of how he'd abducted over a dozen seemingly unconnected people over a period of several weeks. Of how his victims had ranged in age from pre-teen to late-twenties. Of how he'd kept them prisoner, some in cages, restrained with wires so sharp and so thin that any resistance had caused severe injury, blood loss and eventual death. Of how he'd used bags of Hartmann's solution – otherwise known as compound sodium lactate – to keep his victims hydrated and conscious, we suspected to prolong their agony. Plus, glucose solutions. I talked about each victim in detail, their backgrounds, when they were abducted and where their bodies were found. I walked my audience through the related crime scene photos, the scarce evidence and the victimology, with the aid of a gruesome slideshow keeping pace on the big TV screen.

I could see lips curling and body language forming unspoken expletives. I couldn't blame them; it was giving me the creeps trudging over old ground. Like skulking through a cemetery in the dead of night after watching a zombie movie.

Make no bones about it, painting a picture of *The Maestro's* evil activities was like deciphering the hellish images in a Hieronymus Bosch masterpiece.

You didn't want to go there.

Finally, I closed with the discovery of Stevie's body at the 7th Street Bridge and how imperative it was that we find Sheryl Klaussner before she met with the same frightening fate.

"In conclusion," I said as I froze the slideshow on the final image, which was the sketch artist's rendition of *The Maestro* given by Rochelle Lewis over a year ago, "there's a lot we don't know about The Maestro. We don't know his real name, anything about his background, or how he chooses his victims. What we do know is he's male, sixtyish, at least six foot, two hundred pounds, and he's a sadist. He derives extreme pleasure from making his victims suffer as long as he can and in humiliating conditions. We have both the ME's and Sheryl Klaussner's testaments to the fact that his methods are designed to cause the maximum amount of excruciating pain over the longest period of time.

"His objectives are maximum discomfort and degradation. Inflicting pain is paramount to this killer. It's his rapture. That's why he keeps them alive as long as possible. You could say their misery is his ecstasy. He gets off on it." I enlarged the sketchy image so that *The Maestro's* cold gray eyes completely filled the screen. "Take a good look at these eyes. The Maestro is a monster in every sense of the word. He is a torturer, with zero empathy, compassion or conscience for the torment of other human beings. Any questions?"

48

With no urgency to go home to an empty house, I hung around in my new government-funded penthouse long after the sun had sizzled away into the Pacific.

Our team of Feds and cops had disbanded for the night. Gone their separate ways with renewed determination to catch a killer before he struck again. Some working through the night. Others getting some rest before another long day tomorrow. Prior to the case meeting we'd all had different stories in our minds about *The Maestro*. Now we were all on the same page. Working from the same song sheet. The LAPD would coordinate with the Bureau and vice versa. Pool our resources, our manpower and our investigatory expertise.

No one was going to let *The Maestro* slip into obscurity this time.

I stared out across necklaces of streetlights. Fireflies dancing in the deepening dusk. Scatterings of jewels twinkling in the hills. On the illuminated four-oh-five, strings of glowing rubies stretching one way and brilliant white diamonds stretching the other.

It was my first evening back in California and I wasn't in any particular rush to go any particular place.

Maybe that was part of the reason I'd shacked up with Jack. Only psychopaths thrive on loneliness. Positive or negative, experiences are always better shared. Of course, I had friends in the city I could go and spend time with, places I could go and hang out, have fun. But the truth was, I didn't have the heart for it. Losing Hope had forced me to reevaluate life. It had also made me a little more selfish with my time.

I called Grace and explained what had happened and where I was. At first, she didn't sound too thrilled about it. But as I assured her that her daddy was in safe hands she conceded to the situation. Since her mother's murder, I was acutely aware that Grace was down to a single parent. She'd been overjoyed having me move to Florida, where she could keep an eye on me, know I wasn't out dodging bullets. Now that I was on the other side of the country again, chasing the killer who had wrecked both our lives, she was understandably concerned. But she had to accept that I wasn't doing this for me or even for her; I was doing this for her dead mom.

Next, I called Jack.

"What's this, big guy – you missing me already?"

It was late in Florida. He sounded sloshed and sleepy; I must have woken him from a drunken slumber. I told him where I was and updated him on Stevie's body found beneath the 7th Street Bridge.

"Jesus, Mary and Joseph. Talk about bad karma. That place is like the mouth of hell for you, big guy. And you're sure it's him, The Maestro?"

"No doubt about it, Jack. The MO's identical. I could recognize that handiwork with my eyes closed and in my sleep."

"Speaking of which . . ."

"Look, Jack, I'm sorry. I didn't mean to disturb you."

"Hey, it's no big deal; I'm already disturbed. How's tea-and-scones Stone shaping up?"

I smiled. "He's okay. Hard work. Well-intentioned. That said, he seems thorough and knows his stuff. Plus, he's well-respected hereabouts. I guess it's too soon to say much more than that."

"You think he's up to the task?"

"Jack, the whole task force seems in better shape this time. It's me I'm worried about. This manhunt is huge. They've thrown bodies at it like sand bags in a flood defense. I have a good feeling, though. I think maybe this time we'll get him. I think this is The Maestro's last stand."

49

I'd converted the basement of my home in Alhambra into a den a matter of weeks before Hope had died. A big TV and a pair of La-Z-Boys installed for Monday night football. Even a small fridge brimming with bottled beer. Everything a guy and his buddies needed to relax, chill out and put the world to rights. All never used. The beer was a year beyond its recommended consumption date and the cable service had long since expired.

I'd driven aimlessly around the night-washed city – trying to get back inside my old head – before eventually ending up at my home.

I fingered the key to the basement off the top of the door surround and crept down the narrow wooden steps into blackness. Soft timbers groaned. I fumbled in the dark for the cord and pulled on lights.

Bulbs sputtered, and then fired up to illuminate the basement.

The ghost of my dead partner, Harry Kelso, was lounging in one of the big leather recliners, giving me a *'where the hell have you been all this time?'* look.

Harry and I had worked the streets of LA as partners for over four years before gluttony had forced him into hospitalization. The routine bypass surgery had gone well; Harry had been in good spirits and looking forward to resuming his personal patronage of the fast food industry, but then a string of persistent complications – mainly of the infectious kind – had kept him in and under observation longer than planned. In the meantime, the serial killer known as *The Undertaker* had begun executing people across the city. In my haste to capture the killer before he struck again, I'd baited a trap. Used one of my contacts in the local TV media to release a statement announcing the killer's last victim had actually survived and was undergoing emergency medical treatment at Cedars-Sinai. I'd wanted to hook the killer and reel him in while things were still hot. But while I'd been chasing a wild goose to the rooftop of Cedars-Sinai, *The Undertaker* had crept into Harry's room in the County Medical Center and injected him with a lethal concoction of drugs.

My violently executed plan had ended in bloodshed, all right. But the wrong kind.

Harry, my dear friend, had died as a result of my arrogance.

"What are you doing here, Harry?" I continued to the foot of the staircase and lingered on the final tread.

"Lending some urgently-needed moral support. Maybe a bit of comic relief. Aren't you even pleased to see me, buddy?"

"If I hadn't smashed my head against the pavement a couple of days ago, I guess I'd be worried right now. Last time I hallucinated like this was back in college."

Harry guffawed. "Concrete wins out over skin and bone every time. Haven't you learned that one by now? Still, you're looking good. Better than me. Tighter muscle tone. Still like shit, but with a suntan."

I stepped off the last tread. "Whereas you look like you've lost a few pounds."

He patted his paunch. "You figure? I guess being dead does that to a man. You should try it sometime."

I went over to the desk in the middle of the floor and booted up the old desktop computer. Fans whirred. Dust billowed. Something bleeped. The monitor lit up. Harry watched as I powered up the laser printer and set about spooling out documents relating to The Undertaker Case. He didn't say much as I pinned glossy photos, newspaper clippings and copies of handwritten post-its to the basement walls. Then again, neither did I.

By the time I'd finished I'd recreated the serial killer shrine from the office in Fort Myers, and then some.

I stood back and admired my handiwork.

Then I turned and followed my heavy feet back up the stairs.

"Where you going, buddy?"

"For something to eat," I said. "Don't wait up."

Harry waved, but I didn't wave back.

50

I woke to the sound of knuckles rapping hard against glass. At first I was disoriented. Thought I was back home, in Tennessee, twenty years ago: when the Mississippi had flooded overnight and rescue crews had airlifted wet families from submerged homes. Ours included.

But this wasn't my bedroom of twenty years ago. I was in my car. In the parking lot behind *Ralphs*, a mile from my home in Alhambra. Slumped in the driver's seat, with a bib full of broken potato chips and drool dangling pendulously from one corner of my mouth. Vaguely, I remembered feeling ravenous, but the actual drive down to the convenience store was conveniently absent.

I'd been dreaming of Harry and there was a bad taste in my mouth.

The nuisance rapping against the glass rapped a little harder.

I pushed myself upright. Crumbs cascaded to my lap. I was stiff, achy; I must have been here all night. There was bag of potato chips on the passenger seat and an opened carton of milk, already starting to smell, in a cup holder.

A weird sense of déjà vu gone askew settled over me.

The guy rapping against the glass was a dark-haired guy. He wore a fitted tweed jacket over a pink Ralph Lauren polo shirt. Skinny jeans and mirrored Ray-Bans. Fortyish, I reckoned. Behind him I could see a long brown sedan parked across three bays. Another guy inside, plucking food from his teeth. The guy with the Ray-Bans saw me blink against bright daylight and waggled a reproving finger in a circular motion: *roll the window down.*

I did.

He leaned forearms across the rubber sill. I could smell something Mexican on his breath: the tail-end of a tequila and someone with a Spanish name.

"Well, well, well," he began with a toothy grin, "if it isn't everyone's' favorite celebrity cop. Jeez Louise. This is becoming a habit: you, me and this routine. What happened, Gabe – I thought you were dead?"

"I was in Florida."

"Same thing."

I glimpsed an old unshaven and disheveled guy reflected in his silvery sunglasses. Someone I hadn't seen in months. Like Harry said: tanned shit.

"So what brings you back to my neck of the woods? It's great to see you. I heard you quit."

"You heard right."

"So what's the lowdown? You back and on a stakeout or something?"

"At Ralphs?"

He grinned. More tequila backwash. "Now see that – that's what I'm talking about." He punched me playfully on the shoulder. "Jeez Louise, I've missed you, old pal. Life just hasn't been the same around here without you. How've you been?"

I yawned. "What do you want, Tim? I'm busy."

"Too busy to play catch-up with an old friend? I saved your skin. Remember?"

I remembered all right. I didn't want to, but I did.

Briefly, I'd met Tim Roxbury during *The Undertaker* investigation, back in January. He was an Alhambra PD motorcycle cop back then, and a regular at the discothèque run by Stevie Hendricks and her boyfriend, Tyler Cummings. Our paths had crossed a few times. Nothing serious. No real friendship. More of a tolerated interaction. Essentially, I'd gone to the club one night looking for a guy – but not in that way – and run into Tim. Stevie had spiked my drink. Tim had come to the rescue. End of story.

"While you were away sunning yourself down there in the Gulf," he said with a grin, "would you believe I passed the detective exam? Say hello to Alhambra's newest detective." He rummaged in his tweed jacket and brought out a wallet. Balanced it on the sill so that I could admire the badge. "See. It's official. Police Detective Timothy Roxbury, at your service."

I showed him my new shiny shield. "Mine trumps yours, Tim."

Tim's smug grin slid off his face. "Maybe. But you're a ways down the catwalk when it comes to competing on fashion."

I noticed he was wearing several colored wristbands.

"Hey, what's with those?"

"These? These're mementos. Reminders of some clubs I frequent. Some men I'd like to. Christian charities. That kind of thing."

"Show me the yellow one."

"Why? You thinking of switching sides, Gabe?"

"Just let me see it, Tim."

He waggled his wrist so that the lemon-colored band became fully visible. I peered closer, trying to read the indistinct upside-down lettering without the benefit of readers.

Tim sighed, "It says Charity Cop."

"*Charity* Cop? What's that?"

"Exactly what it says."

"Not Celebrity Cop?"

Tim made a face. "Jeez Louise, will you slow down, Mr. Ego? Why on earth would it say something like that? Still thinking the world revolves around you, are we?"

My cell phone chirped on the dash. I picked up: *Mason Stone.*

"Quinn, it's me. Where are you?"

"Stocking up on groceries." I shooed Tim away from the open window, but he stayed put. "What gives, Stone?"

"We have a lead on a suspect. You need to get your arse over here as quickly as you can."

He gave me an address: an abandoned factory in El Monte, east of LA and north of I-10. I knew where the place was; I'd called at the nearby home improvement store once or twice when my life had been ordinary.

"You have him cornered?"

"As far as we know, he's still inside. We're going in," he paused to check his watch, "in ten minutes. Be sharpish and no dallying or you'll miss all the fun."

I disconnected the call and turned the transmission.

Tim didn't move. "Hey, Mr. Ego. I hear on the grapevine you're not the only big player back in town."

"Oh, and who might that be?"

"You know who I'm talking about: The Maestro. I'm willing to bet that's why you're back. I'm right, aren't I? Listen, I can help with the case. I've studied the files. I know it inside and out. Use me, Gabe. I'm telling you, I'm inside this guy's head."

I started to roll up the window. "Tim, I appreciate the offer. But I'm busy."

Tim shifted his arms off the sill. "Oh, I see how it is. Got a shiny new FBI badge and all of a sudden I'm dispersible."

"Dispensable."

"Exactly." He hooked fingers over the glass rim before it reached the top. "Look, Gabe, I've done my homework on this one. Thinking outside the box. I've been looking at similar crimes committed in the weeks preceding The Maestro's first strike. I think I found something."

"Bye, Tim."

He kept his fingers curled over the glass to the very last second, then pulled them away as the window snapped shut.

I saw him mouth the words *'I'll call you, later'* and make a phone gesture.

I was in no doubt that he would.

51

Traffic heading east on I-10 was light. I hammered along with my foot pressed hard against the accelerator, teeth clenched. Could the FBI have *The Maestro* cornered and caged in already? Could anything be that easy? I jumped off at the Baldwin Avenue exit, switched back under the Interstate, then headed north onto Temple City Boulevard.

A half mile later, I eased off the gas as I crossed train lines cutting slantwise through the asphalt. A stocky guy in an FBI vest was in the middle of the road, stopping vehicles and sending them back the way they'd come. I showed him my FBI credentials and he waved me through. Up ahead, I could see two black vans parked against the curbside. Two distinct groups of serious-looking Feds between the vans: one gaggle in white tees, sunglasses and dark-blue bulletproof vests, gathered in the summer sunshine like buddies for a game; the other hard-helmeted and geared up like a military insertion unit readying for combat. Unmistakable FBI lettering throughout. There was a black chopper hovering about two hundred feet up. No sign of any police officers. No police cruisers. This was solely a Bureau tactical operation; they didn't want any gung-ho cops stealing the show.

Hubs scraped the curb. Mason Stone met me as I leapt out. He looked bigger in his FBI vest. A heavyweight champ with a day-old beard speckled with gray. His resemblance to the movie actor Sean Bean was clear as day.

"Nice timing," he said as he handed me a Kevlar vest. "We were just about to go in."

"The Maestro?"

"We believe so. He's holed up, back there." He thumbed over his shoulder to a big, peach-colored building.

Boarded-up windows, overgrown chain-link fencing and the inevitable decay that befalls buildings left to the elements and neglect. A group of three or four sprawling structures in a compound of broken bones concrete and knee-high grasses. One of them had a *For Sale* sign on it. Looked like it had been there for years, color-drained by the unremitting Californian sun.

"What is this place?"

"A disused plating factory." Stone saw my frown and added: "I forget we speak the same language, only differently. It's abandoned."

I looked around the street. There were a few small businesses opposite: a furniture makers and a small food-processing plant, still struggling after the recession. No one on the sidewalks. A Fed turning back traffic to the north of us. A SWAT sniper lying prone on the roof of one of the vans, rifle aimed toward the quiet compound. The quickened heartbeat of the FBI chopper hanging perfectly still directly above: a blot on an otherwise spotless sky.

I ducked into the vest and sealed the Velcro tight. "You sure it's him?"

"We're pretty certain – according to the intel."

In police terms, I knew what *pretty certain* meant: a decent lead based on the best information available. Like the suspicion of weapons of mass destruction when there aren't any. Pretty certain never equates to one hundred percent positive. There is always a margin of error. Sometimes huge.

Stone handed me a sidearm sitting in its holster, together with a spare clip slotted inside a magazine pouch.

"Yours. Be a love and look after it."

I examined the weapon. It was a standard-issue Glock 22 Gen 4 in .40 caliber. Looked and smelled brand-new. I checked to see if the clip was full. It was. Safety on, I attached the holster and magazine pouch to my belt.

"Not exactly a prime location," I remarked. "Care to share what led you here?"

Stone let out a weary breath. "Remember the boy we found in Griffith Park?'

"Zachary Innes."

"He attended the same high school as Marta Chavez."

I felt one of my eyebrows tug itself up my forehead. "As in The Maestro's fourth victim? Why didn't we know this yesterday?"

"An oversight. Anyway, the point is, they both had the same music teacher."

"Marv Connolly."

"You remember him?"

"Too clearly."

Connolly had coached the school marching band and ran an extracurricular music tutoring service from his home in Culver City. We'd first investigated his connection to the original case after one of his students, Marta Chavez, had disappeared the same evening she'd attended his private class. Connolly was a music teacher, with a particular interest in the classical composers. For a time, Connolly had been high on the Piano Wires *persons of interest* list – perpetuated by allegations of sexual misconduct leveled at him by some of his out-of-hours students – but had been subsequently dropped when some of his shaky alibis had found their feet. Connolly was a big redheaded guy with a bad temper, not renowned for either keeping his mouth shut or excelling at self-restraint.

"Connolly was ruled out of the investigation," I said.

"Only because something new came along to point it in another direction. Otherwise he was looking good for it."

"Sheryl Klaussner escaped." I nodded. "She was able to pinpoint the time of her abduction to a period when Connolly was coaching the son of a local councilor. His alibi was airtight."

In spite of all his BS, I hadn't figured Connolly for a murderer. Still didn't. But now he was back under the microscope. Back in the fray. I didn't believe it was coincidence.

"So how did he end up here, in an abandoned factory eighteen months later?"

Stone shrugged. "How does anybody go from a well-paid job with a good pension plan to living in a disused warehouse? Here's how: he hit the bottle and flushed his life down the loo."

"Connolly was a teetotaler."

"Yeah, before the education board fired him following the sex scandal and his wife threw him out."

Stone had done his homework; knew something I didn't.

"Okay, so we know how he got here, but what about you? How'd you come by this location?"

"Quinn, we really don't have time for this. We need to get in there before he gets wind of us out here."

"Indulge me, Stone; I'm a stickler for details."

Stone drew a deep, impatient breath and rattled off the information with the weariness of someone who had told the same story a dozen times.

Here's how it went: FBI techies had trawled through all of the traffic camera surveillance footage of vehicles leaving Griffith Park within a twelve hour period prior to the body of Zachary Innes being discovered. Using license plate information, they'd concentrated their efforts on single male drivers fitting the killer's description, and they'd come up with eleven candidates. Through interview and background checks, ten were ruled out.

Stone pointed across the street. "See that vehicle over there?"

It was a plain black pickup truck parked on the lot outside the furniture makers. A Ford, a few years old. Its wheels and fenders were clogged with hard, tan-colored mud. More of the clayey soil was sprayed up the sides and the doors and onto the filthy windows. The truck had been off-road recently. Maybe more than once. Never hosed down.

"It's registered to some kid called Franklin Forrest. He lives in Culver City. When our investigator asked him about the pickup and the link with Griffith Park he told us he'd reported it stolen six months earlier. We checked his story. He had. Yesterday, we issued a statewide police notice on the registration number – the plates. This morning, a City of El Monte squad car spotted it and called it in."

"And the connection to Marv Connolly?"

Stone's patience was wearing thin, mild irritation creeping through.

"We questioned the owner of that furniture company over there, where the truck's parked. He told us he didn't mind the pickup being parked there because, and I quote: the wino helps us move lumber. He gave us the wino's name and description."

"Marv Connolly."

The nondescript truck connected Connolly to the Piano Wire murder in Griffith Park, Thursday. He'd tutored the murdered boy, Zachary Innes, and a previous victim, Marta Chavez. And I'd ruled him out as a prime suspect.

Coincidences are for those who believe in fairies.

"Now can we please get on with this?"

"Don't let me hold you back."

Stone didn't waste any more time introducing me to his band of resolute colleagues from the Wilshire field office. Five male agents and one female. We'd all met yesterday, in the case meeting.

The armored SWAT team came over as we crowded together for a team huddle.

Stone ran through the plan of attack one last time, mainly for my benefit:

There were several ways in and out of the abandoned buildings. Lots of means to escape. Not just streets leading away from the compound, but also railroad tracks, adjacent factory compounds still in use, and a flood canal running into the San Gabriel River. The plan was, the SWAT team would go in first and sweep the buildings. Our band of plain-clothed agents would hold back and cover the exits. Catch Connolly if he tried to slip away. The idea was if SWAT failed to capture the suspect inside then they'd at least flush him out into our hands. Everyone had instructions to capture Connolly alive. Wound him as a last resort – preferably in a none-fatal area – but take him into custody nevertheless.

It was a solid plan, providing Connolly was even in there.

Stone handed out tactical lights for our firearms. High-power Xenon beams with red-dot laser markers. We clipped them on.

"Okay, people. You all know what you're doing. So let's rock and roll."

One of the tactical guys used long bolt cutters on the padlocked chain holding the main link-gates together, and we slipped into the compound at a run, spreading out, weapons drawn. The black-suited SWAT team followed their MP5 submachine guns into the buildings, silently breaking open doors or entering through large rents in the crumbling walls.

I was teamed up with the female agent, Melody Seeger. She was an inch or two shorter than me. Thirtyish, I reckoned. A girl-next-door with coppery hair scraped back into a tight ponytail. A leanness to her figure that spoke of a healthy gym subscription and counted calories.

"Nice day for a bust," I said as we bounded across fractured concrete. "How long have you been with the Bureau, Agent Seeger?"

"I'm into my second year," she answered. "I got my BA in Japanese from Crimson Tide and spent four years as an interpreter before applying. How about you?"

"My second day."

She made one of those looks that women do when they suspect a man isn't being totally forthcoming with the truth.

We planted our shoulders against rough brickwork, taking positions. We were in the shadow of the third building, covering the doorway where two SWAT members had entered ahead of us. A battered door at the top of a short flight of metal steps, hemmed in by an iron safety rail. Behind us, a ladder climbed up the wall to the roof. A long time ago, the metalwork had been painted bright yellow. Now it was mostly bare with rusty joints. I empathized. There was what looked like a loading dock around the corner from the doorway: a raised, U-shaped concrete platform with thin concrete struts supporting the broken roof. A ramp with more rusting yellow handrails sloped up and in. Years of overlapping graffiti everywhere you could see.

I could smell dry grass and iron oxide. Like blood on a summer's day.

Not much to do but keep our eyes peeled, and wait.

"So what made you plum for the Bureau, Agent Seeger?"

"I guess it was always in the cards. I was raised in a family with deep roots in law enforcement. My stepdad's father was a hardnosed Huntsville cop. His before him. My stepdad wanted to follow in his footsteps, but he failed to make the grade. So you could say I'm living his dream. Why'd you become a cop?"

"Same reason."

We shared a laugh.

She pressed a finger to her ear, suddenly listening to a conversation in her earpiece.

"First building clear," she announced.

"My father was a Memphis beat cop back in the day," I said. "He never made it to detective. Not sure he wanted to. Didn't live long enough to see me make it."

Seeger's smile curled into a grin. "Legacies. You see it all the time – one generation passing the torch on to the next. Is your son living your dream, too?"

I baulked at the question. Right now I had no idea what my son was doing. Certainly not following in my footsteps. If anything, speed-walking in the complete and opposite direction.

Agent Seeger caught my reaction and made note of it.

She pressed a finger to her ear again. "Second building clear."

I began to get a sinking feeling, like we were about to be hit by a big anticlimax.

Then a series of sharp staccato cracks echoed around the cavernous loading dock, and we both jumped to the unmistakable sound of gunshots.

I heard the words '*agent down!*' hollered through Seeger's earpiece, and we reacted automatically. I jabbed a finger toward the doorway and Seeger bounded up the steps as I sprinted into the loading dock.

I stepped through a sliding door, flicked on the tactical light and scanned the shadowy interior.

Several years ago, when the factory owners had cleared out, they'd cleaned out. All that remained of a once busy production facility were hollow rooms and rows of concrete stumps where plating machinery had once stood. No fixtures or fittings other than overhead piping and ventilation ducts. Alternating bands of mote-filled shadow and light where bright sunlight lanced from shattered skylights. Doors off hinges and debris strewn everywhere.

There were discarded spray paint cans and smashed beer bottles. Every vertical surface covered with multicolored street art.

No signs of any movement.

I listened, heard the muffled sound of footfalls coming from a passageway at the far end of the bay. I ran toward it, swept the Xenon beam across every dark recess as I went. The corridor was lined with ransacked offices. Broken glass and ripped-out ceiling tiles piled on the floor.

No signs of Connolly.

Footfalls fading.

I continued noisily across the shattered tiles. Came out into a large open space, interrupted by big vertical pipes that curled down from the high ceiling to form funnels a few feet above the floor. Several rusty orange domes with big iron doors that I guessed were furnaces. Ancient smells of smelted ores and molten metals.

I heard movement on the far side: feet pounding over concrete.

I yelled a warning.

The footfalls stopped.

Then something clanged against one of the pipes directly in front of me. It whizzed past my ear at high speed: a bullet. In the same instant, I heard a series of resonating booms as the sound of the gunshot ricocheted around the pipework like a pinball.

The footfalls started up again.

So did I.

I scurried between the funnels, slipping and sliding over debris. Hadn't gone very far when something like an invisible wrecking ball thumped me in the chest. The impact stopped my upper half dead, but my legs continued to run out from underneath me. The world tilted and my shoulders hit the deck with enough force to blow the wind out of my sails.

Daylight dazzled from a hole in the roof.

I blinked and dragged in air. Glanced at a ragged hole in the Kevlar vest. The glint and smell of hot metal.

Connolly had shot me!

Six inches higher and the bullet would have torn through my throat.

"Quinn!"

I twisted, looked up.

Seeger was on a metal gantry near the high ceiling, holding a hand to her earpiece.

"He's heading for the roof!" She turned and started sprinting along the raised walkway.

I clambered to my feet and headed back out through the loading bay. Saw uniformed SWAT converging across the overgrown compound as I leapt off the raised platform. Plain-clothed Feds were running my way from the other buildings. I reached the metal ladder first. Without hesitating, I stowed the Glock and pulled myself up the side of the building, two rungs at a time.

I didn't give a second thought to whether or not the old metal ladder could take my weight all the way to the top. Maybe I should. The flat roof was at least thirty feet above ground level; too high to jump from without breaking bones and doing serious damage. All the same I scurried up the ladder like I had a demon on my tail. I wanted to get there and intercept Connolly before anyone else got to him.

This was my case.

I'd given Connolly a clean bill of health.

I wanted it back.

I heard Feds jump on the ladder below me.

I was halfway there when several bolts fixing the top of the ladder to the wall decided to shake loose from their moorings. Crumbled cement rained down. I shook my head and blew away dusty debris. Blinked and kept on climbing. When I looked back up I saw the curving top of the ladder had started to come away from the wall. Only a dozen or so rungs to go. I could make it. I kept going.

Heard somebody holler *'everybody off the ladder!'* as the pins came completely out of the crumbling cement and the metalwork leaned a foot away from the wall with a sudden creaking jerk.

In that split second, the way I figured it I had three clear choices: I could cling on to the ladder for dear life as it peeled away from the wall altogether, popping out pins as it angled away, pray that I could drop to safety from a reasonable height; or I could jump now and hope for the best, maybe fracture a hip or bust open my skull, maybe even kill myself or somebody else in the fall; or I could leap, fingers curled like grappling hooks, hands aiming for the crisp edge of the roof.

The split second came and went.

Two more pins popped out right behind my hands.

The ladder let out another agonized moan and angled itself away from the wall.

I bent my knees, focused on the hard line where the top of the wall met blue sky, and leapt.

I swung into the wall with my fingers hooked onto the roof. Banged bones as the ladder fell away. Heard people yell warnings from down below. I heard the metal ladder groan as it collapsed like a felled tree, hitting the compound with a reverberating clang.

Someone shouted *Holy Mother of God!* It might have been me.

I was hanging from the lip of the roof by fingertips alone. Thirty feet in the air. Grip weakening. I must have looked like a complete fool. I think I heard someone below verbally confirming it.

I'd made it this far; I wasn't about to drop out now.

I mustered every morsel of strength I had and hauled myself onto the rooftop.

If anyone clapped, I didn't hear it.

I rolled to my feet, momentarily disoriented, looking around me for signs of Seeger or Connolly.

Keith Houghton

The FBI chopper was directly above. A fierce downdraft blowing loose cement and dust particles all over the place. Ragged insulation flapping noisily.

I squinted against the swirling grit.

The factory rooftop was mostly flat but cluttered with interweaving piping conduits, boxed air-conditioning vents and slender, brass-colored smoke stacks. Most of the glass skylights had been smashed, leaving yawning holes and buckled framework.

Connolly was in the middle of the chaos, in one of the few open spaces devoid of clutter. But he wasn't alone. One of his big hands was clamped around the neck of Agent Seeger, the other pressing a gun against the curve of her waist.

While I had been performing my aerial stunts, Seeger had been taken hostage.

"Stay where you are!" came the amplified instruction from the sharpshooter hanging out of the chopper. "Or we will open fire."

Not while there was a federal agent in harm's way, I thought. And Connolly knew it. I saw him force the muzzle of the gun into Seeger's ribs. Saw her whole body go rigid. There was little chance of her breaking free without Connolly pulling the trigger.

I took out the Glock and hollered *"Connolly!"* against the battering wind.

His bloodshot eyes dipped my way, a look of recognition mangling up his unshaven face. But his puzzlement soon vanished.

"You're making a big mistake, Quinn," he shouted as I worked my way carefully toward him.

"Drop the weapon!" I shouted back. "And let her go! You don't want this, Connolly. This isn't who you are."

I could see he was thinking about making a bolt for it, but the risk outweighed the reward. Two red dot laser sights jiggling around in his eyes weren't favorable odds. I didn't know how he'd climbed up here, but I knew there was a faster way down – one that led straight to the hospital or straight to the morgue.

I was within touching distance, watching Connolly down the sights of the Glock.

I saw his finger tighten on the trigger.

"Shoot him!" Agent Seeger shouted.

Then the roof gave way under their feet.

And Connolly dropped like a condemned man at the gallows, taking Seeger with him.

I reacted instinctively: I launched into a death dive as they plunged through the gaping maw. I dropped the Glock as I sailed through the air and thrust out both hands as I belly-flopped onto the roof. Miraculously, I managed to grab two handfuls of flesh and clothing and clung on: one hand wrapped around Connolly's gun fist, the other hooked into the padded neck of Seeger's bulletproof vest. But Connolly was a heavy guy. Filled with demons and drink. Gravity was sucking him down like a rock in a well. His weight dragged me toward the hole, on my stomach. I tried to dig in toes, to no avail. For a moment I thought I was going to plummet into the maw after them, headfirst onto the uncompromising concrete below, but my Kevlar vest snagged on the rim of the hole and brought me to a juddering stop. Pain ricocheted through my shoulders and into my back as both Connolly's and Seeger's combined weight tried to pry the joints out of their sockets.

I clung on.

Wind from the roaring rotor blades beat down on us.

The roof creaked. I slid a few inches deeper into the abyss.

I heard Seeger release a terrified whimper.

Insanely, Connolly tried to turn his wrist and aim the gun upward at my face.

There was a feral look in his eyes bordering on madness.

I'd been here before: in Vegas, right before *The Undertaker* had taken a thousand foot fall from the Stratosphere Tower, into the glittery night, never to be seen again. I'd hung through another gaping maw then, with the freezing Nevada air blasting tears from my eyes, faced with the choice of who to let live and who to let die.

Connolly strained against my grasp, mustering with all his might to bring the muzzle in line with my white-eyed gape.

I stared into his wild eyes and wondered if he could be *The Maestro*: the killer of my wife.

The Feds thought so.

They were *pretty certain*.

But how certain was I?

I stared down at the big guy dangling like a ragdoll from my outstretched hand.

And wondered.

Right here and now, the easiest thing in the world would be to let go. Let Connolly fall to his death. Save the judicial system a whole lot of time and money spent prosecuting him. I'd be doing everyone a favor. But most of all, I'd be evening the score.

All I needed to do was let go . . .

But Agent Seeger beat me to it. She knew I couldn't hold their combined weight for much longer. She swung her leg and kneed Connolly in the groin. His eyes squeezed shut with pain. His big paw opened, reflexively, and the gun fell out of his grasp. In so doing, it removed the pressure keeping my own grip secure, and his unburdened hand slipped through mine.

He dropped to the factory floor like a sack of wet sand.

I grabbed Seeger's vest in both hands and howled like a dog as I hauled her out of the jaws of death.

52

"We're going to need to bag that vest as evidence," Special Agent Mason Stone told me as we loitered on the sidewalk outside the abandoned plating factory in El Monte.

I was feeling sore. Massaging aching shoulders and listening to cartilage crunch. For sure, both arms were now a few inches longer than they had been an hour earlier.

I shucked off the vest and handed it over. Stone passed it to one of his colleagues, who promptly dropped it into a clear plastic sack. Sunlight glinted off the bullet lodged in the dark blue fabric as he carried it away.

Incredibly, Marv Connolly had survived the fall. But his body had been badly messed up in the process. An ambulance had whisked him away to an Emergency Room close to the FBI field office, and the factory complex had been quarantined. SWAT had already cleared out, with the remaining Feds comparing notes and waiting for the Evidence Response Team to come in and perform a full sweep. Midday sunshine bore down from a cloud-freckled sky.

I noticed Agent Seeger watching from her shadowy perch beneath the open tailgate of one of the Suburbans. I nodded and she acknowledged with a nervy smile.

"Good God, Quinn, you were lucky," Stone was saying. "That bloody stunt almost got you killed. Next time try saving some of the heroics for the rest of us. Come on, there's something you need to see, back inside. I think you're going to like it."

Curious, I followed Stone back into the compound. We headed into the first building. More debris and lively street art. Shafts of light piercing the shadows. We passed through a large open space with a wide trench running down the middle. It was filled with concrete blocks standing in neat rows.

"Remember the eggs in the first Alien film?"

I did. We kept moving. Came to a metal staircase leading to an observation pod overlooking the factory floor. I tailed Stone into the confined space.

The observation pod had once been home to a shop-floor controller. From here, he would have monitored the plating process down below. Since going to rack and ruin, trespassers had smashed its bay windows and gutted wiring from the remains of a control console. Empty liquor bottles were scattered around the place. Several crushed beer cans. Bits of garbage and broken glass. There was a thin roll-up mattress in one corner, stained. A threadbare sleep-bag that hadn't seen a Laundromat in at least a year. An old kit bag stuffed with clothes. Opened boxes of breakfast cereals and other dried foodstuffs that looked like they'd been rescued from a Dumpster.

"Looks like Connolly's been holed up here for quite some time," Stone observed.

But all at once I wasn't listening.

I was gawping at the graffiti on the wall above the roll-up bed.

Over the jazzy murals, someone had spray-painted five horizontal red lines crossed with musical notes.

"Da, da, da, dah," Stone breathed in tune. "See, I knew you'd like it."

53

Marv Connolly was sealed in an observation room in the Good Samaritan Hospital on Wilshire Boulevard, lying prone like a stricken mountaineer. His neck was locked in a stiff brace, limiting movement. One of his wrists was handcuffed to the bed frame, while his other was white-knuckled with pain and grabbing at the air every now and then, as if trying to snatch something only he could see. Connolly had survived the fall, but had broken both legs, a clavicle and several ribs for the privilege. Maybe fractured a few vertebrae. Only the scheduled scan would tell us for sure.

Despite his pain, Connolly was playing hardball. He'd clammed up the moment the paramedics had scraped him off the factory floor, and hadn't breathed an intelligible word since. Basic analgesics hadn't touched his pain. He was demanding something stronger. But we needed him conscious, coherent.

I studied him through the glass partition, trying to see beyond his obvious discomfort. Connolly was in agony and was letting the whole of the Intensive Care Unit know about it. But Stone had said '*no Morphine*' to Connolly's doctors – at least not until we'd finished grilling him. They hadn't been happy, but hadn't argued the point either.

I still wasn't convinced Connolly was the killer we were after.

My *Uh-Oh Radar* was as quiet as a mouse in a library.

The Maestro that I knew was a mastermind. Brilliant at his craft. Meticulous and organized. Able to abduct his victims and keep them locked away for days on end without detection. Sometimes multiple victims at once.

The year before last, he'd given the LAPD and the Feds a runaround for their money. He'd evaded capture and killed more than a dozen people before disappearing into obscurity. He was skillful, canny and extremely dangerous. Nothing like Connolly. Nothing like a down-and-out drunk squatting in an abandoned factory, surviving on handouts. Connolly might have met the criteria on some level – right build, right age group, right place – but his profile just didn't fit the bill.

Unless Connolly was an A-list actor, I wasn't buying a ticket to his execution.

So far, a surface sweep of the abandoned factory had failed to uncover anything to connect him with *The Maestro* other than the painting on the wall. No piano wires. No signs of anyone being held there against their will. And no trace of Sheryl Klaussner. On strict orders from Stone, the boys and girls from the Evidence Response Team were digging deeper, but no one was holding their breath.

I wasn't convinced Connolly was the killer.

But, then again, I wasn't convinced about coincidences either.

Stone joined me at the observation window. "I know what you're thinking, Quinn. It's all over your face. You're thinking he isn't our man."

"We ruled him out the first time," I reasoned. "His alibis were airtight."

"And you and I both know alibis can be faked. Come on, look at the facts. Connolly has connections with two victims. He's a music teacher with allegations of misconduct against him. We caught him on a traffic camera leaving Griffith Park the night before the body was discovered. We found Beethoven's Fifth on the wall above his bed. Need I go on? That's more than enough to quash reasonable doubt."

"Maybe so. But it doesn't add up to make him a serial killer."

I watched Stone stew it over. He'd believed the intelligence was golden. Believed that Connolly was a good candidate for a prime suspect. Still did. Now I was raining on his parade. Now he was wondering why he'd flown across the country and invited me in.

"Let me take a shot at him," I said. "I know Connolly. I'm a familiar face. Let me see if I can find out what's really going on here."

"Do you honestly think he'll open up to you? You do know he probably blames you for the break-up of his marriage?"

"And that could work in my favor. I don't think he can resist unloading all that pent-up anger. Do you?"

And angry tongues are loose tongues.

I exchanged places with the agent in the isolation room and shut myself inside with Connolly. I had a file folder in one hand and a brown paper bag in the other. The Fed had already read Connolly his rights and tried softening him up a bit: talk, confess, shave a few years of a lengthy prison sentence. Get some urgently needed pain relief. But Connolly's lips had stayed sealed. Since he hadn't requested one, there was no appointed lawyer arriving anytime soon.

I walked over to the bed.

Connolly was a manacled bear, prepped for a veterinary inspection. He looked much older than the last time I'd questioned him. Thinner in some parts, bulkier in others. Yellowy, sunken eyes indicative of hard alcohol abuse. Unkempt hair and ingrained dirt.

He smelled of filth and beer.

I leaned over, so that his pained gaze met mine.

"You're in big trouble, Marv. I hear you're being uncooperative. Which surprises me, since I know you're an intelligent guy underneath all that hurt. You must be aware by now that there's no way out of this for you. That the only way you're going to make what's promising to be a difficult rest of your life any easier is by cooperating." I showed him the file folder. "We have you on resisting arrest and the illegal possession of a handgun. And that's just for starters. You shot at a federal agent, and then threatened to kill another. Marv, this isn't looking too rosy, is it? In fact, it's a slam-dunk. I hear the District Attorney is looking to make an example. She takes exception at the thought of some vagrant trying to murder federal agents just doing the public a service. Tell you the truth, it wouldn't surprise me if she doesn't skip the twenty-five to life and go straight for the lethal injection. So it's your choice, Marv. Give me what I need and I'll put in a good word. Get you fixed up. Otherwise, it's the end of the road for you."

Connolly glared with hateful eyes.

He desperately wanted to bite my head off, tear into me for wrecking his life, but stupidity or a warped sense of loyalty was keeping his mouth shut.

"Just imagine," I continued, "best case scenario right now, twenty-five to life, maximum security, with no hope of parole, maybe no visitation rights, nothing but that little concrete cell and the bull males to keep you company at night. Remember, Marv, we're not the only ones who despise child killers; those bull male inmates despise them too." I placed the brown paper bag on the trolley table, swung it around so that Connolly could just about see it above the bed. "Tell you something, I couldn't do it. Caged up like a rabid dog. Praying for the needle. Can you?"

Connolly eyed the bag. Bloodshot eyes straining. Tears of pain welling. I'd scrunched up the paper so that the shape of a bottle was instantly recognizable. Connolly needed morphine, but the part of his brain addicted to alcohol had other ideas. I saw his tongue involuntarily lick his bottom lip. Saw him try to push himself up, and then stiffen as pain pinned him down. He raised his free hand, stretched filthy fingers, but the table remained tantalizingly beyond his reach.

"It's yours, but only on the condition you talk."

I turned as if to walk away.

"I have nothing to say to you, Quinn." The words were spat through gritted teeth browned with neglect.

I turned back. Knew I had to keep him talking. Opening up.

"What happened to you, Marv? You had a nice wife, a good job. The respect of your peers. Plans for a family. Now look at you: you're a disgrace. A drunken wreck."

"You happened to me."

I came closer. "Me? Oh, no. You can't blame me, Marv. I was just doing my job. I didn't put those complaints in the mouths of those kids. That was all you. That's the real reason why your wife left you and the education board fired your sorry ass. You were lucky they didn't take things further."

"You call this lucky?"

I shrugged, "We choose our own path to walk. Like you chose to take the fall instead of facing up to what you've done."

I put my mouth near his ear, whispered: "I really hope you're not the guy we're looking for, Marv – because that guy murdered my wife. Just between you and me, I have every intention of making his life hell on earth, right before I end it. You get me?" I straightened up. "Now tell me about Griffith Park."

Connolly glared. One or two tears leaked out of the corners of his wounded eyes and left tracks in the grime.

I rattled the bagged bottle on the table, repeated the instruction.

"I go there to collect wood."

Each word was an effort, forced through grating teeth.

"Why?"

"Because I get paid for it."

"By who?"

"Chan. *Goddammit!*"

He tried to grab me with his free hand, but winced as pain drew it back.

"Chan?"

"He runs the furniture place across the street from the factory. He pays me to collect stuff for him. He turns them into features or something. I don't know. Coffee tables, or something."

"What about Zachary Innes?"

"Who?"

"Zachary Innes. Remember, he was one of your music students, back in the day?"

Connolly's heavy brow formed deep furrows. Sweat began to pool. It was hard for him to think through all the raw pain. But I had to keep him focused.

I rattled the paper-covered bottle.

"Zachary Innes," I said. "Nice kid with a silver-and-blue retainer."

"Zack? Yeah, I remember Zack. Like you say, a good kid."

I removed a color eight-by-ten from the folder and held it over Connolly's face. It was the image of the blood-soaked boy wired to the tree.

"Take a good look, Marv. Zachary was found murdered in Griffith Park on Thursday, the day after you happened to be there."

Fear flashed across Connolly's eyes.

"You can't think I had anything to do with that!"

"What am I supposed to think? The evidence shows you were there the same time. We got you on a traffic cam fleeing the scene. Zachary's a former student of yours, isn't he? Just like Marta Chavez. You do remember Marta Chavez, don't you? We found her bloodied body bound to a tree just like this."

There was foam in the corners of Connolly's mouth. In spite of all his injuries, the thought of an alcoholic beverage sitting just beyond his grasp was killing him.

"So I knew them both," he growled. "It doesn't make me a murderer!"

"How long have you been holed up in that factory, Marv?"

"Why should you care?"

"I don't. Just curious."

"A few months."

I swapped the picture for another: it was the photo of Beethoven's Fifth, taken in the plating factory. "Recognize this? Who did it?"

"How should I know?"

"Because you're the one sleeping under it every night, that's why. It's newer than the rest of the graffiti in there – so I'm guessing it's been done recently. Work with me, Marv. Think about lessening your prison time. Who did this?"

Connolly clammed up again, stared at me with spiteful and defiant eyes.

I grabbed hold of his free hand and wedged the bagged bottle into it. Instinctively, he tried to force it toward his lips, but I held it away.

"Give me a name," I said.

Connolly pulled. I resisted.

"Give me a name."

"Woody." He growled it under extreme protest, through teeth clenched so hard the gums were white and springing with blood.

"Who's Woody?"

Connolly's eyes were racked with pain and hatred. He screamed. I could see he'd already bitten off more than he could chew, and now the mouthful was stuck in his throat.

"Who's Woody?"

Connolly pulled with all his might, desperately trying to get the bottle to his lips. I resisted. He emitted a defiant roar and thrashed against his shackles.

I heard knuckles rapping against glass, turned to see Stone gesturing that I should cut-off the questioning and come out, immediately.

I let Connolly win the tug of war and walked away. Heard him rummage in the bag like a child impatiently ripping open a Christmas present. I heard him emit a long cry of misery as he discovered the cola bottle inside.

"The ERT found something of interest in the factory," Stone told me as I joined him outside.

"What?"

I could see the whites of his eyes. Something big.

"A cage, with signs of captivity. We need to go back there. ASAP."

54

Let's be straight about this: I wasn't happy about cutting short the interview with Connolly; I had more questions in mind and more information to lever out of him. But at least I had a name. Something to work with. I also knew that if Connolly and *The Maestro* weren't one and the same, then that meant he and the killer had been in the abandoned factory at the same time. Chances were, their paths had crossed.

In which case, Connolly could identify the killer.

We rode back to the abandoned factory in silence. I had the feeling Stone didn't fully approve of my interview techniques. I walked the line and we both knew it. Sometimes either side. Not exactly unorthodox, mind you. But not exactly textbook.

A federal agent wearing blue Latex gloves and an excited grin met us at the factory gates.

"We found a series of subterranean tunnels and chambers," he explained as we climbed out of the Suburban into afternoon heat. "Someplace to run all the electrics and coolants for the plating processes. We came across the cage in a small room behind the main power junction. Almost missed it down there in the dark. Here, you'll need these."

He handed out Maglites.

We followed the techie at pace into one of the buildings, passing through a gutted control room and out into a large open hanger-like space. I could hear birds tweeting in the lofty metal rafters. To one side, a long, downward-sloping ramp was set into the floor. We descended toward a set of double doors marked with faded yellow *Caution* signs, and pushed through into darkness.

We flicked on our flashlights.

The air was stale down here. Dry. I ran a light beam over the walls. We were at the head of a wide passageway. I could see oval lamps behind metal grilles, clamped to the walls every few yards or so – some smashed, all unlit – disappearing into the distance. Dusty pipes pegged to the length of the ceiling. Other, smaller passageways sprouting off into pitch-blackness on either side.

We followed the beams of the Maglites, our shoes skittering over loose debris. We turned down a side tunnel, then another. Up ahead I could see a bright wedge of light illuminating a slice of the passageway. Portable lamps on tripods, powered by batteries. Techies from the ERT in hairnets and plastic slippers, standing around, waiting on us. Lightning bursts followed by the inhuman screech of a recharging flash as photographs were taken.

Another techie approached as we entered the pool of light.

"It's definitely some kind of a detainment area," she said as she handed out pairs of plastic slippers. "We've found signs of human blood and chaffed skin."

We slipped the thin plastic sleeves over our day shoes and ducked through the doorway.

It was a small, square chamber of bare cement walls. No more than three yards on a side. The ceiling was lower than that in the passageway, claustrophobic.

I could smell the sharp tang of metal mixed with the unmistakable reek of sour urine and human feces.

There was another portable lamp in here. Its focus was on the far corner, directed at a wire cage with its door wide open. It was one of those big collapsible crates used by dog owners to stow their pet when out at work. Big enough for an Alsatian and then some. The light from the portable lamp threw elongated, grid-shaped shadows across the walls on either side. Multiple lines of crosses.

I moved closer, using the Maglite to pick out details.

There were lengths of steely cable tangled in the framework of the cage. More of it coiled on the floor in and around, like ripped-out angel hair.

I went down on my haunches to get a better look.

There were dark, misshapen stains on the cement floor. It looked like somebody had spilled red paint, multiple times, and hadn't cleaned it up. Pools of dried blood, still tacky where they touched the bottom edges of the cage. Fluff and clothing fibers caught in the red glue.

And something else. Something hiding within the discarded wires.

I unhooked the sunglasses from the neck of my shirt and reached inside the cage. Used one of the spindly arms to separate the object from the wiry nest.

I heard Stone say: "What've you got there, Quinn?"

I held the find up to the Maglite and turned it over. Thin metal wires glinted.

It looked like a blue metal spider with a clear plastic carapace.

"I think it's Zachary's retainer."

55

She hadn't seen her abductor's face, but she knew who he was. She knew all about him and the evil he perpetrated. Intimately. She knew that he had abducted innocent people before. Some of them children. She knew that in every case bar one they had all died from hypovolemia. The police had found their starved and dehydrated bodies, bound with piano wires, days and weeks after they'd gone missing. She knew the victims had been drained of blood, and that the police had never caught him – that he'd gone to ground after the brutal slaying of Gabriel Quinn's wife. All these things she knew. Intimately. What she didn't know was how long she could hold out before she became another one of the monster's sad statistics.

56

That was it: Stone was convinced we had our man.

But I still wasn't.

Something was bugging me.

Despite the mounting evidence against him, I couldn't begin to believe that Connolly was *The Maestro*. Even sober, Connolly was a coward. The only thing the booze had hardened was his liver. Could he have strung together a complex series of abductions and homicides? I doubt it. Connolly could hardly string a coherent sentence together. Even sober, Connolly was no mastermind.

We left the Evidence Response Team to continue scouring the old plating factory with a fine-toothed comb, and headed out.

The results of DNA swabs, as well as hair and skin sample analysis, would get back to us in their own time. I didn't need a lab on the other side of the country to confirm what I knew: *The Maestro* had kept Zachary Innes in the basement room beneath the abandoned factory in El Monte. Imprisoned in a cage like a rabid animal. Wired, until a combination of blood-loss and organ failure had taken their toll. I had no doubt that the boy had exsanguinated right there, in that underground chamber, probably in the dark, sobbing, alone, too weak to break free, while Connolly drank himself into oblivion upstairs.

Connolly wasn't the man who had killed my Hope.

Try telling Stone that.

We were on our way back to the hospital when a call came through on Stone's phone. It was from Agent Seeger. She'd volunteered to guard Connolly. Something had happened. Something bad. Connolly was in a coma.

"He attempted to take his own life," Connolly's attending physician told us as we arrived back at the ICU after a lightning dash.

"How?"

"By slicing through his jugular."

Stone looked pissed. He had every right to. "How on earth did he manage to slice through his own jugular? He was handcuffed to the bloody bed."

"Only with one hand. Somebody left a soda bottle within reach of his other. He smashed it against the bed frame and used it to rip open his neck."

My stomach twisted into a pretzel.

I glanced through the glass partition at the man lying in the hospital bed.

Connolly was flat on his back, hooked up to bleeping machines. The neck brace was gone. In its place was a block of thick wadding taped to his neck. I could see a red dot in the center of the white cotton. A tube ran from his mouth to a medical ventilator. A black gasket enclosed in a plastic cylinder, concertinaing as it pushed air in and out of his lungs. Digital monitors displaying sorrowful statistics.

When I turned back to Stone, I found him examining me with his meditative gaze. I knew what he was thinking; I was thinking the same thing.

"He lost a lot of blood," the physician added. "His brain was starved of oxygen. Even if he comes through the coma, there's a strong likelihood of cerebral damage. We need to notify his next of kin."

Stone blew out an expletive and slammed a big hand against the wall.

Our prime suspect had just become unreachable. If Connolly had known Sheryl's whereabouts, we'd probably never find out.

"There's something else. He left a suicide note."

We followed the physician into Connolly's room. It smelled of antiseptics and rubber. The sound of the artificial breathing apparatus was unnervingly loud. We followed him to a trolley table, pushed into the corner, out of the way.

"We brought it up here when we moved the patient. We left it exactly as we found it."

There were words scrawled on the melamine tabletop. Red whorls forming letters and shapes. Connolly had used a finger to carve a sentence out of his own blood:

He knows where your children are.

My stomach knotted.

I'd heard a similar statement back in Nevada, on a freezing January night, as *The Maestro* had beaten me to a pulp in Rochelle's gravelly backyard:

"I know where your children live."

This wasn't a suicide message, it was a warning. A threat to back off or risk endangering my own flesh and blood.

As if I could.

Connolly knew who *The Maestro* was.

I should have felt angry, enraged. I didn't. If anything, I was deflated.

Any hope I'd had about Connolly revealing the killer's true identity was suddenly extinguished like Snakeskin's bomb in Jack's freezer.

57

News of the discovery in the underground room had found its way back to the field office ahead of us. We arrived at the federal building to a round of applause from our task force and even one or two cheers. Stone lapped it up. I didn't.

Connolly wasn't our man.

But the general consensus agreed that he was. Irrefutable evidence linked him to both the old and the new homicides. The team was buoyed by the capture. Previously tense faces had relaxed into congratulatory smiles. Pats on backs and *'good job'* compliments. I tried arguing my point, but no one was interested. I was the new kid in town and I was being a killjoy. Sometimes belief overrides reality. Stone told the team that we should now focus purely on finding Sheryl Klaussner before it was too late to save her.

Only half of me agreed.

"Right, people, we go back over everything we know about The Maestro," he said. "Re-interview all of Connolly's old faculty, his friends, his neighbors, his family. Someone knows something. There's a decent chance Sheryl is still alive. She survived once, she can do it again. Let's make this a double victory."

The team dispersed, with a new sense of urgency. There were old witnesses to find and speak to. Old evidence to review. Old crime scenes to revisit and plenty more abandoned buildings to search. It would take time. Maybe even days. Something Sheryl Klaussner didn't have in large amounts.

I could tell Stone was pissed with me for effectively muting our prime suspect. But I didn't care what Stone thought. As far as the Feds were concerned, they had their man. It was like the Harland Candlewood fiasco all over again.

I left them to it.

I was focused on finding the real killer.

58

Backtrack. Go over what you know. Look for inconsistencies, links, patterns, things you may have overlooked the first, the second and even the third time around. Time alters perspectives. Try to view the facts from a different angle. Re-interview witnesses, jog memories, and re-investigate leads. These are what an investigator does when presented with a dead end.

In this case, Connolly's coma was as good as a brick wall. From head to toe: six foot thick. Our investigation had crashed straight into it, headlong, absorbing our momentum. Any hopes I'd had of tracing the killer through Connolly were obliterated in the crash. There was no going through that barrier. If clues to the killer's whereabouts or even his identity were to be found beyond the dead end, then I had to find a way to get around it.

Scaling new heights was one option. Digging was another.

I called at a coffee shop on the intersection of Wilshire and Santa Monica to sate my grumbling belly, and to think. I was being good: a ham and Swiss cheese Panini with an icy Frappuccino to flush it down. A seat by the window with a prime view of the busy crossroads. People-and-traffic-watching – while my subconscious sifted through the information inundation.

See: my mind *was* in a daze.

I slurped ice-cold coffee and forced achy shoulders to relax. I needed to recharge. Rethink. Spend a few minutes breathing and relaxing; two things I hadn't done a whole lot of since coming to LA. Physically, I was fitter than I had been when last I'd walked these streets.

Psychologically, I was still finding my feet. The pace of life was much faster here. My brain had gone soft, trundling along in second gear. Now it was being forced down the fast lane in fifth.

I had to pace myself.

I wondered how Sheriff Torres was doing finding her island murderer. With no ID and no motive to go on, her detectives would be pulling out more hair than extra shifts. I wondered if she'd had any feedback from the APB on Snakeskin, and how things were developing there. Torres was a good cop. I sensed she was also a good person, outside of the job. I didn't know much about her home life, or if she had one. The lack of a wedding band didn't necessarily indicate lack of a relationship. Why was I even wondering?

I wondered if Chief Cooper had discovered my departure yet and, if so, how many heads he'd bitten off. Cooper was a Bullmastiff. Once his jaws were locked onto something, it was game over for that particular something. Right at this moment, that something was me. He wouldn't have taken the news of my leaving very well. I was surprised he hadn't been on the phone or even on the next plane out.

I wondered how Jack was coping with an empty house again. I knew what that was like. Loneliness is a killer. I'd rattled around my own home in Alhambra like a pea in a drum for months following Hope's death. Not good. Jack was used to my company. Then, again, I was used to his. Funny how easily we adapt and grow comfortable. If I knew Jack, he'd be whiling away his time either fishing or getting drunk, maybe both at the same time.

It was hard to believe that a day or so ago I'd been on the other side of the country, facing a whole set of different pressures. In the meantime, the investigation into The Piano Wire Murders had resumed in full flow, taking up the eighteen-month slack in the wake of the Griffith Park homicide.

And I'd been caught up in its slipstream.

Adapt or die.

Truth was, I didn't have time to think about stalker-bombers or even dead bodies washed up on picturesque beaches. Both could wait. I had bigger fish to fry. I had to prioritize, concentrate on my reasons for being here: to find Sheryl Klaussner and to avenge Hope's murder. I knew Torres well enough to know that the moment she found something new she'd be on the phone declaring it. I just had to hope that she wouldn't be too put out when she discovered I'd skipped town.

Inevitably, my thoughts returned to the present. I finished up my pit stop, and then drove southeast to Culver City, windows down, letting the summer air blast at my face. The afternoon was hot and bright. The air conditioning had never worked particularly well in my old jalopy. I'd always meant to get it fixed – along with the million other things in my life. The road to Hell and all that. I had sunglasses on and damp patches under arms.

I ran through the events of the last twenty-four hours.

The Maestro.

My one-track mind needed to stay on the right track. Focus entirely on pursuing the monster responsible for ripping out my heart and trampling it into the ground.

I didn't buy the *Connolly is a killer* crap.

But I did believe Connolly knew the killer.

What did I know that the FBI didn't?

From what I'd seen so far, the Feds were organized. Tight. They had all of our old LAPD case notes, plus those newly created following Sheryl's abduction and Zachary's murder, now supplemented with Stevie Hendricks' killing. Stone's gang seemed efficient. Seemed like they knew what they were doing. Could probably run rings around me in the dark. I wondered exactly why the top brass had insisted on bringing me onboard. I knew my old friend Bill Teague held some sway, but even so, it was stretching credibility. Director Fuller didn't need me to hold anyone's hand, especially Mason Stone's. The guy oozed confidence.

So what did I know that the FBI didn't?

I left the Nathan Shapell Memorial Highway at the Culver Boulevard exit and made a left under the overpass, straight into road maintenance works. I remained in stop-start traffic for twenty minutes, stewing things over. I wanted to know if Connolly had known the killer before Connolly had had his breakdown. Not just from a chance meeting in El Monte. I couldn't ask Connolly himself. But I could ask the next best source. Someone who knew Connolly probably better than he did himself. Someone who needed to know he was in a coma, even if they thought they didn't need to.

The temporary traffic lights changed to green and I made the next right. I parked on the roadside opposite a well-tended park crossed with lines of perfectly-straight pathways. It was a nice neighborhood. Quiet. The house I was outside of looked much as I remembered it: a single-floored, cream-colored affair, with stone cladding around the windows and the doors. A well-maintained lawn out front, with a planted rockery in one corner. I walked up the tiled driveway, feeling edgy.

I'd been here previously: the year before last. Then, I'd brought good news. Now, I was the prophet of doom.

Part of me didn't want to be here. But only part.

I looked around the pleasant street before announcing my arrival.

There was a blonde woman jogging with her terrier through the park across the street. A neighbor hosing down his car and another a few doors down: a thickset youth in a Megadeth tee. He had long dark hair and a goatee, meaty hands buried in the pockets of his loose jeans. He was watching me.

I drew a deep breath and rang the doorbell. Waited. I knew the woman I'd come to see was home; I'd called ahead.

Eventually, the door opened a smidgeon, revealing a slice of pale face through the crack. A long, pearlescent silk robe. A whiff of menthol. When she saw it was me, she pulled the door fully open.

"Hello, Celeste."

There was a long cigarette in her hand, poised near her chin – more accessory than necessity. A pointy elbow resting on the other arm, which was wrapped around her slim waist, holding the silken robe together like drapes across frosted glass. She pressed the cigarette against her lips as I looked on, inhaled, and then blew curling smoke out of the corner of her mouth.

"Hello, Gabriel. It's been a long time. I was beginning to think you were avoiding me. Won't you come in off the street? This heat is unbearable."

When I'd last seen Celeste she'd been a striking woman. Long, wavy blonde hair pooling on slender shoulders. Inquisitive blue eyes and a genuine smile. A naturally good figure most middle-aged women would go under the knife to achieve. But the intervening eighteen months had taken their toll on Celeste. Aged her by a decade. Now I could detect distinct lines around her eyes – eyes that seemed to have lost much of their luster. Golden locks hacked to within an inch of her scalp and combed back. Even her flawless skin had lost most of its sheen.

She looked like Grace Kelly in *Dial M for Murder*.

I caught a stronger scent of menthol as I passed her by. Unlike Celeste, the house hadn't changed much: still cozy, still warm, still inviting. Lemon-painted walls and mahogany furniture. The old upright piano still leaned drunkenly against a wall, its lid closed over yellowing keys. I heard her close the door softly behind me.

She flapped a hand at a comfy chair. I fell into it, sinking into deep foam.

"Can I get you a drink? Something to quench your thirst?"

"I'm good, Celeste, thanks."

"Heat kills, you know?" Her voice was flat, almost emotionless.

She perched herself on the edge of the facing sofa and leaned slightly forward, legs together, elbows on knees, cigarette never moving more than a few inches from her lips. She studied me through cold eyes hardened by pain.

"Is he dead?"

"No."

"More's the pity."

"He's in the hospital, Celeste. The Good Samaritan. There was a fall, through a factory roof."

"Drunken bastard. What did he do this time, trip up over his own tongue?"

So much hurt – enough to bury her feelings under a ton of dirt.

"Celeste, it's bad news. He's in a coma."

I thought I glimpsed a glimmer of compassion pass across her narrow face, but wasn't sure. Celeste had stoic to a tee. Never used to be this way. She used to be vibrant, full of smiles and the joys of Spring. Her cheating, conniving, lying, letch of a husband had ruined all that.

I watched her suck smoke, dispassionately, before blowing it out, sideways. I didn't say her husband had tried committing suicide and that I'd been instrumental in it.

"I cut my losses a long time ago." Celeste flashed a crooked smile, still lacking real emotion. "I'm way past caring."

Anyone who didn't know her might have believed that statement. But I didn't. Celeste had hidden her upset well. But it had made her cool and standoffish. She'd grieved for her marriage as though Marv had already died. So much so, that I figured when he actually did, she'd be no different.

Beyond the protective wall she'd built up around herself, I could see she was still hurting, still carried a dying ember for her broken marriage, and some of the blame for it.

"It doesn't look good for Marv."

"Will he die?"

"Possibly. Right now, he's on life support. Like I say, Celeste: it's bad. I'm sorry."

She smirked, briefly, without any emotion. "Don't be, Gabriel. My dearest husband deserves everything he gets. Would you believe my mother warned me about him? Nothing but bad luck, she said. I thought I knew better. We always do, don't we? Always think we know better than our parents. Hindsight is such a bitch." Another long drag. More curling smoke. Then she got to her feet. "Sure I can't fix you a drink? I'm having one."

I hesitated long enough for Celeste to make up my mind for me. She padded across the carpeting to a glass cabinet. I could see soft curves accentuated under the silk robe as she moved. I watched her place a pair of whiskey glasses on a counter and crack open a bottle of bourbon. Hips seesawed as she poured.

Celeste's mother was wrong. Marv Connolly had been a lucky guy. I'd thought so at the time. Celeste had been a good catch. A fellow schoolteacher, with a long fuse and a warm disposition. They'd had a nice home and a nice life. No kids to spice things up, but a full circle of friends and regular Caribbean vacations. Then Connolly had ruined it all. He'd taken his life and his wife for granted and ended up losing everything. Including Celeste.

I watched her as she blew smoke into the air.

Glass chinked against glass.

Her hips were almost hypnotic.

"Ice?"

"No, thanks."

We'd questioned Connolly as part of the investigation into Marta Chavez's murder, tried to see if he fit into the rest of the Piano Wire homicides. His detainment at the Precinct had sparked a flurry of misconduct claims from several high school students, both male and female. Connolly had tutored kids after school, from his own home. This very house. Celeste's home. It hadn't been our job to determine his guilt or prove his innocence regarding the claims of sexual harassment. That had been another department's job. The media had gotten hold of it and the mud had stuck. Connolly – a recovering alcoholic – had chosen escape instead of facing his accusers like a man.

Turned out Connolly and I had something in common.

Celeste came over and handed me a tumbler: whiskey, two fingers, easy.

She perched herself on the rim of the sofa again and sipped at her drink between puffs of smoke.

She looked frail. A wounded bird. Damaged. Maybe irrevocably so.

"How you doing, Celeste? I mean, really doing."

She drew a long unsteady breath and let it out slowly.

"All things being unequal, as well as can be expected, I suppose. Did they tell you I refused counseling? I couldn't handle it. Couldn't face talking about it with strangers. Making judgments. You know what I mean, don't you? We have that in common, you and me. So I locked everything away, up here." She tapped a fingertip against her temple. "Deal with it when I have the energy and the inclination. I'm still waiting. How about you?"

"Pretty much the same, I guess." I smiled uneasily.

"I heard about your wife."

The smile wilted.

"I sent flowers, to the funeral. I hope you don't mind."

"I know, and I didn't."

"I tried calling."

"Look, Celeste –"

"I'm sorry, Gabe. Really I am. It's just –"

I leaned forward, reached out and touched the back of her hand clutched around the whiskey tumbler. "Celeste, it's okay. Honestly. You don't need to say it."

"That bastard wrecked both our lives."

Not Marv this time. *The Maestro*. Blaming a third party for her husband's own indiscretions was still a bitter pill, but an easier one to swallow than accepting she'd married a pedophile.

"It's why I'm here," I said. "The Maestro – he's killing again."

Celeste's milky complexion paled even more. I saw something like fear creep across her ashen eyes. Two diagonal lines of consternation crossed between her eyebrows. "I don't understand. You said Marv wasn't involved. You cleared his name. Are you now saying that he was, is?"

The thought had lifted the sheets off some of her stored memories. Exposed things she'd carefully covered up. Until this moment, Celeste Connolly had remained emotionless. Now there was the making of fear quickening her pulse. I saw her shudder. She had every right to air her disquiet. She'd been through a lot. We both had.

"I still believe your husband wasn't directly or intentionally involved in the original murders."

An obfuscation. Celeste didn't miss it.

"So what exactly are you saying?"

In the first few days after Connolly had been implicated in the Piano Wire Murders, Celeste had stood by her husband. Kept face and a stiff upper lip in public. She'd defended his character to the hilt. Marv was no killer. He was many things, but not that. Then the allegations of sexual misconduct with teenagers had come out into the open and Celeste had caved under the media pressure. Instead of refuting the claims, her husband had escaped on an alcoholic journey to oblivion. Their marriage had crumbled under the stress. Celeste had kicked Marv out of the family home. He'd lost his job and turned to a life on the streets. Celeste had locked herself away and cursed every day that followed.

I'd felt bad for Celeste. In some way, I'd felt obligated. Still did. I'd linked her husband to the Piano Wire Murders. Elevated Marv Connolly into the world of the serial killers. Where the scum of the earth become celebrities overnight. In so doing, I'd opened a can of worms that had eaten through every fiber of their relationship.

And so, maybe through guilt, I'd visited Celeste, here in her home, once or maybe twice. Maybe I'd been thinking too black and white. Not considering consequences and taking into account her vulnerability. Maybe it was something else. Something I couldn't quantify and conveniently label.

But then something had happened.

I'd sensed the kind of comfort Celeste needed wasn't the kind I was willing to give.

Not then.

Not eighteen months ago, while I was still a happily married man.

Nor in the aftermath of my wife's vicious murder, when Celeste's number had appeared on my answering machine, time after time, with no message left.

But the months had rolled into years and we were no longer the same souls confined to the same set of rules as we were back then.

I still wasn't ready. So why was I really here?

I lifted my hand from hers, withdrew. I snatched a gulp of the bourbon and let it burn all the way down.

Celeste was watching me with eyes that could see through skin and bone.

There was something about her. I'd always thought so. Something unspoken. Something that tiptoed into the subconscious and made itself at home. Nothing bad. Nothing to fear. But I wasn't sure it was anything good either.

"Your husband was living in an abandoned factory," I began. "Out in El Monte. The killer used it to detain one of his victims: a teenager we found dead in Griffith Park this week. They were there the same time, your husband and the killer. There's no way their paths wouldn't have crossed. In fact, we have reason to believe Marv knew the killer. Possibly, back during the original investigation, too. He just didn't make the connection at the time."

And neither had we.

"But now he knows?"

"He didn't go into the coma straight away. He told us something first. Something that links him with the killer."

Celeste tapped ash into a silver dish on a side table. "You need to know who Marv's acquaintances are, were."

Some aspects of Celeste were closed off, but not her perceptiveness. Women are like that. While men bury themselves in their own crap, women see right through it.

I brought out a folded sheet of paper from my pocket, and spread it out flat.

"This is an artist's impression of The Maestro. It's from an unreliable witness, but it's all we have."

Celeste's gaze sank to the hand-drawn image on the paper. She studied it like somebody perusing the Sunday supplements without much interest. The crossing lines on her brow came and went a few times, but the hurt remained.

My cell rang.

I glanced at the number without answering: *Tim Roxbury.*

He must have put it in my phone when I'd crashed at his place, I realized, when he'd rescued me from Stevie's spiked drink back in January. I hadn't noticed.

I looked back to Celeste. Beautiful, but wounded Celeste.

"Does it remind you of anyone Marv may have known? Anyone at all? Please, Celeste, think; this is important. Not just work colleagues, but past acquaintances, people he knew before you and he got together?"

She thought about it as she sipped her whiskey. But she didn't look back at the sketch. Not once. Instead, she kept her gaze on mine.

"No one springs to mind," she said at last. "But, then, clearly I didn't know everything there was to know about Marv. One thing I do know is he had lots of drinking buddies. Most of whom I never had the displeasure of being introduced to. Thank God."

Connolly had had a whole side of his life kept separate from Celeste.

I'd seen it before: with killers.

What did that make me?

"There is one thing," she began as she rubbed the cigarette into the ashtray. "Marv kept appointment books. They go back years, even before we met."

"The extracurricular tuition."

"Yes, and also his private sessions." She saw my raised eyebrow and explained: "Marv tutored adults, too. Even before he started with the kids. This house has seen its fair share of strangers, coming and going over the years. Hard to keep track."

"Can I see them, these appointment books?"

"Better than that – you can have them." Celeste drained the remains of her whiskey and got to her feet. "They're in the closet, his books. In the bedroom. On the top shelf. Would you like to come and take them down for me?"

I watched her walk away. Watched her hips seesaw through the pearlescent silk robe as she floated across the carpet.

I folded up the sketch of *The Maestro* and slipped it back in my pocket. Then I emptied my glass, got to my feet, and followed the scent of menthol to the back of the house.

59

Her mother was visiting her, again, for the third time that she knew of. As with the previous visits, her mother was standing over her. Maybe even floating. Hands clasped in a knitted ball of woolly fingers against her throat. Bright blue eyes glimmering like lake water in summer. A mist of silvery hair floating around a porcelain face. She looked young, vibrant. Illuminated from within like a Chinese lantern.

Her mother's presence was calming, uplifting. Always had been.

Her mother was speaking. Not vocally, but mentally. Her voice as soothing as a mountain stream, bubbling under the skin. Words reassuring her that pain and discomfort were ephemeral. That her suffering was a means to an end. Comparing her life to the journey of a solitary raindrop falling toward a greater body of water. That the briefest moment of impact was the here and the now.

But she wasn't fully listening to her mother; all she wanted to do was reach out and hug her. Smother herself in her mother's glorious maternal warmth.

She hadn't hugged her mother in a long, long time.

Not since the open casket on that bleak winter's day when steel sleet had guillotined from the sky.

60

Ten minutes later, I was stuck in the road repairs on Culver when my cell phone told me I had an incoming call. The screen read: *Tim Roxbury*.

"Somebody's impatient."

"Insistent," Tim corrected. "Gabe, we need to talk. Soon as. I need to speak with you about the case. The Piano Wire Murders. You free to meet for a coffee?"

I watched workmen throw slabs of broken asphalt into the back of a truck.

"Not right now, Tim. I'm busy."

Tim made a disgruntled sound. "How's your new partner shaping up – Special Agent Stone of the FBI? He's British, isn't he? Does he carry a truncheon?"

"Tim, have you been snooping?"

"Absolutely. I've also uncovered new evidence in the Piano Wire Murders. It's what we need to discuss, and as a matter of urgency. I mean it. We need a meet."

A road worker started up a pneumatic drill. I closed the windows.

"No, Tim. If it's so urgent you can tell me over the phone, right now. You have thirty seconds. And that's it. And I mean it."

"Jeez Louise. Your generosity is overwhelming."

"Twenty-seven seconds, Tim."

"Okay. All right. But, listen; this is something I can't tell you over the phone. You need to see it with your own eyes, which means we need to meet. You and me. Face to face. Later. I'll call you back when I've made the necessary arrangements. I expect it'll be in the early hours of the morning."

"Why?"

"Simple. Because if I tell you now you won't come."

"I mean why in the early hours of the morning?"

"Gabe, trust me, you'll just have to wait and see."

I let Tim hear my impatience. "Quit with the cloak and daggers, Tim. What makes you so sure I'll come anyway?"

"Your history and your OCD."

I sighed and made sure he heard it. I didn't like the sound of Tim's plotting and scheming. All the same, I was intrigued. "You mentioned fresh evidence?"

"I did. When I heard The Maestro was back in town, I did some digging. I checked into unsolved abductions in the weeks leading up to the first murder."

"Why?"

"Looking for a pattern. That's what serial killers have, don't they?"

"No, Tim, I mean why did you even think of checking?"

"Because I want to help."

"Even though this isn't your case?"

"Because it's yours, Gabe. And buddies help buddies, right? I have your back. It's the way it is. We make a foreboding team."

"Formidable."

"That's what I said."

I sighed again. I crept the car forward a few feet and pressed the brake. "Tim, we checked all unsolved homicides involving piano wires, or any kind of wire for that matter. We went back twelve months, with no luck."

"I know; I've read the reports. You were thorough. But the original investigation didn't check *abductions* involving wires, where the victim survived. Or did I miss something?"

Our team had never had any cause to think that anyone other than Sheryl Klaussner had lived to sing *The*

Maestro's song. Certainly, no one had stepped out of the wings.

"And so I found a police report," Tim continued. "It was buried deep. Dated a few weeks before the first killing. A teenage boy was abducted, restrained with wires and then raped before being released."

I made a dismissive grunt. "Doesn't sound like The Maestro. Rape isn't part of his MO."

We hadn't found evidence of forced sex on any of his victims, either male or female, and certainly none had been sodomized.

I heard Tim say: "Bear with me." I could hear excitement stirring in his tone. "Do you remember what Sheryl Klaussner said in her statement about background noise during her captivity?"

I did. She'd recalled hearing classical music playing the whole time.

"Well, this boy made the same statement. They match."

A hard-hatted laborer holding a Stop-Go sign started waving our line of traffic through the disruption. I eased off the brake.

"Tim, it's a pretty tenuous link."

"Not when you add into the mix that this kid, the one in question, the one who was raped but survived, was a student at the same high school as Marta Chavez."

Suddenly my interest perked up and took notice. I touched the gas and passed the guy with the sign. "You sure about that?"

"Positive. I double-checked. But wait – it gets even better. Here's the clincher: this boy, the one who was abducted, wait for it . . . he's the grandson of Senator Stone."

Brake lights shone. I pressed the pedal a fraction late, almost ran smack-bang into the car in front.

"As in Mason Stone's uncle?"

"One and the same. Again, I double-checked. I'm thorough, too. So, how's that for a coincidence? Oh, that's right: you don't believe in them. The fact remains – your boss' first cousin once removed is a possible victim in the very case he's overseeing. What are the chances of that?"

I didn't know. Maybe astronomical. It made no sense: Stone's first cousin once removed potentially being a victim in the same case he was now investigating. Professionally, it was questionable. Morally, it was debatable. Failing to mention it at all made it unforgivable.

The car ahead began to pull away.

"Gabe, out of interest, just how well do you know this Stone character?"

I thought about it as I drove back to the field office.

Truth was, I didn't know Stone at all. I knew the basics: he was a Brit with joint nationality. Best of both worlds. I knew he'd been given carte blanche status as a troubleshooter after the Bureau had poached him from a top job at Scotland Yard. I knew he wasn't the kind of investigator who would miss something so crucial. When it came to his personal life, I realized I knew absolutely zero.

"Where's SAC Stone?" I asked the duty coordinator as I came out of the elevator into the busy FBI suite.

"He's out in the field," she answered. "Would you like me to page him?"

"No, thanks."

I made a beeline for my office. Shut myself inside. I stacked Connolly's dog-eared appointment books on my desk and chewed some cud. I didn't know what to make of Tim's discovery – except that Stone hadn't been exactly forthcoming with the information. I could appreciate him keeping private the abduction and rape of his first cousin once removed. Who wouldn't? It was no one else's business. In any other situation I would have agreed. The fact it possibly linked his family directly to our investigation – an investigation he was leading – made it a conflict of interest. And I knew how Stone felt about those.

Why the cover-up?

I logged onto the FBI terminal and checked Tim's story. It took a few minutes to find the LAPD police report in question. It was dated approximately two weeks prior to the first abduction/homicide – just as Tim had said it was. Someone had buried it without doing an exceptionally good job. I put on my readers and looked it over.

Christian Stone – a sixteen-year-old student at the same high school where Connolly had taught music – had been abducted on his way home from a date with friends. His unidentified abductor had kept Christian locked in a darkened room – probably a basement – overnight, before releasing him at a remote location the following day. In the interim, Christian had been restrained with wires – suffering lacerations in the process – blindfolded and raped. Christian hadn't been able to describe his attacker or the location, but he had remembered hearing classical music being played throughout the assault. Interestingly, a rape kit had found no semen or spermicidal fluid, but the medical attendant had noted cuts and bruising indicative of forced penetration. The boy had been referred for counseling and the report had been filed with no action taken. No suspects. No arrests. No mention of it from Stone.

I leaned back in the chair and chewed the arm of my readers.

This was the grandchild of Stone's senator uncle.

Stone's first cousin once removed.

Family.

No way he hadn't known about it.

No way he hadn't seen the connection the moment he was assigned to the Piano Wire Murders.

Why had he kept it out of the case?

270

Out of curiosity, I brought up Stone's personnel file. His brooding eyes stared at me from the screen. I scanned a list of assignments, duties, commendations, citations and career highlights – covering a handful of years since joining the Bureau. Trophies for sharpshooting. Commonwealth Games triathlon medals. An honorary fellowship in music from Cambridge University for his piano recitals. It read like the jacket of a highly-decorated military officer. When it came to case breaking, Stone's delivery record rivaled DHL's. Right now he was the Bureau's golden boy. Success followed him around like a celebratory entourage. He could do no wrong.

But he was wrong about Connolly.

It went against everything I was reading in his file.

Stone rarely made mistakes.

But he'd made one with Connolly.

I wanted to know why.

Keeping an eye on the door, I scanned through his dossier, looking at his prior assignments before coming to California.

61

The devil is always in the details.

I'd made some headway into the second of Connolly's riveting volumes when the office door almost flew off its hinges with a bang. I looked up to see a Norse goddess from Wagner's opera *Die Walküre* storming toward me across the blue carpet tiles.

"Precisely when were you going to tell me you were back in town?" she demanded as she loomed over me like an eagle about to strike its prey.

I closed the appointment book with a snap and pushed back in the chair, out from under her icy stare. "Eleanor . . ."

"Don't!" she cut me off. "Don't you dare. I had to read about it in a memo! How could you, Gabe? Am I that detestable, that forgettable?"

I made a pained face.

My therapist friend, Eleanor Zimmerman, was wearing a gray business suit over a silver satin shirt. A pearl choker. Matching studs. Short, silvery hair styled into a box cut. Pink lips pursed with anger. Cheeks florid. Glacial eyes expecting answers, not excuses. Unquestionably, she was the white Grace Jones. And she was pissed.

"Trust me, Eleanor, you are anything but forgettable."

"Just detestable. Is that it?"

I sighed, "No. Never. That's your word, not mine."

I got up and went over to the door, closed it. One or two Feds were gawking through the glass partitions. They'd heard Eleanor's raised voice, and ears had started tuning in. Systematically, I tilted the blinds at each window to stop prying eyes.

"Eleanor, I was going to tell you. I meant to. It was all last minute. Then one thing after another got in the way, and before I knew it . . ."

My words trailed away as I saw Eleanor's offensive stance slump into emotional defeat. Then a quiver ran through her. I moved toward her, slowly.

Eleanor Zimmerman worked for the LAPD's Internal Affairs Division. For a long time, she had been a close friend and a confidant. A good friend of the family, too. Hope's friend. Not just mine. Then, following Hope's murder, she'd become my designated shrink. I'd gone to hell and back to avoid attending her counseling sessions – even when my evasion had threatened my position with the LAPD. Wrongly, shamefully, I'd treated her with contempt, when all she'd ever done was try and help. While I'd gone off track, Eleanor had stayed the course. Even helped me escape wrongful house arrest in Vegas shortly before coming face to face with *The Undertaker* back in January. There was a long history between Eleanor and me. And it wasn't all rosy.

I reached out, "Eleanor –"

Before I could utter another word, she threw her arms around my neck and hugged me tight. In all the years we'd known each other, we'd never come this close. I felt my own arms slide around her. Pull her body against mine, in that intimate way that buddies never hug. I felt her tremble like a tuning fork in my hands. Her mouth was near my ear, breath tremulous. She was warm, with an aura of expensive perfume.

A warm whisper against my neck: "Gabe, I missed you. Every damn day you were gone, I called but you never answered. Not once. Damn you, Gabe. Damn you."

I felt another quiver run through her body as she hugged me even harder.

"I'm sorry," I breathed.

It sounded weak, pathetic. But I was. Truly.

I felt another tremor course through her.

I should have pushed away. Done the honorable thing. I didn't. We were deep inside one another's personal space. In that no-man's land between attraction and connection where lines get crossed.

"I missed you," she repeated, reinforcing the words with a gentle hand that cupped the back of my head and drew me close.

I was out of practice. I didn't know what length of time a friendly hug was deemed acceptable before it became more than just a friendly hug – or that anything other than a friendly hug was even acceptable. I should have cut it off. I didn't. For long moments I was happy to let Eleanor cling.

Impossibly, it felt good.

We hugged like long lost lovers. We could have been anywhere. It didn't matter. The rest of the world was shuttered out and inconsequential.

Eleanor tilted her head back a little. Brought her face in front of mine. Her arctic-blue eyes were magnified with tears. I had a feeling mine were the same. Until this moment I'd never realized just how beautiful she was, or maybe I had and had denied it along with the rest of everything else I'd disowned.

There was an inch between our lips, if that.

We gazed into each other's eyes, as if seeing each other for the first time. Still locked in our quaking embrace.

No awkwardness.

No expectations.

No way out.

I could feel her heart pounding, then realized it was mine.

All at once, there was nothing left to say that hadn't already been said, or that wouldn't be endlessly analyzed in the cold light of day after this moment, pulled apart and made excuses for.

For once, for the first time in too long, I was happy to drop my defenses, to go wherever this impossible moment led.

Then, just when I thought it wouldn't, the irrepressible magnetism of shared emotion brought our lips together for the first time.

62

Someone was calling my name. Way off in the distance, at first. Then growing louder and clearer, until it boomed around my head like traffic crossing the 7th Street Bridge.

I cracked open a sticky eye, followed by the other, and realized I was slumped over my office desk, face-down on the pile of appointment books – that my romantic encounter with Eleanor had been nothing more than a dream.

"Feeling all right, Quinn? I was about to call an ambulance."

I blinked at the big guy leaning over me. It took a moment to recognize his face. It was Mason Stone, and one of his big hands was hooked over my shoulder.

He released his grip and gave me his trademark frown. "Bloody hell. Have you been drinking?"

Celeste's whiskey was still on my breath. I straightened myself out and wiped away drool.

"Look, seriously, if this is all too much for you –"

"No," I insisted. I checked my watch: almost six in the evening.

Stone was nodding, "One too many Florida siestas, is that it?"

"Something like that."

His look of hesitant suspicion stayed put. "Listen, I thought you should know. Everyone's clearing out for the day. A few of us are going for a pint."

"On a week night?"

"Quinn, it's Saturday."

So it was. Only a three-hour difference between the East and West Coasts; I couldn't chalk it up to jetlag. The trouble with retirement is all the days tend to blend into one.

"You're welcome to join us, if you like."

"What about Sheryl?"

I saw him draw a big breath.

"Half the LAPD are out canvassing everyone and anyone associated with Connolly. We have agents working double shifts through the weekend. Back to back. Knocking on doors and checking into every abandoned building in the city. We can't do any more than we're already doing. Some of us have been working flat out for days. We need a break. We're not all superhuman like you, Quinn; some of us need to recharge our batteries once in a while."

I glanced at the appointment books mounded on the desk. I'd barely scanned through two of the volumes before being pulled into involuntary slumber – before dreaming of Eleanor. So far, all I'd seen were page after page of dates, names, numbers and times. Nothing out of the ordinary. No golden nugget. About as exciting as reading the phone book. It was my thinking that if the killer had met Connolly through his coaching, then there was a chance his name was in one of these volumes. As yet I hadn't come across anything that leapt up off the page. No Travis Kimball aka *The Maestro*. No Woody. No shooter on the grassy knoll. But I had a few more volumes to go.

"Maybe some other time?"

Stone didn't hide his disappointment. Since leaving Florida, he'd made an effort to bridge the gap between me and the rest of the world. With my unbroken record of dead partners, the distance was there to protect us both – even more so, now that doubts had been raised into his integrity.

"There's one thing you need to remember, Quinn: we caught him. We caught The Maestro." His words were measured, each one streamlined for impact before it left his lips. "Actually, you caught him. So take the night off and come with us. Celebrate. Let your bloody hair down once in a while. This job is shitty enough. Moments like this don't come along very often. You should make the most of them."

I didn't have the energy to argue my *Connolly is innocent* plea. Nor did I want to broach the subject of Stone's first cousin once removed, even though I was sorely tempted. Not yet. Not until I knew more, including Stone's motive for keeping it hush-hush in the first place.

Stone saw my darkling look and started backpedaling toward the door. He was smart enough to know which battles he could win. "All right. Have it your way. But don't say I didn't offer. If you change your mind, we're over the road at Westwood Village. The bar on Glendon. The drinks are on me. Ring me if you get lost."

I leaned back and watched the workforce drift home for the weekend.

One by one, the lights went out over the workstations scattered across the open-plan office area as federal agents and government employees packed up and bailed out. It didn't take long for the field office to be whittled down to a skeleton crew.

I didn't believe for one second we had *The Maestro*.

I did believe it highly unlikely that the abduction and torture of Stone's first cousin once removed had no bearing on the case. There were just too many similarities to chalk it up to chance.

What I found hardest of all to believe was that he'd failed to even mention it.

I grabbed a snack from the vending machine and ran a strong black coffee, then set about compiling a list of names and numbers from Connolly's appointment books.

Some people swear by lists. They make lists for every occasion. In police work, making lists is part of the process.

The key is being selective.

Connolly had been a busy guy; there was a lot of chaff to strip away. Over the last decade, he'd devoted at least three evenings each week and every Saturday to providing piano lessons to the local community. Poor Celeste. Straight away, I dismissed any sessions that were clearly a parent and child. As far as we knew, *The Maestro* didn't have kids of school age, or if he'd ever fathered any in the first place. I figured it was a safe bet removing the parent and child sessions from the picture.

I'd scribbled down a half dozen parties of interest when my cell rang. I glanced at the little screen: *Jack Heckscher*.

I stripped off my reading glasses and rubbed the bridge of my nose.

"What's this, Jack – your turn to miss me now?"

"Heck, no. I auto-dialed your number by mistake." He sounded tipsy. I could hear overlapping sports commentaries in the background, drowned out every now and then by waves of people chatter. Very likely the bar near Tarpon Bay. "I thought I was calling that cute little redhead from the shell shop."

I smiled. Didn't ask. "Thanks for caring, Jack."

"Hey, don't go getting all mushy on me. Since we're speaking, how are things panning out in California? You caught this pianist dude yet?"

"The Maestro. And, no, I'm working on it."

I told Jack about our joint task force, about Connolly and the escapade at the abandoned factory, about the Bureau's error thinking they had their man, and about Stone's first cousin once removed.

"Sounds like things are getting a tad complicated out there. You think he's hiding something, this English dude?"

"Jack, to tell you the truth, I'm undecided. Until I've dug a little more, I'm trying to keep an open mind. But the more I think about it, the more it looks suspicious."

"Just don't let him pull the wool over your eyes, big guy. Those Feds can be all secrets and lies. I take it you checked into his whereabouts during the original homicides?"

Again, I smiled. Once a cop, always a cop. Jack knew me well. Suspicion was a way of life to men like us. Guilty until proven innocent.

"I checked the dates of his assignments. Stone was posted in San Diego throughout the time of the first killings."

"Within driving distance."

"I guess, at a push. Jack, what are you implying?"

"I think you know. Exactly how well do you know Mason Stone?"

I grunted. "Strange you should say that. You're the second person today who's asked the same question."

"Oh?"

I told him about Tim, about his antics during The Undertaker Case and now more recently about his interest in this case.

I heard Jack snort. "Sounds to me like you need to keep an eye on that one, too. They're all popping out of the woodwork. Listen to the voice of wisdom, big guy. Anyone who pops up twice in two separate investigations needs their motives questioning."

"You don't need to worry about Tim," I countered. "Tim's a good guy. He's just nosy and trying to get a leg up the ladder. Ironically, he's got the kind of pushy attitude that'll make a good detective. What about things there, Jack – no unexploded bombs in need of defusing?"

Snakeskin hadn't shown his disfigured face in my absence. Jack wasn't sure that he would. As far as he was concerned, we'd scared him off.

But there was a development: "The Island's in total shutdown," Jack told me above the background noise. "We're being hit by T-storms left right and center, one after the other. Wham, bam and thank you ma'am. It's why

I'm hanging out with the boys, down here at the bar. We're making the most of it before the hurricane hits."

I perked up, suddenly thinking about Grace's safety. I'd forgotten all about the approaching storm. "Is that what the reports say?"

"Haven't you heard? It's all over the goddamned TV. We're under a full hurricane advisory down here. They think it could be another Charley in the making. Looks like you got out at the right time, big guy."

I let out a nervous whistle. I knew the weather history – having looked into it when Grace had relocated to the Sunshine State several years ago. Category four Hurricane Charley had made landfall just north of Fort Myers, in Punta Gorda, virtually wrecking Sanibel and Captiva in the process. It had run up a repair bill close to fifteen billion dollars and left the islands looking like Hiroshima after the bomb.

And now there was another monster breathing down their necks.

"Everyone's keeping a close eye on it," Jack continued. "If things go from bad to worse they'll evacuate the coast altogether. Move everybody deeper inland. Before you say it, I know you're worried about Grace. Don't be. If push comes to shove and she needs my help, she knows she's got it."

I thanked Jack for his vigilance, but it didn't quell the worry.

63

Mason Stone raised a sloshing beer and saluted my entrance into the popular watering hole in Westwood Village. It was a little after ten on a warm Californian evening. Perspiring weekend celebrators crammed in every crevice. Raucous laughter and happy chatter. In a corner, a local grunge band was lamenting love lost, their guttural guitars vying for audible dominance. I navigated the busy bar, aiming for the small knot of federal agents huddled around two tables pushed together at the back. Pitchers of frothy beers and stacks of emptied glasses.

Stone scraped out a chair and shouted above the music: "You made it. Nice one, Quinn. I'd all but given up hope on you loosening up and showing your face. What's your poison?"

"Whatever's on tap."

Stone filled a Pilsner glass with an oaky brew and thrust it into my hand.

I dropped into the chair. "I'm surprised you're all still here."

"Don't be a wet blanket. It's a hot summer's night. The end of a long week. And the beer's stone cold. Oh, and did I mention we caught a killer?" He chinked his glass against mine. "Cheers, mate."

"Cheers." I tasted the chilled brew. It was strong and woody. It fizzed around my gums. "I thought you Brits liked yours warm."

Stone chuckled; he was tipsy drunk. His tie was pulled loose on an unbuttoned collar. A sheen of sweat on his big brow. Every one of his big muscles relaxed and soaking up the beer. "Another popular misconception, Quinn. Along with bowler hats and afternoon tea at the

Ritz. And none of us know the Queen. Now drink up; you have plenty of catching up to do. We're about to hit the tequila shots."

I spent the next hour bonding with my new FBI buddies as they savored their spoils. It wasn't awkward; they were a likeable bunch. Talkative and in good moods. Seemed like they drank as hard as they worked. Deserved to, I guess. I hung around on the periphery of their social campfire, happy to be warmed by their high spirits and the alcoholic buzz. I wasn't in a celebratory mood, not particularly, but I kept my misgivings about Connolly to myself. Who was I to spoil their fun? To them, they'd caught a killer. To me, we'd just got started.

At one point, Agent Seeger worked her way over, sharing jokes and jibes with her male buddies as she came. Stone made room for her and she seated herself next to me.

"I haven't had a chance to say thanks," she shouted above the soaring guitars. "For saving my life."

I made a tipsy face. Flapped a hand. "Don't mention it."

"No, seriously. You saved my life back there. I could have ended up like Connolly, or worse, if it hadn't been for you."

I wasn't sure what was worse than Connolly hooked up to life support, broken and in a coma, with a high likelihood of a vegetative existence, but I smiled all the same.

"We did good today," she said, striking her glass against mine. "You're my hero, Gabe Quinn." She leaned over and pecked me on the cheek.

We kept the conversation light, in keeping with the party tone. Once or twice I tried scratching the surface of Seeger's history, but she parried my probes with ones of her own, and I dutifully backed off. She was young and living in the moment; the last thing she wanted to talk about with an old grump like me was her life before the Bureau.

Finally, Seeger got sucked into another conversation with those around us, and my thoughts drifted. I thought about Grace and the coming storm. Thought about my stalker-bomber back in Florida and his deadly intentions. Thought about Torres and the washed-up body on Bowman's Beach. I was missing Florida, but not as much as I thought I would.

Eventually, I made an excuse to part ways and walked back to the federal building on Wilshire with a cloudy head and bees in my ears. It was midnight, or thereabouts. On a bone-dry summer night in LA. All at once I was dog-tired. But Connolly's appointment books were calling.

I went straight to the washroom and splashed cold water over my face. Grabbed a cup of hot black and a Hershey bar from the machine as I passed. Not exactly a saintly diet, but then again I wasn't exactly a saint.

The dimly-lit field office was quiet; a few diligent agents with no lives, catching up on paperwork. Glowing computer screens and the occasional gurgle of a telephone.

I padded back to the glass-paneled office and sealed myself inside.

Before sloping off to the bar on Glendon, I'd compiled a list of a dozen names from Connolly's appointment books. Males of varying ages. People we needed to speak with and ascertain alibis – if I could convince Stone that Connolly wasn't a masterful killing machine. I was down to the most recent volume, marked the year before last. The year when *The Maestro* had popped up on our radar and Connolly's life had fallen apart.

I balanced the readers on my crooked nose and opened the remaining book.

It was more of the same. Dull as dishwater. Names, times, numbers. Munching chocolate alleviated the tedium, but only slightly. I turned pages, sipped coffee, looking for something, anything to snag my attention and keep me from succumbing to sleep.

It was beginning to look like a fool's errand.

Nothing for the first quarter of the year. Then, in the middle week of May, a name that plucked at my heartstrings: Leo B.

Leo Benjamin.

Had to be. *The Maestro's* last victim, the first time round. The boy left beneath the 7th Street Bridge as a distraction to me while the killer had attacked my wife in our family home. What was the likelihood of another Leo B. being connected with Connolly?

I thought about Celeste's husband lying in his hospital bed, on life support. Pictured Celeste by his bedside, holding his hand. Then I scrubbed out the image in my head. Celeste wasn't interested in Marv. He'd shamed her publically and brought disgrace on their marriage. Connolly had been as good as dead to her for over a year. I wondered what it would be like if I were to feature more in her life. Holding her hand. Then I scrubbed out that image, too. It was the alcohol talking. Nothing had happened between Celeste and me, but the electricity was there. Undeniable. Fizzing under the surface. Dangerous. Like playing with live wires.

Sooner or later somebody always gets hurt.

I resumed my research.

Nothing in the following months that rang a bell – until the entries for early August, where I came across a name I recognized instantly: Marta Chavez. I knew Connolly had tutored her privately; it had come to light during the original investigation. I'd been expecting it. But the confirmation wasn't any less chilling. I turned the page and saw her name repeated on the same evening of the following week. Same the week after that. But on the last week in August there was another name next to Marta's, a name I'd heard growled from Connolly's own cracked lips:

Woody.

Coffee burned in my belly. Not wholly because of the connection, but because there was a cell number scribbled next to the hand-written word.

Automatically, I picked up the desk phone and dialed. I pressed the receiver tight against my ear to eliminate the patter of my racing heart.

I knew it was late – or early – but I wanted to see if the number still existed, and if it did, who would answer.

The number rang out.

Still active.

I held my breath, willing someone to answer.

It rang, and rang, and then the connection clicked over to an answering service. A pre-recorded male voice came on the line:

"Hey, I'm busy, dickwad. Call me back later, or not. I don't care. I'm outta here!"

The connection clicked off. I hung up and sucked in air.

Woody – if that's who this was – sounded young, hip, and a bit of an idiot. He'd known Marta Chavez, attended piano coaching with her in Connolly's home, so it was safe to assume he was around her age group. Maybe even attended the same high school, which meant he probably knew Zachary Innes and maybe even Christian Stone.

For a moment I wondered if Woody could be *The Maestro*. Then dismissed the idea. I knew the real killer was my age group. Like Connolly. Big and as bad-tempered as a Grizzly; too much like Connolly – yet another reason why the Feds were so hung up on him.

But I couldn't dismiss the fact that three of the killer's victims were students at the same school, a school where Marv Connolly had taught music. Connolly had tutored Woody from his home in Culver City. And Connolly had snitched on Woody for being the artist behind the Beethoven's Fifth painting on the abandoned factory wall.

Seen from any angle, Woody was a major player in the Piano Wire Murders.

Find him and maybe, just maybe, we'd find the real killer.

Feeling adrenalized, I brought the desk terminal out of sleep mode and logged onto the FBI mainframe. I checked the cell number written next to Woody's entry in Connolly's appointment book. I kept my fingers crossed, hoping for a full name and even an address of registration. But it came up as a non-contract allocation, which was as good as to say it belonged to a disposable phone and was therefore untraceable to a specific owner.

I closed the search window and returned to the desktop. I had copies of the case files arranged on the screen: a column of folders for each victim, in date order, with a strip of folders containing coroner reports, police reports and general investigation notes along the bottom. I clicked on one labeled *Persons of Interest* and was presented with a new pop-up window filled with files. I found the document containing the roll of students under Connolly's tutelage and opened it up.

It was a sizeable list. Arranged in first name alphabetical order. I wondered about the allegations of misconduct leveled at Connolly as I scanned through, looking for anyone with the name Woody.

There was a Wendy, a Wesley, a Whitney and two Wilsons.

But no Woody.

I chewed cheek. I contemplated phoning Celeste. Contemplated asking her if she knew this Woody character and, if she did, could she provide a description and any other identifying information. But it was late. And I had manners. I glanced at my own cell. I was expecting a call from Tim. He'd promised to phone in the early hours. Insisted he had something very important to show me, and that he could only do so under the cover of darkness.

I have never been a big fan of murder-mystery weekends.

The office door opened.

I looked over the top of the readers to see Agent Seeger standing in the doorway. She was wearing the same white shirt tucked into a pinstriped brown skirt as she had done in the bar, but somehow she looked less business-like in the subdued office lighting. Her coppery hair was down, cascading over slim shoulders, with a wave to it that I hadn't noticed before.

"I brought refreshment," she said, holding up a pair of tequila bottles. "I don't know about you, but I'm too wired for sleep."

She slipped off her pumps and padded over. Offered me one of the drinks. I shook my head. She put the shoes and the bottles on the desk.

"Gabe, I didn't get the chance to thank you for saving my life."

"Yes, you did. You bought my drinks. Consider the debt paid and in full."

"No, I mean properly."

She leaned across the desk and dowsed the lamp. The office fell into semi-darkness; lit only by the weak glow of city lights coming through the window.

I straightened in the chair, defensively. "Seeger . . ."

She put her hands on the armrests, preventing my escape, and lowered her face toward mine. It was a move I hadn't anticipated. It caught me off guard. I withdrew, automatically, as far as the padded leather would allow. Not through revulsion – Seeger was anything but repulsive – but because her behavior was inappropriate. Not counting the fact she was half my age.

"Seeger, wait. This isn't right. You're drunk."

She was smiling like the cat that got the cream. Had me trapped. Clearly, she had no concern for what was and what wasn't acceptable protocol between two federal agents caught alone in the wee small hours, inebriated or not.

Her smile didn't waver. "You saved my life. I owe you. Let me make it up to you."

"Not like this." I rolled the chair backward. She lost her grip and I got to my feet.

She looked at me with the eyes of a panther about to pounce.

My cell phone rang on the desk.

"I really need to get that," I said.

Seeger pulled back and smoothed down her hair. "Saved by the bell," she lamented.

I reached around her and picked it up. It was Tim, as expected.

"You ready for some action?" he said.

"So long as it doesn't involve bringing any dancing shoes."

64

Despite its cloak of darkness, the discothèque on Santa Monica Boulevard still looked like a bank. A big black cube with a single splash of neon-pink signage above door. There were people milling about on the sidewalk: laughing, chatting, hooking-up. Mostly men. This was a popular area. Sprinkled with lively bars and rowdy nightclubs. Merry partygoers drifting from one gaudy venue to the next. Blasts of dance music and lines of scantily-clad people behind velvet ropes, waiting to make a red carpet entrance.

Even with the shocking news that his ex-girlfriend had been brutally slain, Tyler Cummings, the owner of the club, had still opened up shop. Sometimes it's the routines that keep us going.

It was a little before 2 a.m. – late, but still early for the eclectic LA night scene.

I had the car windows down, letting the warm night breeze flow through. It carried with it the throb of the clubs and the scents of hard liquor and even harder cologne. It also kept my blood alcohol on the back burner.

A slow-moving black-and-white crept up alongside. The beam of a flashlight swept across my face, then back, and stayed. I produced my FBI badge and they moved on to the next curb-crawler.

When I looked back to the nightclub, I could see a tall, well-built guy in a pink short-sleeved shirt, black hot pants and red cowboy boots scanning the street. The shirt looked like it had been sprayed on, it was that tight. Same went for the Lycra shorts. No modesty there. In my opinion, the crimson cowboy boots were just one step too far. He spotted my car nestled against the opposite sidewalk and crossed the street.

"See what we're forced to resort to when you ignore my calls?" he said as he leaned on the rubber windowsill. He smelled like something with a French name. Something unpronounceable. He noticed my passenger in the backseat. "Hello and hi there. Who's this beauty?"

"Agent Melody Seeger meet Detective Tim Roxbury."

Tim's too-close-together eyes assessed the situation in a blink: a young woman with mussed hair and smelling of alcohol in the backseat of my car; two buttons of her shirt undone; and my cheeks glowing like hot coals.

"This isn't how it looks," I said. "Seeger needed a ride home and that's all that's going on here."

"How chivalrous."

"She's on my team, Tim. You know, I shouldn't have to explain."

Tim nodded like he didn't buy my story. "You're FBI?"

I heard Seeger release a lighthearted laugh, "You're a cop?"

"Touché, sister." Tim reached in and shook Seeger's outstretched hand. "Always a pleasure to make a new acquaintance."

"Likewise."

I could see a few passersby glancing in our direction. My car didn't have a flashing neon on the roof, but it might as well have had.

I popped the locks. "Tim, will you just get in here before the cops book me for soliciting."

Tim opened the door and shoehorned himself into the passenger seat. Tight clothes creaked against the leather. "Okay. Let's go."

"Where?"

"Silver Lake."

"What's in Silver Lake?"

"You'll see."

I sighed.

Keith Houghton

"Gabe, trust me. It'll have intimately more impact if you see it for yourself."

"Don't you mean infinitely?" Seeger asked.

"Not always. Okay, folks, so where's the whiskey hiding? I can smell it. Have the both of you been drinking?"

Against my better judgment, I started the transmission and pulled out onto Santa Monica Boulevard. "Silver Lake it is."

65

In retrospect, I should have gone straight home. Hailed Seeger a cab. Said goodnight to Tim and the prospects of a wild goose chase, and buried my head under a pillow. I didn't.

I wish I had.

We headed northeast instead, through deserted streets lined with shuttered stores and darkened businesses. I wasn't exactly pumped with the thought of our final destination; I wasn't convinced Tim had found the Holy Grail. Many crimes have overlapping characteristics. My suspicion was, he'd put two and two together and found Jesus in a slice of toast.

We cut diagonally across the sleeping city, traveling through neighborhoods free from cloying daytime traffic. Tim and Seeger enjoyed a lively discussion about a fly-on-the-wall TV show that was all the rage right now. Getting on like a house on fire. I didn't join in; I was busy thinking, like I do. We crossed quiet intersections and made rights on reds. Drove through West Hollywood, Los Feliz and finally into sleepy Silver Lake.

"Take the next right," Tim told me.

It was a leafy little hillside off Hyperion. A dozing neighborhood of darkened homes hidden behind walls of greenery, tangled trees and painted cement. Not much in the way of street lighting. No sidewalks lining the narrow roadway. Trimmed lawns and Mediterranean-style rock gardens. Neat little picture-book houses clinging to the hillside overlooking the reservoir. We worked our way along curling roads and switchback lanes.

"Here," Tim said, finally. "Right here. This'll do."

I pulled up outside a property with a pair of big leafy trees straddling a short driveway. It was a Spanish-style dwelling with two floors, terracotta tiles and metal verandas. Walls that were salmon-pink in daylight but just another shade of gray at this hour.

Tim opened the glove box and retrieved my flashlight. Then he got out and indicated I should do the same.

I turned to Seeger. "Stay here. I've got a feeling you won't miss anything. We'll be right back."

"And then what?"

"Then you go home and sleep it off, that's what."

I joined Tim on the street and looked around. It was quiet. Some insect sounds, but not many. Homes deep in slumber. One or two lights still on here and there across the hillside, but mainly darkness. There were a few stars to the north and a faint murky glow to the south hanging over downtown LA.

A whispered shout: "Earth to Gabe. This way. Come on."

Tim was waving frantically from a narrow archway at the side of the house.

I went over, feeling like a cat burglar casing a joint.

"It's right through here." His voice was low, an excited whisper.

I wasn't getting my hopes up.

There was a metal gate across the archway. Tim pressed the latch and swung it open. It complained a little at being disturbed from its rest at this hour.

"Tim, I'm not sure this is a good idea. This is a private residence, and we're men of the law, trespassing."

"It's okay," he whispered back. "I know the guy who lives here. We're cool. Trust me."

"So let's come back in the morning. Do this the right way and the legal way."

"No can do. Gus is jumpy paranoid. And I mean, jumpy paranoid. Soon as he sees the Celebrity Cop on his doorstep he'll go siege mentality. Probably blow a fuse and totally trip-out. Trust me, this is the only way you're going to get to see this. Now come on; stop being a wussy."

Normally, whenever somebody says *trust me,* I start worrying. When it comes from the mouth of Tim Roxbury, I know it spells imminent trouble.

Tim slipped through the entranceway and disappeared into deeper shadow.

I snatched a quick look around before following.

We moved silently along the side of the house in the direction of the backyard, dipping past darkened windows. We squeezed around a pair of plastic trash containers. I was acutely aware that a neighbor's dog might sniff out our intrusion at any second and raise the alarm. My pulse was elevated. How would we explain our presence – an FBI agent in faded jeans and sneakers skulking around in the dark with a plain-clothed police detective wearing an eye-watering getup?

This was insane.

We came to another metal gate. This one was taller, with a padlock on the latch. Tim hooked the toe of his boot into the metalwork and hauled himself up.

"Tim, this constitutes breaking and entering," I whispered fiercely.

Tim continued undeterred. He slung both legs over the top and dropped down onto the other side.

"So arrest me," he said. "Besides, Gus told me I was welcome to visit anytime I liked. To me, that's an open invitation. He didn't put any time stipulations on it."

I looked at Tim's shadowy face through the bars of the gate. "Exactly how well do you know this Gus guy?"

"Not biblically, if that's what you're implying. But well enough. He's a regular at the nightclub. We party every once in a while."

"I need my head examining." I pulled myself up the wrought ironwork, dithered for balance at the top, then

295

dropped down next to Tim. "This better be good. I mean it."

There was a smile widening his face. "Trust me."

There it was again: famous last words.

We entered a paved patio area. There was an outdoor table and chairs set. One of those dome-shaped wheeled barbeques in the corner, looking like a deactivated robot drone from a sci-fi movie. A rectangle of dry lawn, with a three-foot-tall statue of a winged cherub sitting in the middle – a bird feeder with a demonic face.

I followed Tim out onto the grass.

We stopped either side of the small statue and turned to face the back of the house.

In the dark, all I could see were picked-bone walls and eye-socket windows. Nothing special. Nothing that leapt out and cuffed me on the chin. Just a regular home in a nice little neighborhood.

Without powering it up, Tim aimed the flashlight at the house. "This is it, Gabe. Ready for the grand unveilment?"

I sighed at the made-up word. "Do you have to be so melodramatic?"

"Gabe, your life would be duller without it. Here goes."

Suddenly, the flashlight beam lanced across the night-darkened yard and threw a large white splash on the back wall of the house.

All at once I could see why Detective Tim Roxbury had brought me here, to this quiet residential street in Silver Lake on a hot summer's night.

I felt my jaw drop, then tighten as I realized exactly what it was I was looking at.

In the gap between two windows, on a section of otherwise bare rendering, the owner had hung a piece of wire wall art about six feet in length and two in width.

It was a silvery flash, comprised of five horizontal lines crossed with musical notes. It was standing proud a few inches away from the wall, so that the flashlight cast a perfect shadow onto the sand-colored cement behind it.

It was an exact execution of *The Maestro's* bloodied signature, in wire.

"I told you it was good," Tim breathed.

My heart was thumping. "Tim, who is this Gus guy?"

"His full name's Gus Reynolds. Like I say, he's a regular at the club on Santa Monica. That's how I know him. He threw a house party a couple of weeks back. That's when I saw this. It wasn't until I started digging into the Piano Wire Murders that I made the connection."

I stared at the silver wirework. It was a perfect copy of the killer's motif, and very likely created by the same hand.

I was still getting to grips with the discovery when the sun came out. But it wasn't the sun. It was a security lamp. We both shied, instinctively, from the blinding light suddenly flooding the backyard.

"Get the hell off my property!" somebody yelled.

I shielded my eyes against the thousand-watt glare as our shadows ran for cover. Through splayed fingers, I could just make out the shape of a man silhouetted in the hard halogen glow. He was standing on the patio with something long and tubular gripped in both hands, pointing our way. It could have been a yard brush. But I knew it wasn't.

I yelled *'Police'* in the same moment Tim yelled *'FBI'*.

We glanced at each other.

Make no bones about this: being woken by a pair of dumbstruck groupies from a Village People convention in your backyard in the dead of night isn't exactly conducive to a friendly chat over a cup of morning coffee.

The rifle pointing at us crackled. The cherub's hollow head exploded into pieces between us. In the same instant, Tim and I dove sideways, in opposite directions. I hit the bristly grass and loosed some air. Rolled awkwardly to my haunches and had my Glock out and aimed before I came to a full stop. I couldn't see the shooter in all the brilliance, but I could calculate where he was. I dropped the safety and squeezed off a round. I wasn't aiming for the shooter. The security light fizzled and died. The backyard was plunged into dense blackness. I blinked at the red-hot cattle brand still burning a bullet hole into my retinas. Heard something clatter against stonework and then heard Tim shouting:

"He's making a bolt for it!"

I almost yelled *'let him!'* but got to my feet, stowed the Glock and gave chase.

Now we all know foot chases can be hazardous even in broad daylight. Under the cover of night, through unfamiliar territory, they can be deadly.

The shooter had dropped the rifle, bounded across the patio and scrambled up and over the wall separating this property from the next. Why he hadn't rushed back inside the house and bolted the deadlock was anyone's guess.

"Cover the front!" I yelped at Tim.

Lights were coming on in bedroom windows. A dog had started barking farther along the street. Gunshots and raised voices have a way of drawing attention, especially in the dead of night.

Half-blinded, I leapt up and over the wall. The shooter was disappearing over another divider on the far side of the property. I ran and cleared the boundary, coming down heavily onto hard concrete. Something twanged in my ankle. I lost my balance and staggered forward. The ground gave way and I plunged into cool water. A swimming pool. It swallowed me up with a jolt. I took water on board, broke the surface and spluttered it out. A lamp came on in a window at the back of the house. It threw an oblong of light across the choppy surface. Someone shouted and banged on the glass. I saw the shooter clambering up a taller wall at the rear of the property. I dragged myself out and sloshed after him. I got there just as he belly-flopped onto the crest. I grabbed at one of his legs. He kicked out. His foot sideswiped my head. No harm done, but it was enough to keep the leg out of my grasp. I tried to grab his foot again, but it pulled away, out of reach.

I heard him crash down the other side and let loose a howl.

I retreated to the edge of the pool, took a run-up and leapt up the wall, rolled over it and landed on a pile of wooden planks, hard.

I was in the backyard of a house directly facing the reservoir. At the top of a series of garden terraces. I could see the silvery lake through a rectangular gap down the side of the building, and the shape of a man running down a long sloping driveway toward the street below.

I continued the chase as bedroom lights blossomed.

The street where Seeger waited in the car was now higher up the hillside, behind me. I had no idea if she'd heard the gunshots or if she'd even seen Tim legging it down the street in his hot pants and cowboy boots. Chances were, I was the only one in hot pursuit.

Conditioned muscles started burning stored energy. I tucked in my elbows and pumped my knees. The shooter was about to make a dash for freedom across the street, heading for the lake. But he was slowing and I was on a roll. Months of morning runs coming to the fore. I reached the sidewalk as the shooter reached the middle of the street.

Then everything happened in slow motion.

I heard the screech of tires, like the wail of a wounded beast, and saw the car in the last second. I dug in my heels, sneakers squelching. The shooter was frozen in the middle of the road. Spellbound by the onrushing vehicle. The car fishtailed, wheels locked, and then it hit him full on. The shooter splashed up the hood, crashed into the windshield and flew up and over. He cartwheeled through the air like a rag doll and came down heavily, headfirst on the roadway. Meanwhile, the car swerved through a hundred-eighty degrees and rocked to a standstill, headlights illuminating the smashed body sprawled in the street.

My heart was in my mouth.

Not wholly because of what I'd just witnessed, but because it was my car and Seeger was driving it.

"I saw him too late," she gasped as she got out. Her complexion was ashen, eyes wide with fright. "I couldn't avoid him. He just didn't move. I'm sorry."

I dropped to my knees, next to the shooter.

He was a mess. Red-black blood everywhere. One of his legs buckled the wrong way, lying across the other at an impossible angle. His chest flopping around, as though a big fish were trying to fight its way out. The impact had crushed his rib cage and the fall had cracked his skull. There was an expanding pool of black liquid on the road surface beneath his head. More dark blood all over his face. One eye shut and already swelling. The other staring up at me from behind a torn eyelid. Blood-thickened saliva bubbling from busted lips like oil from a tar pit.

"Why'd you run?" I breathed. It was a stupid question, but shock makes us say stupid things.

The shooter coughed out blood. He lifted a weak hand to his broken face and gargled a horrified moan. He was dying. Broken. Lungs wheezing like ripped gaskets. Only seconds left, and he knew it. He knew it.

I leaned over, dripping pool water. "Gus, you need to tell me: who made the wall art, on the back of your house?"

An answer gurgled in his throat. Dark blood bubbled out of his shattered mouth.

I leaned closer. "You got to tell me, Gus: who made the wall art?"

I felt a weak hand grab ahold of my shirt and pull me even closer.

My ear was almost touching his busted lips.

He spluttered, struggling against the inevitable drowning. The unblinking eye was racked with fear.

He tried to form a word, but his throat was choked. He tried harder, bubbling out blood. I caught a whispered name in a dying breath.

Then the grip loosened and all at once his struggle was over.

I fell backwards onto my butt as Seeger began to shake like a leaf.

66

There was a ragged hole in the strip of metallic tape stuck across her mouth. She had no idea how it had come to be there or when it had appeared. Tentatively, she moved the tip of her swollen tongue over it, then forced it in as far as it would go, before retracting it, and sucking in air. Throughout her life she'd always been a nasal-breather, and had found mouth breathing awkward. But during the course of her captivity her nostrils had become inflamed and sore, inhibiting the flow of air into and out of her lungs. Mucus membranes like scorched cardboard. The discovery of the thumbnail-sized hole in the duct tape was like finding a lifeline, enabling her to breathe unhindered once again.

The first thing she did was attempt to scream, but the action caused her to croak and cough instead. The abrupt movement forced skin against wire. Paper-tissue collapsing against a scalpel blade. Gooey blood trickling down her face. She held still, trying to swallow down the fluff. Her throat was bone-dry and scratchy. Hardly any saliva to keep it lubricated. Lack of moisture had also formed crusty rings around the rims of her eyes. Grit that couldn't be blinked away. She'd learned to keep them closed. Now they were sealed with wax.

The first stages of mummification – that's how she thought of it.

Her body had become a dried-out husk. Ballooned hands and feet tethered on slack strings to her limbs. Internal organs struggling for equilibrium. Blood pressure all over the place. And her shrinking brain slowly sinking in a sea of nausea.

She'd thrown up once or twice: searing acid that had scalded her larynx and mouth, before gravity and throat muscles had sucked it back down.

And now it tasted like something had died in her mouth. Maybe her.

Maybe she had died long ago and this is what it was like to rot in the grave.

Maybe this was how it would be, for eternity, trapped in a rotting carcass.

She tried to scream again, but was racked by a fit of painful coughing.

Syrupy blood dripped into her mouth through the hole in the tape.

It tasted like rust.

67

Being instrumental in a fatality brings ramifications. Legally, I wasn't worried about the shooter's accidental death; the Bureau had good lawyers. Emotionally, I was paying the price.

Gus Reynolds hadn't deserved to die for his art.

At 9 a.m. on a pleasant Sunday morning, Agent Seeger and I underwent an unpleasant debriefing with the Assistant Director in Charge of the Los Angeles field office. It was a formality. Brutally sterile. A member of the public had died during an FBI investigation and statements had to be taken. Actions accounted for. Questions raised – such as why I'd used my gun against a man sporting a .25 caliber air rifle. There was a member of the legal office present, together with a somber-faced Mason Stone. I explained our reason for trespassing, for giving chase and for ultimately causing a death by misadventure. Our maverick methods were frowned at and a comment was entered into our FBI records. Then I was asked to leave. Seeger was asked to stay.

Stone caught up with me as I marched back toward my office: "Quinn, you should have come to me. I warned you, told you. This isn't how we do things here. We play by the rules. This isn't the bloody Gabriel Quinn Show."

Everyone was looking our way, responding to raised voices.

"What do you want me to say, Stone? I'm sorry for making you look bad. Believe me, it was unintentional. You heard what happened: it was late; I wasn't sure what Tim wanted to show me, possibly nothing. Maybe we all had a little too much to drink and our perspectives were warped. I don't know. Everything went from zero to sixty in three seconds flat. There wasn't any time to okay things first, or even call for back-up."

Sometimes bad things just happen.

Sometimes we cause them.

"Who the hell is this Tim person anyway? I know he's a rookie detective, but what's his interest in this case?"

"He thinks he's helping."

"And that's the kind of help we can do without. Quinn. There's a fine line between helping and hindering. And this Tim character definitely hasn't done you or this investigation any favors. Have you even considered he may have an ulterior motive for poking his nose in? You admitted you hardly know the bloke. God knows what you were thinking."

He caught me by the arm and drew me to a stop.

"Look, from now on, I don't want this Tim person anywhere near this case. The ADIC's given you a second chance and I'm all right with it. I don't want this to come between us. All I'm asking is that you be up front with me."

"I'm still looking for the killer."

Stone let out a frustrated sigh. "Why, when we have our man?"

"Because Connolly's a fall guy. You and I both know Connolly can't even tie his own shoelaces. I'm telling you Stone, Connolly's a scapegoat. You've seen him. He's a washout. The Maestro is a mastermind."

"We need to concentrate our efforts on finding Sheryl."

I went to say something, but Stone cut me off:

"I mean it, Quinn. No more action hero antics. I can do without the headache. We have a missing person to find. Once that's done you're free to do whatever the bloody hell it is you like. Now go and do something constructive."

68

Rebellious ways seldom win friends.

I had no intention of towing the line. Some lines are meant to be crossed. The whole of the task force were focused on the search for Sheryl Klaussner; they didn't need me getting underfoot.

The Maestro was still out there. I was sure of it. I could feel it. I had no idea where to start looking, but I had to start.

I'd entered the empty elevator carriage and pressed for the ground floor when a hand caught the doors before they closed. Agent Seeger slipped inside. She looked shaken, but not as shaken as she had done down by the reservoir.

"I'm out of here," she said as the doors closed. There was a tremor in her voice and tremble in her shoulders.

"They suspended you?"

"Pending an investigation. I've been asked to go home until further notice. Reflect." She hit me with her melting-chocolate eyes. "Gabe, I didn't mean to kill him. Really, I didn't. I responded to the gunshots. I saw Tim running down the street. I guess I figured I could close the loop. But Reynolds just came running out. I didn't expect it. There was nothing I could do. Believe me. I tried to swerve out the way –"

I reached out. I shouldn't have. It was an automatic response. Paternal. She came into me, slid her arms around my neck and nestled her warm face in the curve of my neck. Then she clung to me for comfort while the quakes ran through her body and the floor numbers dropped away.

"It's okay," I said, knowing full well that it wasn't. An innocent man had lost his life and I was the last person who should have been consoling her. Seeger was beating herself up from the inside out. I knew how she felt; I'd visited that painful place more than once. "You don't have to explain."

Seeger tilted her face so that she was looking directly into my eyes. In them, I could see a desperate longing, underpinned with need and fear. Black holes sucking everything in. The most destructive force known to Man.

"Gabe, come home with me," she whispered. "Please. I don't want to be alone right now. I'm scared." She stroked my lips with her fingertips. "Please, Gabe. I'll make it worth your while."

"What is it with you, Seeger?" I forced her to arms' length and let her see the full length of my frown.

"I just want to . . . I don't know . . . you saved my life."

"And you bought me a beer. Now we're even."

Suddenly Seeger stared at me with spiteful eyes. "Screw you," she breathed as the doors hissed open. "Who do you think you are, my damned father?"

I watched, numbly, as Agent Melody Seeger turned on her heels and stormed away.

69

All fired-up and ready to blow – that's how Seeger left me. I was furious with myself for failing to see it coming.

I needed air. Room to breathe and to think, to focus on catching a killer.

I commandeered a Tahoe from the FBI motor pool and drove eastward on Wilshire. Thoughts tangled. *Eye of the Tiger* roaring in my ears from the stereo. I paid no attention to the passing scenery; I was too embroiled in trying to figure things out. I needed to speak with this Woody character, about the murders. I had a strong feeling he was involved. I didn't know why or how, but I knew he was. I kept driving and thinking until I found myself outside the abandoned plating factory in El Monte.

Why had my subconscious brought me here?

I got out and followed my feet to the padlocked gates. *The Maestro* had used this place to cage Zachary Innes underground. He'd let him bleed to death while Connolly had stood lookout upstairs.

I hooked fingers around the aluminum gate and scanned the abandoned buildings.

What did I know?

Both Zachary Innes and Marta Chavez had been students at the same high school. Both Zack and Marta had come into contact with Connolly, their music teacher. On their deathbeds, both Connolly and Gus Reynolds had given up the same name: *Woody*. Woody had attended extracurricular piano lessons with Marta Chavez in Connolly's home. It was fair to assume that Woody had known Zachary Innes. But, aside from a sculptor of metals, who was Woody? Was he *The Maestro*? If so, it would mean rewriting our description of the killer. And I didn't feel comfortable doing that. *The Maestro* had lived with and been the lover of Rochelle Lewis before she'd upped sticks and relocated to Boulder City. Neither her account of their relationship or her description of the killer had led us to believe he was anything but a sixtyish traveling salesman with no ties to the LA community. So what was I missing?

I turned and pressed shoulders against the gate.

Tim had mentioned Gus being a regular at the discothèque on Santa Monica Boulevard. That would have brought him into contact with Stevie Hendricks, the killer's last victim. Could she have known Woody too, and that was her link to being chosen by the killer? Was Woody a regular patron of the nightclub that disguised itself as a bank? More worryingly, did Tim know him?

The more I thought it through, the more I got to thinking that this Woody character was the linchpin keeping the wheels on the killing machine.

But who was Woody, if not *The Maestro?*

My phone shrilled: *Sheriff Torres.* I ignored it. I wasn't being ignorant; I'd seen something across the street. Something that reached out and prodded at my gut.

There was a black Ford pickup, sprayed with dried, orange-colored mud, parked in the shade outside the furniture makers. A truck used by Connolly, according to Stone.

I crossed to the other side of the street and tried the driver's door. It creaked open, unlocked. I scanned the untidy interior: bits of stale food and crumpled trash in the foot spaces; a jumble of unclean clothes and shoes on the backseat; the regular accumulated filth that working trucks attract, together with the smell of labor and sweat. I opened the glove box: a few rusty tools, including wire cutters. I walked around to the back, examining the vehicle as I went. There was a stained tarp stretched tight as mottled skin across the cargo bed, held in place by twisted wires running through fixing points. I dropped the hatch and peered under the tarp. The cargo area was mostly empty: some splinters of wood, dried leaves and ridges of brown soil; several coils of silver wire near the far side; an old paint can with dried red runs. Smelled earthy.

I stepped back and closed the hatch.

And that's when I saw them: the Alabama plates.

Hot adrenaline blossomed in my chest.

I'd seen this truck before, I realized. Not here. Not even in California. In Nevada. On a cold winter's night. On an edge-of-town circular in a newish housing development in Boulder City. Back then it had been parked underneath a sunshade attached to Rochelle's place. It had been cleaner. But it was the same black Ford, a few years old. The same pickup driven away by *The Maestro* after he'd mashed me to a pulp in Rochelle's backyard.

The Maestro had used Connolly's truck.

I fumbled my phone out of my pocket and dialed Stone's number. He answered after two rings:

"Quinn? Is everything all right? Where the hell are you?" He sounded rushed, breathy.

"I'm at the abandoned factory, with Connolly's truck."

"Bloody hell, Quinn. I thought we agreed –"

"Listen to me, Stone. This is important. Remember you told me Connolly had stolen the pickup?"

"No. I remember telling you the owner reported it stolen and that Connolly was using it."

I frowned at the technicality. "When?"

"Right before the assault on the factory."

"No, I mean when was it reported stolen?"

I heard him think, then: "Sometime in late February. I'd have to check the logs to be sure on the exact date. Look, some of us are busy trying to save a woman's life here. Is this line of questioning going somewhere?"

My heart was racing, pounding. *The Maestro* had driven the pickup back in January, out in Nevada, a whole month before it had been reported as stolen.

My pulse was playing *Chopsticks* in my throat.

"You said it belonged to a kid from Culver City. What was his name – Lake or Park or something?"

"Forrest," Stone corrected. "The boy's name was Franklin Forrest. What are you getting at, Quinn? What have you found? More importantly, do I need to worry?"

70

I had butterflies in my belly, but not of the happy bunny kind.

Franklin Forrest's home address resolved to a house three doors down from Celeste's place, near the neatly-tended park in Culver City. I should have been surprised. I wasn't. Fate has an ironic sense of humor. Get used to it.

The house was a single-floored clapboard affair, painted olive green, with white window frames and an overgrown front yard. Layers of dried oil and grease on the driveway where multiple vehicles had been tinkered with over multiple years.

I pulled the Tahoe behind an identical vehicle parked five dwellings away from the target premises. Mason Stone had got here ahead of me. Over the phone, I'd told him about the incident at Rochelle's place, last January. I hadn't wanted to. No choice. If I wanted him on my side I had to be accommodating. Stone knowing about my encounter with *The Maestro* in Nevada was my leverage to get him here. He'd listened intently, then made it clear he wasn't happy about it being kept out of the case files. I'd snickered at his hypocrisy. But the news of the pickup being used by the killer in Nevada, before it had been reported stolen, was enough to make him overlook the irregularity and come see for himself.

We climbed out of our vehicles, simultaneously. His white shirt gleamed. Pressed suit pants with knife-edge seams. I must have looked like a bum in comparison.

"Where's the cavalry?" I asked.

"You're looking at it. It's just you and me, Quinn; everyone else is out in the field looking for Sheryl." He nodded toward a house just up the street. "Bit of a coincidence don't you think: Forrest and Connolly being neighbors?"

"I'm more surprised it wasn't picked up the moment your boys ran the plates."

I could see it was an embarrassing point. Until now, no one had noticed that the truck owner lived two houses away from the guy suspected of stealing it.

Sometimes oversights can make or break a case.

"And before you say anything," I added, "I know how this looks: it's a cut-and-dry case of Connolly stealing his neighbor's truck. From the sidelines I'd say it's a reasonable play. Even I could buy into it – except for one thing: Connolly wasn't living here at the time. He'd already been kicked out of the family home the year before. His wife had filed a restraining order. He had no reason to come back here, least of all to steal some kid's ride. Plus, the killer drove it to Nevada a whole month before Forrest filed the grand theft auto."

Stone didn't seem fazed by my reasoning. "It makes perfect sense if Connolly's the killer."

"He isn't."

"So you keep saying. Level with me, Quinn. Are you really one hundred per cent certain it's the same vehicle?"

What were the chances of another Ford truck with Alabama plates figuring in the investigation?

There was a note pinned to Stone's face that read *it's your move.*

His cell tinkled something by Mozart. He looked at the screen, then tilted it my way. I could see the photo of a thickset kid, late teens, with shaggy shoulder-length hair and a goatee.

"Franklin Forrest," he said. "His DMV mug shot."

I grabbed the phone and peered closer.

This wasn't the first time I'd seen Franklin Forrest, I realized. I'd clocked him before, outside the house when

I'd visited Celeste, yesterday: the big youth in the Megadeth tee and the loose-fitting jeans. One of those apes where it is impossible to state with any certainty where the neck ends and the head begins. Maybe steroids. Maybe one too many happy meals. He'd seen me, yesterday – must have known who I was – and hadn't flinched one bit.

"Doesn't look like a killer," Stone commented as I handed back the phone.

"Neither did Ted Bundy. Proves nothing."

"Okay. Fair enough. This chance encounter with The Maestro in Boulder City – the one where this truck allegedly made its first appearance – did you happen to see his face?"

"It was dark."

"But you got as close to him as we are now."

"Closer. But he took me by surprise and attacked me from behind."

"And you're absolutely certain it was him, The Maestro?"

"Without a doubt."

"How?"

"Because of the things he said, and the fact he was skulking around his ex-girlfriend's house."

"But you didn't actually see his face."

I sighed, "No, Stone, I didn't actually see his face. The guy in Rochelle's yard was built like Connolly. Same age, same beery breath. I knew it was him."

"In other words, Connolly could have borrowed Forrest's truck in January. Then, when he was supposed to return it, he didn't – forcing Forrest to file the stolen vehicle report."

"It wasn't like that. Why are you so fixated on Connolly anyway?"

"Because he ticks all the boxes. And the fact of the matter is, we don't know what condition he was in seven months ago – physically or mentally. If he had Forrest's truck back then, and you swear it's the same one, then that puts Connolly out in Nevada. And that makes him the killer. Unless you're mistaken."

Stone's logic was as impeccable as his suit. I couldn't argue it. But I knew he was wrong.

"One way to clear this up," I said. "Let's just go speak with Forrest."

We went up the front walk. Stone rapped his knuckles against the front door. We waited. He rapped again. I leaned across the nearest window, cupped a hand against the glass and peered in. A living room: brown fabric furniture facing a big LCD TV. A games console on the floor. Heavy metal magazines scattered like dragon scales. An electronic keyboard on a stand in the corner. Some metal art hung on the walls. No signs of life. I heard Stone bang a fist against the wood.

I stepped off the porch. "I'll check the back."

Down the side of the house, a short driveway led to a separate garage building. There was a basketball hoop jutting out of the wall above the battered garage door. No sign of a car. I rounded the corner. The backyard was overgrown with weeds. Not a whole lot else. I heard Stone shout *"FBI – open up!"* as I reached for the backdoor handle, tried it. It was unlocked.

Sure, I was tempted. But I knew without a warrant to back me up, a case for entering the property under probable cause was tenuous if not vaporous. Plus, I didn't want to aggravate Stone any more than I already had.

I retreated a few paces and peered through the grubby kitchen window. There was a row of cereal boxes on the windowsill, bookended with cookie jars. Used crockery mounded on cluttered surfaces. Open cupboard doors revealing shelves stacked with stuff. A pet crate over on the far side.

Stone popped his head around the corner. "Come on. It looks like Forrest's out somewhere. We have work to do."

"The backdoor's unlocked," I began.

Stone joined me in the yard. "Forget it. We'd need a warrant."

"Not if we hear somebody inside who needs our help."

"I can't hear anything."

"There's a pet cage in the kitchen."

I saw a frown pass over his face. I wasn't making much sense.

"No signs of a pet," I added. "There're no dog toys in the yard either. No food bowls on the kitchen floor."

"So?"

"So it's the same kind we found in the abandoned factory."

Stone was shaking his head. "It's just not enough to go on, Quinn. Look, I gave you the benefit of the doubt, but that's it: we're done here. We need to stop wasting time and find Sheryl. This is getting beyond the joke. I'll get someone to check on Forrest later."

I wondered if Stone was deliberately trying to steer me away.

"Have you seen the garage door?" I said.

Stone turned and looked at it.

There was a series of padlocks and chains fixing the battered door to the concrete driveway. Five in total.

"A little on the overkill side," I said, "don't you think? As far as I know, this isn't a bad neighborhood. So who needs to lock their garage up like Fort Knox? Make the call, Stone. Prove me wrong."

Stone was smart. Smart enough not to place any bets he wasn't guaranteed of winning.

He spoke to the ADIC at the field office and explained the urgency of our situation. His boss instructed us to hold back until the expedited warrant arrived. In the meantime, Stone retrieved a pair of long bolt cutters from his SUV, and then we waited. It felt like an hour. Midafternoon sun beating down. The occasional passerby glancing our way before moving on.

Fifteen minutes later, Stone's cell played its piano melody. He stood on the cigarette he'd been smoking and smiled as he read the incoming text message. "Okay. That's it: we're good to go." He offered me the bolt cutters, "Would you like the honor?"

One by one, I cut through the padlocks. I dragged rusty chains out of metal loops bolted into the concrete driveway. Cast them aside. Then I curled fingers under the rim of the door and hauled it upward, into the roof space.

I didn't know what I was expecting to find. A car maybe. Tool benches. Junk, in the very least. Certainly not emptiness.

But that's all I saw.

With the exception of a large sheet of brown cardboard spread across the middle of the floor, the garage was absolutely empty.

I looked at Stone. He was looking at me.

The anticlimax was palpable.

I wandered inside. Stone followed.

The garage was a long empty container, with bare walls and a smooth cement base. It looked like it had been cleaned with a toothbrush. Spotless. A complete opposite to the messy kitchen behind us in the house. No tool racks. No workbenches. No storage boxes. No household maintenance equipment or accumulated junk of any kind. In fact, just about the cleanest garage I'd ever seen.

But there was something in the empty space. Something invisible and everywhere.

An odor.

It was thick, potent. Like baked iron oxide in an Arizona junkyard.

I went down on my haunches and hooked fingers under the edge of the thick cardboard sheet. There was writing on it: technical specs and the image of a projection TV. Stone stepped clear as I peeled the flattened packing carton away from the floor and flipped it aside.

"Bloody hell."

Stone's astonishment was mutual.

Franklin Forrest had used the TV box to hide a hatchway in the concrete garage base. It was a plain wooden panel set flush with the cement floor, about ten feet in length and four feet wide, split into two halves, crosswise, with an inset metal handle on each of the doors where they met in the middle.

I reached for the nearest handle. Stone grabbed the other. Together we pulled the doors up and open. They leaned back on strong hinges to reveal a rectangular pit ten feet in length, four in width and about five deep. A grave-shaped recess cut into the surrounding concrete.

Stone unclipped a Maglite from his belt and shone it into the hole. The beam illuminated wire meshing, throwing grid patterns across the walls.

"Looks like we just struck gold," he breathed.

He wasn't wrong.

Franklin Forrest had installed a pair of pet cages, pushed into opposite ends of the trench, and facing each other. Both were identical to the one we'd seen in the abandoned factory. Both empty. I watched the beam flicker over crisscrossing wires, across walls, then down onto the base of the pit, where it revealed multiple puddles of gelatinous red fluid pooled on the cement floor. Congealing, thickening, hardening at the edges. Older stains visible between the cages. Red-rust discoloration on the metal mesh.

"There's you're reasonable doubt," I said.

Franklin Forrest, the youth in the Megadeth tee, had been caught red-handed.

Stone couldn't cling to his *Connolly does all* theory any longer.

71

The grisly discovery in the garage in Culver City proved beyond doubt that Franklin Forrest had played a key part in the Piano Wire Murders. Even Stone couldn't dispute hard evidence. The killer's mortifying MO was right there, buried in the floor. Just how big a part Forrest had played, we were yet to determine. Safe to say more than Connolly, by the looks of things. We knew Forrest was a kid. I knew he'd attended at least one piano tutorial with Marta Chavez in Marv Connolly's home. We knew Forrest had once owned the truck driven by Connolly. Until the background checks came through, that's all we knew.

I decided not to wait.

While Stone was on his cell – calling in the troops and issuing a citywide all-points bulletin on Forrest – I entered the residence through the backdoor.

The Evidence Response Team would conduct a full search of the entire premises once they got here, but I wanted to inspect the place first. See if I could figure out how a knucklehead teenager like Forrest fit into the killer's methodology.

I followed my Glock into the stuffy kitchen, slowly, quietly, ready to react to the slightest whiff of trouble. No one had responded to Stone's repeated rapping on the front door, but I wasn't taking for granted that nobody was home.

The sunlit room smelled of rotten food and general uncleanliness. Ingrained cooking odors and years of layered grime. There was a dining table buried beneath a pile of junk. Newspapers, food packaging, beer bottles. The dog crate without as much as a dog hair snagged in the wire.

I entered a short hallway and paused at the first door. It was a small workshop, with various hand tools pegged to the wall above a long workbench: cutters and shapers. Rubber clamps thumb-screwed to the wooden top. Drums of cables, a plastic bin filled with aluminum, and what looked like a portable welding machine.

I moved on.

The next doorway along led to an untidy bedroom. An unmade bed under the window. The stench of stale sweat and old cigarette ash. Empty beer bottles crowding a nightstand. Playboy posters plastered to the walls and the ceiling. I glimpsed a nameplate tacked to the bedroom door as I moved out. It was a rectangular ceramic plaque with a leafy design painted around a name formed from cartoonish sawn logs.

Franklin Forrest had a nickname, I realized.

Turned out I'd been too absorbed trying to unravel his relationship with Connolly that I hadn't seen the Woody for the Forrest.

72

She was dying, again. This time she was sure of it. Drowning in a delirium, and only able to surface for the briefest of moments — just long enough for her murky mind to recollect her terminal predicament before the burning fever dragged her back to hell.

Nightmares borrowed from a lunatic's imagination.

When she did waken, she was aware of vague movements outside of her. Shadows with substance. Cold competing against heat. Light lancing through dark. It was impossible to say where her tortured body ended and the rest of everything else began. She floated in an unending limbo, where the line between her physical self and her eternal soul had become fudged, indistinct. No telling that she even had a body left at all. No telling that there was anything left of her but her frightened thoughts, for eternity.

The pain had gone.

The fear had gone.

She was gone.

All that remained was for her to accept the inevitable and let go . . .

73

Multiple blood profiles from multiple victims over multiple months. That was the first impression given by the FBI forensics team as they began the arduous task of processing the garage. Old trace that could date back to the original homicide spree. Fresher blood that pointed to more recent victims, possibly in situ a matter of hours prior to our arrival at the Forrest residence. It was too soon to assign names; even submitted with top priority, it would take the rest of the day and into tomorrow to run the DNA profiles, and even then there was no guarantees.

If Sheryl Klaussner had been imprisoned here, we'd missed finding her by hours, and there's was no way of knowing if she were alive or dead.

The burning question was: where had Forrest taken her?

We left the crime scene to Forensics and returned to the field office to coordinate the continuing search for Sheryl.

Now that we had a name, our team set about canvassing everyone associated with Franklin Forrest, lifting up the lid on who this kid was. That meant analyzing credit trails, medical records, and interviewing anyone who we thought might have some idea where his favorite hangouts were.

Forrest had taken Sheryl somewhere. That somewhere was unlikely to be someplace he wasn't familiar with. We are all creatures of habit. Serial killers are no exception. But no one knew anything.

Then we got out first nugget of luck: a neighbor reported seeing Forrest driving a white van, coming and going over the last week or so.

A DMV check failed to come good on a vehicle registered in Forrest's name, other than the Ford pickup used by Connolly. Agents telephoned rental agencies and bingo: the kid had rented a GMC Savana Cargo from a Culver City operator. Odds were that Forrest and Sheryl were in that van. Trouble was, according to DMV records, there were thousands of similar trucks in California.

Time was ticking.

Both the description and the license plate details were broadcast through the police dispatch system. It was our hope a patrol car would spot the van before Sheryl exsanguinated to death.

Every abandoned factory, warehouse and business premises in the city was checked for signs of the white van. Checking abandoned housing would prove a greater challenge, and impossible to complete in one afternoon.

Every passing second swept us closer to a frightening conclusion: if we did find Sheryl, it'd be too late.

And I was kicking myself for missing the link.

I'd been by there, yesterday, within touching distance, when visiting Celeste. Every damn likelihood Sheryl had bleeding out in the garage pit three doors away.

The father in me wasn't in a forgiving mood.

I thought about Sheryl's divorced mother, being fed palatable tidbits of information from her US Marshal Liaison. Wondered how she was coping with the abduction of her daughter, for the second time. I hadn't met Mrs. Klaussner during the first investigation; she lived in the Deep South and hadn't followed her daughter to California to live her dream of becoming a nurse out here. As with her daughter, she'd trusted us to do our job and had waited on pins from afar. Now she was reliving that nightmare all over again.

My thoughts turned to my own daughter, a thousand miles away. I was conscious of the hurricane rushing up the Gulf.

I went online and checked the news feeds.

It didn't look good.

With every passing hour, the hurricane was wheeling closer and closer to an inevitable Florida landfall. Expected Monday morning. Tomorrow. Already, it had wreaked havoc in Jamaica and then Cuba. I watched a video clip of rain-driven winds battering shanty buildings to a pulp, peeling off corrugated roofing and turning the debris into deadly projectiles. Anyone caught out in the open didn't stand a chance. The lesson here was get out or dig deep. Fearing the impending threat, the Florida Governor had issued a State of Emergency and advised everyone to prepare for the worst. Citizens and businesses were being encouraged to shut down, shutter up and shift out. I watched its predicted path on an Internet weather channel – a red dotted line curving steeply inward toward the Fort Myers area – then called Grace.

"Daddy, I'll be fine," she assured me. "I know it'll do no good telling you not to worry – that's your job, I know – but I promise I'll do everything I can to keep out of its way. They're used to these things down here. We're prepared. We have a storm shelter in our building, food and water. If push comes to shove, I'll go down there and cower. I promise I won't come out until it blows over. I promise."

I told her I'd asked Jack to keep an eye on things, and her.

"Yes, he called," she confirmed to my relief. "I told him I'd let him know if I needed his assistance. But honestly, Daddy, I'll be okay. I've told Jack he's welcome here, but it looks like he's staying where he is, even though most islanders are evacuating. Daddy, you should see this place: it's gridlocked."

I'd seen it on the news: the evacuation was slow going, with thunderstorms impeding everything. Landfall was predicted somewhere around Cape Coral. Hopes were that the category three monster would downgrade significantly over the next twenty-four hours. If it didn't, if it grew in power, then . . . well, let's just say I didn't want my little girl to be standing directly in its path when it hit the coast.

I made Grace promise to keep me posted, told her I loved her at least four times, then called Jack.

"Will you relax, big guy. I've got this baby covered. Sure, they're advising everyone to clear out, but I'm staying put. Yes, you heard it right. Freedom of choice and all that. I've battened down the hatches and dug out my snorkel gear. So quit worrying about me. It'll take more than a bit of hot air to uproot this old fart."

I wasn't happy with the prospects of my only daughter and my closest buddy being exposed to the hurricane. But I didn't have much choice either way.

At around four o'clock, I was handed a dossier on Franklin Forrest.

I stared for long moments at the enlarged DMV photo pinned to the cover, musing murderous thoughts.

Was this the person instrumental in Hope's death? Had she been strung up and left to die by this teenage slab of meat?

With a sickly stomach, I put on my readers and opened the file.

Franklin Forrest was nineteen, almost twenty. Born and raised in Los Angeles. Former student at the same high school where Connolly had been a member of the faculty, before dropping out. Neither surprised me. I'd seen his nickname in Connolly's appointment book and made the assumption.

According to the IRS, there was no record of employment against his social security number. Or college enrolment records for that matter. He did have a bank account with a nice six-figure balance. I wondered about that. Not bad for a kid his age with no obvious income. Household bills were being paid by electronic debit. No debt or even credit cards to speak of. Interestingly, both of

Forrest's parents had died in an automobile accident the year before last, in late September, mere weeks before *The Maestro* had begun orchestrating his killing spree. I knew from experience that sudden tragedy can make a man venture along a path he would otherwise have given a wide berth. I wondered if the death of his parents had acted as the stimulus behind his involvement in the Piano Wire Murders.

The death of my wife had triggered demons in my own flesh and blood.

The hard way, I had learned never to underestimate the power of anger.

Forrest was something of a metalsmith. Examples of it were hung up all through his house. He'd put together the artwork in Gus Reynolds' backyard. Reynolds had been a regular at the nightclub on Santa Monica Boulevard, a nightclub run by the latest victim, Stevie Hendricks.

I didn't know how Forrest knew Reynolds, not exactly. I had my suspicions – namely, that Forrest had frequented the nightclub himself. It would have brought him into contact with Stevie. There was also a possibility that he'd been there on that night in January when I'd gone looking for Tim Roxbury and got my drinks spiked. He would have known who I was. Seen the connection. Known that Stevie had shown more than a passing interest in me.

It was beginning to look like everything revolved around Forrest.

But Forrest wasn't *The Maestro*.

I was at it again.

Neither him nor Connolly.

I was convinced. And my tune wasn't for changing.

So what did I believe?

According to our profile, Forrest wasn't smart enough to orchestrate the abduction/homicides by himself. And that was the critical factor. His academic records of achievement spoke of below averages in all subjects. The killer I knew was clever, deceptive, cunning. Anything but Forrest. The solitary brain cell belonging to Franklin Forrest looked like it spent most of its time searching for another to rub up to. He was more the kind of lackey who delivered the meat to the butcher, rather than the man that wielded the blade.

As for Connolly, he was a drunk and a coward. He lacked the courage to face his problems, let alone the will to kill. He had the brains but not the balls. He was more excuse than reason.

I thought about my scrap with *The Maestro* in Rochelle's backyard on that freezing Nevada night back in January. Everything I knew about the killer's physical make-up pointed to a guy older, tougher and bigger than me. Connolly was the right build, the right generation, but he was as tough as wet tissue. Forrest was the right build, wrong generation, and about as soft as an enraged bull in a rodeo.

Individually, they made lousy soloists. As a duo, they played all the right notes. But neither had the measure to compose harmoniously.

The only way this unlikely pair could match *The Maestro's* kill rate was if somebody else was doing the conducting.

And that's the person I knew as *The Maestro*.

Suddenly it clicked like a light bulb popping on in my head:

There was a third person.

It made sense: someone pulling strings – or wires, in this case. Directing from the wings. The beat keeping the rhythm. Without a third person – the brains – Connolly and Forrest were just a bad double act in need of tuning.

I went over to the window, all out of musical metaphors.

Late afternoon sunshine was pulling out perfectly-straight shadows from the headstones in the Veteran's Cemetery. Orange sunset reflecting off the Getty Center.

It had never occurred to me that the killer might not be acting alone.

Nothing had led us to believe more than one killer had undertaken the original killings.

Is that why I'd never managed to catch *The Maestro*, because we were looking at a team rather than a single serial killer?

I was giddy with the thought.

History shows that serial killer teams fail. Mainly thanks to clashing egos. All those sociopathic brain cells competing for control simply culminates in a clash of characters. Invariably, one of the components becomes disenfranchised and breaks ranks. The dismantled team is less efficient. Mistakes are made. The only time serial killer teams persist is where one party completely controls the others – either through fear or even with love. It is true that we are at our most vulnerable during each of these emotional states. And that's when the psychopath strikes.

I watched the red-and-white lights moving up and down the four-oh-five, and started formulating a theory.

Here's how it went: Connolly and Forrest were the front men, the hired muscle, working under the supervision of a third person – *The Maestro* – who was the real brains in the outfit. *The Maestro* directed Connolly to source out suitable victims (and possibly suitably abandoned detainment sites), while Forrest provided the brawn and performed the abductions themselves. This explained away Connolly's alibis during the original investigation, and explained why several of the victims were connected to him. Forrest's brute strength would be used to restrain the victims. A kind of meathead gofer. As for the wrapping of the wires, the torturing, that would be conducted by none other than *The Maestro* himself – simply because that particular sadism was his purpose, his drive. In other words, he got off on it.

That gave us three distinct band members: Connolly on bass, Forrest on drums and a third man on lead.

It didn't give us a name for *The Maestro*, or where we could find him.

But we were getting closer. I could feel it.

At 6 p.m., the local news channels ran a *'Have You Seen This Man?'* bulletin, released by the Bureau. It showed the same picture of Forrest that I had on my desk. They played taped footage from the Forrest residence in Culver City: FBI techies garbed in white coveralls, scouring the property for clues. People crowding the police tape. I looked, but didn't see Celeste. The bulletin ended with a brief press statement read by the Special Agent in Charge, Mason Stone. He was standing outside the federal building, this building. His eyes looked sunken, weary. The heavy night in Westwood Village was beginning to exact its price.

"I cannot stress how important it is that we speak with Franklin Forrest sooner rather than later. This man is dangerous. We're urging the public to be vigilant and report any sightings or information pertaining to his whereabouts straight away, either by contacting the police or our dedicated FBI hotline. I repeat it is of the utmost urgency that we speak with Franklin Forrest of Culver City as soon as possible. A woman's life hangs in the balance. Thank you."

We were getting desperate. It showed.

The accompanying press release made no mention of *The Maestro* – just that Forrest was suspected of abduction and was wanted by the FBI – but the press agencies were anything but slow on the uptake. Despite Stone keeping me out of the picture as far as the media were concerned, I knew it was only a matter of time before they put two and two together and linked our manhunt with the Piano Wire Murders.

No one was going home tonight. Maybe not for days.

Our section of the FBI suite was a hubbub of activity: agents answering phone calls from frightened citizens, agents chasing down possible sightings, information being passed in, through and out with the speed of light.

Daylight faded into dusk and twilight succumbed to night.

Through my office partition, I spotted Stone handing out instructions to a group of attentive agents. He saw me looking and nodded an acknowledgement. I wondered about his first cousin once removed. I remembered Jack's damning indictment that Stone could play a bigger part in the case than met the eye, and not just from our side of the fence.

I watched the Brit as he directed his underlings with aplomb, shirtsleeves rolled up, tie pulled loose, sweat beading his brow despite the efficient air conditioning. Stone was bigger than me, heftier, my generation, smart and, when it mattered, in the vicinity of every one of *The Maestro's* crime scenes. I hadn't ran any deep background checks on Mason Stone. Hadn't had the time or the inclination. Maybe I should have. Maybe I should have gotten Dreads to lay him bare. In the very least, I should have broached the subject about his first cousin once removed. Confront him in public and catch him off-guard.

For a disturbing moment I had the sudden feeling that the elusive third man was in reach and that I was looking at him.

Could Mason Stone be *The Maestro?*

74

Then, at 8:15 p.m., we got the call we were waiting for:

A person fitting Forrest's description had been sighted on scrubland in the Hollywood Hills. The suspect had triggered a motion detector on Mount Lee and been caught on closed-circuit security cameras after trespassing into protected parkland. The park security had sent several blurry gray-tone night-vision images for us to check out. The face in the frames fit Forrest's perfectly, and our team scrambled for the elevators. Both the rangers and the police were told to hang back until we got there. We didn't know if Forrest was armed. We did know he was dangerous. We were also acutely aware that we had to capture him alive at all costs if we wanted to find Sheryl.

Our FBI posse tore northeast on Santa Monica, ignoring traffic signals, with Stone and me in the lead vehicle. A half dozen black SUVs with patriotic lights crackling against the night. Several police cruisers joined the stampede, their sirens wailing as they cleared a safe passage through the city streets. Our speed was dangerous, but so too was our destination.

I watched Stone, occupying the other end of the backseat, as we were chauffeured at a lightning pace. I didn't really know much about him, I realized – other than the official spiel and what had come from his own mouth. I had no idea what his interests were outside of the Bureau. No idea what terrible thing had happened in his past to forever alter the way he viewed the world. What possible motive could he have to orchestrate a series of cruel abductions and homicides?

"Do you mind?" Stone asked as he rummaged out a crumpled cigarette packet. "I'm a bag of nerves."

I shrugged. I watched him ignite the cigarette with his Zippo and suck deeply.

"You don't strike me as the nervous type, Stone," I said.

Stone lowered the window halfway and blew smoke into the night. "Don't tell me – I exude confidence."

"Something like that."

"Then that makes two of us. I bet you're also good at poker."

"I've been known to win a few hands in my time."

Stone nodded. "On some levels we're the same, you and me. Our über confidence is a cover. Like wallpaper over cracks. Realistically, it's impossible to reach our age or our status without hoarding secrets."

But Stone didn't know mine. Any of them. He thought he did. I could see it as he studied me through his halo of smoke. But he didn't. He had no idea. I had a dark secret worse than any Stone could dream up. And there were only two people in the whole world that knew the absolute truth. I was one and the other was being tracked down by Hives – the private investigator I'd hired on Sanibel to help do my dirty business.

But I knew Stone's secret. I knew about the abduction and torture of Christian Stone, his first cousin once removed – very possibly by *The Maestro*. I just hadn't figured out what had happened that night, or why, and what part Stone had played in it. I knew Stone deliberately kept the information out of the investigation. Keeping it hushed-up the way he had was smart. It meant he had unquestioned command of the case and was able to steer our team in the direction he felt best. Like convincing everyone that Connolly was the killer. Like keeping me close so that he could keep an eye on me.

If Mason Stone were *The Maestro* he would do everything in his power to point the finger of blame elsewhere. Misdirect. I was keen to see Forrest's reaction when he saw the Brit gunning for him.

We made the left onto Gower and headed north, as fast as the darkened road conditions would allow.

Stone flicked his cigarette through the window and answered a call on his cell.

I didn't mind the lack of polite chitchat; I was focusing on catching a killer, even if that killer was within arms' reach.

Our driver made turns and the roadway started to incline as we entered the Mount Lee foothills. Up ahead, I could see blood red lights throbbing on the radio tower sprouting out of the summit. A faint gray impression of the famous Hollywood Sign lurking beneath. The rest of the hillside was shrouded in fuzzy darkness.

"He's up near the sign," Stone declared. He tapped our driver on the shoulder. "Head for the security gates at the end of Deronda Drive. We're taking the fire road to the top."

We climbed away from the city, our flighty speed drastically reduced by the narrower suburban lanes. Red-and-blue lights splashing across hillside homes. No sirens here, but folks coming to their windows to investigate all the same.

Stone was in a conference call with other agents, issuing instructions into his cell: we were to apprehend the suspect and take him into custody; no one was to make a fatal shooting, but shoot to wound if it meant protecting or defending innocent lives; this was a Bureau-led engagement and the LAPD were to act in a support capacity only; an airborne SWAT unit was minutes away and would provide weapons cover and visual guidance from the air.

I checked my Glock as the Suburban switched back and forth along the quiet residential lanes. I hadn't used it since shooting out the security lamp in Gus Reynolds' backyard. The pool water had long since dried up. I'd re-lubricated where necessary and checked the firing mechanism. It was good to go. But was I? I knew Sheryl's life hung in the balance. Forrest was our best and possibly our only shot at rescuing her alive. But if he'd been instrumental in Hope's death, could I trust myself not to seek the death penalty, tonight – judge, jury and executioner?

I sounded like a vigilante. And maybe I was.

Eighteen months ago, I'd made a promise. A vow. A pact with the devil to kill *The Maestro* and avenge my wife's murder. When it came to the crunch, could I do it?

I looked again at Mason Stone and wondered about my theory.

What if Forrest, Connolly and Stone had all played their part in my wife's murder?

Was I prepared to take three lives for one?

We arrived at the restricted area access gates at the head of Deronda Drive. There was an FBI vehicle parked next to a white GMC van – Forrest's van – with agents poring over it with flashlights.

A dutiful ranger swung open the gates and waved us through. We began the winding ascent along the unlit mountain fire road, into darkness. Our driver had his headlight beams on full – so, too, did the five SUVs tailing us. Two-dozen white lances roved across the hillsides like super troupers at a motion picture première, revealing glimpses of steep wooded gullies and brush-covered ridges.

The roadway climbed steeply as it zigzagged around the mountainside. Tight curves and treacherous drops. Spectacular views over the city. Finally, we arrived at the station compound to find it crawling with cops. A half dozen black-and-whites and a couple of rugged off-roaders belonging to the rangers.

We bailed out into hot evening air and ducked into bulletproof vests.

I could hear the rhythmic beat of approaching rotor blades and the squawk of police radio chatter.

A burly police sergeant from Hollywood Division came directly over to us.

"What's the situation?" Stone asked as he accompanied us to the chain-link fence lining the edge of the roadway.

"The suspect was last seen down by the sign. I have men posted all along the access road and units covering the trails exiting the park. Canine units are on standby. If he tries to make a run for it, we're well-placed to intercept him."

"Thanks," Stone said. "We'll handle it from here."

The police sergeant nodded and returned to supervise his men.

I looked beyond the fence, down the steep, dark hillside to the sprawling cityscape glowing in the valley below. Closer to home, where the mountainside fell away, I could see flat, geometric shapes towering out of the rough scrubland. Dark gray panels fixed to scaffold supports. We were right behind the Hollywood Sign, I realized. Right behind the letter Y, in fact. Higher up. Closer than I'd ever come before.

A helicopter thundered overhead, low. Dust and grit blasted our faces. We all ducked instinctively as it swooped out over the drop-away.

It looked like a TV news chopper.

Stone was shaking his head. "That's all we bloody need."

He barked orders to one of our team as the helicopter slowed and turned on a dime about a hundred yards out. Now it faced us, slightly higher. A powerful search beam burst into life and dazzled our eyes before dropping to the Hollywood Sign.

A Fed came over with a tablet PC. "Boss, this is going out live all across the networks."

We stared at the bright screen.

It was a real-time view of the Hollywood Sign, being streamed from the helicopter hovering in front of us.

I could see the tall white letters illuminated within the intense searchlight. Sharp-edged shadows scrambling around in the brush. The word *'LIVE'* posted in the top corner of the shot and a red-and-white *'BREAKING NEWS'* ribbon across the bottom of the picture. Within the surrounding darkness, I could just make out our huddle of Feds gathered up near the top of the frame.

The TV news had got to the story first. But that wasn't the worst part. Not by a long shot. The worst part was far worse. It drove hot nails into our guts and ripped them out.

In the anemic glare of the spotlight, it was clear to see that someone had hung something against the letter Y, about a third the way off the ground. Right in front of us.

With a jerk, the TV camera zoomed in.

It was a woman.

She was naked – except for her bra and panties, the color of which was impossible to determine beneath her varnishing of wet blood. It looked like her skin had been peeled. She was hanging from the white-painted steel vertical. Legs bound together with coils of wire. Arms angled out and above, wrists looped with thin metal filaments, so that her pose mimicked the letter to which she was attached. More steely cables were wrapped around her midriff and the panel behind her, holding her in place like a steely spider web. Wires crossing her face at the bridge of the nose, glinting in the luminous searchlight. The downdraft from the chopper was blowing her long coppery hair across her face like a sea anemone in a strong current.

Even so, it looked like Sheryl Klaussner.

My heart was on fire.

"Will somebody get this off the air," Stone breathed through clenched teeth. "Now!"

75

This was it.

No idea where Forrest was hiding.

No waiting for the SWAT helicopter.

It was now or never.

I grabbed a pair of bolt cutters from the Suburban while Stone hollered commands to the team, then we fanned out, taking different routes to the sign. The plan was to cut off any hopes Forrest had of fleeing the scene. Capture him and rescue Sheryl. Sounds straight forward, right?

I slung the heavy cable cutters over the chain-link fence, then curled fingers into the crisscrossing wire and scaled it clumsily. I crashed into the rough chaparral on the other side, almost losing a sneaker. I got out my Glock and activated the tactical light. Stone dropped down a yard away, nimbly for his size, and flicked on his Xenon beam.

"I'm going for Sheryl," I said as I gathered up the cutters.

"Right behind you."

The terrain was steep, dropping at an increasingly sharp angle to the base of the sign. The brilliant beam connecting the letter Y to the hovering chopper impaired night vision. Even with our tactical lights, we were as good as blind. We ran, scuffing and tumbling our way through coarse scrub, skidding on the loose soil.

We couldn't see Forrest, but we knew he could hear us coming. He'd also be aware of the canine units sweeping up the hill from below; I could hear their faint barks coming to us on the night breeze. The noose was closing in on Franklin Forrest. He was trapped.

My foot snagged a root and I slid the last few yards on my butt, into the shadow behind the enormous letter Y. Stone wasn't far behind, sending pebbles skittering noisily into the metal support struts.

Above us, the Hollywood Sign towered forty-five-feet into the inky night sky. The whole of the giant letter was a jet-black silhouette framed by brilliance.

No signs of Forrest. But plenty of shadows and crevices to hide in.

With Stone covering, I stowed my Glock and worked my way beneath the huge letter, blundering out the other side into the blazing light.

Dust swirled. Grit clattered against metal.

I backed down the slope a little to get a better viewing angle on Sheryl; to see if she were still breathing.

She looked like she'd been crucified.

She was covered from head to toe in blood. Some of it splashed on the sign. More below her feet where her killer had scrawled five parallel lines with crossing musical notes.

Forrest had desecrated the iconic Hollywood Sign.

But something was wrong with the picture.

Something that didn't look quite right.

I was still gawping when the freight train hit me from the side.

I didn't see it coming; everything outside the cone of light was sheer blackness.

My attacker came thundering out of the dark and hit me with enough force to bowl me off my feet and knock the air from my lungs. We went crashing into the prickly Manzanita. Strong arms wrapped around mine as we rolled and thrashed through the brush. I sucked in air and wrenched an arm free. Elbowed him in the side of the neck. We rolled. I came on top. I grappled for my attacker's face. Felt a knee strike my ribs. Momentum rolled him on top again and he dug in his knees, bringing our cartwheeling to a stop. I went for my gun. A big fist came down and collided with my skull. Stars spangled. He was straddling my chest, pinning me down, silhouetted against the blinding glare coming from the helicopter's searchlight. The beam was on us, I realized. Transmitting our scrap live on TV for all the world to see. The Celebrity Cop being mashed to death by a brute twice his size. I coughed out dust from the downdraft. Brought up a knee and thumped it into his back. He didn't buckle. Not one bit. I couldn't see his face – just a blur of rotor blades around his shadowed head. I raised an arm to sock him in the throat, but he knocked it aside and planted another pulverizing mitt into my face. My vision crackled like one of those movie techniques that mimic a TV signal interruption. I blinked. I went to slug him with my other fist, but caught another knuckle hammer in the teeth for my efforts. I tasted blood. Spat it out. I was having difficulty breathing, crushed by his weight. I saw him reach aside, into the brush, gather up a big slab of sandstone in both hands and heft it above his head. A lump of sedimentary rock the size of a gravestone. He was going to plant it down on my head, crush my skull, and bury me here beneath the famous Hollywood Sign. I tried twisting, reaching for some kind of a weapon, but couldn't move an inch. He was too damned heavy. Squashing me like a bug. His arms arced backward as he heaved the huge tombstone into the air, stretching for the optimum impact trajectory.

It was all happening too fast. I'd be dead before I could make even one last desperate ditched effort to save myself.

This was it: I was going to die here. On live TV. The end of a cop's celebrity. Broadcast to the entire world.

I saw a red dot play over his shadowed face.

Then a clap of thunder rang out across the hillside.

My attacker hesitated, with the whirling chopper blades rotating in slow motion behind him. His arms quivered. For a heart-stopping moment it looked like he was about to drop the slab on my head. Then he was falling back, pulled down by the sheer weight of the rock. His crushing weight lifted and I scrambled to my feet as he fell clear. I coughed out dust and blood and got out the Glock.

Franklin Forrest was on his back in the scrub. Unmoving. Eyes blank and staring. A black hole in the center of his forehead.

I heard the noise of somebody plunging through the chaparral from behind. I whirled round. Then realized it was Mason Stone. He appeared out of the dark, squinting against the glare. There was a gun gripped in his fist and a look of grave determination creasing his face.

"Is he dead?"

"I expect so; you shot him right between the eyes. Witnessed by millions."

He holstered his firearm. "At least we have Sheryl."

I stared at Mason Stone with a plume of lava rising in my throat. "It's not her," I breathed. "It's Seeger."

"Agent Seeger?"

"Take a look for yourself if you don't believe me. She's the same build, same hair as Sheryl. But it's Seeger. She's dead and Sheryl's still missing." I spat out blood and goo. "Congratulations, Stone. You just killed our only hope of finding her alive."

76

Sure, I was grateful to Stone for saving my life. But I was pissed at him for killing Forrest.

We had our killer, or at least the guy I believed was the hired help. We'd caught him red-handed. No question about his guilt. I was confident the DNA analysis taken from his Culver City home and the abandoned factory would link all of *The Maestro's* latest victims with Forrest, and possibly those from the original killing spree the year before last. There was no doubt in my mind that Forrest had played a huge part in the Piano Wire Murders. But still I believed he was just an underling carrying out his master's bidding.

The real mastermind still walked free.

And Stone had killed any chance I'd had of squeezing an identity out of Forrest.

I blinked as the flash from a camera lit up the immediate hillside.

The stricken Franklin Forrest was still sprawled in the scrub with his brains pulped. I could see how Forrest had been able to abduct and carry his victims with ease, even hoist Seeger up the Hollywood Sign: he was a giant redwood, toppled by Stone's death shot. A six-foot-five, three hundred pound mass of muscle and madness. One of those big-boned kids who outgrows his clothes faster than he wears them out. As for Stone, he was coordinating the cleanup from afar. Every now and then he glanced in my direction. He knew I was pissed and was keeping open ground between us. If his bullet hadn't killed Forrest when it had, my head would have been mashed into Mount Lee. No question, I owed Stone. But I couldn't help wondering about ulterior motives.

What better way to silence his disciple than by placing a bullet between the eyes?

Was Stone the ringleader?

If he was, I'd find out, somehow, soon enough. Maybe through his second cousin once removed. And when I did he'd know about it. He'd pay for killing Hope, even if that meant crossing every line.

There were people up on the scaffolding behind the Hollywood Sign, using cutters to free Seeger. There was a lump in my throat the size of a clenched fist as they lowered her body to outstretched hands. We were all shell-shocked by the discovery. None of us knew why Forrest had targeted Seeger. No idea how he'd even known she'd been working the case. What we did know was that he had abducted her sometime today, while we were all preoccupied searching for Sheryl. He'd snatched her up in his nondescript white cargo van and strung her up to die.

The universe seeks balance and Seeger was dead.

And somehow, perversely, I felt responsible.

77

I grabbed a ride back to base in any FBI vehicle that didn't have Stone in it. I didn't want to speak with Stone any more than I had to. Not right now. I didn't want to be in his company, not especially. The more I thought it through, the more I was beginning to believe he'd silenced Forrest deliberately. I couldn't ignore the possibilities stacking up in my head. Stone had been within striking distance during the original homicides. There was a strong likelihood his first cousin once removed was a victim of *The Maestro's* master plan. I didn't know why. Add a mop of unruly hair and Stone fit the description we had for the killer. Plus, he had the brains and the means to pull it off. If he were *The Maestro*, I'd find out sooner or later. Either something would give or someone would slip.

Or I could push.

In the meantime, I wasn't letting him out of my sight.

Did Mason Stone kill my wife?

There was a tangible atmosphere of doom and gloom in the field office. Our spirits should have been high – we'd taken a killer off the streets – but everyone was on a downer. Deflated by the fact we'd failed to find Sheryl Klaussner and by the slaying of a colleague. We were all conscious of the pressing time and the fact our best lead to Sheryl was dead. Time was against us and everyone was feeling the pressure.

No time to grieve for Seeger.

I felt bad.

A preliminary analysis of Forrest's van showed no signs of blood trace on the metal flooring. There was, however, evidence of spray bleach. It looked like he'd used it to transport Seeger to Mount Lee still alive. Maybe sedated. Then tied her so tight to the sign that she'd bled out within minutes. The rest of the van was clean. No fast food receipts. No parking violations. Nothing to give us a sign pointing to where he'd stashed Sheryl.

We'd come to a dead end.

Stone put in a requisition to Caltrans – the traffic camera network – in the hope they could find images of the van during Forrest's route from Culver City to where he'd dumped it on Deronda Drive. It was a long shot, but we were desperate.

If Sheryl were still alive she wouldn't be for much longer.

We had to find her, and fast.

At eleven twenty six, something made me check the weather forecast for Florida. Like here, things were looking grimmer by the hour on the Gulf Coast, but for different reasons. The hurricane hadn't downscaled in the slightest and was expected to collide with the coast around ten in the morning, bringing with it one of the worst storms this decade. Barrier islands protecting the mainland from storm surge had been evacuated, and were already being battered by torrential rain and gale-force winds. Towns up and down the waterfront were in lockdown, with residents advised to remain indoors, preferably in watertight storm shelters.

The live satellite feed showed a huge, bubbling white disk whirling in the Gulf. It resembled a buzzsaw blade with its teeth about to gnaw through the Floridian coastline. The Doppler radar imaging depicted its predicted path, with figures ramping it up to a category four by daybreak. Nervously, I watched a news clip of storeowners boarding up storefronts, while rain lashed the streets and broken palms arrowed through the leaden sky.

It was bad.

I thought about calling Grace, then realized she was three hours ahead. It was likely my worry was out of proportion. Being a parent does that. Grace was a big girl; she could look after herself. Heck, she'd been looking after me for months! I had no choice but to sit it out. There were no missed calls on my cell or worried voice messages. No news is good news, right?

Close on midnight, I spotted Mason Stone heading for the elevators. I waited until he'd entered the carriage before scooping up my stuff and following.

78

What were the chances of an FBI agent being *The Maestro* – not just an ordinary FBI agent, but also a case-breaker in charge of the very same case?

Didn't make sense.

So why was it eating away at me?

I asked myself the question over and over as I shadowed Stone into the silent parking garage. He was on his own. Jacket slung over his shoulder. A smoldering cigarette jutting out of the corner of his mouth.

It didn't seem likely. Federal agents were handpicked. They had to pass rigorous psyche evaluations designed to weed out the undesirables, and be shining examples of law enforcement. The possibility that a homicidal and sadistic psychopath had slipped through the tight recruitment net was slim.

But it wasn't impossible.

The trouble with psychopaths is that some of them are pretty good at fooling the exams. Plus, I had to remind myself that Mason Stone had been invited to join the Bureau. He'd come in through the backdoor. Like me. And I know I wouldn't have passed the psyche evals. I was a loose cannon with an FBI badge. An unknown quantity let loose with absolute authority.

Could I say the same for Mason Stone?

I waited until he'd headed out of the underground parking structure in his black Mustang before commandeering a motor pool vehicle and giving pursuit.

Did I really want to believe he was the killer of my wife?

Could I ignore it if he was?

On her deathbed, I'd promised Hope I'd avenge her.

If it came to it, could I kill Mason Stone?

I sifted through the few facts I knew as I tailed the Brit through the lamp-lit streets of LA, heading south.

Out of habit, I had the windows down – letting the warm night air flush through the car.

I had a strong suspicion that Connolly had groomed the victims – mainly through his work with the school and his extracurricular coaching. I didn't know exactly where all of the victims had come into contact with him, but I was pretty sure that if I dug deep enough I'd find it. I knew Forrest had acted as the go-between – the hired muscle who abducted the victims and transported them to their incarceration. Frankenstein's monster, so to speak. I had an undeniable feeling that there was a third person, the orchestrator, directing Connolly and Forrest. This was *The Maestro* – the sadist who derived perverse pleasure from binding his victims with razor-sharp wires, then watching them bleed to death in agony as they struggled to survive.

The Maestro was intelligent and able to coordinate his kill team efficiently. He was somebody who had endured life long enough to perfect his twisted fantasies and then seize the opportunity to see them play out. He believed he was better than the average Joe. Beyond the arm of the law and smarter than those chasing him. *The Maestro* was as hard as stone. I smiled at the analogy.

Stone had brought me into his fold, where he could keep an eye on me. Keep your enemies closer, as they say. His uncle's grandson had been abducted and assaulted by someone whose MO resembled *The Maestro's*. Something wasn't right. I had to know if he was my wife's killer. Rule him either in or out. And that meant a confrontation.

A showdown.

I had no doubt Stone would deny it, do everything in his power to persuade me otherwise. But I wasn't in the best frame of mind to take his BS right now. Something had snapped in my head. An elastic band, stretching too far under pressure. I was *this* close to finding the murderer of my wife. And the thought was all-consuming.

Stone wouldn't go down without a fight.

Then again, neither would I.

79

It was a hotel situated directly on the harbor front in Marina Del Rey. A swanky, upmarket property supplying lavish accommodations for people visiting the seaside community. Until now, I hadn't given much thought about Stone's living arrangements here in Los Angeles. Didn't know where his real family home was, other than back in England. This place looked expensive. High-roller expensive. Didn't matter; Uncle Sam was footing the bill.

I slowed the vehicle to a crawl against the curbside as I watched Stone turn his beloved Mustang over to a kid working the overnight valet. I hung back until the Brit had disappeared through the hotel's main entrance before leaving my ride in the public parking across the street.

I crossed empty lanes toward the marina.

This time of night, the hotel lobby was quiet. Most guests either in bed or watching on-demand movies. I padded over thick carpeting toward the front desk. A wafer-thin male receptionist with short blonde hair came out of a back office. He was wiping crumbs from the lapel of his smart blue jacket. He looked about sixteen.

"Hey." I showed him my FBI badge. "You have another federal agent guesting here by the name of Mason Stone. I need to know which room he's staying in."

The kid smiled cockily, pale eyes narrowing with suspicion. It looked like I'd just interrupted his midnight snack and a feet-up with the comedy channel.

He nodded at the badge. "Is this for real, this shield?" He had a Slavic accent – maybe Russian. I'm not good with accents.

"As real as this." I indicated the Glock attached to my belt.

The kid was smirking, "Ah, yes. My cousin, he has similar setup. He picked it up, cheap on eBay. Very good deal." The kid appeared nonplussed by my glower. "Only his shield, it looks – how you say – less false?"

I let out a weary breath.

"You have warrant, to go with it?" he smirked.

"Do you have a green card?"

"Actually, I do. I also have fascination with American dollars."

I slid a twenty onto the counter.

The kid looked offended. "Really? Something tells me you are able to do much better than this."

"That's it. Or I'll take you in for racketeering."

The kid made a tight noise and tapped at a keyboard. "Let me see. Ah, yes. Mr. Stone, he is in one of our eleventh floor suites. Room eleven-fifteen to be exact. But he is not there."

"Oh? I just saw him coming in."

"As you say. But he is in the pool area. Smoking." The last word came with a curl of his lip.

"Give me a key to his suite – or we can discuss your taking bribes, downtown."

The kid was frowning. "This is entrapment."

He didn't like it, but he fired up a keycard all the same.

"And when you see him," I said, "no mention I'm here. Got it?"

The kid put the twenty in his pocket. "My mouth is considered closed. Long live capitalism."

Frowning, I rode the elevator to the eleventh floor, not fully knowing what I intended to do once I got there. What was I hoping to find in Stone's room – irrefutable and incriminating evidence linking him to the Piano Wire Murders, case closed? Was anything in life that simple?

I let myself into Stone's suite and flicked on lights. It was a series of opulently-decorated rooms, each with panoramic views out over the marina. The place looked like something straight out of a French Renaissance château. Heavy brocade drapes, thick carpeting and real wooden floors. Foreign landscapes in gold frames against embossed wallpaper. Palatial furniture throughout. There was even a grand piano with its lid raised.

Nothing out of place. Not a speck of dust.

Either Stone was a tidy freak or the maid service here was first class.

I went over to the piano and peeped under the angled lid: no strings missing. What did I expect? There was a page of sheet music on the rack. Something by Liszt. I didn't recognize the piece by looking at the arrangement – probably wouldn't have recognized it even if I'd heard it being played. I preferred my piano music more Joplin than Chopin.

I inspected the bedroom. A four-poster with Egyptian linens. Dark suits hung in a hardwood armoire. A stack of crisp white shirts still in their plastic sleeves on a shelf. Colored ties hanging on the inside of the wardrobe door. Shone shoes sitting in pairs on a tilt stand and casual clothes folded in the drawers. Everything this season. It was like a page from a Ralph Lauren brochure.

There was a suitcase at the back of the walk-in. I unzipped it. Nothing inside except for a thick file folder with my photo pinned to the cover.

Bingo.

I went back into the living area and laid it out on a glass table, opened it up. The first page was a summary. Not just my career in law enforcement, but also personal details pertaining to my life outside of the force. Stuff about my parentage, my upbringing in Memphis, Hope and the kids.

The words *Celebrity Cop* had been written in red pen and underlined twice.

I got the feeling I wasn't going like what I was about to read inside.

"I hope you've found what you came looking for."

I spun on the spot, gut burning, to see Mason Stone standing in the guest room doorway. His trademark look was pulling down his long face. He stepped inside and slung his jacket over a chair.

"Go ahead," he said, "take a good look. It's your file. Nothing you don't already know about."

I made no reply. Made no move. I was acutely aware that I'd been caught red-handed, trespassing in my immediate line commander's personal domain. It didn't look good.

Stone's hands moved to his firearm.

Mine was out and pointed at his chest before he could pop the safety stud on the holster.

Stone laughed, "Bloody hell, Quinn, relax with the cowboy antics, will you? I was just taking it off. It's been a long day. I'm knackered and I need a shower. Stop being so bloody paranoid."

I told him to sit on the couch, and gestured with the Glock.

Stone sighed heavily and perched himself on the arm. He slackened off the knot in his tie, slid it from around his neck and proceeded to wrap it around his knuckles. "You know, you didn't need to sneak in here and snoop around behind my back. If you'd asked, I would have invited you over. The whiskey here's first rate." He looked at me down the length of his nose. "Are you going to tell me what this is all about?"

"I think you know."

"Do I?" He leveled his dark gaze on mine.

"Your connection with the case."

"My connection?"

"Don't play dumb, Stone. It isn't you. You know exactly what I'm talking about."

Stone placed the rolled-up tie on the couch. "I think this case is getting the better of us. It's been a rough couple of days. Losing Seeger hasn't helped. I don't know about you, Quinn, but I could murder one of those whiskies right now. Fancy joining me in one, maybe two?" He started to stand up.

I flicked off the safety and told him to stay seated.

Stone raised his big hands and lowered himself back onto the arm. "All right. Don't get excited. I was just trying to break the ice. But obviously you've got a bee in your bonnet."

I fingered a set of handcuffs out of their pouch and tossed them into his lap, told him to cuff himself to the leg of the grand piano.

He looked at me like I'd lost my last marble. "Are you serious?"

"Deadly."

"This is silly. Your paranoia. Your obsessive nature. I knew it was bad, but I thought you could at least hold it together until the case was over. It's gone far enough, Quinn. It's time you got some help. First thing in the morning I'm going to recommend you see a professional."

I stepped closer. Leveled the muzzle. "Put them on."

"Or else what – you'll shoot me?" Stone cast the cuffs aside. "Grow up, Quinn. This is ridiculous. I refuse to play this childish game. I don't know what's gotten into you. Perhaps it's the case. You're too involved on a personal level. Opening up an old wound has got you seeing spooks in every shadow. Your trouble is, you over-think things. You see patterns where there aren't any. Connect the dots and make up your own picture. Now look where it's got you: breaking and entering and threatening your superior with deadly force. Bloody hell, Quinn, pull yourself together."

His hand moved toward his weapon again.

I stepped in and knocked him on the temple with the butt of the gun. Stone's eyes rolled back in his head. He released a lungful of hot air and collapsed sideways onto the couch.

No turning back now.

80

It was reactive. Spontaneous. Probably, I'd live to regret it. Strangely, in the heat of the moment, I couldn't care less about consequences. If I was wrong about Stone, then the worst that could happen was my being turfed out of the Bureau before the closure of the case, and a charge of assault being leveled my way. I could live with that. If I was right about Stone, then I was now in a better place to extract a confession, and to limit his capacity to retaliate with his own deadly force.

I was still sifting through the file – my file, two inches thick – when Stone came to. The material was pretty exhaustive, even to the point of delving into the adult lives of my children. I saw his face screw into a frown as he realized he was on the floor, handcuffed to the piano.

"Bloody hell, Quinn, I can't believe you pistol-whipped me. You crazy bastard. How long was I out?"

"Fifteen minutes."

He touched a tentative finger against the bruise on his temple, winced. "Have you lost your mind? This doesn't bode well for our continuing relationship, you know. You've overstepped the mark this time."

I threw the file onto the couch. "Why?"

"Why what?"

"Why have you been keeping tabs on me, compiling statements from people in my life, digging into my private affairs?"

He inched himself into a seated position. "There's no big conspiracy here, Quinn. I make it a point of thoroughly vetting all the people I work with. No prejudices and no exceptions. If I know what makes you tick I'm less likely to be caught by surprise."

"Didn't work out for you this time. That file contains everything, Stone. And I mean everything. Warts and all. My whole life history. Not just my time in law enforcement, but from before I joined the Memphis PD. My school records are in there. Clubs I joined. Girls I dated. Every case I've ever worked. More than you need for a damn character reference. Give it a preface and you could call it a biography."

"So shoot me; I'm thorough." He raised his hands as far as the handcuffs would allow and made a whimsical face. "I'm joking . . . about the shoot me part."

"You didn't need to poke your nose into the lives of my children."

Stone shrugged, unimpressed by my snarl. "What do you want me to say? We're both guilty of excess. It's what men like you and me do every day of the week. In the name of justice, or fairness, or payback, or simply because we can. We push the envelope. Go where others fear to tread. That's what defines us, people like you and me. It separates us from the pack. We make the decisions others deem too tough. Then we act on them. Worry about the consequences later. Let's face it; half the bad guys we put away would still be roaming free if we didn't make those kinds of judgment calls. It doesn't mean we're wrong. It means we're good at our jobs. Sometimes the lines are there to be crossed. The world is a safer place because we do."

"Not with my kids. Even I know which lines are out of bounds."

Stone snorted. "Drop the holier than thou attitude, Quinn. You're no better than me. You've done your fair share of snooping around, using unconventional means to make your ends. We're the same, you and me. Cast from the same mold. You were in here prying into my personal things long before you discovered that file. I also know you checked out my FBI file on the system. So get to the point. I'm guessing there must be a good reason behind your

Bruce Willis impersonation. I'd like to hear it. See how well it defends this little breach of protocol."

I leaned forward, elbows on knees. "Why did you kill Forrest?"

"Because he was about to kill you. Obviously."

"You could have winged him."

"Aren't you glad that I didn't? He had a boulder hanging over your head, Quinn. If I hadn't killed him when I did, you'd be dead right now and we wouldn't be in this fix."

"You were wrong about him. The same way you were wrong about Connolly."

"And how on earth do you come to that conclusion?"

"Because Connolly and Forrest were stooges, working for a third man."

Stone drew an exasperated breath. "For the love of God, is that what this is all about? First you question the Connolly capture. Now you're saying Forrest wasn't the only killer. And, let's remember, that's taking into account everything you've seen with your own eyes." He looked at me with a look bordering on incredulity. "Bloody hell, Quinn, are you for real? Take a step back and look at the big picture. Everything points to Forrest being The Maestro. Everything."

"Same thing you said about Connolly."

"So they were in cahoots. Forrest went to the same school as half the victims. He knew Connolly. Connolly used his truck. He used Connolly. He had him guard the abandoned factory, while he tortured Zachary Innes. We found evidence of incarceration in his garage. Multiple blood trace. He murdered one of our agents in cold blood and hung her out to dry. You said yourself that Connolly wasn't capable of killing. We both know Forrest is – was. All the evidence points to him being The Maestro."

"Aside from the fact that Forrest wasn't smart enough."

There was a wry smile beginning to break on Stone's face. "Here's news for you, Quinn: not every killer is a genius. Sometimes being capable is all it takes."

"Even so, Forrest doesn't fit the visual description we have for The Maestro."

"Which description is that? The one that came from the only person to see his face and speak about it? And who would that be, Quinn? Rochelle Lewis? His girlfriend? Good God, has it ever crossed your mind that she may have played you?"

I didn't answer. Not because I didn't want to, but because I didn't have one.

Pretty much the whole of our artist's impression had come from Rochelle's description. Rochelle had known the killer by an alias: Travis Kimball. He was an on-the-road piano parts salesman, ostensibly supplying outlets up and down the West Coast – at least that's what he'd told her. One night in a bar in downtown LA, they'd gotten a thing going on. Rochelle had moved him in the very next day. According to her story, he'd used her place as somewhere to crash whenever his work brought him to town. A few weeks here and there over the course of a couple of years. Under interrogation, Rochelle had given up a good description of the man she knew as Travis Kimball: a well-built male in his late fifties, with a slight southern twang. Under protest, I'd made her sit with a sketch artist until he'd perfected the killer's likeness on paper – or at least the likeness Rochelle had wanted us to have. Since we'd had little else to go on, Rochelle's sketch had become the face of *The Maestro*. The face of our investigation. But Stone wanted me to believe she'd misinformed us from the get-go, that my image of the killer was a fake one.

"When did you shave your head?" I asked.

Stone snorted again, this time with surprise, "I'm sorry?"

"Your hair. When did you shave it all off and get your crew-cut?"

"What's that got to do with anything?"

"Because with hair you're not a million miles away from matching the artist's impression we got from Rochelle. Plus, your build and your age group are the same."

Stone's eyes squeezed into narrow slits. I sensed his mental cogs moving up a gear. Then his eyes flared wide and realization sparked in his pupils.

"Bloody hell," he began, "now I get it. You really are out of your mind, Quinn. You've convinced yourself that up is down and down is up and now everything's arse over tit."

We stared at each other for a moment. No give. No compromise. Stone was as set in his ways as I was. Two juggernauts rushing headlong toward an imminent collision.

"I know about your first cousin once removed," I said.

Stone's frown returned. I watched him do the math in his head, then smile brightly through his gloom.

"So you think you have it all figured out. Well, bully for you, Quinn. Now I understand what got you acting like a nutter. You think I'm involved in the murders. You think I'm him, don't you? After all we've been through. After everything that's come and gone, you think I'm this mysterious third person, don't you? You think I'm him. You think I'm bloody The Maestro."

The truth was out. No going back. Cards on the table. Face-up.

We both knew where we stood.

Somebody was going to lose.

"You were in San Diego eighteen months ago," I said, "during the first killings. Within driving distance. Your cousin's son was possibly the first and only victim to be released alive. That links you directly with the case,

Stone, *before* the original homicides. You tried pinning the blame on Connolly. You probably had Forrest kill Seeger because she'd embarrassed you, or she found something out. Maybe I was next. But then you were forced to silence Forrest before he could identify you. You even have piano ringtones on your phone and a baby grand in your hotel room. You're the right age, the right build. You certainly have the mental capacity for it. Add a mop of hair and you'd look the part. Then you went and got yourself assigned to the case the moment The Maestro popped up again. And I don't believe in coincidences. You can appreciate how it looks."

"And I suppose if it wasn't for my giveaway British accent, I'd fit your mental picture perfectly."

"I'm sure if you applied yourself you could fake a southern twang."

Stone nodded thoughtfully. "It's an interesting theory, Quinn. Completely wrong, of course, but certainly interesting. I can see how you'd arrive at the conclusion you have. It makes sense, from your blinkered point of view. But it doesn't mean you're right just because you think you are."

"So enlighten me."

Stone shrugged a lip. "Is there any point? It looks like you've already made your mind up. Judge, jury and executioner."

"Try me."

"For a start you're wrong about Christian. There's no big mystery there. I kept my cousin's son out of the investigation as a favor. My cousin asked me to keep it hush-hush. Asked me to keep Christian's rape out of the public arena."

"Why? To protect your cousin's father: Senator Stone?"

"No, Quinn, to protect his son. His vulnerable teenage son, who was abducted, tortured and brutally sodomized. Good God, Quinn, you're unbelievable. My cousin was concerned that our bringing it to the fore would have ruined his son's academic and social life. So I respected his wishes. And I would have done the same even if he hadn't been related to me. You have a son of your own. How far would you go to keep his secrets and protect him from public humility?"

There was an invisible hand choking my throat. A clammy claw strangling the life out of me. For a fearful moment I wondered how far Stone had dug into my own son's history. Wondered which skeletons he'd exhumed and run DNA tests on. In his own words, he was thorough. Had he unearthed my son's terrible secret? Did he suspect or even know the truth?

"I read Zimmerman's psyche evaluations," Stone continued. "I know you think everything's connected, that everything happens for a reason. The trouble with that conviction is that it makes everything contrived. It removes randomness and replaces it with purpose. Suddenly the insignificant becomes important. You start seeing patterns in the chaos. You become paranoid. Delusional. You start believing your own conspiracy theories. That's why you think I'm The Maestro, the man who murdered your wife in cold blood. Not because you have undeniable evidence, but because your overwhelming refusal to deal with reality has effectively blinded you to the truth. Your lines got blurred, Quinn. You crossed them without even realizing they were there."

I picked up the Glock.

"And now you're going to kill me in cold blood, too, in revenge for your murdered wife. Go ahead, Quinn. Man-up and pull the bloody trigger. It won't be the first life-changing mistake you've ever made. And I guarantee it won't be the last."

I raised the gun and pointed it at his face. "I want to hear it from your own mouth. A confession."

"Never going to happen."

My cell jangled in my pocket. I ignored it. It jangled some more. I ignored it some more.

"You should answer that," Stone said. "No one rings this time in the morning unless it's an emergency."

The phone continued to ring.

I leaned back in the chair, keeping the gun aimed on Stone while I glanced at the display on the cell: *Grace.*

My heart burned. I jammed the phone to my ear.

"Gracie, is everything okay?"

"Daddy." She sounded upset, distraught. Like she'd been sobbing uncontrollably.

"Gracie? What's happened? Is it the hurricane? Are you okay?"

Suddenly my mind was overrun with all kinds of scary thoughts about the approaching storm and Grace being in dire straits. But then a new kind of fear gripped me as I listened to her next words:

"Daddy. The Maestro is here. You have to come to Florida. Please hurry. I love you, Daddy. Please hurry!"

The line went dead.

I stared at the screen as a volcanic geyser of fear and rage plumed in my chest. Every thought in sudden disarray. Every nerve vibrating.

The cell buzzed in my hand. A text message, sent from Grace's phone:

'Listen to your daughter. If you want her to live, you will do exactly as I say. Do not call this number until you arrive in Florida. Be here in five hours or Grace dies.'

It was signed with the letter X.

Two crossing lines – like the signature marks on the faces of every one of *The Maestro's* victims.

81

A woman's whispering voice, not hers:

"*Let go . . .*"

Her struggle was over. Her strength sapped. Her will to cling to this crumb of an existence crushed by defeat.

Her end was near. Her transition from this world to the next all but transacted.

A woman's whispering voice, not hers:

"*Let go . . .*"

Her time had come.

Her finger-hold on reality slipped and the darkness swept her consciousness away.

It was strangely exciting.

82

All flights coming in and out of Southwest International in Fort Myers had been cancelled or rerouted. All aircraft already on the airport apron had been grounded until further notice. The worst storm this decade was bearing down on the Florida Gulf Coast, making air flight a virtual impossibility. Only the brave or the foolhardy would risk flying through wind speeds in excess of ninety miles per hour, straight into the fury of a hurricane. I didn't know which category I fell into. Definitely of the desperate kind.

My attention was divided between the unrelenting turbulence buffeting the Gulfstream jet and Mason Stone who was sitting facing me, eyes closed.

The plane was pitching and yawing like a raft on a swollen sea. Dropping hundreds of feet between wind gusts, only to climb steeply and fall again. It was gut-wrenching, nauseating stuff. Worst rollercoaster ride in history. Stone had slept through most of it, napping like a baby as the jet had rocketed over the southwestern States and careened out across the wind-whipped Gulf. I hadn't.

My fingers were coiled around the armrests. Had been all the while. I could taste something nasty in the back of my throat, but not wholly thanks to our seesawing ride. I was desperately aware of each minute slipping by. Each minute bringing me closer to the deadline thrown down by *The Maestro*. A deadline involving the death of my daughter. The closer we got, the steelier became my resolve to end his reign of terror once and for all.

My befuddled brain still couldn't compute the fact that the killer had Grace. But it did confirm my theory of a third person controlling Forrest and Connolly. While we had been sidetracked with his underlings, *The Maestro* had fled California and turned up in Florida. It was all part of his dance macabre of killing Hope, then my children, then me.

As personal as it gets.

I hadn't let Stone off the hook. Not entirely.

The Maestro had abducted Grace. I couldn't dispute that fact; I'd heard it from my daughter's own lips. But my gut still told me I couldn't trust Stone. Receiving a call from the killer while I was interrogating Stone seemed convenient, farfetched, planned. I wasn't buying Stone's innocence. There was something he wasn't telling me. I could sense it. Feel it. Maybe he was the orchestrator, *The Maestro*, and there was a fourth member of his kill team waiting for us in Florida. Someone he'd sent out there to misdirect me and throw me off the scent. A confession wasn't imminent. And proving it would take precious time I didn't have.

I'd asked God to forgive me for abandoning Sheryl, but my priority now was saving Grace. Retribution came a close second.

I'd called LAX Departures from Stone's hotel suite. Learned there was a flight lockdown on all southeast air traffic. Nothing coming in or out because of the hurricane. Stone had suggested we use the FBI charter – on the condition he came along. I'd mulled it over, for about five seconds. The Bureau could overrule the flight ban. We could enter the no-fly zone, at our own peril. But the jet wouldn't fly without Stone's approval. It was the only way I could get there ahead of the killer's deadline. I'd removed Stone's cuffs and kept a safe distance between us. He'd called a truce and then driven us at speed in his Mustang to LAX. I'd kept his Glock on him the whole time. Hadn't given it back. We hadn't spoken more than a handful of words in almost four hours. I didn't mind.

Sooner or later I'd uncover his role.

I watched him as he dozed. No snoring. I wasn't sure if he was really sleeping or just avoiding having to face my accusations.

Stone had instructed the pilot to get us to Florida without delay. The pilot had taken the Gulfstream to its maximum altitude – an almost vertical climb before leveling out. The thinner atmosphere meant less drag, and less drag meant quicker speeds. He shaved a whole thirty minutes off the normal flight time, which was then gobbled up as soon as we descended into the turbulent skies clogging up the Gulf.

The whole flight, I'd wrung hands and run through all kinds of scenarios in my mind. Chastised myself for failing to protect Grace better than I had. By resuming my hunt for *The Maestro*, I'd allowed a killer into her life. Now he was threatening to do to her what he'd done to her mother. And I couldn't get there quick enough.

My child needed me. I'd do whatever necessary to protect her. Kill, if I had to.

I spent the final descent urging time to slow down. It felt like the jet was about to be crushed by the violent winds and sent plummeting into the wave-torn waters below. It was impossible to see where the thunderstorms gave way to the hurricane. In some fairy tale rendering in my mind's eye, I had imagined being able to see the gargantuan wall of cloud being rotated by ferocious winds. But this was no tornado. Twisters are localized, causing immediate destruction within seconds to everything they touch. We've all seen them on the TV, gobbling up barns and throwing around cars as if they were toys. Hurricanes are different. They are mostly wind and rain. Their destructive force comes through prolonged pressure, usually against manmade structures. Their influence is widespread and can be accompanied by storm surges in sea level. This particular hurricane had a diameter greater than a couple of hundred miles. Even at this distance, the weather system tearing up the Gulf was a single dark gray

Keith Houghton

malevolent mass. Shapeless up close. Every so often I glimpsed sheet lightning briefly illuminating chaotic cloud decks. It looked like a scene from a disaster movie.

Our descent forced us through clouds moving so fast they blurred. The jet slewed and shook. Metal creaked. Cabin lights blinked. I pulled my safety belt tight enough to cut off circulation. Gripped the armrests with white-knuckled claws. The plane lurched and recoiled as the winds tried to snatch it out of the sky. Visibility zero. The pilot slapped the plane onto the runway so hard it jarred bones. The jet bounced a few times and fishtailed all over the tarmac before the brakes grabbed the wheels and burned away our speed.

I swallowed down acid.

Stone's eyes flickered open. He yawned and checked his watch. "Bloody hell. We couldn't have cut it closer if we'd tried."

It was almost six in the morning, California time – almost nine in the morning here in Florida. Minutes to *The Maestro's* deadline. I speed-dialed Grace's cell number while the jet taxied toward the terminal building.

Her phone rang twice before she picked up.

"Grace, it's me. I'm here, in Florida. Against all odds. Are you okay? Grace, tell him I'm here. I made it."

"Daddy." She sounded scared. No tears this time. Just fear choking up her voice. But she was alive. "You have to come to the island. Please hurry."

The line went dead.

83

Before leaving LAX, Stone had called ahead to the Miami Field Office. Requested a man and a car to be ready at our disposal. Our pilot popped open the Gulfstream's hatch and we scurried through torrential rain toward the waiting Dodge Durango.

The sky was a cauldron lid, marbled with feathers of whiter cloud, moving fast.

"Sanibel Island," I told the driver. "Fast as you can."

The driver hit the gas and we sped out of the airport, hurtling westbound on Daniels Parkway through a driving downpour.

Bullet rain peppered the windows, reducing visibility.

We raced along deserted streets toward the barrier islands. Stores and businesses shuttered and braced against the fierce weather. I could see trees bending backward under the force of the winds, then snapping straight and bending the opposite way. Leaves and loosened debris swooping though the air. Traffic signals jiggling on plucked cables. The storms had turned the roads into rivers. It was after nine in the morning but it looked like nine in the evening. Dark as dusk. Last time I'd seen this place it had been melting under a sweltering sky. Now it was drowning under a deluge of razor-wire rain.

A text message chimed on my cell. More instructions from *The Maestro*. It was the image of a street map seen from overhead, copied from the Internet. I recognized the layout: the Sanibel road system, with Periwinkle Way cutting through the middle. There was a red marker in the northwest quadrant. A red flag halfway along Wildlife Drive. It was the wooden observation tower in the Wildlife Refuge.

Be here within the hour or your daughter dies.'

"Go faster," I urged at the driver. "Don't stop for anything."

The only other vehicles out and about were police cruisers and EMS vehicles, their roof lights flashing bright against the twilight as they rushed to one emergency after the other. We were doing eighty, easy. We had our grille lights blinking and the cops turned a blind eye as we raced southbound on the rain-slicked US-41. We shot past the hotel where Snakeskin had partaken in a lethal drug-and-sex bondage party, just days ago. Lights out everywhere. Drainage systems struggling to draw off pooling water from the curbsides. No one on the streets. No traffic. Everything braced for impact. End of the world.

The Maestro had abducted Grace from her apartment in Fort Myers and taken her to Sanibel. Probably kicking and screaming. I didn't know why, except as bait to get me here. Then what?

I didn't want to think any further. My first and only priority was ensuring Grace lived. Call it parental prerogative. If I became a casualty of the war to keep her alive, so be it. My child's life was worth more than mine, any day.

We hit the final stretch before the Causeway.

I was as tense as a coiled spring and grinding teeth.

Our driver notched the Durango's speed into triple figures. The sound of rainwater spraying out from beneath the tires was like nails against a chalkboard. Once or twice the vehicle aquaplaned as it flew through flooded intersections with signals blazing red. All the while I clung to the door handle, the clammy claw still clutching at my throat. I didn't want to die before saving Grace.

I caught a glimpse of wave-peaked waters through oscillating trees: a roiling, cratered moonscape of battleship gray flecked with white.

Through sheeting rain I could see the toll station up ahead. There was a police cruiser parked across the SunPass express lanes, its red-and-blue light-bar illuminating the darkened checkpoint. Our driver eased off the gas and slowed our mad dash. A cop in a weatherproof smock emerged, waving a flashlight. He struggled over to the window.

I rolled it down. Rain blasted into the cabin.

"No access beyond this point," he shouted.

I showed him my FBI badge, yelled: "Federal emergency."

He shook his head. "You don't understand. There's a jackknifed semi on its side, halfway up the first bridge. It's wedged in tight against the retaining walls. You can't get through until it's been cleared. And we can't get a lift in here until the storm passes."

"Let us through," Stone shouted. "We'll make our own way round."

"All right," the patrolman nodded, "but it's your funeral."

I slid the window shut. The cop struggled back to his cruiser and backed it out of the way. We accelerated though the toll point and started to climb the first and highest humpbacked bridge leading to Sanibel.

A panorama of gray-black chaos opened up around us. Tormented waters and tormented skies. Impossible to determine where one ended and the other began.

About fifty yards from the apex, a silver tractor-trailer with a big red engine lay on its side, completely blocking the roadway.

Our driver hit the brake a few yards short.

I forced open the door and climbed out into the battering gale. Heard Stone doing the same. Rain roared. Wind tried to blow me off the bridge. I stooped over to the crashed rig, drenched to the bone within seconds.

The semi-truck had been caught by a sudden gust as it had cleared the crest. There were skid marks and abrasion scuffs all the way down the incline where it had slid downhill before jamming itself tight against the walls. Behind it, a line of abandoned vehicles trailed all the way back up the bridge and down the other side, their occupants long since evacuated on foot.

There was no way through – at least not by car.

I checked my watch. Forty minutes until *The Maestro's* deadline. Forty minutes until he killed Grace. And at least another six miles to go, and in calamitous conditions.

We wouldn't make it.

Grace wouldn't make it.

"Quinn!"

I turned to see Stone holding a bulletproof vest, with another tucked under his arm. He was soaked, like me, shirt clinging, rain dribbling down his screwed-up face.

"Your jacket said you were a runner," he yelled. "Any good?"

"Good enough," I yelled back. "How about you? Your jacket said you used to do triathlons. Reckon you can run six miles in a hurricane?"

"I'm English, remember? Rain is in my blood. If not, I'll die trying."

We sealed ourselves inside the blue Kevlar vests.

Stone stuck out a hand. "Give me my gun." He saw my distrusting look and added: "Don't be a fool, Quinn; this has gone far enough. I can help. Let me. If he really does have Grace then we're going to need all the firepower we can get. If your suspicions about me turn out to be correct, you have my permission to shoot me."

Reluctantly, I handed it over.

Stone instructed our driver to go find the nearest shelter. Then we clambered through the couplings connecting the silver trailer to the tractor rig and started the long run to save Grace.

84

It was like running in lead-lined boots while elastic restraints pulled first one way and then the other. Hard wind smacking the air from our lungs. Windswept rain stinging our faces. Five feet forward, four feet back.

Out in the Gulf, the hurricane was close to making landfall. Close to slamming headlong into the Florida coastline like an ocean liner running aground. Ripping up anything not properly secured.

And we were running to meet it head-on.

What made us think we'd fare any better?

We descended the incline, passing the long line of abandoned vehicles, fighting against the fierce gale tying to pluck us off the bridge. It was strength-sapping stuff. Horizontal rain hammering like shotgun pellets. The intracoastal waters flowing northward around Sanibel were crashing into the causeway cays and sweeping over the roadway. We splashed our way across, dodging javelin palm fronds as we went.

I ran in sneakers weighted by water. Half-blinded by the relentless rain. Keeping pace with Stone. Head down. Pounding the road. Even so, it took over ten minutes to reach the middle bridge. Already, I was feeling the strain. Stone looked like he had more miles left in him. At this rate we'd never get to Grace in time. Running five miles in this storm was impossible.

Then something occurred to me. It came from nowhere. A spark of inspiration. I dug out my phone and called Jack. I had no idea if he'd answer, or if he'd kept to his word and stayed on the island despite the evacuation order. But if he had and he was mobile, he could come pick us up.

Miraculously, he answered after a dozen rings.

"Jack. Where are you? Tell me you didn't leave the island and you're still at home."

He was. Second miracle in a row. He was barricaded in the house on Rabbit Road, like a fugitive hiding from the authorities. Hurriedly, I explained the situation. Shouted it above the wind roar, then strained to hear Jack's words drowned in hiss and crackle. After several expletives, he told me he'd be with us just as soon as nature would allow.

"Your island buddy?" Stone shouted as we attacked the second bridge.

"Jack Heckscher's a good friend," I called back.

"Can you trust him to get here in time?"

"With my life."

I could see small boats on rolling swells. Yachts with broken masts, loosened from their moorings and being carried away by the fast-moving water. One or two capsized, colliding with the bridge supports.

In the far distance, cowering behind a gray shawl, I could see Sanibel Island being consumed by the hurricane's ravenous maw. A speckled cloud of broken vegetation and airborne debris swirling above it like forest-fire smoke.

"You still think I'm The Maestro, don't you?"

I glanced at Mason Stone. He was breathing easy – clearly fitter than he looked. Fitter than me. Everything fluid. "Let's just say I'm reserving judgment."

"You're wrong, you know."

"Maybe."

"We don't all have dark secrets, Quinn."

Again, I glanced his way.

Suddenly, Stone slowed and came to a stop.

I continued a few yards on.

"I know about your son," he called.

Then I dug in my heels and spun round to face him.

Raging wind clawed at us. Stinging rain sleeted against our skin. Water swirled across the slick road surface, forming miniature tornados.

We faced each other like two gunslingers in a shoot-out, sodden and disheveled, with a half dozen yards and a thousand lies between us.

"We don't have time for this, Stone."

"On the contrary. I think now's the perfect time. Out here. In the middle of nowhere. Where there's no one to eavesdrop."

"Leave it, Stone. We need to go. Right now. I'm serious. Grace's life is on the line."

"I know about his condition," Stone breathed. His words were torn from his lips and smacked against my ear. He waited for a response. When it didn't come, he continued: "I know he walked out on his wife and son – your grandson – and has never been seen or heard from again since. I know he has a dark secret, Quinn. Your boy. I know what he's done. And I know you've covered it up."

I was stunned by Stone's revelation. I felt exposed, violated. Most of all, I felt caught. "How long have you known?"

"Long enough. It's over, Quinn. Finished. For both of you. When we're done here, I intend to make it my priority to hunt your son down and bring him to justice. You can bank on that."

A red mist descended over everything.

Stone knew my son's terrible secret. *My* terrible secret.

Without rational thought, I got out the Glock and unloaded the full clip into Stone's chest.

85

The gunshots were lost in the howling wind. As each bullet slammed into him, Stone was jerked backwards across the bridge. Blue fabric puffed on his Kevlar vest. I stepped forward, repeatedly squeezing the trigger. Aim deadly in spite of the gale. Like a marionette whose wires were being reeled in, Stone staggered under the force of the impacts. The back of his thighs hit the concrete retaining wall. He stared with a mixture of shock and confusion as another succession of rounds buried themselves into his sternum. Then momentum was pulling him over the edge. He started to fall. I kept pulling the trigger, walking toward him until the clip was empty. His legs came up, and then gravity sucked him down, over the bridge. I reached the balustrade in time to see him hit the bloated waters far below. A small white splash, then nothing.

What had I done?

86

The swift current swept him under the bridge. I ran slantwise to the opposite side of the roadway and peered down at the churning water. I didn't know if Stone had survived the fall, or if he could even keep afloat in the stormy surge. If he were alive, surely it wouldn't be for long. No one could survive in that swollen sea. Not even with a bulletproof vest acting as a life preserver. Rip currents were creating treacherous whirlpools. Waves blistering and crashing into one another as the advancing hurricane strangled the intracoastal waters, forcing more volume into the channel than it could cope with. I ejected the spent clip and replaced it with a full one. Stowed the Glock and gripped the concrete wall as I scanned the writhing waters below. I thought I caught sight of Stone as the surge swept north – an arm and a fragment of blue vest being sucked beneath a swell – but I couldn't say for sure.

What had I done?

87

I ran on. Fast as I could against the switchback winds. Pulled to and fro. Eyes stinging. Legs pumping like pistons. I was ignoring the searing acid building up in my muscles. Making painful headway. No time to think about anything other than the coming encounter.

But I couldn't help it.

I had just killed a federal agent in cold blood.

A moment of pure madness, unforgivable.

A death penalty for the criminally insane, for sure.

All to protect my children.

How could I even begin to explain my actions?

I'd murdered an innocent man.

It was indefensible.

How could I live with myself after that?

I'd had a choice, but I wasn't giving myself any option.

I had a deadline to beat.

I had a daughter to save.

My own freedom was a small price to pay for her life.

Demons snapped at my heels as I sprinted toward the coming storm.

88

I noticed the headlights of Jack's Range Rover long before I saw the vehicle itself. It came tearing down the middle of the final bridged roadway like a lime green bowling ball. I stood stock still with one foot planted either side of the unbroken divider lines, and waved tired arms, gasping to keep the air in my lungs.

I'd cleared the remainder of the middle bridge and the second swamped cay in little less than fifteen minutes. It was like running through syrup.

I was desperately aware of the precious seconds slipping into history.

Still so far to go and so little time to get there.

The Range Rover performed a perfect half pirouette twenty yards short and came sliding to a standstill, facing the opposite way.

I loped over and yanked open the passenger door, crowded inside. I was saturated, dripping rainwater all over the leather upholstery, panting. I must have looked like a drowned rat. Maybe I was.

"Welcome back to Florida, big guy." Jack shouted as he stamped on the accelerator.

The SUV slithered back toward the island. Back into the jaws of the hurricane.

The windows started steaming up.

I put the air-conditioning on full heat and full fan, and mopped rain off my face.

Jack glanced my way. He was wearing a black wet suit, with his shaggy gray hair fixed up in a short ponytail. "Jesus, Mary and Joseph, big guy," he said, "what the hell happened back there? You okay?"

"I'll live."

"I thought you had company? What happened to the other guy?"

"Something unexpected," I answered flatly.

I sensed Jack's questioning eyes search for an elaboration, but my eyes were fixed on the road ahead.

By now, a drowned Mason Stone would be on his way to Captiva or even snagged up somewhere in the mangroves. Maybe at the head of the Wulfert Keys Trail. A broken body, suspended in the watery stampede. Another bloated corpse, destined to be washed up on a picturesque beach and pecked at by gulls.

With my bullets buried in his Kevlar vest.

What had happened to me?

I'd snapped. It was inevitable, I guess. I'd run away to Florida, hoping to keep a lid on the pressure pot boiling away inside of me. Something had to give. In time, everything does. The only thing required is a weak vessel.

I'd killed Mason Stone.

In cold blood.

I was no better than any of the evil lowlifes I'd made a career out of putting behind bars.

"Big guy?"

I blinked, refocused. "What's with the wet suit?" I asked.

"Survival. I figured I could cope better with the storm surge if I dressed appropriately. I even have flippers in the trunk. This is seriously screwed up. You know that, don't you, big guy? Where's he holding her?"

"The observation tower on Wildlife Drive." My voice was a monotone, my gaze distant.

"Great. He would go and choose just about the hardest place to get to right now. You better hold tight there, big guy. Half the island's under water; it's going to be a fun ride."

Water drilled out from under the Range Rover's wheels as we sped onto the island.

Sanibel was a mess. It looked like a bomb had gone off. Splintered trees down all over the place. Sparking power lines draped across the pavement. Snapped power poles. Windblown debris flapping in the sidewalk vegetation. Storefront awnings dangling pendulously on wire tethers. Holes in roofs where loose tiles had flown away like startled birds. Altogether, a disaster area.

The partnership of torrential rain and storm surge had all but submerged the roadway. At best, it was under a foot of muddy water. At worst, it was deep enough in parts to kill the electronics in the Range Rover's engine.

Jack found a solution: he avoided the deeper pools by mounting the sidewalk. Broken palms everywhere. The Range Rover crunched its way through, headlights picking out debris. Hard rain clattering against the windows. Ballistic branches slapping against the metalwork. The approaching hurricane was a gathering growl, louder than the in-car air-conditioning, reducing visibility down to just a few yards.

This was madness. I was keenly aware of the seconds ticking by. Even if we managed to save Grace from *The Maestro*, we still had the impending hurricane to contend with. We'd be lucky to come through the other side alive and in one piece. Maybe we wouldn't. Maybe we'd join Stone in his watery grave. Maybe it was karma.

I kept hold of my bile and clung on. Rightly or wrongly, I pushed Stone's falling body and his wounded expression to the back of my mind.

Finally, we arrived at the wildlife refuge.

The wire-mesh access gate at the head of Wildlife Drive was half-open. Jack didn't slow. It clanged deafeningly against the hood as we barged through. The tires found a better bite on the asphalt conglomerate lining the dike and we accelerated out into the bayou.

No flooding up here – which meant Jack could floor it. And he did. The Range Rover sprinted along the Drive, punched by wind and pelted by rain. The deadly combination of high tide and storm surge had swollen the previously shallow mangrove waters surrounding the dike. Now they were almost level with the elevated road surface – a choppy inland sea covered in floating flotsam. Mangroves half-submerged. Reed beds completely drowned. No signs of any indigenous wildlife whatsoever.

"You going to answer that?"

I glanced at Jack. "What?"

"Your phone. It's ringing. It could be Grace."

I hadn't heard it warbling away; too busy thinking darkling thoughts. I jammed it to my ear without checking the caller ID.

"Quinn. Can you hear me?" The line was bad. Crackling. "It's Sheriff Torres. Are you there?" Her voice ebbed in and out. "Quinn?"

"I can hear you – just about. This is a bad time. Can I call you back? I'm right in the middle of a life and death situation."

"That's why I'm calling you, Quinn. Don't hang up on me; this is important. I mean it. I know it's all action stations at the moment, with the state of emergency, but I made you a promise and I'm keeping to it." She heard my silence and added: "The body washed up on Bowman's Beach – the DNA results came in."

"I really don't have time right now –"

"Quinn, hear me out. Don't hang up. I mean it. You need to know this. The DNA profile corresponds to a retired police officer. A cop from Houston." There was a pregnant pause filled with surging static. "Quinn, I don't know how to say this except to just say it. This retired cop from Houston – the body on the beach – his name was Jack Heckscher."

89

Far away, I heard Sheriff Torres say: "Quinn, are you there? Quinn? Answer me, dammit! Quinn!"

Her voice was lost in the tornado screaming between my ears.

My mind had hit a brick wall and rebounded with a bang. Instantly punch-drunk. Brain-mashed. Everything reeling. Thoughts taking flight and beating it like spooked birds. It felt like God had reached down and squeezed the life out of me.

"Trouble?" Jack asked as we bounced over a humped crosswalk. "Big guy?"

"I'm here," I breathed into the phone.

Sheriff Torres sounded troubled, "Quinn, listen to me. There's no mistake. I checked twice, personally. It's his DNA. It matches his police records. The corpse currently residing in the Lee County Coroner's Office is that of Jack Heckscher. Your roommate. Where are you?"

My words came out of their own volition: "On Sanibel, heading for the observation tower on Wildlife Drive." It sounded like somebody else's voice. Somewhere far away. Grave.

Everything was spinning.

Torres sounded panicked, "Oh my God. Quinn, you need to get off the island! The storm's going to hit any minute! What are you doing out there?"

"Saving Grace from The Maestro."

I tossed the phone onto the dash and turned to face my friend, the man I knew as Jack Heckscher.

The clammy claw wrapped around my throat reached in and punched me in the gut.

90

The sky was almost black, crossed by lines of fast-moving vapor streams.

The hurricane was poised for impact. So was I.

In the distance, out toward San Carlos Bay, I could see whole stretches of mangroves being torn from their sediment beds and sucked skywards before being ripped apart by the high-speed winds.

We were on a collision course.

No backing down now.

We'd come too far.

Do or die.

We rounded a curve in the Drive and hit the long meandering straight leading to the cross-dike. Wheels slithered over littered leaf debris.

The heel of my palm was on the butt of the Glock.

Jack became conscious of my staring. "What?"

"When were you going to tell me?"

"Tell you what, big guy?"

"That you killed the real Jack Heckscher."

Jack – or at least the person I'd come to know as Jack – glanced my way, gray eyes narrowing. He kept his foot planted firmly on the gas. Big hands wrapped around the steering wheel. Knuckles white. There was a deep furrow screwing up his brow and bewilderment contracting his pupils.

"What's that supposed to mean?"

"You know exactly what I'm saying."

"No, no, I don't. Okay, I get this is a high-stress situation, but you're talking like a crazy person. You take a knock to the head on your way here, big guy?"

"That was the Sheriff," I said, coolly. "The DNA results just came back for the body washed-up on Bowman's Beach. Remember the body? You should do; it's your body, Jack."

A confused glance. "That's impossible."

"Is it? You tell me. The results don't lie. According to Torres the DNA's a perfect match. She double-checked. Who are you, really?"

Another glance: this time I could see fear leaking through the confusion. "Look, Torres has got her lines crossed. Either she's mistaken or somebody's messed up big time. I'm Jack Heckscher. It's me, big guy: your best buddy. You have to believe me. Jesus, Mary and Joseph, this is crazyville on crack. Gabe, you know me: I'm the dude who saved your life, remember?"

"I remember. I also remember Doc Osman guesstimating on the timeframe when the body went in the swamp, which wasn't long after I came to Sanibel. You kept it in the chest freezer, didn't you? Under the house. You killed the real Jack Heckscher when you came to the island. Assumed his identity. Then when you asked me to move in, you had to get rid of the body. Cart the corpse down the Wulfert Keys Trail and dispose of it. Hope the gators would eat the evidence. The wristband they found didn't say Celebrity Cop. It said Charity Cop. Something a real cop might wear – even a retired one."

Jack's complexion was insipid. "So now you take Torres' word over mine?"

"You can't dispute DNA."

"You can if it was faked." His eyes flicked from the road, to me and back. "Will you look at us? Fighting when we should be concentrating on saving Grace. For chrissakes, big guy, can't you see what's happening here? I'm being set up. The both of us. Someone's switched the results."

"Why would anyone do such a thing?"

"To plant doubt in your mind. Turn you against me. See, it's worked, hasn't it?"

"Who would want to do something like that?"

"Somebody with an ulterior motive, that's who. Somebody with access to the FBI database. Somebody who could switch the records around. Make you believe anything they wanted you to."

"You have a particular somebody in mind?"

"Yeah. That British guy: Mason Stone. You said he was good for all this. He's the one. He must have caught you snooping and sent you a red herring."

Mason Stone. The mention of him brought with it a flood of icy guilt. It washed over me, bitter to the taste. Left me feeling chilled despite the heat coming from the blowers.

The Range Rover flew over the speed hump where the cross-dike met the Drive. Our heads almost collided with the roof.

The estuary was unrecognizable. Impossible to define where the swamp ended and the open waters began. The storm surge had breached the silt islands protecting the bayou from Pine Island Sound and started to flow inland, drowning the mangroves in swirling saltwater.

Suddenly the observation tower was in sight through the downpour. In spite of the wild winds it was still standing: a two-tiered wooden construction of platforms, slopes and steps, topped with a pointed canopy.

There was a car parked alongside it: a dark red sedan.

Jack stood on the brakes and the Range Rover slid to a standstill. I popped my seatbelt. He went to unbuckle his.

"Don't," I said.

"This is all about saving a daughter," he growled. "We can iron out our petty differences later."

I showed him the heel of my Glock. "Don't force my hand, Jack – or whatever your name is. This is my fight.

Not yours. Stay here. I mean it. Or you'll pay a high price for crossing me. I'll deal with you when I get back."

"You need me, big guy," he breathed fiercely as I shouldered open the passenger door. "We're a team."

I ignored him, and bailed out into the screaming mouth of hell.

It sounded like a dozen jumbo jets screaming by overhead all at once. Machine-gun rain firing on flat trajectories.

There was a human shape on the uppermost platform, under the wooden canopy.

I bounded straight for the steps, clattered up the creaking woodwork. I cleared the first platform and hauled myself up the next flight to the second floor, came out onto the slippery top deck a foot behind the Glock.

"Daddy!"

"Gracie!"

My daughter was alive! Her kidnapper had tied her to a thick stanchion supporting the canopy and the wraparound handrail. Wires fixed her wrists and ankles to the waterlogged wood. She was wringing wet. Blonde hair plastered to her head and face. Tears mixed with rain.

But she was alive!

I started toward her, then stopped, dead, when I realized there was another person standing to one side, holding a gun to Grace's head.

It was her abductor: *The Maestro.*

But this wasn't the craggy, middle-aged murderer. This wasn't Rochelle's artist impression incarnate, or even the guy who'd beaten me to a pulp in her backyard.

It was another of *The Maestro's* brainwashed accomplices:

A woman, wearing a windbreaker and an arrogant expression.

Someone I recognized instantly.

Someone who should never have been here.

I raised the Glock to head height and leveled it at the grinning face of Sheryl Klaussner.

91

"You made it!" she hollered above the gale. "And just in the nick of time, too. Way to go, detective. That was some trip, wasn't it? Congratulations! It's great to see you again, by the way."

My thoughts were all over the place, like the windblown wreckage careering across the malevolent sky. I was unable to process the reality standing before me. One of those moments where the jaw drops and refuses to come back up.

It had never occurred to me that Sheryl – *the one that got away* – had been instrumental in the Piano Wire Murders, and clearly still was. Never crossed my mind that her tale of abduction, torture and plight for freedom had all been a cleverly-constructed act, designed to mislead us and send our investigation in the wrong direction. A ruse. But that's exactly what she'd done. I knew that in the first moment I'd laid eyes on her. Sheryl Klaussner had played us all with her frightened victim routine. Most of all, she'd fooled me.

I rocked on squishy heels, shifting weight and balance to compensate for the violent gusts trying to rip my clothes off.

"I can see it's going to take you a while catching up, detective," she shouted. "Heck, I bet I'm the last person in the world you expected to see here. You thought you were coming to face-off with my father, didn't you?"

"Your father?"

More information that made about as much sense to me as Mandarin.

"Your nemesis," she explained, the words being torn from her lips by the wind. "The one you've been tirelessly chasing all this time. Don't you get it? My father's The Maestro. You could say we're a father and daughter kill team." She beamed. It looked demonic. I didn't like it. "Wow, that feels so uplifting finally admitting it out loud."

I trained the iron sights on the shoulder of Sheryl's arm holding the gun to Grace's head. "Let my daughter go!" I ordered. "I mean it, Sheryl. We all need to get out of here, right now. The full force of the hurricane's about to hit. If we stay, we're all going to die. Now let my daughter go!"

"Or you'll do what – you'll shoot? That's a pretty risky thing to do, detective. Unless you're a crack shot, this wind will have its own way with your bullet. Very likely take your daughter's head off. Besides, you're not exactly in a position to make demands now, are you?"

I felt something cold and sharp press against my windpipe.

"Don't even think about it," a gruff voice barked in my ear.

I moved a fraction of an inch, involuntarily, as the wind thrashed. The sharp object stung my skin, drawing blood. It was a blade. Tempered steel. I saw a long arm reach over my shoulder and pluck the Glock from my hands. Then my assailant came round to face me, keeping the nasty tip of a long Bowie knife needling at my throat.

"I believe the two of you have been introduced already," Sheryl shouted against the thundering gale. "But maybe not properly. So allow me to do the honors. Detective Quinn, aka the Celebrity Cop, meet my father Jacob Klaussner, aka The Maestro."

I stared at the man I knew as Jack Heckscher – at the man I had grown to think of as my closest friend in the whole of the world – at the man who had killed my wife and my life.

The blood in my veins was just about reaching boiling point.

92

All this time Hope's killer had been right under my nose. Within touching distance. Breathing the same air. Living under the same roof. Taking up my time in more ways than one. The realization was razing. I'd befriended her murderer. Lived in his home. Guzzled beer and shared banter like old time buddies. Confided in him. Trusted him. Built up a relationship. Become good friends. All this time Hope's killer had been right under my nose. Within touching distance. Sharing the good times. Empathizing with the bad. The comprehension was crippling.

93

The man I'd known as Jack Heckscher kept the knife-tip pressed against my throat. "No more shadow-boxing," he shouted. "The truce is over."

It was an effort to keep the blade there in the writhing wind. One especially strong gust and it would take a slice out of my Adam's apple.

"Feels good, doesn't it?" he continued. "Kind of liberating. No more secrets. Everything out on the table. Like the weight of the world just got lifted." He studied me with his cold gray eyes. Raindrops slithering down the black rubber of his wetsuit. "Didn't I tell you I knew where your children lived, and that if you came looking for me there'd be a mighty price to pay? But you couldn't leave it alone, could you? You just had to continue your personal crusade, no matter what the cost – to you or your kids. Now look where it's brought you. A whisker away from death, and not just yours. Well, I sure hope it was worth it, big guy. You're both going to die here today. Happy now?"

Far from it. Betrayed. Used. Cheated. Belittled. Deceived. Any number of bad feelings were bombarding my brain and sucker-punching everything I thought I knew into everything I knew I didn't. There wasn't a single molecule of happiness in any fiber of my being right now. Just a geyser of pure hate surging to the surface.

"Why?" I breathed.

One word, demanding a thousand in answer. I wanted to hear it from his lips. Learn why this man who I had trusted with my life had led me a merry dance the way he had. Why he'd killed my wife, then befriended me, then betrayed me. For the life of me I couldn't think of a believable motive other than sheer evil.

A smile pulled at his lips, "Because."

"Because, what?"

"Because, that's it. No big mystery. Just because I could. Let's just say the temptation was too great. When you showed up on the fishing pier that day I almost leapt in the water. When I realized you weren't there because of me, well, I guess you've heard the phrase about keeping your enemies closer." He rotated the Bowie knife so that it gouged a nick out of my neck. "Now take out your handcuffs."

"That your plan?" I growled. "To leave us here for the hurricane to tear us limb from limb?"

"Why, do you have a better idea?"

My fists were balled. Pulse throbbing. I wanted to tear his head off. Beat his sick brain to a pulp. Stamp him out of existence. I hadn't bargained on this: on being the gazelle, staring into the merciless eyes of the lion. Not just me. Grace, too. My stupidity had gotten us both killed.

No father should ever feel those feelings.

I couldn't let it happen.

I stared into *The Maestro's* cold gray eyes as the granite wind tore at us and the barbed rain whipped at our faces.

Behind him, on the far side of the deluged estuary, the sky seethed. I could see a storm surge bulldozing toward us, drowning everything in its path.

Not much time. Minutes, if we were lucky.

Insanely, I leaned into the blade. Sharp pain leapt up my neck as the tip sliced through skin.

The Maestro rocked back on his heels under the sudden pressure.

He was expecting me to lie down, to die.

I wasn't the only one here to be wrong.

The last thing he expected was a comeback.

He should have known better. He didn't.

In desperate hands, the element of surprise can be a mighty weapon.

Pushing into the blade knocked him off balance. As the wind pulled him back, I jerked my head the opposite way and the knife-tip popped clear of my skin. In the same instant, I threw up an arm and swept his hand aside. The blade jumped out of his clutch and was snatched away. It skipped across the decking and caught in the wood near Grace's feet. Startled, *The Maestro* brought the Glock round for a shot. I didn't give him the chance. I kicked him in the groin, hard, very hard – as if I were attempting a field goal from my own end zone. No sportsmanship here. This was a fight to the death. I saw his face screw up as he folded forward, automatically, his smashed testicles screaming for attention. The gun dropped from his hands and skittered across the boards. I didn't stop there. I clasped fists together and brought them down on the nape of his neck, with as much force as I could muster. *The Maestro* collapsed to his knees. I lifted a leg and kneed him in the face. His head snapped back. Blood flew from his busted nose. He flattened onto his back on the wet wooden timbers, dazed, shaking his head like a boxer knocked to the canvas. Then I dropped onto him before he could gather his senses and regroup. Straddled him at the waist and planted a hammerhead fist into his blood-covered face. Followed it with another. Then another. Four, five, six. Felt knuckles crack against teeth and bone. I didn't stop, despite the excruciating pain.

This wasn't Rochelle's backyard. This wasn't seven months ago. I'd come a long way since our last bout in Boulder City. I was fitter, healthier, angrier. No longer dancing to another's tune. This was my song now. *The Maestro* was softer, older, weaker. The tables had turned. He'd been victorious in round one, but round two was about to have a new champion: the comeback kid.

I raised a bloodied fist, poised for the prize-winning punch.

The knockout.

"You should have killed me in Boulder City when you had the chance," I howled. "You should have quit while you were ahead. This is for Hope and every other innocent life you stole."

My bloodied fist curled into a sledgehammer.

Then something struck the back of my head. Felt like a ton of bricks. Dropping through a thousand feet from high in the leaden sky. Lightning crackled behind my eyes. The world spun. I rolled off my opponent, sprawling on the wet planking, momentarily dazed.

Sheryl Klaussner was standing over me. Blood dripping from the heel of her gun.

I blinked against needle rain. Summoned clarity. I saw *The Maestro* flop onto his side like a landed fish; begin to push himself to his knees. Not done yet. Still game.

I was down but not out. Unfinished business. I flung out a foot and caught Sheryl on the knee. Her leg buckled backward at the joint. She let out an agonized scream and toppled to the deck. I shook the world into focus, then wrested the gun from her weakened grasp. I rolled to my feet – in the same instant *The Maestro* scooped up my fallen gun and got to his.

What followed was a surreal moment of stillness.

It was a cessation in the thunderous squall as our gazes met and the rest of the world spiraled out of control around us.

Mirror images of hate and loathing.

Guns gripped in bloodied fists held at arm's length.

Sights aimed and locked.

Friend and foe, interchangeable.

Face to face – with the hurricane breathing down our necks.

Fingers half-squeezing triggers.

Stalemate.

I heard Grace cry: "Shoot him, Daddy! Shoot him! He killed Momma! Shoot him!"

But I couldn't take the shot. Not because I didn't want to kill *The Maestro* – far from it – but because Grace was just over his shoulder, in the line of fire. Like Sheryl had said: no telling how the wind would alter the bullet's trajectory. I couldn't take the risk of hitting my own daughter. Grace pulled against her metal restraints, shaking her head vehemently. Wet hair clinging. Blood on her wrists.

"Just shoot him!"

Not just the line of fire – my hands were all busted up after pounding *The Maestro's* face; the very act of holding the gun and keeping it steady was grueling. No saying where my shot would land.

The Maestro began to backpedal. There was nothing stopping him from taking my head off – nothing except his warped vision that involved making me witness my daughter die first.

I kept the iron sights trained on his bloodied face as he backed right up to Grace.

Sheryl elbowed me in the foot. She was bemoaning her busted knee, her lower leg twisted at an unreal angle. I kept my eyes and aim locked on her father as I reached down and grabbed a handful of hair close to the back of her scalp. She screamed and floundered as I hauled her to her feet, her broken leg hanging limply.

The Maestro had the muzzle of my Glock pressed against Grace's temple. He was going to blow her brains out with my own gun.

Two could play at that game.

I yanked Sheryl's head back and jammed her own firearm into the soft tissue under her jaw line. She tried to pull away, but my grip was viselike in spite of my busted knuckles; she'd have to scalp herself in order to break free.

"This is sweet!" *The Maestro* shouted. "Why haven't we done this family stuff before now? All those times we were hanging out and drinking beer together, we were missing out on this: the real fun to be had with our kids."

We faced each other across the creaking observation platform. Two fathers threatening to kill one another's daughters. Sheer insanity, whichever way you looked at it.

The tower was trembling – or maybe it was my legs.

Out of the corner of my eye I could see a huge bulge of water gathering momentum out across the estuary. It was a tsunami being forced our way ahead of the approaching hurricane.

Barely a minute or more until the observation tower and everyone on it was smashed to smithereens.

"So this is how it ends," he called back. "We kill each other's children. Then we kill one another. Has a weird kind of symmetry to it, don't you think?"

I saw his finger tighten on the trigger.

Mine did the same.

Then the strangest thing happened.

Something whistled past my ear. Too fast to see. In the same moment, the Glock in *The Maestro's* hand disappeared. It didn't pop out of existence like part of a magic trick. It simply leapt at speed from his hand and flew over the handrail.

It was as if an invisible wire had yanked it loose.

The Maestro looked equally bemused.

Two more shrill whistles followed in rapid succession.

A hole appeared in his wetsuit, just under his left clavicle, immediately followed by another a few inches to the side, near the arm. *The Maestro* fell back against the handrail, looking confused, and then slumped to the deck.

What the . . .

I twisted round to see Special Agent Mason Stone standing on the topmost step behind me. His Kevlar vest was gone. So, too, were his shirt and shoes. There were cuts and abrasions on his arms and torso – as if he'd been flogged. A bloodied welt on one cheek. His big fist was sporting a standard-issue Glock. He looked shattered, beat, like he'd just completed the toughest triathlon of his life, and probably had.

"Don't just bloody well stand there gawping," he gasped. "We have to go, now; the sky's about to fall."

I forced Sheryl into his arms. "Take her. She's his daughter. She masterminded the latest killings. She's your killer, Stone. Now go! Get out of here!"

I didn't know how Stone had survived the storm surge. Had neither the time nor the capacity to work it out. Not here. Not right now. Realistically, he shouldn't have made it. He should have been drowned and broken. Beached like driftwood. But he hadn't. A miracle had happened. Somehow the currents had swept him into the bayou and washed him ashore against the road-dyke, a stone's throw from our location. The coincidental nature of it was mind-numbing, unbelievable. And yet here he was, an impossibility, in the flesh. And I was off the hook for murdering a federal agent. So why didn't the sight of him ease my sense of shame?

Stone manhandled Sheryl down the steps as I rushed over to Grace. I plucked the Bowie knife out of the splintered board and used it to cut her wire ties. Freed, she collapsed into my arms. She was exhausted, scared, soaked to the bone and quivering. She clung to me for dear life and sobbed. I let her, for a few seconds at least, all too aware of the tidal wave rearing its ugly head as it steamrollered toward us across the submerged bayou.

I cupped her face in my hands. "Gracie, listen to me. You need to go down to the car. Right this minute. Wait for me there. I have to finish what I started."

She began to protest, but I levered her loose and forced her away. "Now, Grace. Go! I mean it!"

I watched her drag herself hand over hand along the wooden rail, fighting the maelstrom that had begun to shake the platform like a child's rattle. I could hear wood splitting under the pressure, and imagined nails popping out. The whole structure was swaying, coming loose from its moorings. Undulating like a ship in a strong swell. Only a matter of time before the fierce wind broke it into a million splinters. Us with it.

I waited until she'd disappeared down the steps before turning my attention on the man lying prone at my feet.

Just the two of us, now.

The best of friends and the worst of enemies.

Bruised and battered beneath a bruised and battered sky.

The Maestro was gazing up at me, blinking through blood and rainwater pooling in his eyes. His fight was over. Spent. Two expertly-aimed gunshots had taken him down. He was through. Bleeding. Condemned. All that remained was for me to undertake a promise I'd made in a Los Angeles hospital eighteen months earlier, a vow I'd made as my wife had finally succumbed to hypovolemia, at this man's hands.

I knelt down on the trembling timbers. Thrust the muzzle of the gun in the gap between his swollen eyes.

I'd planned for this moment since Hope's death. Dreamed it. Over and over. Worked out what I'd do, in every conceivable detail. How I'd exact my revenge. Make her killer wish he'd never been born. And yet, now that it had arrived, it was nothing like any scenario I'd imagined.

I had thought I'd feel something – relief, happiness, vindication – but I was numb.

Traumatized emotions canceling each other out.

I leaned on the gun butt. Felt his skull grate against the steel.

This man had murdered my wife.

Vicious and vindictive.

Deliberately.

He'd crossed a line that day.

But now that the fantasized payback moment had arrived, I wasn't sure if I could cross it with him.

The Maestro spluttered out red rainwater. "What you going to do, big guy – kill me in cold blood? You're a loose cannon all right, but it's not your style. Don't forget you owe me; I saved your bacon back there with pizza face. If it hadn't been for me, Freddie Krueger would have blown you to hell."

I pressed harder. "You're forgetting you did that to me already." My voice was a howl, baying for blood. I leaned on the gun, finger hooked around the trigger.

"You haven't got the balls," *The Maestro* shouted defiantly.

I willed for the strength. I really did. I prayed for the conviction, for the courage to do what needed to be done. I stared into his bloodied mask and imagined his evil brains splattered across the wet timbers.

But we were poles apart.

Opposing forces.

Nothing is ever how we imagine.

I stowed the gun and got out my handcuffs. Looped them around a wooden strut and snapped the manacles over both his wrists. Then I got to my feet, counteracting the lean of the tower; everything on a twenty-degree tilt.

The Maestro tugged against his shackles. "Finish the job, you coward!"

But I backed away in the direction of the steps. "You're on your own," I called back. "You can duke it out with the hurricane. Let God decide your fate. You don't deserve the waste of a good bullet."

By now, the entire platform was swinging from side to side. Stanchions splitting as the tower began to list into the lapping waters undermining its foundations. With an almighty roar, the canopy ripped itself free and blew away like an umbrella caught in a gust.

"Dammit! Come back here!" he screamed as I put a foot on the first tread. "Let's finish this like men! Untie me, you coward!"

I hesitated and looked back one last time, had one last look at the bloodied face of the man who had ruined my life. "Maybe I am. But I'd rather be a living coward than a dead one."

Then I turned my back on him and walked away.

94

Done.

I left my best friend and my worst enemy to the elements and battled my way down the juddering structure, hand over hand. Struts and railings buckled and cracked as I went, tearing loose. I shielded my face against flying splinters. I didn't look back. Against the thundering gale, I could hear Jacob Klaussner screaming:

"This doesn't end here! You hear me, Quinn? This doesn't end here! You'll be seeing me again! You can bet your life on it!"

The rising sea level had breached the embankments and engulfed the dike. Deepening by the second. The Range Rover was sitting in two feet of water. Engine running. Headlights throwing twin beams across the tower.

I jumped the last few steps and splashed my way over, hunching against the wind. I fell onto the backseat next to Grace. Stone was in the driver's seat, with Sheryl riding shotgun. He'd cuffed both of her wrists to a handle above the door. Her face was pressed against the glass, staring mutely at the swaying tower. Her father was up there and she couldn't take her eyes off it. Grace slid across the seat into my arms as the door locks went *thwunk*.

Then Stone was spinning the steering wheel and standing on the gas. The vehicle fishtailed, tires scrabbling for purchase on the submerged composite. It rotated through a half circle, and then came to an abrupt stop. Stone floored the accelerator again, but nothing happened. He threw it in reverse and spun the wheel. The Range Rover skewed backward this time, squealing. The back end snagged on the looser surface at the edge of the roadway and started to sink, fast. The hood came up. The front wheels lifted clear of the water. Headlights illuminated the top of the stricken structure. Stone stamped his foot and wrestled with the steering wheel. The engine whined. The front wheels whirred freely in the air. No give. No grip. We were stuck. Sitting ducks.

Through the rear window I could see the mucky-gray tidal wave about to strike the dike. A towering ten-foot-tall cliff of churning gray and white, seething with mangrove debris. It drew itself up to its full height as it hit the submerged embankment and rolled upward like a striking cobra, curling, blotting out the blackened sky.

"Hold on!" somebody yelped.

The storm surge crashed over the Range Rover with a deafening roar. A collapsing wall of watery rubble. The vehicle lurched and bucked as the force of the water threw it about. We were slammed around inside. Holding on for dear life. The vehicle groaned like a stricken animal. It sounded like bits of it were being ripped off. Metallic nails scratching off paintwork. Flotsam smashing against the doors. A torrent of filthy water washed over the windows. Something hit the glass near my face. It looked like a drowned raccoon. Its lifeless eyes caught mine for a brief moment before the animal was swept up and over the roof. I felt Grace's grip tighten. The back wheels caught against the rocky embankment again and the Range Rover hunkered down as the deluge washed over it.

Then, as fast as it had come, the flood was receding. Subsiding. Sluicing over the hood and the glass. The water level dropping as the swollen head of the surge rushed away from us across the bayou.

The shadowy sky reappeared through the windshield.

We were back on a tilt. The back end sunk in silt, with the underneath of the vehicle wedged tight against the embankment. Dirty water halfway up the windows. Some of it beginning to penetrate the seals and pour into the cabin. Unbelievably, enough of the engine was elevated above the water line to keep it running. Headlights still striking the stricken observation tower – or what was left of it.

But the worst was yet to come.

Behind the storm surge came the full brunt of the wind.

It impacted the dike like a bomb going off.

The Range Rover shook as if it were a flimsy foil and balsa replica.

We clung on. Teeth chattering. Bones grinding. Somebody whimpered.

Metal creaked and protested. Water spouted through gaps wrenched open where the doors met the bodywork. Gushing into the foot spaces and filling them up.

I wrapped bloodied hands around my daughter and held her close.

It was like a scene from a disaster movie.

I heard Stone shout: "She's breaking up."

Not the car. The observation tower.

All eyes zoomed in on the wooden structure as brutal wind collided with it. The platforms crumpled like paper. Screwed themselves up and blew away. The steps twisted and flapped loose one by one. The ramps writhed like things alive. Planks and rails wrenched apart. We all stared, wordlessly, as the whole structure was ripped away from its foundations with a resounding roar and was scattered to the four winds.

I thought I saw *The Maestro's* body being blown away as Sheryl Klaussner wailed like a banshee.

95

I should have felt something other than guilt. I should have felt something other than remorse. I should have felt something other than regret. I should have felt something. I didn't feel a damn thing.

96

The emergency services arrived three hours later; ours was not the only life and death situation demanding attention in the aftermath of the hurricane. The barrier islands had weathered the worst storm in a decade. Widespread structural damage. Boat canals swamped. Homes shredded, some washed away. Trees uprooted or snapped in two. Streetlight poles folded in half. A power outage running a fifty-mile stretch of the battered coastline. It was a disaster zone.

We waited, stranded on the flooded dike, with water sloshing at our heels, as the surge waters slowly dissipated to reveal a wrecked bayou of trampled mangroves and piled driftwood.

There was no sign of the pulverized observation tower or of Sheryl's rented red sedan. Both had been taken by the storm. No sign of *The Maestro's* broken body.

Just devastation as far as the eye could see.

We were lucky to be alive.

Physically, we were tattered and torn. Bedraggled. Emotionally, our brush with death had muted us. Tongue-tied and tearful.

We had plenty to say, but none of us spoke it.

We all knew where we stood:

Sheryl Klaussner would be read her rights and taken into custody, grilled, processed and charged with several counts of murder one. Then she'd be incarcerated, with no chance of getting out of a guaranteed death penalty. She'd spend the remainder of her days knowing that I had killed her father. She'd grind her teeth until they fell out one by one, and rue the day she'd crossed my path. Grace, my beloved daughter, would go to the hospital, get checked out, receive a clean bill of health, go home and recoup. She'd return to normalcy, to work, to her life without her Daddy getting underfoot, and maybe shed a tear whenever she thought about how close she and her father had come to joining her mother on a stormy day in August. Stone would graciously accept yet another glittering commendation for capturing another public enemy. He'd face the cameras and the press with assured aplomb, then return to troubleshooting unsolved cases, and collect more accolades, maybe even smile with irony once in a while when he reflected on his calamitous experience with the Celebrity Cop in a hurricane on Sanibel Island.

And as for me . . . I went home.

But not without first sitting in on Sheryl's in-flight interrogation as we returned to California. A recorded session where she confessed point blank to all her charges, and then some. With the death of her father, the fight had gone out of her. No point being uncooperative now that her secret was out – might as well get credit for something she could claim as her own while the limelight dazzled.

Stone and I listened with mouths pressed into hard lines as she imparted her horror story into a video camera. No holding back. No emotion. No remorse.

None from me either.

She spoke of how she'd left the sticks behind, following her childhood sweetheart to Los Angeles on the back of a job offer. She told us how she'd enrolled in a student-nursing program, and how she'd befriended Franklin Forrest by chance at the nightclub on Santa Monica Boulevard. Forrest had told her about his dark fantasies, one of which involved a boy at school who he had a crush on. Together they'd abducted Christian Stone and sodomized him, just for the fun of it. Sheryl had gotten a buzz from the experience – especially the torture aspect – and had shared her story with her doting father.

She explained how she'd procured her daddy's help to feed her addiction. Jacob Klaussner loved his little girl, even her psychotic tendencies (probably because they had them in common), and had agreed to aid and abet her burgeoning curiosity.

As their warped fantasies had taken shape, Forrest had suggested they use Marv Connolly to source out suitable candidates. Forrest had had something on Connolly – she didn't know what – and had used it to coerce his cooperation.

She told us how she'd masterminded the abduction/homicides the year before last, and how she'd posed as a victim in order to distract our investigation. She told us how she'd planned to murder my wife, not only in a bid to throw us off track, but to get one over on me, just because.

But things hadn't gone as expected.

Her father hadn't agreed with killing Hope. They'd fallen out because of it, and he'd gone his separate way. In the face of her loss, and still in victim mode, Sheryl had accepted the offer of relocation from the Department of Justice. But she wasn't a happy camper. The killing and the torture had satisfied something deep inside her brain. Something that needed sating. She was smitten, and it was hard forging a new life without the regular kill-thrill.

As the months passed, the craving had become unbearable. Finally, she'd returned to California to take up where she'd left off. The kill team had reformed. She'd recruited her childhood sweetheart, Melody Seeger, into the kill team. Sexual coercion being a powerful thing.

She explained how she'd had Seeger silence Connolly in his hospital bed, and how Seeger had silenced Gus Reynolds to stop him pointing a finger at Forrest. Apparently, Forrest had known about my visiting the discothèque a year after the first killings – looking for a different killer – and my encounter with its owner, Stevie Hendricks. Sheryl told us about her idea to use Stevie as bait to lure me back into her evil game, and how, most of all, she'd believed that if I were back on the scene, it would act as the catalyst to force her doting father out of his Florida retirement and back into her life, back into her beloved kill team.

It was all bullshit.

Sheryl Klaussner had had everything planned. Everything under control. Her father – the man I had thought to be a solitary serial killer – had been nothing more than a reluctant accomplice, pandering to his daughter's extreme demands. He was no less guilty, but not solely responsible for killing Hope, as I'd thought.

Didn't lessen my loathing for him.

Sheryl was the real brains behind the Piano Wire Murders. Not her father. Not my dead enemy friend.

There was only one mastermind, playing me from the start:

Sheryl Klaussner – *The Maestro*.

Case closed.

And so I went home.

But not because I was through with Sheryl and her psychotic world of delusions and attention-seeking – which I was, bellyful – but because of her closing confession:

That there existed one final undiscovered victim, hidden in the very last place I would ever think of looking.

Sheryl's screwy idea of poetic irony.

And so I drove the rental recklessly along Valencia Street, with the speedometer's needle teetering on fifty. Blood pricking through the bandages wrapped around the knuckles of each hand. I leapt out of the car even before it had fully crunched to a stop, half on the sidewalk outside of my house. I sprinted up the overgrown front walk and shouldered open the front door. Sprang up the staircase three at a time. Heart thrumming. Blood pumping. Nerves jangling.

Sheryl thought she owned me. Sheryl thought she knew me. Sheryl thought she'd got one over on me. She was wrong on all three counts.

I rushed along the short landing toward the master bedroom. I didn't place a hesitant hand on the brass doorknob, feel the metal that was chill to the touch. I didn't press my other hand against the green-painted wood, and then follow it with my brow. I didn't let the door take my weight. I didn't close my eyes, summoning – as I had done countless times before – the strength to turn the doorknob, to go inside the place where Hope had been brutally attacked and left to bleed out.

I'd failed every time.

Not this time.

I threw back the door and rushed inside.

The child in me scurried into the corner and covered his eyes.

Eighteen months ago, *The Maestro* had painted a musical motif on the wall over the master bed: five red parallel lines crossed with notes. Drawn in Hope's blood. My dying wife, spread-eagled on the mattress, with cruel wires slicing through her wrists and her ankles. More crisscrossing wires pinning her down to the bed frame. Two particularly vicious filaments forming an X over her face. She'd lost a lot of blood trying to wrench free – while I had been elsewhere, futilely trying to save Leo Benjamin from the same fate beneath the 7th Street Bridge. She'd been weak and unconscious, her organs and brain damaged by exsanguination. No hope. She'd died a week later in Cedars-Sinai, having never woken up. I'd never entered this room since that time. The killer's signature ought to have faded in the interim, dulled, blended itself into the paintwork. It hadn't.

More recently, somebody had broken into my home and repainted the motif with fresh blood. Not Hope's this time. It belonged to another woman – who was lying naked and spread-eagled on the mattress, with cruel wires slicing through her wrists and ankles. A web of steely filaments crisscrossing her body. Dried blood everywhere.

Déjà vu.

She'd lost some blood trying to tug free. But not enough to kill her. There were two intravenous drip stands near the headboard, one on either side of the bed. An empty fluid bag hanging from each, connected to her inner arms with clear plastic tubing. Several empty saline bags scattered on the mattress around her, like gutted fish.

I pressed two shaky fingers against her neck. Detected the very faintest of pulses. She was extremely frail, severely weakened by days without proper nourishment. Gaunt and skeletal. Dehydrated to the point where her pale skin had transformed itself into tissue paper. Shredded beneath the taut spider web of wires.

But she was alive.

Outside, I heard the first of the EMS vehicles screeching to a halt. Sirens wailing. Doors opening. Paramedics jumping out. A gurney clattering against the pavement.

I leaned over and peeled the duct tape from Eleanor Zimmerman's lips.

EPILOGUE

I didn't go home again for another three days. Not until my dear old friend from Internal Affairs had resurfaced from her coma. Days again before she'd find the strength to recount her ordeal – if she ever did. Thankfully, Eleanor's long-term prognosis was positive. I wasn't so sure about mine.

There was a polybag propped up against the front door of my home in Alhambra when I got there. One of those plain gray packets with white USPS stickers. I picked it up, examined it. My name and address was printed on a little sticky label. Post-dated the day before last. A Virginia postmark. Not heavy, with contents protected by bubble wrap. I carried it inside.

The house smelled of disinfectant and antiseptics.

I tore open the seal as I wandered into the living room. Pulled out the padding to reveal a gold-colored DVD disk in a transparent plastic case. No note. No letter. No writing on the disk. I slipped it out, holding it by its edge, and inspected it. It looked like a regular DVD. No fingerprints. No marks of any kind. Curious, I powered up the TV and let the DVD player gobble it up.

The picture flickered, then focused.

It was a home movie. Shot in what looked like a warehouse – most likely from a camcorder mounted on a tripod. Fixed viewpoint. I could see red metal beams and sheet metal walls. A corrugated roof, in shadow. Shafts of sunlight slanting from skylights. A smooth concrete floor. Nothing else in the frame except a guy in a chair.

He looked familiar; in fact, I recognized him.

I crouched in front of the TV, curiosity mutating into trepidation.

He went by the name of Hives. He was a three-hundred pound African American private investigator with a French bulldog face: roundish and flat with bulging eyes that seemed too close to his ears to provide proper stereoscopic vision. The protruding eyes were a product of proptosis, rather than the fact he was tied to the chair with loops of nylon rope. There was a bleeding gash on his brow and purplish bruising on his cheek. The makings of a black eye. Silver duct tape covering his mouth.

He was staring at the camera with big bloodshot eyes.

I felt the hairs on the back of my neck do handstands.

I hadn't heard a peep from Hives since coming to California. The task he'd undertaken on my payroll couldn't be considered an overnight flash-in-the-pan. Tracking down somebody who didn't want to be found took time, patience.

What was he doing tied to a chair in the middle of an empty hanger?

Had he caught up with *The Undertaker?*

Then another figure appeared in the shot and suddenly the pieces all fell into place.

Again, it was someone I recognized, instantly.

He was of American Indian descent, with a melted face and a milky eye. Nightmarish. Unforgettable. Snakeskin.

He came around from behind the camera. There was a red five-gallon jerry can in his hands, like the kind used to store gasoline. I felt my stomach clench. I saw the big black guy struggle against his bonds as Snakeskin hefted the heavy can into the air.

"We reap what we sow, Quinn." I heard Snakeskin say. "This is all on your head."

Without hesitation, he drenched Hives in the flammable liquid. It splashed all over him, soaking through his suit and shirt, pooling on the warehouse floor.

Mesmerized, I stared, aghast, glued to the horrifying display as Gary Cornsilk emptied out the can's entire contents. Hives fought against it, screaming behind the duct tape as the gasoline seared into his wounds and eyes.

I didn't want to know what was coming next, but I did. So, too, did Hives.

Snakeskin discarded the can. It clanged across the warehouse floor, echoing. Then he stepped back – an artist admiring his work – and struck a match. Hives' bulging eyes flared even wider. I felt the breath harden in my throat. Heard a whimper escape my lips as Snakeskin tossed the lit match onto Hives' lap.

The unbelievable happened:

The gasoline exploded into bright orange flames. Hives thrashed as the fire engulfed him. Hands grappling against the chair arms. Feet trying to force the chair on its side. But his struggles only seemed to fan the flames. They intensified, fed by his clothing, raging several feet into the air, churning out a thick plume of black smoke.

I swallowed thick, acidic phlegm. It stuck halfway down like a ball of barbed wire.

My pulse was thumping in my throat.

Snakeskin approached the camera, coming so close that his liquefied face completely filled the screen. I could hear sizzling sounds behind him. Fat popping.

"That's what happens when you fuck with me, Quinn," he said. "From here on in, I'm in the cremation business. Anyone who crosses my path will go the same way as your private dick." He leaned into the lens. "I'm coming to get you, Quinn. You and everyone close to you. I'm going to make you pay for what you did to me. You and The Undertaker. Make the both of you feel my pain. Then I'm going to kill him first and then you. So break out those marshmallows, detective; your life is about to become a living hell."

He disappeared from the shot, leaving the horrific view of Hives enveloped in his raging inferno. He was no longer resisting. He was gone. Fat burning into a human candle.

I should have stopped the recording then and there. I didn't. We are all victims of morbid fascination. I let it play out. Intentions hardening. Focus coalescing.

Then I grabbed up my car keys and headed out.

The Undertaker, the serial killer responsible for ruining both of our lives, may have deserved to burn in hell, but it wasn't Snakeskin's call to make.

It was mine.

I pulled open the front door and stopped, dead in my tracks.

There were two dour-looking men in dark suits and wayfarers butted-up to the doorstep, blocking my path.

In unison, they held up FBI badges.

"Gabriel Quinn, you are under arrest for the attempted murder of a federal agent. You have the right to remain silent. Anything you say can and will be used against you in a court of law –"

I flapped: "Is this some kind of a joke?"

"- You have the right to consult an attorney. If you cannot afford an attorney, one will be appointed for you . . ."

The agent's Miranda recital trailed away as I realized there was another suit observing from the sidewalk. He was a well-built guy, with a sprinkle of salt-and-pepper hair shaven close to match the thick stubble coating his jaw. A couple of inches over six foot. Heavier than two hundred pounds. No fat. Just loose muscle. Early fifties, I reckoned. One of those dilapidated faces that looked like several hapless tenants had lived in it.

And he was smoking.

I stared at Special Agent Mason Stone as my rights were read out loud, my ears deafened by the din of demons celebrating my detainment.

I thought about running. I really did. But I'd already tried it, only succeeded in tripping myself up.

Sometimes standing still is all that stops us from falling down.

Words from the Author

Thank you for reading my novel!

If you liked it, you will love the prequel and the follow-on

And if you did enjoy this book, please consider writing a quick review on Amazon for me.

Great reviews help other readers decide on my books and hopefully enjoy them as much as you have!

Simply go to the book's Amazon page, scroll down to the review section and click on **Write a Review**. Or log into your Amazon account and add it from there.

You don't need to write a long and rambling review, a few short words will do the trick.

Thanks!

I really appreciate feedback about my books, and love hearing from readers.

Please stay in touch and be the first to hear about my new releases by leaving your email on my website or by dropping me a quick 'hello' to:

contact@keithhoughton.com

Now you can be entered into my exclusive **Reader Competitions** automatically (such as winning signed copies of my books, or even having your name as a character in a future novel) by adding your email address to my spam-free mailing list at:

www.keithhoughton.com

Simply look for the **Author Updates** box on the right-hand menu and add your email.

You will qualify for all **Reader Competitions**, plus you'll receive a very occasional email update from me about upcoming projects and new releases.

Some secrets are better left buried . . .

Eighteen years ago, Jenna Luckman disappeared, presumed murdered. Her boyfriend, Jake Olson, hasn't been home since. Now he's coming back to find her killer.

Since he last set foot in Harper, Minnesota, Jake's whole life has changed beyond recognition, but the place seems just as he left it. Small-town politics and gossip rule, and his return is big news.

When a body is discovered at the frozen Hangman Falls, Jake is beset by a snowstorm of anger and revenge. Hounded by grudges and feared by the townsfolk, Jake is determined to uncover the truth behind his girlfriend's disappearance. But he still has enemies in town and they have other plans for him.

Betrayed at every turn and unsure whom to trust, Jake's quest for the truth rekindles old rivalries and rouses ghosts that should never have been disturbed. He wants above all to find the peace of mind that has so long eluded him. But no man can escape his past.

Join me and Gabe's fans on social media

Twitter
https://twitter.com/KeithHoughton

Facebook:
http://www.facebook.com/KeithHoughtonAuthor

Gabe Quinn Fan Group
https://www.facebook.com/groups/gabequinn

Thanks for all Your support!!

Keith

Made in the USA
Middletown, DE
24 December 2020

30034815R00250